A Lamb in Wolfe's Clothing
A Novel by
S.L. Shelton

The first novel in the Scott Wolfe Series

For CLAUDINE!!
I miss working with you. Thank you
for all the years of fun.
with much Love Sean

For my wife, Diane

Thank you for your constant and loving support.

Prologue

August 11, 2008 - Gori, Georgia (The country, not the state.)
Russian invasion of South Ossetia.

LIEUTENANT STEVE MARSH of the US Navy led his team of "military advisors" down a side street in Gori. They had walked in across the bridge before sunrise and had stayed as far from the bombing as they could. But the CIA agent in charge—Miller—had been urging them closer throughout the morning…and Marsh still didn't know why Miller wanted the squad from SEAL Team 9 in the city.

The Russians' air bombardment had intensified over the past couple of hours, but the focus of the attack seemed to have shifted almost entirely toward the Georgian military base, one street and one row of buildings beyond where they were currently huddled.

The explosions shook dust and loose masonry down around the squad as they took a short break from their forward movement.

"Nightshade. Arrow," Marsh said into his radio mic,

speaking to the sniper who was perched on a rooftop somewhere above them.

"Go ahead, Arrow," the sniper replied.

"How's it looking across the parade field?" Marsh asked.

"Well, Arrow, there are a lot of explosions and fire and smoke," came the reply. "I'd have to say it looks like a big fuckin' mess—yes. Definitely a huge, gigantic, dangerous fuckin' mess."

Marsh figured there wouldn't have been any change. It was pointless to have a forward observer during an air bombing. None of them were happy about being there, but Nightshade should have known better than to use an open channel to relay his frustration at having been ordered to do something stupid.

"COM discipline, Nightshade," Marsh said into his mic.

There were two clicks in his ear, confirming receipt of the order.

"Hey, Skipper," said Petty Officer Egermayer, who was crouched against the wall next to Marsh. "Remind me again why we're here."

"Because 'God' wants us here," Marsh replied, referring to Miller, the agent in charge.

"And why was it again that he wanted us here?" Egermayer asked, one eye closed and his face screwed up in a tight pucker which could hardly be confused with a smile.

"He didn't say," Marsh replied quietly as he turned his head toward a noise in the street.

"And what's the target?" Egermayer pushed.

"He didn't say," Marsh replied again, his attention still down the street.

"Then how will we know when we are done?" Egermayer asked, a grin spreading over his face as Marsh turned to look him in the eye.

"He didn't say," Marsh replied.

Egermayer was about to ask another annoying question when Chief Petty Officer Seifert spoke up from across the street.

"Hey, Boss," Seifert hissed loudly, holding up a guide book he had lifted from a gift shop when they entered the town. "It says here that Joseph Stalin was born here, and also some guy named Alexander N-A-D-I-R-A-D-Z-E."

"That's nice, Majesty," Marsh replied. "Would you mind looking in that building and seeing if Deadeye is…"

"For some reason, this Noddradaze guy must be important," Seifert continued, interrupting. "Because it's supposed to be some big deal that he worked here until his death."

"Until whose death?" came the voice of Petty Officer Cooper—Deadeye—as he appeared in and then climbed through the window above Seifert's head. "Oh. Skipper, the front wall on this building is collapsed. No way through."

Marsh nodded.

"Whose death?" Cooper repeated.

Seifert replied, "Some guy named Nodderize, Nadereyes—"

"Nadiradze," Cooper corrected, rolling the "R" perfectly.

"Yeah. That guy," Seifert said.

"He was the father of mobile ballistic missile technology," Cooper continued. "What about him?"

All three men turned to look at Cooper at the same time.

"What?" he asked incredulously. "You don't learn a language in a vacuum, you know."

"Where did it say he worked?" Egermayer asked Seifert.

Seifert flipped a page back and forth and then looked up at Marsh, a stunned expression on his face.

"The base on the other side of this blown-out building we're leaning against, apparently," he replied, jerking his thumb over his shoulder.

It suddenly dawned on Marsh that it had gotten quieter. "Nightshade, what's going on up there?" Marsh asked into his throat mic.

"Arrow, it looks like the bombers are done," the sniper replied.

"Roger. We're moving up," Marsh said. "Cover us."

"You're clear to the east," came the sniper's reply. "I've got you."

"Come on, boys," Marsh said. He stood and then slapped the masonry dust off his shoulders. "Let's see what all the excitement was about."

"Hey, Boss," Egermayer said as he stood and adjusted the strap on his M4 assault rifle. "You don't think there are still any nukes over there on the base, do you?"

"Nah," Marsh replied, stepping carefully through the rubble. "The Soviets would have pulled them out when they left."

"Not necessarily," Cooper said as he turned to check the street behind them. "The Russians didn't exactly make an orderly exit."

"Looks like they changed their minds and want them back," Egermayer replied with some snark.

"When did they leave?" Seifert inserted.

"It was like, ninety, or thereabouts," Cooper said. "Why are you asking me? You've got the guide book."

"Just curious. The book said Nodderadaze, Naderoddeyes—"

"Nadiradze," Cooper corrected again as the four man team started walking east along the street.

"Yeah. Him," Seifert said. "The book said he died in eighty-seven."

"Eighty-seven was a rough year for Georgia and Soviet relations," Cooper said. "They started forming their own political parties that year. Russia didn't like that."

"Okay, guys," Marsh warned with a hiss. "Cut the chatter."

"But do you think they got their nukes out before they left?" Egermayer added in a whisper from across the street.

Marsh shot him a harsh look.

"Skipper, I just want to know why we are walking freshly-bombed streets with no direction from God." Egermayer said.

"Arrow, this is God." Miller's voice came across the command channel.

"Speak of the devil, and he will appear," Marsh muttered as he switched his broadcast to that channel. "God. This is Arrow. Go ahead."

"It's gotten quiet up there," Miller said. "Can I get a SITREP?"

"Wait one," Marsh replied.

He hated that Miller had chosen "God" as his call sign. Not because he was religious, but because it reinforced his doubts of the man's abilities and motivation—it meant he thought too much of himself.

Marsh flipped back to the team channel. "Nightshade, we're coming up on the corner across from the base. Anything new to report?"

"Arrow, Nightshade. Yeah, a bunch of civilian vehicles are picking their way along the road at the edge of the base," the sniper replied.

"Heading out of town?" Marsh asked.

"Negative, Arrow," Nightshade replied. "They are moving to the base entrance…two columns."

That's different, Marsh thought to himself.

"Arrow, this is the Lord Almighty. Where's my SITREP?" Miller's voice sounded impatient.

Marsh scoffed at the message before clicking over to the command channel again.

"God. Arrow. We have two separate columns of civilian vehicles moving back into town toward the main base entrance. Over."

"Arrow. How many vehicles?" Miller asked.

Marsh moved out into the street and looked up at the sniper who had been covering their movement from the roof of an apartment building. He flashed a "C" signal to the sniper, indicating that he needed to switch over to the command broadcast channel. When he got the thumbs up from his sniper, he clicked his mic open again.

"Nightshade. Arrow. How many vehicles returning to the city?"

"Arrow, I've got four coming down the western road and five on the southern road. Trucks and school buses," the sniper replied.

"God. Did you get that?" Marsh asked into his mic.

There was a momentary silence.

"God. I say again, four west and five south. Do you copy?" Marsh said.

"Arrow, they are more than likely just looters coming in to clean up before the Russians reach town. Let them be. Come on in, those tanks will be rolling over the hill in a few minutes," Miller replied.

Egermayer whipped his head around to look at Marsh upon hearing the new order.

"What the fuck?!" Egermayer said in a low voice. "He sent us out to stroll around Main Street while it was being bombed, and *now* he wants us to come back in?"

"That's fucked up, Skipper," Seifert added.

"God. Arrow. They are in formation. Are you sure you don't want us to take a closer look?" Marsh asked.

"I'm sorry. We must have bad COM. I said to leave them the fuck alone and come back to FOA. The bombing has stopped, and the ground troops will be coming over that hill in a few minutes," Miller replied.

"Acknowledged. Arrow out," Marsh responded. He looked at Chief Seifert and Petty Officer Egermayer and then shook his head. "Looters don't travel in convoys and certainly don't coordinate divergent approaches," he said quietly. "Something is going down, and I want to know what it is."

The rest of the men looked at him hesitantly. "God wants us off the streets, Boss," Egermayer said.

"Something stinks with this Miller character," he said, pausing to think. Then, switching to the team frequency, he leaned out so the sniper could see him and flashed the signal for that channel.

"Arrow, you wanted a private conversation?" the sniper called over the team channel, his tone dripping amusement.

"What do you see up there? Over," he asked the sniper.

There was a pause, and then, "Arrow. Three trucks and a bus just turned onto the base. The rest are still outside of the city but moving fast toward the main gate. As fast as you can through popcorn anyway," he said, referring to unexploded cluster bomblets.

"Nightshade. Acknowledged," Marsh said and then hung his head, running his fingers through the stubble on the back of his neck. "Let's see if we can get some Georgian attention over here. We wouldn't be interfering if they happened across a column of looters and took them into custody. And if it ends up being more than that, we'll report back to 'God' on the Langley channel so Papa has the head's up," he said, referring to the Deputy Director of National Clandestine Service (NCS) at the CIA in Langley, Virginia.

He looked from face to face, seeing approval, so they rose to move across the street. There, a Georgian military command car was abandoned near the entrance of the base. Seifert and Egermayer took up guard positions, and Marsh climbed in to check the radio for functionality. It seemed to be working, so he handed the mic to Petty Officer Cooper, who spoke Georgian like a native.

Marsh nodded, and Cooper began broadcasting.

"Ch'ven mimdinareobs daeskhnen! Dakhmareba! Dakhmareba! Avtori bazaze!" Cooper pleaded into the Georgian radio. "Isini mkvlelobashi ch'vent'vis." He was saying, essentially, that armed men were attacking them, shots were being fired, there were casualties, and that they needed help.

As soon as a voice responded, Cooper smiled and turned the radio off. The team looked at each other, smiling, pleased with their deception, and then moved back across the street and into a three-story apartment facing the base. They sat in the window and watched.

After a few moments, they saw two armored troop carriers zooming down the edge of town toward the entrance to the base.

"Here come the cops," Seifert said, calling attention to the Georgian military presence.

"They look pissed," Egermayer replied.

They watched as the second convoy of civilian trucks and busses broke formation, turned in the street, and then sped back down the road they had come in on.

Their retreat was cut off by another group of Georgian armored vehicles.

The two units of carriers converged on the convoy and then began firing. Shots were returned from the civilian vehicles, but several men were caught in an explosion when the Georgians fired a rocket. That knocked the wind out of the fighters from the convoy. The survivors quickly dropped their arms and were overrun by the Georgian army. The captives were thrown to the ground, zip cuffed, and then roughly shoved into the armored transports.

"Should we let them know about the ones on base?" Cooper asked, but Marsh's answer was cut short when an explosion on the parade field had all eyes looking north. Gunships appeared in the sky over the ridge north of town, followed by the unmistakable rumble of an armored column rolling hard and fast across the hill. Their turrets turned toward the base and surrounding streets then began a massive bombardment as they rolled down Gorijvari Street.

"Nope," Marsh replied. "It's too late. The Russians will get 'em now if they don't vacate."

The Georgians from the armored personnel carriers rapidly mounted their vehicles and left, shoving the now-empty civilian convoy vehicles to the side with their heavy metal bumpers. They quickly disappeared into the city, heading toward the river crossing.

As soon as the Georgians were out of sight, the first civilian convoy group rolled out of the base. The three trucks made the tight turn onto the street, but the bus swung wide. Its front tire hit a bomblet just as it was making the turn, and the resulting explosion flipped the bus on its side, and it slid through a storefront on the opposite side of the street.

The trucks paused for a brief moment, but then hurried on their way out of town as the Russian tanks began to rain shells down on their location.

Lt. Marsh stood up. "Okay, boys! Our work is done. Let's di di mau the fuck outta here," he yelled over the shelling, borrowing a colorful phrase from another generation of fighters. He clicked his mic open. "Nightshade, we're moving out."

"Roger, Arrow, on my way down," the sniper said. They exited the building out the rear and made for the river crossing. The team waited for Nightshade's arrival before continuing across the bridge.

"That armored column went right for the base," the sniper, Petty Officer Monroe, said as he arrived to join his teammates.

"Let's hope they stop there," Cooper replied as the team walked carefully across the bridge, being careful not to accidently step on unexploded bomblets. "This is pretty far from the Russian border. All we need is another Cold War."

"Well at least we wouldn't have to worry about being 'down sized,'" Egermayer responded with some snark.

"Unless you step on some popcorn," Marsh snapped, pointing at the ground at Egermayer's feet. "Watch your step."

By the time they were across and out of the war zone, the Russian tanks were starting to set position on the edges of the town.

**

August 21ˢᵗ, 2008 - Ten Days Later

AGENT DWIGHT MILLER had just received bad news. Days after the fighting had ceased, the Georgians discovered the looters they had captured were actually members of a group of Bosnian Serb mercenaries and arms dealers led by Goran Jovanovich—a man wanted for war crimes and for selling illegal arms to terrorists.

Miller was copied on the memo. It read:

> *The looters the Georgian Army captured in Gori before the Russians moved in are Bosnian Serb Nationals. They belong to Goran Jovanovich. State wants them. They've arranged NATO transfer. If we can get info on Jovanovich from them, it would be a big feather in our caps. We need a win after all the black eyes over Iraq and UBL. We should have someone there to babysit during the handover.*

"Oh, fuck," Miller muttered to himself as he read the message.

Miller knew very well who was in the convoy. He had set it up, and he had been paid handsomely to do it—paid by one Heinrich Braun, the head of security for one of the richest men on Earth.

The sudden realization that part of the team had been captured sent a chill down his back. "Why didn't Jovanovich tell me some of his people were captured?" Miller mumbled to himself.

He had made exchange arrangements for the four warheads the Serbs had captured only four days ago.

This complicates things, Miller thought.

He sat in an empty house near the Armenian and Georgian border, waiting for the appointed hour of the hand over. Somehow he had to get the warheads, clean up the mess with the captured Serbs, and make it back to Germany without giving himself away.

If he screwed up any part of this plan, he could be imprisoned by the US on charges of treason, killed by the Serbs or, more likely, Heinrich Braun would—quite literally—have his head on a spike.

Miller copied his CIA station chief in his reply.

I wish I could be on the escort team since I was on site when the arrests were made, but I've been detained in Turkey. If it's okay with everyone, I'll meet up with the interrogators after the hand-off.

It was only a few moments before his phone rang.

"Miller," he said into the secure satellite phone.

"Why are you in Turkey?" The voice of his boss came from the other end.

"I was following up on a lead with the Serbs myself," he lied.

"What lead?" his boss asked.

"Serb chatter that popped up after the invasion," he said, expanding his lie. "Nothing solid yet. That's why I'm here, following up."

"Make sure you log it," came the reply. "I didn't even know you were there."

"Sorry, Boss," Miller said contritely. "Won't happen again. When are they supposed to transfer the Serbs?"

"In the morning," his boss replied.

Tension filled Miller's chest. There wouldn't be much time to fix the problem.

"Tie up the loose ends, and get back to Germany," the station chief said. "I want you on the interrogation team."

"You got it," Miller said.

The call ended abruptly.

Miller immediately dialed Jovanovich's number.

"You could have told me your guys got popped in Gori," Miller said accusingly as soon as the phone was answered.

"That is our problem," Jovanovich said coldly. "Not your concern."

"It's bloody well my fucking problem if they say why they were in Gori!" Miller retorted.

"Who will they tell?" Jovanovich asked incredulously. "The Georgian army?"

"Try the CI fucking A." Miller spat. "Georgia is handing them over in the morning."

There was silence at the other end of the line.

"Uh huh," Miller said with arrogance. "Different story now, huh?"

"They won't talk," Jovanovich said more quietly.

"You're damn right they won't," Miller said. "We have to change the exchange time."

"And the location," Jovanovich said. "Some of those captured know that location is ours."

"Where then?" Miller asked.

"I'll have to let you know," Jovanovich replied. "In the meantime, don't do anything stupid."

"Fuck you," Miller replied. "If you want your money, you better get with the program."

"You've been warned," Jovanovich said and then ended the call.

"Motherfucker!" Miller exclaimed, kicking his chair over. He grabbed his bag from the floor and stuffed his phone and netbook into it and then stomped outside to his beat up SUV.

"Don't do anything stupid, my ass," Miller muttered, and then yelled, "Who the fuck does he think he is?" He pounded on the roof of his vehicle, punctuating his words.

He was a mile down the road before he calmed down

enough to form a plan. After a moment of gripping the wheel and getting his temper under control, he decided it was up to him. The Serb prisoners had to be killed before the transfer team got their hands on them.

"Time for a night op," Miller said as he pushed his foot down harder on the accelerator.

**

August 23rd, 2008 - Two Days Later, in Germany

Miller had just returned to his duty station at the field office in Berlin. He was exhausted. He had nearly been discovered while slipping into the Georgian military prison and had actually been detained on the way out. He had been able to talk his way through the gate by showing falsified NATO ID.

Crossing the border into Turkey had been the hard part. That had been twenty-one hours ago, and the only sleep he had gotten in two days was on the flight from Trabzon, Turkey to Berlin. He was still trying to sew together his cover story for the station chief when he walked into his office carrying his travel bag.

"When are the Serbs being transferred?" Miller asked his boss.

"You didn't hear?" the station chief asked.

"No," Miller replied, setting his bag down. "What's up? When do we start interrogations?"

"We don't," his boss replied. "Unless you can squeeze information out of a corpse."

Miller's face displayed confusion, though he knew exactly

what was going on. "Why? What happened?" he asked incredulously.

"Poisoned. All seven of them," the station chief announced. "In their evening meal the night before handover."

"Fuck me!" Miller exclaimed in disbelief. "Was it Jovanovich's people?"

"We don't know, but that would be a good guess."

That's good news for me, Miller thought. "So, what now?"

"Nothing, unless you got a solid lead in Turkey," he responded.

"Nope," Miller said, looking genuinely perturbed. "That was a dead end."

His boss shook his head and then sat back in his chair, taking a deep breath and blowing it out slowly before continuing.

"Why the hell were they in Gori?" his boss asked quietly, as if to himself.

Miller shook his head.

"Jesus, Dwight," the chief said abruptly. "You look like shit. Go get some sleep."

Miller nodded. "Okay, Boss. Thanks," he replied sincerely. "I'll try to pick things up again in the morning when my eyes are fresh."

Once back in his quarters, Miller pulled the curtains closed tight and lay down in his bed, still fully clothed. He had just drifted off when his satellite phone chirped. He reached for the flashing light next to his bed, and he answered.

"Miller," he said.

"We are still awaiting delivery of our packages," the voice at the other end said coldly, mechanically.

Braun, Miller recognized the speaker immediately by the thick German accent. "We're going to have a problem with that," Miller replied. "They've gone off radar. I think the Russians have put the heat on them, and they aren't going to trust anyone after their buddies were poisoned in jail."

"That is unfortunate," Braun replied. "How do you intend to rectify the problem?"

Miller thought quickly. He knew that if he didn't answer correctly with something that satisfied the caller, he might be forfeiting his life. He was well aware that there were very few places one could hide from the people who had financed the raid on Gori.

"I can use the information we have and put the Agency on Jovanovich's trail. But there's very little hope of finding him before October." Miller replied.

"Are you suggesting we serve him to the CIA on a silver platter?"

"No. Not at all," Miller replied quickly. "If he is captured here, the investigation and handover could be managed by someone at State. I'm certain you have people in place who could guide him through the system to 'friendly' hands."

"So someone else should then complete the arrangements we made with you." Braun said snidely. "And receive your payment, I would imagine."

Miller bristled at that suggestion. He was on the outside of this arrangement and playing catchup. *That fucking Jovanovich,* Miller thought. *If he had just kept his people clear of the Georgians, this wouldn't be happening.*

"If I had more details, I might be able to come up with something," Miller replied defensively. "You've had me working half blindfolded from the beginning."

"You were hired to facilitate a recovery and an exchange," Braun said coldly. "Nothing more. Why should we trust you with more information when you have so far been unable to accomplish that?"

"Fuck it, then," Miller said, testing his room to maneuver. "*You* find Jovanovich. He's got your 'merchandise.'"

There was another brief pause. "We have no one at State in a position to do what you suggest."

"Then put me in at State," Miller said, reaching for a long-shot solution.

"How would that benefit us?"

"I'm assuming you have the ability to sway minds in the Executive branch. There is no reelection for the current administration. They've nothing to lose. Place me in The Hague at the Embassy...in a position high enough to affect a decision," he said, sewing his plan together as he spoke. "I'll put Jovanovich on the radar with the CIA before I leave Berlin. They'll find him eventually. When they do, I'd be in a position to work Jovanovich for the deal."

"That will not deliver our packages by October."

"That isn't my fault. It was the delay in the Russian invasion and the fuckin' Serbs getting captured. They were your pick, remember?" Miller snapped back. "I *can* get them back, but it will take time."

There was silence at the other end for some time before a reply came. "Very well, do what you must. We will simply have to alter course on our October plan."

That statement disturbed Miller. *What's in October?* he wondered. Suddenly the term "October Surprise" came to mind.

It's an election year! he thought. *Could these greasy bastards be planning a fake terrorist attack a month before election?! With a Russian NUKE?!*

He took a second to calm down before continuing. He was suddenly very aware of his treason up to that point. If his guess was right, and if he remained silent, he could be classified as an enemy combatant and relegated to the dark confines of a cell at Guantanamo.

His only visitors would be his interrogators—the ones who would waterboard him for information morning, noon, and night. They would continue long after he had no information left to give. He knew this because he had been on the interrogation side of the table enough times to know that's how it worked.

A cold shiver worked its way up his spine.

In a moment of decision, the one that committed him, he decided his patrons were more powerful and had a better chance of finding and killing him if he betrayed them. He quickly banished thoughts of Gitmo and the imagery of his face covered in a wet cloth with buckets of water spilling over it.

"Give me two weeks to get the ball rolling on the search

for Jovanovich," Miller said, avoiding acknowledgment of the mention of October or any possible surprises. "Then get me as high up at The Hague as possible without raising too many eyebrows. The bigger the signature on the orders, the easier it will be to avoid questions."

"Very well. We will move as you suggest." Braun ended the call.

"Okay. Bye then," Miller said into the severed connection. "Creepy old fucker."

**

HEINRICH BRAUN was pissed off. As soon as he hung up on Miller, he walked into the office of his employer, William Spryte—one of the famous billionaire brothers and the executive officer of a little-known fraternity called Combine.

Spryte was watching stock market indicators on his desk monitor when Braun entered the office with a subtle clearing of his throat. Spryte motioned him in.

After closing the door, Braun went over and stood rigidly in front of Spryte's desk—an old habit from his Stasi days.

"Well? Is it worked out?" Spryte asked without looking up.

"I'm afraid not, sir," Braun replied. "It may yet. We have time, but it would appear the Serbs have disappeared with the devices."

Spryte set his jaw to the side like a young boy about to throw a temper tantrum.

"I thought we had eyes on them," Spryte said, withholding his ire.

"The Georgians captured a handful of the recovery team," Braun said without emotion. "Our man on the inside was in no position to intervene."

Spryte slapped the surface of his desk with the palm of his hand. Braun didn't even blink. He had seen the rage this man had to offer. He knew he could handle anything thrown at him.

"Prepare a message for the board," Spryte said, after regaining his composure a bit. "If the polls look beyond our ability to manipulate, we'll burn the house down behind us."

Spryte was clearly talking about the economy. If their presidential candidate couldn't win, even by rigging the election, then Combine would insure the new President's only job for the next four years would be digging the world out of financial collapse.

"Yes, sir," Braun replied and then turned to leave.

"And Heinrich," Spryte added as Braun reached the door. "Make sure it's clear that everyone is to participate—all fifty members."

"Yes, sir," Braun replied and then left the room.

**

September 29th, 2008

WILLIAM SPRYTE read the fresh set of polls as he ate his breakfast—they showed what nearly everyone was already thinking—the US would have its first African-American president.

This angered Spryte beyond words. The message was sent to all members of Combine, telling them to deepen their sell off.

By the time the new President was sworn in, the world would be deep in recession—possibly depression.

Spryte sat in his study, watching the markets sell off on the TV and his computer. He smiled as wave after wave of stocks lost more than half their value. When the tension became too great, he rose and walked to his window overlooking Central Park.

He looked down on the masses, scurrying about the street below—on their way to either consume or produce. Each one, in some direct or indirect way, had added to his wealth just by being alive.

He had rarely felt such a visceral physical response to his own actions—it was nearly euphoric. He spoke to them, his subjects. "It's time to remind you who is really in charge."

one

Twenty-Two Days Until Event

April 24ᵗʰ, 2010 - Twenty months later, at the REI in Fairfax, Virginia

"Scott." I heard my name called from a couple aisles over. "Paging Scott Wolfe."

The voice belonged to the woman I had been dating for the past couple of months, Barb—Barb Whitney.

"Over here," I called out.

A moment later she came around the corner to see me holding the harness I had just picked out for her. A climbing harness.

"Is that for me?" she asked with a flirty smile.

I grinned back. "It *is* your birthday," I replied.

"Can I try it?" she asked, her flirting becoming more

pronounced.

I bent to let her step through the leg holes and helped her position it correctly before tightening down the straps.

"Oh!" she squealed as I cinched the butt straps tight.

"It has to be tight," I said preemptively, in self-defense. "You don't want to slip out."

"No. That wouldn't do," she replied wistfully. "Though it would be poetic to die on my birthday."

"That's dark," I joked.

She slapped me playfully.

There it was again…the playful whack when I said or did something she didn't like—a slow training process, teaching me how to behave around her. I'd seen it in other relationships. But it was a first for me.

"In a cute way," I continued, testing the theory…again.

She leaned over and kissed me on my cheek. *Yep,* I thought. *The carrot and the stick.*

But Barb was gorgeous, smart, ambitious, and very giving—and I was really bad at relationships—so I had decided weeks ago to see how far we could make it.

Barb was on a break from school. Not spring break—more like an extended mental health break—that long, deep breath one takes between a masters and a doctorate.

"Are you sure this will hold me?" she asked, tugging at the various loops and straps on her harness.

"No doubt," I replied. "Trust me. I've been climbing since I was ten."

I actually remember more about my first climb than anything else about 'ten.' Something had happened to me that year, and all my memories before it were a jumble of violent images and bad dreams culminating in the death of my father. I had trained myself to avoid thinking about it.

"What about a pouchy thing for the chalk?" she asked, looking at her harnessed behind in the mirror by the racks.

"You mean a chalk bag?" I joked.

She slapped me again, 'playfully,' as she giggled.

"Yes," she replied. "That's what I said. The pouchy thing for the chalk."

"Yep. Right over here," I said, reaching for the wall. A cascade of colors assaulted my eyes in a visual hallucination—typical flowchart visualization—this time with a color schema attached to it. I grabbed a pink and purple one, her favorite colors, as confirmed by my internal flowchart.

She smiled and leaned on my arm, kissing me on the cheek.

Once I had paid for her new toys and a pair of decent climbing shoes, we drove up the beltway to Carderock, just west of DC on the Maryland side of the Potomac. It was one of my favorite places to climb.

**

"Can we try something harder this time?" she asked as we

shouldered our equipment in the parking lot of the park.

"Absolutely," I replied, always happy to increase the difficulty of a challenge—one of my personality flaws.

In less than thirty minutes, she was cursing that request.

I was on belay at the foot of the cliff as she attempted her ascent, and I was enjoying the gorgeous shape of her behind as she moved with frustrating slowness to her next hand hold. It was too far for her to reach. I knew it. She knew it. But she tried for it anyway.

Pop. She came off the rock. I caught her weight immediately. She dangled there for a few minutes, swearing under her breath.

"Hey there," I yelled up to her.

"What?" she replied, clearly annoyed.

"To your left is a flake. It's off route, but it still has a 5.8 rating," I offered. "If you stretch your left foot out as far as you can reach, and then get your fingers in that flake, you can make it up the rest of the way and still have finished the hardest climb you've ever done."

She looked down at me, thinking that over. "You don't think I can finish the one I started?" she asked, pouting.

"The shoes I bought you are good...they aren't magic," I replied with a mischievous grin. "If you do it my way, you'll have made a two point jump past your best climb."

"Would you still respect me if I gave up on this one?" she asked jokingly.

"A two point bump in rating after five climbs? Hell yeah. That's very respectable," I replied. "That and I might actually get to climb today."

"I see right through you, Scott Wolfe," she jabbed playfully and then looked at the rock face again. After a moment of reflection she set her jaw. "I'm going to try this one once more."

I nodded, knowing it had been a losing suggestion to begin with. "What a surprise," I muttered to myself.

"What was that?" she called down.

"On belay!" I said back.

I let the resulting memory trigger from that word wash through my brain without fighting it. I discovered long ago that it's over faster and with less disruption if I just let it happen.

Merriam-Webster
Belay - verb or Noun \bi- 'lā

> *1: the securing of a person or a safety rope to an anchor point (as during mountain climbing); also: a method of so securing a person or rope*
> *2: something (as a projection of rock) to which a person or rope is anchored.*

The words, formatting, indentation, and inflection scrolled through my head as if I were reading them from a page or a computer screen. More than likely a remnant from the first time I looked the word up. If I had needed context for when the memory had occurred, that would have popped up as well.

It was quite annoying to have a brain that acted like a golden retriever in a park full of squirrels. But it was also the secret to my success…as a software developer, not as a boyfriend.

She dismissed my comment—and apparently my split second vacant stare, as well—and attempted her original ascent path once more. Within moments she'd popped off the rock again with another squeal of frustration. She dangled in her harness for a few seconds, shaking the tension from her hands.

"Are you ready for the other one?" I asked.

"Yes," she said reluctantly.

Within moments of getting back on the wall, she was past the crux move and moving her way to the top.

"Yay," I yelled up to her as she touched the snap-links at the top of the climb.

"Yay," she mumbled.

She walked down the cliff backwards as I lowered her slowly. When her feet touched the ground, she unclipped the rope and stood, looking up at the climb she couldn't finish.

"Two points on the maiden voyage of your new shoes," I said, consoling. "That's quite a prize."

"The other one would have been better," she said quietly, her jaw set in frustration.

"Patience, young one," I said soothingly. "All things in their own time."

She turned and looked at me for a moment, measuring my comment, and then slapped me on my shoulder—playfully.

"It's my birthday," she said finally, breaking into a broad grin. "Buy me cake."

No climb for me.

**

Back at my condo in Fairfax a few hours later, we had decided that we would bake a cake together. I'd convinced her to try the gluten-free cake mix; she convinced me to frost it with canned frosting. Compromise—the secret to any healthy relationship.

Dinner was spectacular, if I do say so myself. Pastured steak, parsnip and sunchoke shoestring fries, and fresh spinach and sunflower seeds sautéed in extra virgin olive oil. The wine was from a local Virginia winery. Not bad either. By the time we got to the cake, we had emptied the bottle and were both feeling quite playful. A little smear of frosting on a nose and then a bit on the chin and then the nape of the neck led to an obvious conclusion for the evening.

I was starting to see this girl, this woman, as more than a fleeting interest. But I also didn't like feeling I was being maneuvered. That thought alone kept much of my heart in reserve.

**

Evening of April 24th, 2010 – Bruges, Belgium

Satellite surveillance had been placed on one of Jovanovich's senior lieutenants, Vukasin Popovich. He and his driver had been active for two days, but had done nothing to indicate they were in physical contact with Jovanovich.

SEAL Team 9, 2nd Platoon had been brought into Belgium—the CIA station chief in Paris was certain that this would be their best opportunity to capture Jovanovich.

In the briefing, Langley had made it clear that if Popovich didn't lead them to Jovanovich soon, they would make the call to capture him for interrogation.

Shortly after night fall, the plan solidified. Popovich's Land Rover had pulled into a parking structure with just him and his driver. When they emerged from the other side, there were four people in the vehicle. That was the break the team had been waiting for.

A flurry of communication began as soon as the Rover reappeared on the street. Lt Marsh's team was on the ground in Bruges, and the Deputy Director of NCS at the CIA was running the operation personally back in Langley, Virginia.

"Arrow, this is Papa. Can you confirm that's our target rolling? Over," came the voice of Deputy Director Burgess through Lt. Marsh's tactical headset.

"Papa, this is Arrow. Confirmed. Primary target is outbound. That's our guy. Over," Marsh replied.

"Acknowledged. It's about time. The call is yours. Over," Burgess replied.

Marsh looked at his teammates. They all nodded. "Papa. We are go. Over," Marsh replied.

"Acknowledged. See you on the other side. Papa out."

That would be the last contact they had with Langley until after the mission unless something went wrong.

Four members of the SEAL team were in a nondescript minivan, following the Rover at a respectable distance. There was a second squad watching the safe house that had been used by Popovich the night before.

"Arrow. This is Stinger. We are standing by to assist. Do you need us closer?" Marsh's second-in-command asked from their stationary position outside the Serb safe-house.

"Negative, Stinger. You are too far out. If they slip through, they will more likely head your direction. Keep that safe house buttoned up. I don't want any reinforcements spoiling our surprise party," Marsh replied.

Two clicks on the COM confirmed the command had been received.

Their spotter, one of two snipers set up for the operation, was perched on a crane next to the canal. His elevated position—and his scope—gave him the perfect vantage point to follow the target over quite a range of distance.

"Arrow. This is Hawkeye," the sniper said. "Target has just turned onto service road at the docks. West Point. You're gonna miss your turn unless you cross two lanes right now."

In the van, Marsh slapped the driver in the shoulder indicating he should try to make the turn. "I always wanted to go to West Point," the driver said.

"You wouldn't meet the height requirement," Marsh said. "You have to be short enough to kiss ass without bending over." A moment of panic seized Marsh when it dawned on him that the Deputy Director of NCS was no doubt listening to their chatter—and he had been a West Point grad.

Through their earbuds, they heard the unmistakable sound of someone clearing his throat. Marsh dropped his head as a sheepish grin appeared on his face.

"I guess you're passed over again, Skipper," the driver

chuckled.

"Arrow. Hawkeye. They just stopped outside a warehouse at the point. No other traffic in the area. Over," the sniper said, snapping everyone back to focus.

"Hawkeye. Arrow. Acknowledged. We are one mike behind them. FUBAR that truck on my mark, and we'll come in hot," Marsh said.

He heard two clicks in his ear-piece confirming receipt of the command.

"Go dark now," Marsh said to the driver.

He counted down contact. "Twenty…fifteen…ten…five…take the truck."

A shot from the crane above the night skyline sent an armor-piercing round through the engine block of the Land Rover.

"Three…two…one…"

The van skidded to a stop next to the vehicle, its passengers already on the ground with their weapons trained on the occupants of the Rover. But as soon as the engine had been struck by the .50 cal round, Popovich had drawn his weapon, and he already opened the Rover's passenger side door. The other occupants of the vehicle weren't quite as fast, but they attempted to follow suit.

Popovich dropped to the ground as the minivan pulled up, firing two shots at the feet of the exiting occupants. One SEAL was struck and fell to the ground, leaving his head a target to the efficient Bosnian Serb killer. Popovich didn't hesitate for a second—the SEAL never even got a chance to steady his weapon.

The SEAL squad opened fire immediately, killing the driver as he drew his weapon. The passengers in the rear of the vehicle quickly ducked down, shooting back through the window and rear hatch from below the window level. Lt. Marsh tipped his rifle at an angle and shot down into the back seat, striking one of the men in the leg. When the wounded Serb raised his head in pain, Marsh noted it was not Jovanovich and put two bullets through his temple with his silenced rifle.

Pop. Pop.

The single remaining vehicle occupant placed his hands on his head and screamed "Surrender!"

The SEAL who had gone around the opposite side of the Rover was caught in the chest with small arms' fire. His body armor absorbed the impact, but the blow sent him to the ground. The second of peace Popovich bought himself was all he needed to make it to the edge of the dock. As he dove in, the sniper got off a third shot, striking Popovich at an angle across his head. He disappeared into the dark water

"Hawkeye. Arrow. Did you get the fourth bad guy?" Marsh asked into his throat mic.

"Arrow. Hawkeye. I got a piece of him. But I lost him in the water," the sniper replied.

"Shit!" one of the other team members exclaimed behind Marsh.

Marsh turned to look as Jovanovich's head was being black bagged and his hands zip tied. He saw the fallen team member—Petty Officer Mickelson. The dark hole in the center of his forehead precluded any question as to his condition.

"Papa. This is Arrow. Target acquired, kicking. Two bad

guys down, one unaccounted for," Marsh said. Then, after a second's pause, "One casualty."

"Arrow. Papa. Acknowledged. Bring it in. Over." Burgess replied with a somber tone.

"Roger. Out," Marsh said.

**

Back at Langley, Deputy Director Burgess walked upstairs to his office rather than taking the elevator. As soon as the door to the stairwell closed, he paused on the stairs, took a deep breath, and muttered, "Fuck."

two
Eight Days Until Event

4:00 p.m. on Saturday, May 8th, 2010 - 400 block of Singel in Amsterdam, Netherlands

Sjaak Visser was very happy. It was Saturday, and he was always happy on Saturday. He was the owner of a small fleet of canal tour boats in Amsterdam, and he worked very hard all week, managing bookings, taking reservations, and when shorthanded, even piloting a tour boat.

But today he was happy, and it was not because his job was so rewarding. He hated his job. He didn't like dealing with idiots, foreigners, and especially tourists. What made him happy was that all week long, while reservations were made and prepaid with credit cards, those who hadn't thought ahead paid cash at the time of service—untraceable cash. Cash that didn't go on the books.

With his coffers full, he looked forward to Saturday, when he would go to the office, reconcile the books for the week, and then pocket the unrecorded cash. It wasn't a fortune. Not enough to escape his life. But it was enough for him to buy a generous portion of hash, smoke it with his friends, and then amble, blurry eyed, down to his favorite Italian prostitute, Nella, who was always waiting with a smile and her ample bosom to soothe his worries away.

"Next Saturday, then?" Nella asked as Sjaak stumbled to the door, still trying to fasten his pants, the sweat of their passionate business exchange still clinging to his cheeks.

He looked up and smiled. "Yes," he replied. "We will run off together next Saturday."

Nella laughed. "I don't think your wife will like that very much," she said. "Besides, I am too expensive for you to hold on to every day."

"I would buy you the biggest diamond in all of Amsterdam and settle our tab up front," he gushed, a silly grin on his face.

Nella laughed again. "You should wait until your hash wears off before making promises like that," she said, giving him a wet kiss before shooing him out the door.

On the lazy walk home, he fantasized about a small house in Italy with a buxom new wife—Nella—and the leisure that would come from not having boats, employees, a family, or dealings with tourists.

By the time he reached his house he was completely immersed in the dream. As he put his hand on the door knob of his home on the 400 block of Singel, the bitterness of his reality began to creep back, harshing his buzz.

Upon opening the door, his hash- and sex-induced euphoria was further harshed, in a way quite different from the usual disgusted ranting of his wife.

Four men were standing in his parlor. Two of them were

standing behind his two children, who were seated on an oversized ottoman in the center of the room. The other two men were seated on the sofa, one on each side of his wife. His wife had blood trickling down from her hair line and an angry abrasion on her lip, which was starting to swell at the corner of her mouth.

He paused as he came into the room. His fuzzy head cleared very quickly when it finally dawned on him something was terribly wrong. "What is this? Why are you in my home?" he blurted in a nervous attempt at anger.

"Calm down, Mister Visser," came a voice from behind. Three more men had appeared behind him.

"We have a task that requires your assistance to be successfully completed," the man said. He was in his late thirties, average height and weight, with dark black hair and what appeared to be a thick scar on the right side of his neck and jaw, running from his ear to his chin like spilled wax.

"You have reservations for thirty people to take a canal lunch tour Monday morning at eleven o'clock a.m.," he continued.

"How do you know this?" he choked out indignantly.

The man walked calmly over to Sjaak and then hit him hard across the face with the back of his hand. Sjaak just stood there, dumbfounded.

"You will not speak. You will listen," the man continued. "You will take these passengers aboard your boat, *La Belle Époque*, and proceed toward Nieumarkt Square. Before arriving at Nieumarkt Square, you will pass under Jodenbreestrat Bridge. When the entire boat is under the bridge, you will stop. We will do our business, and then you will continue on to Nieumarkt Square. Now repeat to me what you will do."

"On Monday, thirty people. *La Belle Époque.* Go to Nieumarkt. Stop under Jodenbreestrat," he repeated nervously.

"Very good Mister Visser," the man said, smiling and patting him on his shoulder. "And in return for this simple service, we will return the lives of your wife, your daughter and your son—unharmed—with a very interesting story to tell when they grow old."

"You," Sjaak choked, "you are taking my wife and children?"

"Only borrowing them. For a short period of time," he replied with a gentle and understanding smile. "But make no mistake," he continued, his face turning somber, "if you fail me in any way, my friends here will take great joy in raping and then disemboweling each of them, slowly, one at a time, in front of each other, beginning with your son and ending with your wife."

The shock on Sjaak's face made it clear that he understood this was not to be fouled up. He nodded quickly, adding, "You have my word. I will do as you say. Please don't take my children from me."

"I'm glad we have an understanding, Mister Visser. Your wife and children will be back home by dinnertime on Monday if you satisfy the terms of our agreement," he said and then turned to go out the back door. "Good bye, Mister Visser. It has been a pleasure doing business with you and your lovely family."

The other men assisted his wife and children to their feet and then hurried them along toward the back door, following the dark-haired man with the scar on his jaw. As soon as the door closed, Sjaak dropped to the floor and began to weep. He felt this was his punishment for seeing Nella. He resolved that when he saw his wife and children again, he would be a changed man. He would no longer spend his Saturdays with whores. He resolved to give up the hash.

And then a soul crushing thought occurred to him.

What if I never see them again?

**

8:05 a.m. on Saturday, May 8th - Fairfax, Virginia

My phone rang, waking me. I was in a cold sweat, again, having had another disturbing dream about my father, again.

I looked at the time on my iPhone, seeing it was just after 8:00 a.m., before answering it. The caller was Barb.

"Good morning, sleepyhead," Barb chirped before I even managed a "hello." But I snapped out of my fog immediately—there was an edge to her voice that I had not heard before.

"Good morning to you as well," I replied, sitting up and wiping my eyes.

"Do you feel like having breakfast with me?" she asked.

It was not an invitation—it was a diplomatically constructed command.

"Sure," I replied. "Holy Natural?"

"Sounds good," she replied, trying to keep her voice pleasant, but I could tell that whatever was waiting for me would not be. "Nine o'clock?"

"Sure," I replied, swinging my legs off the bed. "See you in a bit."

The tension in her voice produced a mirrored tension in my chest. And as I prepared to leave, it built on itself until I found that I was quite worried—as well as a little annoyed.

**

The restaurant we met in was my favorite weekend breakfast spot. The owners went to great lengths to make sure everything was organic and local, but I ate there because the food was fantastic and the waitress always had some new, friendly tidbit about how to eat healthy. I noticed my climbing performance improved when I implemented her recommendations, so I was always happy to hear her preachy sermon about the evils of processed food.

It worked for me. Why argue with success?

I had brought Barb there on a number of occasions since we had started dating. As she sat across from me, carefully dissecting her grapefruit with her spoon, I could feel the tension build between us. She was going to drop a bomb on me.

"The grapefruit is bitter," she stated matter-of-factly. I didn't know her to complain about trivial things, so it threw up a red flag.

"I'm sorry," I replied soothingly. "Would you like me to order some orange slices instead?"

She toyed at the grapefruit with her spoon for a second, contemplating her response.

"Scott...how many girls have you brought here to eat bitter grapefruit on a Saturday morning?" she asked gently with a mischievous grin on her face. But beneath the grin there was tension that I just knew was going to ruin my day.

"A couple," I replied. "This is my favorite breakfast spot. But you're the first I've brought here more than once." I winked at her.

Her smile softened a bit, but I had only delayed hearing what was on her mind, not avoided it. Between the tension and the bad dream, I knew I wasn't prepared for what she felt she had to say.

I had been dating Barb for about three months—which in itself was a bit of a record for me the past few years. But now we had entered that clumsy period in the relationship when we were more than dating but still in that fuzzy gray area and unsure about what was next.

"No," she said absently, responding to my offer of oranges, changing the subject back to food. "It's not terrible. Just a bit tart." She paused and scooped another spoonful into her mouth, prompting the puckered sour face. "I should have eaten it before I sipped my latte."

She sat her spoon down in her bowl and picked up her coffee.

She was a beautiful woman. One of the few *women* I'd ever dated. I mostly went out with girls—the same age, some beautiful, some talented, but almost always frivolous, distracted, shallow girls... not women. Barbara was different. I knew it as soon as I saw her arguing agriculture subsidies with lobbyists at a bar in Georgetown.

"Do you think you'd be interested in heading up to Carderock today? I'll let you climb first." I said, baiting her with a combination invitation wrapped in a dare.

She tipped her head to the side and smiled at me through suspicious eyes and paused for a second. "Have I changed since we started 'seeing' each other?" she asked, using air quotes, referring mockingly to my description of our relationship.

She was working me. I knew this ploy—answering a question with another question which had nothing to do with the first.

"I'm almost certain I've seen you in more than one outfit...yeah, in fact, I'm positive I've seen you in at least three different things," I replied, straight face melting into a mischievous grin.

She rolled her eyes and shook her head, smiling. "Such a witty boy."

My friend and workmate Bonny—Bonbon to her friends and family—had introduced us one night at Clyde's. The bar had been noisy and crowded. Barb had been loudly though intelligently explaining to a group of agri-lobbyists why the ratio of nutrition-to-subsidy dollar was backwards when used to support grain and soy production. As soon as I realized who her audience was, I respected her.

Bonbon had warned me in advance that if I started a relationship with this one, I'd meet my match with regard to fickle relationship play. There's nothing like a challenge to pique my interest in something. Plus I realized that I was feeling a desire to settle into something more real. I had no idea I was being herded so effectively.

I met her smile and then got up, walked over behind her, leaned forward, and wrapped my arms around her. Then, kissing her on her cheek, I said "You are more wonderful now than you were then...I just didn't want to give you a big head."

I kissed her cheek again. "I'll be right back. Think about climbing," I said, walking away, giving her time to formulate what she wanted to say—and giving me time to brace myself.

Bonbon joked about our quasi-relationship frequently in her machine-gun communication style: "The code for the new interface is ready for testing. Not that it's any better than the old code. But it's fresher. Probably won't make it past the end of the month. When's the wedding? I'll let Storc know you're doing QA on it so he'll relax. He needs to get laid." Her dialogue would pour out in her raspy, mousy voice without so much as a breath between sentences. Sometimes it would be minutes before her whole conversation would sink in.

I stopped in the restroom before paying the bill. I stood in front of the mirror for a moment and looked at my reflection, trying for a moment to see myself as she did. I'm tall—taller than average anyway. Blue eyes, dark hair, square jaw, strong chin. I could be confused for good-looking.

I never saw myself that way, however. It had taken all my objectivity just to stop seeing the gangly, awkward nerd I had been in middle school: knobby knees, arms, and legs that had gotten too long, too fast, leaving me clumsy and self-conscious.

I washed my hands, ran them still wet through my hair, and then went to the counter to pay our bill.

When I arrived back at our table, Barb had clearly decided to abandon the grapefruit, having covered it with her napkin, and was sitting back in her chair, cradling her latte with both hands.

I watched her from behind for a few seconds before returning to the table.

The only thing that was really allowing me to stay objective was her fickleness regarding what she wanted to do between her masters and doctorate. She wasn't sure if she was going to be in the area or not, and in the direction this was going, I didn't want to jump in head first if she was then going to up-and-leave. Plus, I wasn't sure I liked the idea of having to constantly be on guard for manipulation. Eventually, if we stayed together, she would learn how to circumvent my awareness of it. That scared the shit out of me.

So for the moment, I was content to 'see' her and introduce her as 'my friend Barb.'

I sat down and smiled at her. She cocked her head to the side, squinted at me, and asked, "Did you pay our bill already?"

I smiled. "No, ma'am. I was thinking we could slip out the back and become fugitives."

"You did too," she replied accusingly, but smiling. "You always do that."

"Well...I am the one with a job, you know".

She replied by throwing an empty straw wrapper at me.

"Are you ready to go?" she asked.

"Yep. Did you decide if you want to go climbing or not?"

"I'd rather take a walk first, if you don't mind. Can we walk down by the water at the government center?" she asked.

The tone in her voice made it clear she had organized her thoughts. Though she was trying to disguise the seriousness of her tone, I could tell we were going to have a talk.

"Sure," I said, smiling.

On the short drive to the Fairfax Park Authority and Extension Center, we rode in silence for a few minutes before

Barb spoke up.

"Daddy's leaving for the Netherlands on Monday," she said softly, leaving the statement hanging for a few seconds before adding to it. "He asked me if I wanted to come with him."

She was baiting me to start this "talk" she wanted. I didn't bite.

"What's taking your dad to the Netherlands?" I asked.

"I think I mentioned he works for the State Department," she said. I nodded. "Well, he does legal work. And there was a recent capture of a war criminal—you may have seen it in the news—Jovanovich."

"Oh, yeah!" I replied. "I did hear about that. What's your dad have to do with that?"

"The trial at The Hague is going to start soon, and Dad is on the State Department's liaison legal team."

"That's exciting," I said. "Sounds like something out of James Bond!"

"Eh," She replied mildly. "It's mostly lawyer stuff. The exciting part was the capture. Now it's just lawyers, jurisdiction, and judges and trying to keep the witnesses from changing their stories before the trial starts. He just does legal support. No spy stuff."

"Still," I said smiling. "International war criminal, European crime boss—sounds pretty exciting to me."

We arrived and parked and then walked slowly along the park path to the pond and fountain on the other side of the building, holding hands as we went. As we came around the corner of the tall county building, the air became cooler and moist. The wind was picking moisture off the fountain and gently moving it in our direction. The park and surrounding trees were in full bloom.

It was mid-spring, and the temperature was pleasantly warm. I had been wearing shorts since March, but today it seemed everyone was wearing them. Barb was in a skirt and blouse— flowing and airy just like the day.

She was quiet for the longest time—or what seemed like the longest time. I was at a loss. Anything I said would have come across as awkward silence fodder, so I kept quiet. She leaned over as we walked and put her head on my shoulder, drawing me closer.

We walked around the pond once and ended up back at the steps in front of the fountain.

"Let's sit," she said finally. Without waiting for me to respond, she kicked off her sandals, hiked her skirt up to her knees, and sat on the edge of the fountain, letting her feet dangle in the chilly water, flicking at it with her toes.

I sat next to her, shoulder to shoulder. "What's up?" I asked gently. Letting her know by the tone in my voice that I sensed her distress.

She drew her knees up close to her and hugged them, laying her head down sideways on top of them, looking at me. She sat that way for a moment and then gently, lovingly, bumped me with her shoulder.

"I'm sad," she stated simply.

I remained quiet, letting that statement sink in for both of us. After a moment or two she continued.

"I really like you, Scott Wolfe."

"I really like you too, Barb Whitney," I replied with a grin.

"Hush," she snapped but quickly softened it with a smile. There was a short pause. "I really like being with you. I like it too much."

I remained quiet. I knew what was coming next, and I had to hold on tight or risk overreacting. It already hurt, and I hadn't even heard the words yet.

"I have to go back to school soon," she continued. "The past three months with you have been wonderful. The best I can remember. But I can't hold off my whole life's plan for something that *might* happen."

I pulled my knees up like she had, resting my chin on them. I remained quiet. This was her moment. She had built up to it, and I wasn't going to derail her momentum.

She watched me for a few seconds, looking for my reaction, and then she went on.

"I don't know if it's just timing, or if we're going slow for a reason, or if this is just as far as you and I can go…" she paused again, reaching for her words carefully. "But I don't feel confident that…" A long pause. "I don't feel confident that you can commit to this relationship enough to justify staying here and missing another semester of school. There. I said it." She looked at me for a moment, and then said, "Damn…that was way worse than it had sounded in my head."

There was obviously a battle going on in her head between logic and emotion. I looked at her sideways for a moment and then spoke slowly, purposefully, and gently.

"I understand. You have a lot of time invested in your future, a clear direction, and a strong momentum," I said, pausing to let that be felt. "But I want you to know, that if you decided to stay in this area to finish your doctorate, I would remain your understanding and supportive..." I stopped. *Uh oh,* I thought. *I've created a verbal booby trap. I have to define what I am to her.*

"Stop," she said suddenly.

That was it. I hesitated at a moment when she needed certainty. I had just closed the door she cracked open.

I dropped my head. She smiled. Then everything shifted to a very pleasant get-together between friends. I had my opportunity, and now the moment was gone—and so was she, emotionally anyway.

"Dad invited me to go with him to the Netherlands before the summer semester starts. So I probably won't see you for a few weeks. But we should get together when I get back...before I have to pack up and leave for school."

And that was it. The deed had been done with no tears, no yelling, no drama—just a heart-wrenching yank and the slow vacuum of cold air backfilling the void that had just been formed.

The ride back to my condo was a theater of friendly conversation. I could see the glassy sheen on her eyes, but she would not cry and would not stop chattering like we were college roommates catching up on everything before summer break.

"So when we get to Amsterdam, Dad has a couple of days to do the whole 'tourist thing' before he has to jump into the trial," she said, having obviously, recently decided to go on the trip with her father. "I'm looking forward to some time with him. We've both been too busy recently."

Ouch. That was aimed directly at me.

"Maybe the change of scenery will help me figure out if I'm going to expand on my masters' dissertation linking failed federal corporate regulation with the collapse of corporate lobbying rules, or if I will change course and go for 'International Trade agreement, '" she said, but I saw her lip quiver. She was obviously now addressing everything she had put on hold because of me.

"Besides," she continued. "It's time to aim this expensive education at something like a career. I just have to decide if I'll follow Daddy's footsteps or go for a lobbying job."

By the time we got to the condo, I was nearly desperate to say good bye. I had an overwhelming urge to grab her around the waist, tell her not to go to Amsterdam, finish her doctorate at Georgetown instead of Harvard, and move in with me. But that would have only been my reaction to her, not how I truly felt.

Fuck. Fuck, fuck, fuck! I hate guilt, deserved or not.

Objectivity was nowhere to be found as I hugged her goodbye. "Have a safe trip," I said before she stepped into her little sports car and drove away. Outwardly though, I could feel I was smooth and unreadable as ever—an asshole.

As soon as she turned off my court and onto Fair Ridge Drive, I took a deep breath, shoving down my ache, and then turned and went inside.

I plopped down into my overstuffed green chair and swung my feet up onto the ottoman. I immediately felt a mild sense of relief lurking there under the ache. I surfed through all the TV channels twice before realizing there was nothing to hold my interest.

Only a few seconds after I had turned the TV off, my phone rang. It was Bonbon. I didn't really want to answer it because I knew she would already be aware of this morning's breakup. Barb would have been on the phone with her as soon as she pulled out of the parking lot.

"Hello," I said sleepily.

"Do you have something to tell me? Something to say? I'm sure you do. Think about it for a second, and it will come to you," she spilled out in a single breath, her tone bitter and accusing.

"Bon. I'm not in the mood." I said, plainly with an edge in my voice.

"Mood?" she questioned sarcastically. "What are you in the mood to do? Are you in the mood to ruin a perfectly good relationship because it's moving a bit too fast for you? Are you in the mood strain a friendship? Are you in the mood to—"

"Stop. Please," I said, interrupting her tirade before it could gain more momentum. "I'm not in the mood to be guilted for a tough decision. Mine or hers."

"That's all fine and good," Bonbon said. "But there are other things at stake here. She was crying."

"I don't know if she shared this with you or not, but she is the one who decided to leave for the Netherlands and then head back to school in Massachusetts. Not me."

"You didn't give her much choice, did you?" she said, clearly having picked a side in this debate.

"Bonny," I said, slowing down the momentum. "She has her own speed, needs, and expectations, and I have mine. She clearly doesn't think they jive."

"Whatever," she said flippantly.

What? I thought. *There was no way I just derailed Bonbon with the, "Everyone makes their own decisions" argument. Be careful, Scott. It's a trap.*

"I'm sorry, Bonbon," I said softly. "I really would have liked for her to stay in the area. She just needed more of a guarantee than I could give. That's a heavy burden to put on someone after three months."

"Again. Whatever," she replied coldly.

"Okay. Well since this isn't going to be the supportive conversation I need after a hard breakup, I'd rather just hang up and sit here alone for a while," I said, reminding her that she was my friend too, and that this hadn't been easy on me either.

There was a long pause and then, "I'm sorry, Scott. You're right," she said sincerely. "I was just really hoping you two would make it."

"Me too, Bonbon. I promise," I said. The exhaustion from the conversation was already creeping up on me.

There was another pause. She was planning her next line of attack. The frontal didn't work, so she needed a flanking move now.

"Me, Storc, and a couple of other people from work are going out tonight. You should come with us. Get your mind off it," she said finally. I could tell by the tone of her voice that there was no use trying to resist. She would have her way.

"I'm so tired, Bonbon. I don't—"

"We'll make it an early night. I promise," she said, knowingly lying to me.

"Okay. For a couple of hours. But when I'm ready to leave, I'm just leaving. Okay?" I said, setting up my exit unapologetically.

"Okay. Deal!" she said excitedly. "Ultrabar. 9:30. No, better make it 9:00," she said quickly.

"Alright, Bonbon. I'll see you then."

"Don't back out. I'm serious. I'll come and get you," she said threateningly.

"Okay. Bye," I said and then hung up.

A long sigh escaped me. It made me tired just thinking about going to a club tonight, but if I hadn't agreed to do it, Bonny would have hounded me until not only would I have gone, but I would have been more tired and more miserable from the resistance. She had us all very well trained.

**

11:45 p.m. on Saturday, May 8th - Amsterdam, Netherlands

VUKASIN POPOVICH sat quietly on a stack of crates in the corner of the warehouse where he was meeting with members of the Amsterdam Russian mob. He didn't like relying on the Russians for this operation, but time and resources were limited— he had little choice. Keeping them in line would be the hard part.

"So we steal truck, we provide security, we burn evidence, and Serbs stand around looking pretty," said the grating Vova— the second in command of the local mob family.

"Quiet, Vova," hissed his boss—Rodka.

"Why I be quiet?" Vova protested loudly, trying to show he wasn't afraid of Popovich as the others were. "Is our risk, our resources, and if they fuck up—" he said, jabbing his finger in the air toward Popovich, "it's us getting caught!"

"Is good deal. You need to stop," Rodka said, putting his hand on Vova's chest, trying to get him to calm his tone—but Vova was on a roll.

"Why I stop?" Vova said incredulously. "Everyone acting so afraid. Is bad plan, is bad deal, and these are Serbs—in old days this would not happen."

"So you think it's a bad plan?" Popovich said, rising from his stack of boxes. "What do you think we should do instead?"

He walked over in front of Vova with a calm, questioning expression on his face. "Please. This is not the army. If you have a better idea, let's discuss it."

Vova opened his mouth to speak, but he never got to say what he intended. Popovich's arm lashed out with the speed of a cobra, striking Vova in the throat with the edge of his hand. Vova's eyes flashed wide, and his own hands went to his throat as he fell backwards onto the concrete.

A few of the other Russians went for their weapons, but while Popovich stood over Vova, watching him turn blue and twitch, the rest of the Serbs in room quickly raised their weapons at the remaining Russians.

"*Hvatit!*" Rodka yelled at his men, his face twisted into a snarl. "Do nothing!"

The remaining Russians tensed on the edge of violence as

Rodka stepped between them and Popovich.

"Vova brought it on himself," Rodka said and then looked down at the now-still Vova on the floor. "This is the deal. We agreed to it. This isn't game."

"You take this?" one of the other Russians asked incredulously.

Anger spread across Rodka's face, and he slapped the big man who had questioned him.

"Enough, Daniil!" Rodka yelled. "We are in this now. We do what Popovich say."

The big Russian looked down at Vova's lifeless body and then down at his shoes. "Yes, Boss," he said pitifully. The rest of the Russians relaxed their stances after that, though they were still fuming over the assault.

"We'll need someone else to steal the truck now," Popovich said with a smug grin on his face. The big Russian—Daniil— looked up and glared at him, but he didn't make another move toward violence.

"Elvis," Rodka said, turning to one of the other men. "You will Sunday night find box truck and take to safehouse on Amstel. You stay until we arrive."

"Yes, Rodka," Elvis replied meekly.

"Take plates from another truck and cover back," Rodka continued. "No mistakes."

Elvis nodded his understanding, trying hard not to look at Vova's body or Popovich.

"Truck will be taken care of," Rodka said. There was hate in his eyes, but Popovich knew he wouldn't risk his whole family over the execution of one man—the lesson had been effective.

The other Russians had already begun to leave when Rodka motioned them toward the door. He stayed a moment longer, watching them depart, and then turned to Popovich once they were out of earshot.

"Vova was your pilot," Rodka said, anger still boiling in his eyes.

Popovich smiled and watched as the Russians dragged Vova's body into the back of their van. "As I recall, you did a fair amount of flying in the army as well."

It was clear that Rodka had hoped that information had stayed forgotten. But Popovich didn't seem to forget anything. Rodka reluctantly nodded his acceptance and then turned to leave. When he was halfway to the van, Popovich called out.

"Rodka," Popovich yelled across the floor of the warehouse. He waited for the other man to turn. "Let's have no more need for lessons. These are your men. Next time I will hold you responsible for their disrespect."

Rodka looked as if he were on the edge of saying something, but he suddenly turned away, obviously thinking better of it, and then joined his men in the van. As they drove out of the warehouse, Popovich smiled with satisfaction.

"It's best to keep livestock in line before the slaughter," he muttered as he walked past his men. They chuckled at the comment.

**

8:55 p.m. on Saturday, May 8th - Ultrabar, Washington DC

I took the metro into the city and got off at Metro Center and then walked the three blocks or so to the club. It was 8:55 p.m. when I arrived, but 9:10 p.m. before I got in.

Bonny had failed to mention which part of the club she would be in, so I wandered for a while, getting a beer from the bar before I set off looking for her. In one of the dance areas, I bumped into Stacy, a girl I had dated a couple of times. She danced up to me.

"Hey ya, Scott! How are you doing, baby?" she yelled at me over the music.

"I'm well!" I said, smiling. "I'm looking for Bonny and Storc. Have you seen them?"

She thought for a second. She was drunk already, and the evening had just started. "Nope! Haven't seen them," she said. "Why don't you just hang out with me for a while and let them find us?" she said, rubbing her hand across my arm and chest, bouncing to the music. I smiled.

"Sorry," I said. "Maybe later. I have to find Bonny and Storc."

She kissed me on my cheek, and I wandered away.

The drinking had been the reason I didn't go on more than a couple of dates with Stacey. She was very sweet, but I felt there was something painful enough in her life that required nearly constant self-medication.

I don't mind going out and drinking to have a good time, but I refuse to drink so that I can allow myself to have a good time. It results in too many hangovers, damaged brain cells—

which I prize above all other cells—and very little free time to improve myself. To date her would mean spending all my time drinking or, at the very least, watching her drink.

I wandered into another dance area. My beer was empty, so I pushed my way through to the bar to get another. As I leaned into the bar, someone came up behind me and put her arms around my waist. I turned.

"Hey Bonny!" I yelled over the noise.

"Hey Scottman, Scottmiester, Scott-a-lama-dingdong!" she slurred. It appeared as though Stacey was not the only one drinking for a goal tonight.

Storc followed behind her, reaching for Bonny quickly to keep her from tipping us both over.

"Hey! Easy there, Bonbon," Storc cautioned. "Let's get you back to the table."

"I wanna dance!" she yelled, protesting.

"Later," Storc said. "The night is young."

"And so are we," she sang in response, but she followed him as he made a path back to the table our friends from work were sitting at.

When we arrived at the table, Bonny plopped down on the bench, bouncing on the cushion once before settling. Storc squeezed in beside her. I sat on the opposite side of the table, purposely trying to avoid Bonny in this state. It would only be moments before she would remember the reason she asked me to come out, and a drunken Bonny was not someone you wanted a serious conversation with.

I sat next to Tina and Janet, the "twisted sisters," as they were called at work. Though not sisters, they were rarely seen outside of each other's company, and though they looked nothing alike, they spoke sometimes in unison, as twins often do.

They too had been drinking heavily. I found it amazing that in the time it took me to get into the club and drink one beer, nearly everyone at the table had managed to consume a half dozen drinks each…everyone but Storc, who, in chronic worrier fashion, was the self-appointed designated 'sober thinker.'

"How long have you all been here?" I asked over the loud house beat that was vibrating every surface.

Bonny leaned forward and yelled, "An hour or two." She was clearly unaware of the time.

Stoned as well, I thought.

Storc shook his head. "Forty-five minutes," he corrected.

Bonny proceeded to argue the point as Storc patiently nodded, agreeing with her, having learned long ago that arguing with Bonny is pointless, and that arguing with Drunk Bonny is dangerous.

A passing waitress stopped at the table. "What can I get you?" she asked.

"Something dark on tap," I replied.

As soon as the waitress departed, another girl I knew wandered up to the table, dancing.

"Hey, Scott," she said as her body rippled to the techno beat.

"Hi, Claire," I said back, over the roar around us.

"Come and dance!" she said seductively. Her friend, whose name I could never remember, stepped up beside her and started bumping hips with Claire. They both reached out to try and pull me from my seat, but they were interrupted by an angry Bonny, who was climbing across the table, spilling drinks and bottles across the surface.

Both Claire and her friend took a giant step backwards as Bonbon poured herself over the edge of the table toward them and fell onto the floor. Storc and I quickly lifted her and checked to see there that was no bleeding.

"I'm fine," she screamed, shaking our hands off her and then turning her attention to Claire. "I've got business with the Flying Scott-man...man," she slurred. Claire took a step toward Bonny. For a brief second, I thought there was to be a girl fight.

Claire leaned over and whispered something to Bonny that made her mouth drop open, and Bonny suddenly began to giggle uncontrollably. Claire touched Bonny's face with her hand, kissed her on the cheek, very close to her mouth, and then turned and left.

"I even got game with the bitches, bitches," Bonny crowed, and then she began climbing back across the table again. Storc stopped her and guided her around the edge of the table back to her seat. As soon as she was seated, she glared at me through accusingly narrowed eyes.

"Hey!" She yelled across the table at me. "Why don't you like Barbara anymore?"

All eyes got wide and turned to me.

"You broke up with Barb?" Janet asked.

I was suddenly very uncomfortable. "Something like that," I mumbled.

"Oh! She broke up with *you*," Tina threw in knowingly.

"Something like that," I repeated.

"Hey!" Bonny yelled at the two girls. "Bonbon is talking with the Scottmeister." Then back at me. "Scott! Why did you break up with Barb?"

"Bonny," I said, with annoyance and anger in my voice. "Barb broke up with me. I'm not happy about it, but I'll live. Thanks for asking. If this is what you plan on making my night about, I will leave now. I can afford a six pack for every beer I buy here, and then I could take it home and drink it in peace and quiet."

"I'm sorry, I'm sorry," she said quickly. "Don't leave. Please don't leave."

I couldn't believe it had been that easy to derail her. She attempted to get up on the table again to crawl toward me, but she was restrained by everyone, so instead she crawled under the table, pushing legs and purses out of the way as she went. She still managed to spill every drink on the table.

When she popped up on my side, she tried to get Janet to move over. When Janet refused, Bonbon sat on her lap, resulting in a giggly squeal from both girls as Janet and Tina began pinching and tickling her to get her off.

The sight of three pierced and tattooed girls, each with a different unnatural hair color springing somewhere from their heads was interesting enough. But seeing them twisting and turning, laughing and squealing while they maneuvered for space was quite the comedy—and something that made me laugh. I was grateful for that.

Once the seating arrangement had played out, Bonny looped her arm through mine and hugged me close.

"I'm so sorry, Scott. I thought you two would be great for each other," she said sincerely—as sincere as she could be in her current state anyway.

"It's not your fault, Bonbon, but thank you," I replied.

"You know. I've always liked you, Scott," she said and then quickly added, "I mean you're totally *not* my type. Way too straight for me."

"I know. And you're way too dark for me," I said, joking with her.

"The only reason we come to these techno meat factories is for you guys," she said, pointing at Storc and me and then waving her arm around the table at a couple of our other workmates. "This shit makes our ears bleed."

"We've been to your dungeon clubs before," I reminded her.

"They're called 'steam punk,'" she corrected.

"Right."

"You don't even have any tattoos. You and Storc are the only people we hang out with who don't have tattoos," she whined.

"I do too have a tattoo!" Storc complained.

Bonny looked at him condescendingly. "Birthday bar codes don't count. You have to show them! Be proud!" She lifted her shirt, revealing a knot of Celtic vines emerging from her waistband and winding their way up under her black bra. She then reached for Tina's neckline, pulling on her shirt to reveal the frogs tattooed on her breast, prompting a squeal and another giggly battle beside me.

Tina smoothed her shirt and shoved Bonny into my side, sending me to the floor. Tina and Janet thought it was funny, so they bumped Bonny and sent her over the edge on top of me. She laughed as she struggled up.

The light-hearted ruckus improved my mood dramatically, and within an hour, I was out on the floor dancing with an alternating lineup of Bonbon, Tina, Janet, Claire, and her friend whose name I could never remember. Even Storc danced, demonstrating that a computer geek can learn rhythm given the appropriate motivation—five cute girls.

By midnight, Bonbon and Claire were making out in a corner. It wasn't the first time I'd seen Bonbon hook up at a club, but it was the first time I'd seen her displaying her sexual diversity in front of people from work. She was really drunk. I would be surprised if she remembered it the next day.

Around 1:30 am, I was starting to nod off when it occurred to me that I still had to catch the metro back to the commuter lot in Fairfax. I started to say my goodbyes.

Bonbon saw me moving for the door, broke her embrace with Claire, and ran to me, amazingly without falling over anything.

"You can't go yet! We haven't talked," she whined.

"It's really okay, Bonbon. You're busy anyway," I said, winking and nodding toward Claire pouting in the corner.

Bonny dismissed my comment with a wave of her hand. "She'll get over it." Then a serious look washed over her face. "Are you two really done?"

"I think so, Bonny," I replied. "Bad timing."

"That makes me sad," she replied with a pout on her face.

"Me too," I said.

She hugged me and then sent me on my way with a pat on my behind.

three
Seven Days Until Event

Sunday Morning, May 9th, 2010 - Fairfax, Virginia

I wasn't sure where I was. I was breathing heavily, my legs were taking short strides, and no matter how hard I tried, I couldn't seem to move faster. I looked down and saw feet—a child's feet.

I looked over my shoulder and saw my father running behind me. My heart jumped, and I pumped my legs and arms harder, trying to pull ahead. He seemed to be toying with me. I could tell he could catch up to me anytime he wanted.

I came to a clearing and looked up. It was night, but there was a full moon. I could feel the cold stone before I recognized what it was. In my confused state of mind, my first thought was that it was a sleeping giant. It quickly dawned on me it was a giant stone rising up out of the side of the river bank. To my small eyes it looked as if it were a thousand feet tall.

I looked back and saw my father paused at the edge of the clearing. I thought that perhaps I had lost him, but he turned and laid his eyes right on me. My heart skipped a beat again. I was afraid of my father. He had done something—though I couldn't remember what—to make me fear him.

I put my hand on the cold stone, and a sharp flash of pain shot up my arm. I looked at my hand and saw a gash across my palm. But fear drove me forward, and I began to climb up the rock. I looked down over my shoulder and saw my father pursuing me.

I increased my pace, grasping the rough stone with my small tender fingers. I looked back again and saw shadows on the ground. Ghosts, phantoms, demons—I wasn't sure which, but the fear swelled up in me, and I felt like my small chest would explode from the thundering heartbeat contained within.

I had just made it to a ledge halfway up and looked over when my father's hand grasped the edge. He tried to pull himself up, but his eyes closed tightly, and he seemed to slip. Fighting past my fear, I reached out and grabbed his hand. I began to go over the edge, dragged down by his weight.

I sat up in my bed, drenched from head to toe in sweat, with my sheets tied in knots around my legs.

The dream of my old playground along the Rappahannock River in Spotsylvania County was becoming more vivid of late. In the dream, though I had climbed the rock face many times since I was ten, it seemed unfamiliar—and my father was always in pursuit.

After spending a few moments calming my breath and heart rate, I flopped back down in my soaked sheets and looked at the clock. 5:03 a.m.

"Uhg."

I drifted back into an uneasy sleep.

**

I woke slowly. Over a period of about thirty minutes I opened my eyes to an overly bright, overly loud experience. I had a mother of a hangover. I lingered in bed for another twenty minutes before the nausea in my stomach forced me to rise and dash to the bathroom.

Note to self: breakup, beer, tequila shots, and Bonbon are a bad combination. My joints ached, my head hurt, and my eyes felt like I had slept with sand paper in them. *This is going to be a long day.*

I looked at the clock and realized I had slept half of it away. "Not *such* a long day," I said aloud. *Oh shit,* I thought. *I sound as bad as I feel.* I resolved not to speak again until my throat felt less like gravel. It was too creepy.

I slowly got dressed and then made my way into the kitchen. The trip took far too long. *Coffee,* I thought.

I sat and waited for the coffee to brew. It was taking infuriatingly long to produce as I sat watching it from one of my kitchen bar stools, head cradled in my hand. After a few moments, I realized it was not plugged in.

This is going to be a long day, I thought again.

I finally got the coffee pot functioning properly and decided it would be best if I didn't stare at it. I plopped down heavily into my overstuffed green chair and flipped the TV on. I surfed through the channels once and then gave up.

"Why do I even have a TV?" I asked myself aloud. It occurred to me that my voice sounded better. I turned the TV off and instead opted to check my email on my new iPad. This little devil had me totally absorbed. The company had bought it for me so I could test apps. It had become my go-to computing device when not at my desk.

I scanned my email and saw one from Bonny. *Later*, I thought. *It's too early for her*.

I found one from Storc. He had uploaded a new app to the server. He wanted me to look at it. I checked the time on the email and was *not* surprised to see that it had been sent at 4:30 am. The man never slept. I downloaded the app and installed it, but I decided to check it out later—I smelled coffee.

I felt much better after my first cup. By the time I reached the bottom of my second cup, I was feeling almost human. I decided I needed to get out of the house. Without thinking too hard on the subject, I put on my climbing clothes and then ran downstairs, grabbing my climbing gear out of the downstairs coat closet on the way out. I needed rock under my fingers.

**

Carderock was a line of beautiful schist and quartz sticking up conveniently just across the river in Maryland—less than thirty minutes from Fair Ridge where I lived. I had been climbing there several times a week since I moved to Fairfax five years earlier.

The climbs were short in height yet challenging—for the first year. But by the time I was working at TravTech, I had to make them harder than they were by avoiding important holds. Today I would be challenging them right back. I had some poison I needed to work out of my system. All the words, emotions, and alcohol I had swallowed were now turning sour in my stomach, and I could feel everything leeching into my muscles. I needed a workout.

I roped up the tallest nubby face available on the busy pathway above the rock. There were too many climbers and gawkers wandering around below to toss a rope, so I snaked mine down instead.

Though I had been fairly confident I'd be able to find someone I knew to partner with, I was disappointed to discover everyone I knew—at least everyone I knew who I was also comfortable with belaying me—was already paired up with someone else. Instead, I looped a pair of ascenders through my harness, clipped a third one to my climbing rack, and started up the hardest part of the face.

The quartz had been worn smooth with nearly one hundred years of climbing, and the routes were harder and harder to ascend each year due to that wear. I had long since stopped looking at the climb ratings and instead simply climbed. Today I was ignoring handholds and toe holds any larger than my thumb. That should give me the distraction I was looking for.

I had been rock climbing since I was ten years old.

It was also around that time that my father had died, so there had been many changes in my life. Not the least of which was the discovery of my skill and passion for climbing—which had, for some reason, always been tied to thoughts of my father's death, though I'd never been sure why.

Except for a few years when I took karate lessons, the only physical activity I'd consistently, religiously practiced had been rock climbing. Each climb was a puzzle waiting to be solved—and some would have to wait until a new level of physical strength or agility had developed. There was always a new challenge.

Two hours into my climb, I had popped off the rock sixteen times, ripped a small corner off of one fingernail, and rolled the sharp edge off of one side of my right climbing shoe. I was doing damage.

On my seventeenth pop, I saw Lily out of the corner of my eye, standing below me and looking up. I had climbed with Lily many times in the last five years. She was tall, thin, and strong, with dense ropes of muscle visible through anything she wore. She was a few years older than me and took great pleasure in keeping my ego in check. She did not disappoint today.

"Hey there, youngster!" she yelled up, displaying her wide, toothy grin. "You missed a few holds. Are your eyes going out on ya?"

"I'm looking for an upgrade on this route," I replied. There was no need to yell, the rock wall carried every sound clearly over the river with just a speaking voice. I believe she kept her voice raised to bolster her mocking.

"Then you should climb back over your path," she yelled up again. "You've smeared it with enough blood and skin to upgrade it to a 5.14."

She had successfully knocked the wind out of my sails. I lowered myself down, slowly, feeling the ache in my body completely as gravity greeted my feet touching the ground. I sat down against the cool rock face without unhooking, and Lily handed me her water bottle.

I took it gratefully and pulled on it deeply, swishing a bit around in my mouth when I was done.

"Thanks," I said as I passed the bottle back to her.

She had dropped her climbing pack next to mine while she was watching me. She tucked her bottle back into a side pocket and hefted it up onto one shoulder by both straps.

"Don't climb angry," she said with a wink as she walked past me and headed for the walking path to the top.

I just nodded. Good advice any day. I was done.

After a brief rest, I packed up my gear and hiked to the top of the rock wall to retrieve my rope and anchor straps. Lily, already at the top, had just finished coiling her rope and anchors and was stuffing them into her pack.

I plopped down on the sun-warmed stone cross-legged and began carefully winding my own rope around my legs to form a neat coil. Lily hefted her pack on her shoulders and walked in my direction, dropping her pack next to mine once more. She then proceeded to untie my anchor straps from the trees and boulder that I had tied to. I smiled at her weakly. When she was done, I had wound only a little better than half my rope, so she dropped down next to me with a grunt.

"Thanks," I said mildly.

She nodded in reply, smiling, and then sat drinking from her water bottle while I continued to wind my rope.

She watched me for a few moments before she finally spoke.

"Did you break her heart as much as she broke yours?" she asked.

I was taken a bit off guard by the question, but I wasn't completely surprised. I wasn't the only person who could follow obvious clues and cues to a simple hypothesis.

I smiled sheepishly and without looking at her. "Yeah. I'm pretty sure I did," I heard the sadness in my own voice; I knew she did.

"Well," she began, "I'm not the best person to offer

relationship advice, that's for damn sure. I'm thirty-four and have been married and divorced twice," She paused to take another pull on her water bottle and then wiped her mouth with the back of her hand. "But it's been my experience that if two people are both broken-hearted about a breakup, a little more work could have kept them together."

I let that seep in for a moment as I tied the end of my rope coil.

"I'll agree with you to a point. But that's not to say that both people are able or willing to work a little harder," I replied.

"True," she said.

"And it's not always so easy for some people to wait around while personal baggage is being dealt with by one or both people," I said giving her an insight into what was going on with me.

"Ahhh," she said with irony. "That is their first mistake. Personal baggage is much easier to carry with two than it is with one." She smiled.

"You have to know someone for a while before—"

"Details," she interrupted. "There are a million details in a relationship, like a bag full of excuses waiting to be popped open and fished out."

I looked at her for a moment, letting her words sink in.

When I didn't respond, she continued. "A relationship is about emotion—nothing else. When you get scared by something in a relationship, you start fishing for those details so you can convince yourself you have a reason to leave. All you are doing is letting the fear in your head try to outwit your heart. Sorry...all *they* are doing is letting *their* heads try to outwit *their* hearts."

Her insight had seemed to awaken something in me. I smiled. She patted me on the leg as she rose, grabbing her pack. She slung it across her shoulder. "Good luck, youngster." She turned onto the path and marched away toward the parking lot.

I sat for a moment longer, contemplating Lily's words—and my next step. Fear welled up in me as it dawned on me that none of my insight made any difference if Barb wasn't willing as well.

"Details," I said aloud. With that punctuation, I suddenly had the energy and the courage to try.

"Thank you, Lily," I yelled into the woods in the direction of the path.

I heard a burst of laughter echoing back at me from the woods.

It was getting late in the day. The daytime crowd at Carderock had started to thin out, and the teenage tourists were starting to show up. They stumbled down the rock pathways to the river, clowning on the boulders and showing off for their girlfriends. Some even attempted to imitate the climbers by trying to stick onto the walls of rock, only to pop off after a few seconds when their weak, soft hands and their soft-edged basketball shoes failed to cling.

I pulled my phone out to call Barb's number when I realized the time. She would be getting on her flight soon. I hit dial, and it rang four times before going to voicemail.

"Hi, this is Barbara. Leave a message," her voice chirped. *Beep.*

"Hi Barb. I know you are probably at the airport and this message would have been better delivered in person, or even better, on Saturday morning when it would have mattered.

"I'm sorry. The words 'being supportive and understanding' should have been seamlessly and effortlessly followed by 'partner, boyfriend, or significant other.' I failed miserably in telling you where I stood.

"It's an old habit I believe our time together is making obsolete. I'm sorry I sound so pathetic right now, but I hope it underscores how much you mean to me."

I paused, suddenly remembering I was talking to voicemail. I punched end on my phone, leaving my message as it stood, for better or worse.

I leaned back on my pack and let the late afternoon sun warm my face. The breeze, carrying cool air from the Potomac, was starting to win its battle against the heat of the day and was sending little puffs of cool air across my bare legs—warm then cool, warm then cool. I must have drifted off for a few moments because a chirp from my phone woke me out of doze. It was a text from Barb.

It read, *"Taking off in a few minutes. Have to turn off phone. Your timing sucks ;) We'll talk when I return."*

four
Six Days Until Event

Monday, May 10th, 2010 - Schiphol Airport in Amsterdam, Netherlands

BARB WHITNEY wasn't happy when she arrived in Amsterdam.

"You're kidding me, right?" Barb said to her father as they made their way through customs in Amsterdam. "I just want to go to bed!"

"You'd be doing me a huge favor," her father, Robert, said. "The ambassador's daughter is only a couple of years younger than you and is the only person close to your age in the group from The Hague. The charge d'affairs made a special request for you to go with us. He's giving up his own ticket so you can join the group."

"Okay," she said with resignation. "But you have to promise that as soon as we are done, you'll take me back to our hotel. I didn't sleep more than two hours on the flight."

"Deal," Robert said. "Thank you, sweetheart. I will make it

up to you, I promise."

As they emerged from customs into the reception area, there was a man in a black suit holding a sign for 'Whitney.' He loaded their luggage on a cart and led them to the car waiting for them. Once in the car, Barb leaned over and put her head on her dad's shoulder.

"I'm sorry for being such a princess back there," she said.

"I know, sweetheart. It was a long flight, and you have other things on your mind besides protecting the ambassador's daughter from a bunch of old people," he replied, referring to their earlier discussion, which had been brief and lacking in detail, about her 'boyfriend' dilemma.

"So what is this thing that we're doing with the embassy staff and their families?" she asked.

"It's a canal lunch tour on a restored, Victorian-era boat, more of a floating restaurant, named *La Belle Époque*," he replied.

"Hmmm. Could be fun," she said as their car merged onto the highway to take them to the NH Hotel in the center of Amsterdam.

Upon arriving at the hotel, they immediately checked in. It was all Barb could do to keep from falling asleep at the counter. When they were done, they climbed into the elevator and rode to their floor, where they separated and went into their rooms.

Without pausing, she dropped her bags in the floor of her room and headed directly for the shower.

"Heaven!" she exclaimed as the powerful jets blasted away at the exhaustion in her body. She spent nearly twenty minutes under the powerful heads of water. Each moment seemed to improve her sleep-deprived mood. By the time she got out, she was excited about the canal lunch tour.

She pulled out her laptop and started it up while she dressed. In the mirror, she stared at her naked form before dressing. There was a bruise on her bicep where she had bumped into the rock wall when climbing with Scott the weekend before. It had nearly faded, but the yellow and a trace of purple were still visible. She poked at it with her finger. It was still a little tender.

That line of thought led back to Scott. She wished she had more control of her emotions regarding him. Something about him made her feel safe and in danger at the same time.

What does Scott see when he looks at me? Does he think I'm smart? Devious? Does he think I'm pretty? Does he think I'm hot? She realized she had been standing still for several minutes.

"Damn you, Scott Wolfe!" she exclaimed aloud. Smart, handsome, motivated, generous. Scott seemed to have it all, just like her father. But underneath there seemed to be...something.

Could it be violence? "No," she said aloud. *He's too kind,* she reassured herself.

Whatever it is, I can help him fix it, she decided as she pulled fresh clothes on.

After dressing, she quickly sent an email out, letting everyone know she had arrived safely, and that the showers at the NH were magical, and that the coffee was even better.

She debated on whether to copy Scott, finally deciding she would, and then clicked his address and hit *send* before she could change her mind.

After sending the message, she regretted not sending a

private update to him and decided she would send him a brief note to let him know he was special...but not *too* special—after all, she was still quite upset with him.

She sent the message off, closed her notebook down and finished getting ready for her boat ride. She would be having lunch with the people who she might be working for eventually...or who might be working for her eventually.

"We must present our best face," she mumbled as she reapplied her makeup.

**

ROBERT WHITNEY was in the lobby and becoming impatient. He was about to call up to the room when the elevator opened, and she strode into the lobby. *So like her mother,* he thought. *An international flight and two hours of sleep, and yet she is able to look like she spent the day at a spa and the hair dresser.*

Robert missed his wife. It had been hard to lose her. The cancer had progressed so quickly that there had been little time to emotionally prepare for her absence. Barb had become the woman of the house, too early and far too efficiently. He was saddened by her lack of a complete childhood but was so very proud of what she had become.

He hoped she would choose to follow his footsteps into the diplomatic corps. Unlike her mother, she had a diplomat's wits. She could be just as charming and elegant as her mother had been, but beneath that charm was a mind that could apply enough subtle pressure to bring nearly anyone around to her line of thought. She would be a keen negotiator.

"I'm ready, Daddy," she chirped as if she had a full eight hours of sleep behind her. "Let's get this show on the road."

He was not unconscious of the immediate shift in his attitude. A moment before, he was frustrated because she was late. After she arrived, not only had she made him forget he was agitated, but she had shifted the burden of their lateness to him. *She will be a* brilliant *diplomat,* he mused silently.

**

6:01 a.m. on Monday, May 10th - Fairfax, Virginia

I was awoken around 6:00 a.m. by the trill of the text tone on my phone. It took a few moments to clear the cobwebs and roll to the other side of the bed to reach it.

It was from Barb. I smiled and then opened it. "*Tajen ogg boT,*" it read.

"What?" I said out loud and then typed the same thing into my phone in reply.

I sat on the edge of the bed rubbing my face and eyes with my hands, and then scrubbed my scalp and hair with my fingers in an attempt to bring soberness to my sleep-addled brain.

I picked up my iPad and disconnected it from its charger and then lay back against my headboard, relaxing into the stretch and letting the ache in my back sink and dissolve into the cushion of my bed.

There were two emails there from Barb. I clicked the first one open and saw it was an update on her trip. She had addressed it to Bonbon and carbon copied all of her friends—that made me feel less than special. It read:

> *I was SO tired when we landed. Had nearly ZERO sleep on the plane. And now I have to go on a canal boat tour with people from Daddy's work. Ugh. Diplomats on no sleep—*

this should be an experience.

BUT—on a positive note: eight shower heads with killer pressure, and Amsterdam coffee is like rocket fuel. I think I should be able to power through okay. I'll catch everyone up with pictures and stories if anything interesting happens.

Love,
Barb

The second email was addressed to me. My finger hovered over the message for a few seconds, hesitantly, and then finally, as if by its own will, clicked it open. It read:

Thinking, thinking, thinking. You sure don't make it easy on a girl, do you? I was happy to get your voicemail. It made me smile. Just when I think I have you figured out, you change my mind. You were nowhere to be seen when I left the country... Maybe you could make up for it by being there when I arrive back home. ;)

I sat for a few moments staring at the phone after I had read her emails, expecting a text reply, but none came. My bladder had reached critical mass, so I got up and went into the bathroom to prepare for work.

My morning checklist was progressing: empty bladder—check, shower—check, shave—check. As I wiped the residue of shaving cream from my face, I heard the trill of my phone again.

"grn turk," it said.

I quickly did the math in my head for the difference in time and realized it was too early in the day for Barb to be drunk. *Stoned maybe? She is in Amsterdam.*

I dismissed that thought immediately. *Not Barb—and certainly not while she is with her father.* I was confused.

"*I don't understand.*" I typed in my reply and then waited.

No reply.

I got dressed and headed out the door.

Arriving at work, I walked through the parking lot and entered the building. Bypassing the elevator, I ran up the stairs and through the door of TravTech.

TravTech occupied the top three floors of a building in Reston, Virginia. It was one of the many tech companies that managed to pull the pieces together after the dot com crash, building itself up using the remains of companies that weren't so lucky.

The foyer of TravTech was like many in the industry, with large glass doors and a reception desk just beyond. The waiting area was appointed in modern faux-leather and chrome furniture, with flashy and inspirational landscape photos and large flat screened TVs stretching across each wall.

As usual, they were tuned to financial or news network channels so those forced to wait never felt like they were missing anything by being kept in queue. This morning, however, I was greeted by a large group of employees gathered around the TV screens. Bonbon saw me coming through the door and ran up to me. She had tears in her eyes.

"Scott," she sobbed. "It's so horrible. I just know she's okay...somehow."

Confused, I looked at the screen, tuned to CNN: *Breaking News. Amsterdam Tour Boat with US diplomats aboard explodes.*

My heart felt like it had stopped in my chest. The texts this morning. She was in trouble, trying to reach me. I could feel the blood draining from my face.

The female anchor was giving the scant details of the crisis—repeating the same information over and over in different configurations trying to make it sound as if they had more information than they did.

I gleaned that the explosion had occurred at 11:15 a.m. Amsterdam time in a canal next to Nieumarkt Square. The explosion knocked out windows on both sides of the canal, injured several people on the street and in the square, and though details were slow in coming, it appeared that no one could have survived the blast, as there were pieces of the boat strewn across the canal and streets.

I turned and ran to my cubicle, dropping my pack heavily on my desk as I flipped my computer on. Bonbon was close on my heels. While the computer was running through its start up routine, I pulled a pad of paper from a shelf and began to scribble down the two messages I had received from Barb.

Bonbon slumped down with a thud, leaning against my cabinet drawers and sobbing. Storc walked over, stepped into the tight space, and sat next to her, putting his arm around her shoulder to console her.

"What are you doing?" she cried out pitifully, wiping her nose and eyes on her sleeve.

I ignored her for a moment as I scribbled out the words and tried to decipher their meaning. "*Tajen ogg bot*" meant "Taken off boat," I quickly realized. "*grn turk,*" though…could she mean green truck?

"She's alive," I stated calmly yet confidently, staring at the words. Bonbon and Storc both quickly rose from the floor to hang over my shoulder.

"How do you know?" Storc asked.

I held out my phone and showed them the two texts.

"Texts from Barb this morning. One at 6:01 a.m., and more importantly, one at 6:33 a.m. this morning. That's 11:01 and 11:33 a.m. Amsterdam time. The explosion happened at 11:15 a.m. Amsterdam time."

Bonbon let out a squeal.

"Shhh," I hissed sharply. "Listen. The news says the diplomats were on the boat. If Barb wasn't on it, and the networks don't know it yet, let's just keep it to ourselves for the moment."

"Right!" Bonbon and Storc said in unison.

I looked at Storc. "The phone GPS hack you built. Bring it up—here on my system."

He sat down in front of my computer, and his fingers began to fly across the keyboard…first establishing an encrypted tunnel, signing into the proxy server, entering a secure session, and then popping open an interface. "Phone number?" he asked mechanically.

I reached over his shoulder and punched in Barb's phone number and hit Enter. The map of our area disappeared, and a new map popped up to replace it. Amsterdam. The location icon was flashing, pausing, moving, and then it settled on the outskirts of the city at what appeared to be a residence on the Amstel River next to a small, manmade cove.

We looked at each other for a moment.

"Call her!" Bonbon exclaimed, as she started to draw her phone from her pocket.

"No!" I said, placing my hand over her hand and phone. "If she somehow managed to hold on to her phone, calling it could give her away."

Bonbon chewed on her lip.

"What are we going to do?" Storc asked pleadingly. "Should we call the FBI or something?"

I looked at the ceiling for a moment as my flow chart kicked into overdrive.

Leaving out the complex weighted percent averages regarding human behavior, which could be a book by itself. The best way to explain is with simple process flow.

Object = Barb

Definition: very important to me. Not as important to everyone else as diplomats on a boat.

Action = She was kidnapped.

> *Supporting data:*
> - *Tajen ogg bot and Grn Turk, texted to me because I was the last text on her list, putting me at the top of the list.*
> - *If she kept her phone, she was probably hiding that fact, thus the rushed, misspelled texts.*
> - *Phone is still active, thus not blown up. (Does she still have it? SHIT! Did I give her away when I replied?)*

> - *Most likely a collateral hostage, not a primary one.*

Origin of action = Assumption: Serbs

> *Supporting data:*
> - *Her father was in Amsterdam as part of US team helping with the trial of Serbian War criminal/arms dealer. It was probably related. (There is no such thing as coincidence.)*

Historic precedence of US response = The US does not negotiate with terrorists. [Insert loud noises here]

Flow: Barb is with her dad, who happens to be a diplomat. The "terrorists" aren't actually terrorists; they are criminals who want their boss back. The US will not bend to that demand. They will send in a SEAL team or Delta. Massive amounts of explosives, automatic weapons fire, different languages, and two groups of men with a penchant for being very good at violence, surrounding a group of untrained, scared men and women in the presence of their families.

The odds of me seeing Barb again are about 3.5 to 1. Acceptable odds for special ops. Horrible odds if one of those hostages was there because I was responsible for upsetting her and chasing here away to begin with.

No good. How can I improve the situation?

Alternate Flow Chart:

One puzzle master (me), finding the location of the hostages, using skill in observation and problem solving to formulate least-risky method of contact. Formulate a game that the terrorists must *play. While game is in play, the underlying, Scott-manipulated game plays out, freeing the hostages with*

SEALs or Delta as a backup resource for escape.

Odds of freeing all the hostages: even money. With a massive fall-back option if no rescue possible of calling in the cavalry anyway.

Much of the information I required to complete the chart couldn't be obtained until I reached Amsterdam. So I mapped out my first eight moves and laid down the outline for a few more. I'd have to make myself a controlling variable as well as a player— flowing through the game and making alterations to the rules as I went.

There it is, I thought. *Guns or Brains.*

All of the information played out before my eyes as a twisting, turning play of process flow lines with abrupt endings and the lines turning angry red. And it did so in a matter of five seconds as I was standing in front of my desk, staring at the ceiling.

I knew what I was going to do; I just needed the moment to mentally squeeze the trigger. That took another five seconds.

That's a damned big decision, I thought to myself. *Maybe I should just call the FBI and let them know about the texts. But then again, she wouldn't be there if it hadn't been for me being such a crappy boyfriend.*

"Scott," Bonbon said gently, having seen me go "vacant" on her before.

I looked them in the faces, took a deep breath, and said, "I'm going to get her."

Fear and excitement flashed across both of their faces. After I spoke the words out loud, my heart started pounding.

Somber, sober Storc looked at me intensely and with a lowered voice asked, "What do you need from us?"

"Give me a minute to think," I said as Storc got up, and I sat down with a thump in my chair. Suddenly the weight of this was on me—this beautiful, crazy thing I was going to do.

"I will have to give you both more details as they come to me, but the first thing I want you both to do is to *not* talk to anyone about this. It's critical." I stared directly at Bonbon and paused to let that sink in. She was the gossip, and she knew it. But I was positive, with Barb's life in the balance, that she could keep her mouth shut.

"Bonbon," I continued. "I need a secure website, key and IP access only. And I need it to be bulletproof, and by bulletproof I mean bomb proof, and by bomb proof I mean nuke proof."

"Bomb proof?" she repeated. "Who am I securing against? The terrorists?"

"Think NSA," I replied.

"Ahhh. Gotcha," she said, thrilled with the assignment.

"I'll need secure FTP access, messaging, and a forensic-level wipe app for my tablet and phone. Before you make any system changes to these devices, make a full restore point copy for both of them, including logs." I handed them both to her.

I hoped I wouldn't have to, but if I was going to Europe with illegal software, involving myself in an international incident, and laying a path to terrorists, I needed to be able to cover my tracks. With the push of a button, my smartphone and my tablet could be wiped clean and restored to their present condition—including the removal of any connectivity logs and phone calls.

She nodded and hurried off to her cube down the hall. I looked at Storc and smiled. "Whatever the highest number of bounces you've ever done on proxy paths, I want you to set up a path to triple it, with at least three dynamic, encrypted loops. If you or Bonbon send anything to my phone or iPad, or if I send anything to you, I want it to be completely invisible. Remember who we are trying to hide from."

"That will slow down the connection considerably. It would be best to stick to Wi-Fi when you can. Otherwise you'll be receiving at dial-up speeds," he warned.

"I know. But security will be important... You know they'll be scanning everyone going into Amsterdam," I replied.

"Will do, boss," he said with a smile and a wink.

"When Bonbon has my site up, I'd like to have as near to real-time updates on Barb's phone as possible," I said, pointing at the computer screen. "I also need you to modify a couple of my apps. I'll be able to do some of them myself on the flight, but I won't be able to do it all in the time we have."

He nodded, started to turn, and then stopped and looked at me very seriously. "You, my friend, are Batman. I've always wanted to do something like this."

I smiled and put my hand on his shoulder. "I always thought of myself more as Sherlock Holmes."

"Lame," he said and then turned and headed down the corridor to his servers in the NOC.

I walked down the hall to the first glass-windowed office outside the developers' cubicle farm—the office of my boss, Danny Habib. Danny was a tall, round-faced, smiling fellow with a sharp wit and tongue, but he was likable none the less.

We had an agreement. He keeps other managers, departments, and executives off my back and out of my face, and I make him the highest-producing department head.

He liked that arrangement... though sometimes he paid a pound of flesh for it. The higher-ups had little to complain about when it came to Habib's results, though, so they too had learned to ignore the complaints of the other departments when it came to my interdepartmental boundary crossing.

"Hey, man," I said, poking my head into his fishbowl of an office.

"Hey. What's up?" he said, half distracted by something on his computer monitor.

"I've got four weeks of accrued vacation time. I need to take an open-ended vacation starting today," I stated plainly.

His attention shifted to me fully. "Dude! I can't let you do that. There are too many projects we haven't finished for the next release yet. I need you here."

"Then I quit. Effective today," I said, turning to go back to my desk. Before I had gotten four steps from his office, he was at his door, calling after me.

"Hey, man. Take as much time as you need. I'll cover for you." His response echoed across the cube farm.

"Thanks, man," I said over my shoulder, dripping sarcasm.

I got back to my cubicle and started arranging for my flight and hotel. A few minutes later, Bonbon returned with my tablet and smartphone.

"Okay! The program is running right now to compile and compress your current drives. It should only take another hour or so for it to finish. It's a standard back up with a couple of changes," she said, handing them to me.

"Okay," I replied, chuckling at her machine-gun speech.

"Don't power down on either of them until they are finished," she continued. "Once that's done, I wrote a script, excluded from the backup, which downloads two new apps, installs them and sets up a secure link to a website—which I haven't set up yet, but will set up as soon as I'm done here.

"The first app is the restore point app, which will wipe both drives as long as they are in Bluetooth range of each other. Then, it takes the backup that's running right now and ghost copies it, sector by sector, to its original state. Don't power down, or you'll have to sync to your computer to restore. I kept a backup copy for you. I'll put it up on the website when I've secured it. I haven't yet, but I will, as soon as I'm done here."

"What about—"

"Hush! I'm not done yet," she said, shutting me down. "If you need to wipe, hit the wipe app button and enter your code. It's the one with the skull and crossbones. You don't have a code yet. The app will ask you for it after it installs. Don't forget your code. If you forget your code, you won't be able to wipe it," she paused for a moment, thinking. "Oh yeah! The second app. It's your standard FTP app. Except I made a copy of it and wrote a script that forces it to use an encryption path sequence to hide your location, to use whatever magic road Storc is writing for you, *and* to erase the log.

"You can use the script manually on another system if you need to. But it's automatic on your phone and iPad...*and* if you do have to wipe everything, I figured you'd need it back at some point, so I made it so you can restore everything—including all the new apps and security from the secure server. But you'll have to enter all the proxy stuff by hand. Just tunnel through to the site, and you'll find an executable file to restore your toys."

She had been looking down as if she were speaking to the phone in my hand. I reached over and lifted her chin with my finger and made her look me in the eye.

"Thank you, Bonny," I said, smiling. "I couldn't do this without you."

She lurched forward and threw her arms around me. "I'm gonna cry," she said.

I patted her back and said, "It's going to be okay," and then gently detached her.

"I hope I did everything right. I've never done this spy crap before. I'd feel like shit if it didn't work and you or Barb..." Her voice trailed off, and then she threw her arms around me again. "I'm gonna cry," she said again.

I peeled her away again and looked her in the eye. "You have a job to do here. Barb and I are counting on you. You can't give yourself away by crying every five minutes. But I'll tell you this—I wouldn't trust anyone but you and Storc to run this operation from here." I hugged her again.

I needed to give her something else to do, or she would chew her fingers off trying to stay quiet after the secure site was up.

"Jovanovich," I said.

"Jovana who?" she asked.

"Jovanovich. Bosnian Serb war criminal," I replied. "Find every scrap of information you can on him and upload it to the secure server."

She nodded.

"And anything you can find on modern tactical hostage rescue. SEAL or Delta—not SWAT. I need specific history on US military hostage interventions."

She nodded again.

I grabbed my pack, kissed her on the cheek, and walked down the hall to Storc's cube where he was furiously typing away on his keyboard. All three of his monitors had streams of code running on them.

"I've got an 'update' script. It can send coordinates every ten seconds. You can access them from the website, and they'll update your map on both your iPad and your phone—as soon as Bonbon has the website up and running. Default will be current, but you can step it backwards as far back as you need to, starting from the first set we got on your desktop. The first ones are already saved and will be uploaded with the first live feed," he said and then paused thoughtfully as something profound occurred to him. "Dude!" he exclaimed with a startled look on his face.

It was clear the weight of what was going on had just washed over him.

I smiled. "I'll be fine," I said and put my fist out for a bump. His hand came towards mine palm first and then clumsily closed, his palm to my fist.

"When I get back, we are going to practice that until you get it right," I said with a smile. I turned and walked out. I could hear Storc's fingers clacking away on the keyboard before I was out of his cube.

**

On the drive back to my house, I spent the entire trip working out the path to Barb. If this happens, then this is the response, else, that response. If this data is present, use it for this, otherwise, continue to the next point.

I ran into the condo as soon as I arrived and began packing, quickly trying to anticipate my clothing and equipment needs. As soon as my bags were packed, I hopped back into my car and drove to the bank. I emptied my savings account and converted most of it to traveler's checks.

I mentally went over my inventory as I drove to Washington Dulles Airport, but I was distracted by a chime from my phone. Bonbon's script had finished running, and all the new apps had been installed.

I parked in long term parking and then ran to the check-in counter, seeing that I was running behind. Once I made it through security and to my terminal, I breathed a little easier and checked my messages again. Bonbon and Storc both had texted me letting me know their progress.

Two more apps were done, and the website was up and secure.

I attempted a login from the airport Wi-Fi to test security and mapping. Both worked flawlessly. I tested the connections immediately by downloading Bonbon's research files. One hundred and seventy-five megabytes of web-captured files began loading to my iPad.

Perfect. There are advantages to working with industry-

leading talent, I thought as boarding was called for my flight.

I took a deep breath before rising and grabbing my bags.

"Here we go," I said aloud and then got in line to board.

It was a red-eye flight, so there were quite a few neck pillows being pulled out by the other passengers, but it wasn't a crowded flight. Probably due to the fact that the destination city had just suffered a horrific terrorist attack. I had the short row next to the window to myself.

As soon as my bag was stowed, I immediately laid my head back and closed my eyes, letting the flow chart of the timeline of events spread out over the inside of my eyelids. The line extended from the time of the first email from Barb to the moment I boarded the plane.

Little pieces of information branched off from the timeline and were categorized. Major events that had occurred were categorized with a thick unmovable lines with headlines in bold text next to them—such as the explosion and the timing of the messages from Barb.

Other information was movable, like: Who sent the texts if it wasn't Barb? Was her phone moving? How much battery life did it have? If she was alive, was she alone or with others? Lines sometimes faded out only to reappear further along. Those lines would hopefully be filled in later as more information was collected or as I moved the pieces around in my head.

I was rarely lacking in data. My mind stored nearly everything it saw, heard, touched, smelled, or tasted. Even random thoughts were categorized and stored as data.

But even so, I would have given anything to be able to forget that it was me who was responsible for Barb being there.

That little tidbit kept popping into the flow chart whenever it got to something potentially dangerous as an outcome.

That's not helpful, I thought to myself.

When it was clear I wouldn't escape the guilty taunting of my own flowchart, I decided to do more research. I pulled out my iPad and began scanning through the information I had downloaded on Jovanovich and military hostage rescue tactics. I worked on that until my eyes were too tired to focus.

As I drifted off in my seat, I heard Barb's voice.

"This is your *fault, Scott Wolfe," she said accusingly.*

"I know," I replied.

** **

Early afternoon on Monday, May 10th - CIA Headquarters, Langley, Virginia

Intelligence agencies all over the world were buzzing. Everyone had their eyes on Amsterdam. From the CIA to Mossad to the German BND...even the Japanese DIH was monitoring incoming and outgoing information.

Deputy Director Mathew Burgess, Head of the CIA National Clandestine Service, called in all of his section chiefs—half of whom were on conference call from overseas locations. There had been an immediate lock-down of all State Department facilities and all other US interests were put on high alert. No one had claimed responsibility for the attack, and no red flags had been raised from the usual sources to indicate anything was being planned.

This attack had caught everyone off guard.

"We know the drill people," he said, winding down the meeting. "I want everyone in and out of that city with same-day ticket purchases to be flagged unless they are family of the deceased or news crews." Then he thought about it a moment. "Scratch that. Flag the news crews as well."

"Get all analyst shifts in. I want backgrounds on them all, with non-family, non-news personnel sitting on top of the pile. John, I want you to manage the ground game," he said, speaking to John Temple, his most senior agent, on video from Germany. "Pull in all the help you need from the region. I want eyes on everyone until we know who's responsible. Work out of the consulate in Amsterdam. The consul general is a friend; she'll give you all the support you need."

"Yes sir. I've already contacted CG Martin. She's expecting us," John replied.

"I want full and seamless liaison with Justice, NSA, State, and Homeland. No dick measuring on this one. Pardon me, ladies. This is team USA, not team CIA," Burgess cautioned.

He paused, looking at all the faces. Satisfied he had gotten his message across, he stood, ending the meeting. "Alright folks. Get to work."

As the room started to clear out, Burgess looked at the video screen and raised his finger, indicating John should stay on line. Once the room was cleared, he closed the door.

"What's it look like so far, John?" Burgess asked.

"It's hard to judge. It's spook central downtown already. I'll be there in about two hours, and then I'll be able to take a better reading," he replied.

"Who's missing from the party?" Burgess asked.

John shook his head. "So far, sir, it looks like the Serb Network are the only ones not popping their heads up to sniff the air."

"That's what I was afraid of." Burgess said. "Get with the station chief, and see if we can smoke some of them out and lean on them."

"Yes, sir," he replied "Oh. And sir, CG Martin said she wants to be kept briefed on everything...she asked as a personal favor. Not through the agency."

Burgess nodded. "Bev's a good girl. Give her what she wants until it keeps us from getting what we want. I love the straight arrows, but when it's this hot outside, a little shade can keep you alive."

"Roger that, sir," John said.

"And Captain...try not to get yourself killed. Guys like you and I are too old to be running around in the field. Let the young fellas do the heavy lifting," Burgess said, alluding to John's dangerous proclivity to join the tactical operations.

John smiled. "Speak for yourself, sir. I'm just getting warmed up."

Burgess laughed as he ended the connection. On his way back into his office through the connecting door, he shook his head. "Fucking Serbs."

He had a sick feeling at the pit of his stomach like this was the beginning of something, not the end. He felt bad for all the families of the State Department people, but he had a nation to protect. He couldn't focus on the losses—he had to focus on preventing more.

five

Five Days Until Event

Tuesday, May 11th, 2010 - Schipol Airport in Amsterdam, Netherlands

As soon as I was through customs in Amsterdam, I steered my way to the currency exchange booth where I converted four thousand US dollars into euros. The next stop was the electronics kiosk, which was present in every modern airport. There I found a prepaid smart phone like mine and paid an exorbitant price for it in cash. I opened it, discarded the packaging, and tucked the phone and the charger into my pack.

Outside the airport, I hopped in a cab and said, "*Dam en Warmoestraat, alstublieft. In De Wallen,*" with nearly perfect Dutch pronunciation, giving him the cross street closest to my hotel in the old, walled city.

To his credit, he took the highway to the closest exit to my destination. That was one of the reasons I always learn navigational key words in the language of the country where I'm traveling.

The illusion is destroyed if they decide to carry on a conversation with me once we are underway. But that minor embarrassment can usually be avoided by placing my phone to my ear during the entire trip and muttering as if I were having a private conversation.

When we arrived, I looked at the meter, pulled out the appropriate fare and a modest tip, and said, "*Dank u wel*," the equivalent of "Thanks a lot."

I stepped out of the cab, hefted my pack and duffel on my shoulder, and walked the short distance to the alley my hotel was on.

I walked in to find a modern building, tastefully, though not expensively, appointed. I walked to the desk and cleared my throat. A young woman appeared from around the corner and came to the desk, smiling.

"*Goedemorgen*," she said.

"Reservation for Wolfe?" I said and handed her my credit card.

"Good morning, Mr. Wolfe," she said with a thick accent. "Yes. You are booked for four nights. I just have to make an imprint of your card."

While she did that, I looked around the lobby, noting the security system on the door as she continued her check-in speech.

"There is no room smoking except on the balcony," she said. "If you have entry after midnight, you will need your room key to open the outside lock. You may have additional keys if required. Breakfast is served beginning at seven until ten."

"Your website said you have Wi-Fi," I said.

"Yes. Instructions for logging in are here to the back of

card," she replied, handing me an instruction card. "Do you require assistance with your bags?"

"Nope. I'm good," I replied. "Thanks."

"Thank you for staying at the Old City Hotel," she said as she handed me my room key card.

"Thanks," I said and then walked up the three flights of stairs to my room.

It was a small room by US standards but average for a European hotel. I had a small alcove with a small sink and a microwave, unusual for European accommodations, and my own bathroom. I had stayed in Amsterdam before and had to share a bathroom with several other guests, but most hotel rooms had been updated to include their own in recent times.

I didn't bother unpacking. I took my new phone from my pack and immediately plugged it in to fully charge. Once that was underway, I checked my email.

There was a message from Bonbon:

Hi Scottmeister,

I hope your flight was good. I just wanted to let you know that Storc got a new car. He says you can take it for a spin whenever you like. Have a good time in Amsterdam. Don't get into any trouble. :)

-Bonbon

This, of course, was code for "my other apps are ready to download at my leisure." I proceeded to do just that. Upon logging into the secure website Bonbon had set up, I discovered the two new apps.

I started the install routine and activated them one at a time as they each finished loading.

The first was a fine piece of spyware courtesy of Storc. It was a modified Bluetooth wireless decoder and emulator which would detect Bluetooth devices, scan them for their linking codes, and then provide an interface to emulate them without disconnecting the original. It would allow me to listen in on Bluetooth headsets and mimic wireless keyboards and mice.

The second app was an instant messaging app that tied into the encrypted website Bonbon built. It would allow me to text with Storc and Bonbon over an encrypted channel. I was starting to feel like I was James Bond after all.

I took a short shower to help clear my head and then walked back into the room feeling much better. I pulled on my clothes and checked the charge on the prepaid phone. Discovering it was fully charged; I disconnected it, tossed it and my iPad into my pack, and slid my smartphone into the pocket of my jeans.

I opened my bag, pulled out a worn green hoodie, and then put it on over my black t-shirt. As I headed to the door, I caught a glimpse of myself in the mirror. My eyes had dark circles under them, and my face was covered with stubble. I didn't mind the stubble, it would grow much heavier before I was done. But the bags under my eyes indicated that I was already exhausted, and I'd only just started.

Going down the stairs, I pulled a knit beanie over my head and pulled some strands of hair out in a couple of places. I needed to look like a disaffected European hipster student, not an affluent American tourist.

As I hit the second floor landing, I passed an older couple coming up from their breakfast. They moved to the side and gave me a not-so-subtle look of disgust. Perfect; my image was a success.

As I entered the lobby, I pulled out my phone, loaded the most current GPS coordinates for Barb's phone, and saw it had moved back into the city. Only ten or eleven blocks from my current location.

I walked out the front of the hotel and then paused on the sidewalk to get my bearings. I was about to head in the direction of the arrow on my map when a girl sitting in the doorway and smoking a cigarette, spoke to me.

"American?" she asked as my foot hovered over the cobblestone of the alley. I paused. *Damn*, I thought to myself.

"Yeah. American. What gave me away?" I needed to correct the tell immediately.

She pointed at my backpack. "Your bag. But don't worry, you look more like a European who stole it than an American. It's a nice bag," she said, smiling a flirty smile and then winking at me.

She was an attractive girl. Maybe a little younger than me, though I couldn't say for certain. She had long, curly blond hair and was wearing a pair of olive green army pants and a pair of unlaced combat boots. The freckles on her face seemed to be at odds with her nose ring and her large gauge ear piercings. Her accent seemed more German than Dutch, though I am no linguist.

"Thanks," I said in reply. "Is there a secondhand shop nearby?"

She shot me a quizzical look.

"Used clothing?" I continued.

"Ah. Yah. On the next canal. Over there. By the University," she said, pointing over her shoulder back toward the entrance of the hotel and down the street in the opposite direction I wanted to go.

"*Vielen Danke*," I said.

"*Bitte*," she replied with a mildly surprised smile. "I'm Kathrin," she said, extending her hand as I started to leave again. "I'm staying here with some friends for holiday."

"Cott-rin?" I asked, confirming the pronunciation and extending my hand as well.

"Yah" she explained. "In America, it would be pronounced 'Catherine.'"

"Ah." I said, nodding my understanding. "I'm Scott. Also here on holiday."

"You picked a bad time to holiday—we all did. Police everywhere, shops closed. My friends are talking of leaving *und* going to France," she said and then made a sour look, like she had just taken a bite of lemon.

I looked up and scanned my surroundings. I saw no police at that moment, but I knew she was correct. I returned my gaze to her.

"Yes. It's the story of my life, wrong place, wrong time..." *Wrong things said,* I continued in my head.

I looked at her worn shoulder bag. It was the same olive drab color as her pants, but it was much older. The color was worn nearly white where it had rubbed against her hip, and there were a couple of threadbare edges where it folded and where it snapped closed. I pointed at my pack with my thumb. "Do you like this pack?" I asked.

Her eyes lit up. "Yes. It is a very nice bag—very American."

I pointed to her bag. "Trade?"

"Yah!" she said excitedly and pulled it from around her neck. She dumped its contents on the ground between her feet, pulled it open to make sure nothing had stayed concealed in its many interior pockets, and then handed it to me.

I emptied the contents of my pack directly into the new shoulder bag, checking my interior pockets as well, and then handed it to her.

"*Dankeschoene!*" she exclaimed giddily, giving me a hug and a kiss on my cheek. Then she proceeded to scoop her belongings into her new prize.

"*Bitteschoene,*" I replied.

I shouldered my new bag, was donning my round-framed sunglasses, and was about to step off the curb a third time when she spoke again.

"Did you miss breakfast like I did? There is a pastry shop on the corner. We could get danish *und* a *koffee,*" she said hopefully.

I smiled. "Thanks for the offer. But I've got some things to do this morning," I explained. "Maybe later."

She looked disappointed but kept the smile on her face. "Okay, dude," she said awkwardly. "Catch you later."

I discovered long ago that Europeans my age like to practice their 'American' with Americans. And the last thing I wanted to do at the moment was to appear conspicuously American.

I walked down the alley to the corner. The smells from the pastry shop were making my stomach grumble. Fresh bread, sugar, frostings, and the smell of fresh, strong coffee were making my mouth water, and I wished I could stop. It was a mild blow to my ego that I was being tempted by something as frivolous as bread. But then again, no one is perfect.

It had been a while since I had eaten, but I was still within sight of the hotel—and Kathrin—so I pushed on. I needed to pick up the trail on Barb's phone.

It seemed unlikely to me that Barb would still be in the city. Now that I was out on the streets, I was seeing the police presence that Kathrin had mentioned. Police boats were slowly cruising the canals, and the compactly styled police cars and emergency vehicles were driving by with fairly regular frequency. I couldn't imagine keeping hostages in the city with all this activity. But until I found her phone, there was no way to be sure.

I pulled out my phone and checked Barb's phone's location again. It had not moved since I arrived in Amsterdam. I walked along the west side of the canal, Oudezijds Voorburgwal, as I made my way closer to the mark on my map.

When I was within a block of the location, I crossed the canal and began walking down the east side. From there I could still see the street on the other side of the canal, and I planned on finding a spot to sit and watch for a while. I continued to walk north for another block and then spotted the building the GPS mark was resting on.

It was across the canal and on the corner facing Oude Kerk.

I didn't pause long looking at the building; instead I turned to my right and saw a Rasta coffee shop.

When I walked through the door, the first thing I noticed was the strong smell of pot. I ordered a coffee and two breakfast muffins out of the display case and then sat down at the window bar where I could see the building across the canal.

The shopkeeper was a very pleasant black man with dreads tucked into a black knit cap. He came to me frequently to refill my coffee. The shop was empty except for the occasional customer who came in to buy some pot, but no one lingered.

The streets were very busy, with people walking here and there, but most did not seem to be tourists, and there wasn't much shopping going on. Of course it was still early in the day for the red light district, but it was clearly not business as usual.

It took me what seemed like an hour to figure out that most of the foot traffic was nothing more than locals and police, who were walking slowly, visually inspecting everything. The shopkeeper—Reggie, I heard a customer say—came up beside me.

"De shops was closed all day an' all night, las' night," he said in a thick Jamaican accent. "Not a big deal on a Monday night, 'specially wit de police snooping around. But business is off today as well."

I nodded my understanding of his predicament.

After another two hours of waiting, I suddenly began to get impatient. I checked the time on my phone.

Shock flooded my body. It had only been about thirty minutes since I sat down at the window. A sudden flash of panic hit me, and I spun around to look at the snack display.

"Dude!" I exclaimed to Reggie. "Did you sell me hash muffins?!"

His look of confusion quickly shifted as he leaned over the display case. "Oh, mon!" He said as he reached behind the counter and grabbed the display placard for the case and stuck it on the glass. "I'm so sorry! That was my bad."

I also realized I was still famished. Embarrassed, I looked at Reggie. "You don't by any chance have food that *isn't* psychoactive, do you?" I asked.

"Sure, mon," he replied as he pulled out a stack of boxes. "Just got deez delivered."

The boxes were filled with pastries, pretzels, and muffins. They were still warm, and the scent wafted across my nose like perfume when he tipped one box my direction to inspect the contents.

"I'll take those," I said pointing at the box as I unsteadily returned to my stool. "And more coffee, if you would please."

"Are ya okay?" he asked sincerely as he brought me a plate with the pastries on it.

"Yeah. I'm fine...but I need to get straight quickly as possible," I stated firmly.

He set some sort of detox energy drink next to me. "Guaranteed to put ya straight faster than anyting," he said.

When I pulled out my cash and I handed it to him, he said, "Naw, mon. These are on me."

"Thanks," I said as I continued to stare at the building across the canal.

"My name is Reggie, by the way," he said as he pulled up a stool next to me.

I reached my hand out "Scott," I replied with a smile—I think I smiled. Honestly, it felt like my jaw was floating down my neck.

"What's so interesting across de canal?" he asked. "Are you wait'n for de windows to open?"

I looked more closely at the building and realized there were a series of glass doors and windows at street level. They were a few of the Red Light District's famous red light windows. "No," I said. "Not exactly."

"I'd go to udder windows anyway. De Russians run doze. De girls aren't always dare of day own will," he explained.

"Really?" I replied. "I thought prostitution was regulated in Amsterdam."

"Oh. It is mon. But de cops do de regulat'n—and you know where dares a cop, dares a hand out and a crime wait'n to happen."

"I see," I replied thoughtfully. Then, before my brain could veto my mouth, I spouted out, "My girlfriend is missing, and her phone is over there." I immediately regretted what I had said, but for some reason I felt as if everything was gonna be alright—that I shouldn't worry.

Reggie raised his eyebrows. "Is she American too?" he asked.

"Yes," I replied, resigning myself to my lapse in judgment.

"*Don't worry...about a ting,*" I heard sung over the store

speakers through my fog.

"Is she missing, or did she disappear?" he asked, insinuating that there may be something more typical going on.

"The last text I got from her was that she was being forced off a tour boat. That was yesterday," I explained, fudging some details. I was having a hard time remembering what I had already told him, and I didn't want to come across as insincere.

"A lot goin' on yesterday. Dat boom put me on the floor and knocked stuff off de wall. Until de policemen showed up, you could'a smuggled an elephant in de neighborhood and no one would know it."

I nodded my head in understanding. He disappeared for a moment to tend to a customer who had walked in and then returned to the stool next to me.

"Whatch you gonna do?" he asked.

"Watch the map on my phone until this icon moves, and then I'm going to find out who has my girlfriend's phone," I said.

"Dat little arrow?" he asked, pointing down at my phone.

I looked down and saw that the arrow had moved from the back of the building to the front of it. I looked out the window and saw a thin man with dark, greasy hair and a leather jacket coming out of one of the glass doors facing Oude Kerk.

"That's my cue. I've got to go," I said as I started to rise.

Reggie put his hand on my arm. "Don't waste your time mon. Dat's Elvis. He's on his morning run to the chicken shop. He got the munchies."

I sat back on my stool and watched the man leave the building across the canal.

"He came in here this morning and bought a big bag o' weed. Probably been up dare smokin' all morning," Reggie continued. "He'll be back in ten minutes with chicken and ribs. Jus' watch."

Just then an idea came to me.

"Elvis, you say?" I asked, looking at him.

Reggie shook his head and then leaned in close, lowering his voice. "Look, I don't know what you plan on doing, but I've been across from that corner for a few years now and know those are some bad dudes," he said, his Jamaican accent suddenly vanished.

"DC?" I said, asking about his accent.

"Baltimore," he corrected.

"Fairfax."

"Word." He put his fist up for a bump.

"Let's go upstairs," he said and then called someone from the back of the shop to cover the counter. I followed him up the stairs to an apartment.

"What's going on here?" he asked as we entered the apartment. It was decorated in Scandinavian birch, glass, and chrome. "I'm all about hooking a brother from the States up with some good bud, but I ain't down with gettin' mixed up with those Russian gangsters."

I had to make a judgment call on Reggie, and I had to do it

right then. He managed to keep his Rasta persona rolling well without giving himself away. I had no way of knowing if I could trust him, but my instincts said I could. He broke character to express concern for my safety. That wasn't the mark of a player.

I decided to test the waters. "My girlfriend was on the boat that blew up yesterday," I said.

His eyes went wide. He sat down, still staring at me, wrapping his head around that bit of information. I pulled a photo of her up on my phone and showed it to him to deepen the sense that this was real.

"I'm sorry, man, but revenge won't get you nowhere. I know from experience," he said.

"This isn't about revenge," I said, and then sat down across from him. "If she were in the explosion, her phone wouldn't be on Elvis over there," I said calmly.

He wrinkled his brow for a moment, tilting his head sideways and letting that information filter in. "Man...I don't know," he said. "Elvis is about as dumb as a box of rocks, but those other guys are worse than anything I saw in Baltimore. These are some serious cold-blooded bastards."

"Well...Elvis has the phone. I need to get him alone—away from the other guys," I said confidently.

Reggie stared at me for a moment. Several times he looked as though he were going to speak, but then he stopped. I could see when the set of his jaw changed that he had made up his mind. "What's de plan, boss mon?" he finally asked, slipping back into the character I had met downstairs.

We spent the next hour or so refining the plan I had started in my hash-addled head while we were watching Elvis leave the brothel. "I just need to find out where he got the phone, and if Barb is still in the city," I said as my high started to dissipate. "If I can con him into meeting with me, I might be able to get more information. If nothing else, I can follow him and see where he goes."

"How do you plan on getting him to meet you?" Reggie asked.

"Well, he's into drugs and prostitutes…money should be a good motivator."

Reggie nodded and then looked up suddenly. "He's a fool for good weed. If we can we can get him interested in blazing up with us, I've got something that will loosen his tongue."

"How pliable would it make him?" I asked.

"If you told him his hair was on fire, he'd beat his head against the wall to put it out," Reggie said with a grin.

"Like what I had for breakfast?" I asked with a grin.

"Better," he replied, rising from his seat and going over to a cabinet.

When he returned, he had a vial in his hand. "And this will seal the deal," he said, holding it up for me to inspect. "A couple drops of this in a joint, and he'd tell you his credit card PIN."

"Excellent," I replied. "Okay. Let's get him lubricated with your chemical wizardry, then make him think he's about to be busted. If I can sneak him out the back, he might lead me to Barb."

"I'll need to get Cleavon and my girl Aimee involved," he said. "But I'm tellin' you, it's not going to be hard to fool this guy. You almost don't need the drugs."

"That's what I wanted to hear," I said and then looked at him a little sideways. "What's with the Rasta persona?"

"Marketing," he replied. "Cleavon and I bought this place a few years back. He's the front man, I'm the grower."

"If you don't mind me asking, what brought you here?"

"Legal weed, mon," he said with a broad grin. "I always had a green thumb, but when my brother's gang wanted to pull me in, my momma put her foot down."

I nodded my head. I was familiar with troubles in the DC and Baltimore area.

"So she got this big settlement from the insurance company and told me to get out and make something of myself," he said.

"So you came here and started growing pot?" I asked.

"Not just pot," he said with a little indignation. "The artful and highly prized designer bud that brings people back. Any fool with grow lights can cultivate ditch-weed and call it product. I coax magic out of the seeds, generation after generation."

I had no idea there was such artistry involved.

"Over the last five years, I've managed to turn that small investment into a thriving business. I send money home to my momma and my sister, so they don't have to live where anyone is going to be giving them a hard time."

I was impressed. A real case of the American dream…sort of.

Once we had the plan down, he introduced me to his best

friend, Cleavon, and his girlfriend, Aimee. He filled them in on what was going on and told them that if they were up to it, we had roles for them to play. Cleavon smiled and bumped elbows with Reggie.

Aimee teared up and looked at me. "I'm sorry your woman is wrapped up in all dis," she said gently. "If those gangsters was involved in killing all dem people yesterday, I'll help any way I can."

I smiled and thanked her and then looked at Reggie quizzically.

"She's de real ting, mon," he said smiling.

We spent a few minutes catching-up Cleavon and Aimee on their roles and prepping for our sting. Aimee brought in some food for us to munch on while we talked. A roasted chicken and some roasted fingerling potatoes. Much more satisfying than the pastries from earlier.

My high was gone, but the calm remained. Reggie said that feeling would last a while...he'd used his most mellow blend for the muffins. Once we had eaten and were confident about what each of us had to do, it was time to set it in motion.

We went downstairs and assumed our positions.

**

I seated myself in front of the window I had been sitting at earlier this morning. I pulled out my prepaid phone and sent a text to Barbara's number.

It read, "*Hey there! As promised, I have your money. Where do you want to meet to get it?*"

I set the phone on the counter and sipped coffee while I waited to see if there would be a reply. After a few moments, the phone vibrated on the counter. I picked it up to read the response.

"*Whoz this? Wat money?*" it asked.

I thought about the best way to reply to set the hook firmly. I wrote: "*Alex...from the tour. You loaned me 2000 euros,*" I typed and then hit send.

There was a longer pause this time, and then the phone vibrated. Elvis replied, "*I send my boifrend. Ware r you?*"

I replied, "*RLD. A rasta coffee shop near Oude Kerk*"

I didn't even have time to set the phone down before it buzzed again. "*Im close. Five minutes.*"

I set the phone down on the counter and waited. I watched as Elvis came out of the glass door across the canal, walked to the end of the block, and then crossed the bridge. I lost sight of him before he turned onto the street but spotted him again as he came around a van. He hurriedly strolled up to the door, looking in all directions before coming in.

As he walked in, Reggie looked up from the counter where he was helping a customer pick some pot from the menu. "Elvis!" he exclaimed. "How are ya, mon?"

Elvis smiled and put his arms out wide. "Reggie, my nigga. Wazuuuup," he spouted boisterously with a thick accent, walked up to the counter, grabbed Reggie by the hand, and drew him in for a 'bro hug.' Judging by the curl at the edge of Reggie's lip, I could tell he wasn't pleased by the greeting. As he broke away, his smile returned.

"How can ah help ya, ma friend?" Reggie asked.

Elvis lowered his voice "I'm here to see someone about some money."

Reggie nodded in my direction.

Elvis turned and looked me over for a few seconds to determine if I was a threat and then walked over to me.

"You have money for me," he said plainly, false bravado oozing from his every move. He was not a confident man, but he had been in the company of confident men for some time and had learned, though poorly, how to slip on the tough-guy suit to get his way.

I looked at him as if taken off guard. "I'm sorry? I don't think I know you."

"You know my girlfriend. She loaned you money. She sent me here to get it back," he said, puffing up his chest and leaning onto the bar threateningly close to me. His eyes were glazed, bloodshot, and not focusing well. This guy was still very stoned.

Excellent, I thought.

"A doctor of public policy who lives in Washington DC is *your* girlfriend?" I asked incredulously.

He blinked hard for a few seconds. His tone softened when he continued. "She is more of a friend than a girlfriend. She stays with me when she is in Amsterdam," he said and then paused, sorting out his story. "She needs the money for...her mother. She is sick," he said, smiling, clearly pleased with the elaborate tale he had woven on the spur of the moment.

I picked up my prepaid smartphone and opened the dialer as I said, "You don't mind if I verify that, do you?"

He looked very nervous. "She is in the shower. That's why she sent me," he said nervously, feeling his two-thousand euros slipping away.

"Okay. We'll wait a few minutes to call her, then," I said, setting my phone back down on the counter. Relief flowed across Elvis's face.

Reggie appeared over our shoulders. "Did I hear ya say ya got some time ta kill? 'Cause I got me a new strain upstairs. It so potent I been 'fraid to put it out till someone aside me an' Cleavon smoked it."

Elvis saw an opportunity to turn things back in his favor.

"Reggie, my brother," he said, smiling. "I will like to blaze your new weed with you, but I don't want to leave my new friend 'Alex' down here all alone waiting for a silly woman," he said slapping me on my shoulder "Women can take years in the bathroom," he said and then turned to Reggie for support. "Am I right brother?" he said flashing a greasy smile, lifting his brows, begging for help.

"Das right, mon. A woman can live in da batroom," he replied, throwing his support behind Elvis.

"You see!" Elvis exclaimed. "Even Reggie knows. Let's go upstairs and smoke some of this magic weed." Then he put his hand under my arm to help me from my seat, not wanting to give me an opportunity to change the plan.

"Okay," I said hesitantly. "I guess it would be okay for a while. Then we can call her after."

"That's right. After, after," he said patronizingly. "But first we smoke."

Reggie called to Aimee to watch the shop while we went upstairs. Reggie walked ahead of both of us, followed by myself, and then Elvis brought up the rear to make sure his investment didn't slip away. We arrived at Reggie's apartment, and Elvis plopped down in the big, overstuffed easy chair across from the sofa, spreading out and draping his arms against the back of the seat.

"Reggie grows the best weed in Amsterdam," Elvis said. "I only buy from him. I must be his best customer. He's my best home nigga," he exclaimed.

Reggie was behind him, twisting up his face in a disdainful snarl, but he said, "Dat's right, mon. Elvis is ma 'home nigga.'" This made Elvis laugh.

Reggie arrived at the seating area with a tray of large joints. He stopped in front of Elvis first, who scooped up three, putting two in his pocket and the third to his lips. As Reggie turned my way, his body blocking Elvis's view of the tray, I saw his hand deftly scoop up the remaining joints and then drop several more in their place. He sat next to me on the couch, and then he and I both picked up one each out of the new pile.

The three of us blazed up. I was not what you would call a casual smoker, so I had asked Reggie to roll something for me that wouldn't dull my senses but would pass as pot. He rolled mine with Siberian motherwort, a medicinal herb that has some of the calming effects of marijuana without any THC.

My first tokes were coughed out immediately. Elvis and Reggie laughed.

"Yankee can't hold his smoke," Elvis roared before taking another long draw from the large cigarette. He held it for a long time and then blew the smoke across the room. "You see... Russian lungs are like iron," he said, pounding on his chest.

After the third toke, Elvis started to stare into space. "This is strong shit," he said weakly to no one in particular.

Reggie sat back against the cushions of the couch and smiled. "Do you like it, mon?" he asked.

Several seconds went by and then he mumbled, "Good shit."

Reggie and I leaned forward. "Your blunt is goin out," he said. "Better take another hit." Elvis complied absently with a weak hit. "You call dat a hit, mon?" Reggie asked, laughing, prompting Elvis to take another toke, deeper this time.

Reggie leaned over to me and said, "That's it. We got this now." Then turned to Elvis. "So where's that girl of yours?" Reggie asked with a knowing inflection.

"I don't have no girl. Nothing but whores in my life," Elvis said, sounding sorry for himself.

"I bet that pretty girl who gave you that phone likes you," Reggie replied after a few seconds, his words soothing and supportive.

"She's was pretty," Elvis said, staring dreamy-eyed, a smile creeping over his face. Then a crease formed on his forehead. "My brother took her. Rodka. *Zalupa.*" He sounded more and more pitiful with each passing moment. I had to stop myself from jumping across the table and shaking the rest of the information out of him.

"Zalupa?" I asked.

He looked at me and smiled. "Dickhead," he said,

chuckling like a boy, pleased to have insulted his brother in English as well as Russian. A rare indulgence, I think.

"Your brother? You let your brother steal her from you?" Reggie asked. "That's just wrong," he said.

His brow crinkled. "Rodka always takes everything from me. He gets the best whores first. He drives the fancy cars and leaves me with the twenty-year-old Fiat." He paused for a few seconds, thinking about the other ways his brother had slighted him. "He carries around a shiny gun under his jacket, and then tells me all I can have is this." He pulled a switchblade out of his pocket and flicked it open. Reggie and I looked at each other for a second, but Reggie shook his head indicating not to worry about it. "He says I'd shoot my foot off if he gave me gun. One time...just one time I shoot hole in floor, and he never lets me forget."

He closed the knife again and set it on the table in front of him. "He gets to take his pick of all the loot in warehouse, but I'm not allowed to touch," he continued, dropping his fist onto the arm of the chair. "Says I can't be trusted."

"Mon, that's just wrong," Reggie said sympathetically, gesturing for me to voice my support as well.

"It's not right how he treats you," I said, adding my words to the growing supportive soup in his chemically-addled brain.

"He has the best stuff," Elvis said and then remembered something and pulled Barb's phone out of his pocket. "He always had better phone than me too. Then yesterday, at the...this place we were at, he handed me bag of phones and computers and stuff and said 'burn it.' I looked in bag and Rodka hit me—here," he said, rubbing the side of his face.

"He says, 'Don't open it. Burn it.' So he gets in truck and drives off with..." He hesitated, censoring himself. "And drives off with the pretty girl, and I'm standing there pouring gasoline on bag filled with better stuff than I got." He paused to rub his jaw again.

"But I outsmarted him," Elvis said grinning. "While bag was burning, I hear noise. So I go over and look in grass and there it is," he said, turning Barb's phone over and over in his hand, admiring it. "It wasn't in bag. So I didn't break his rules. Now I have better phone than he does."

"Good for you," I said supportively. *Very good indeed*, I thought. "But why did you let him take your girl?"

"He didn't just take her, he took them all. Him and the Serbs," he said, and then his face got angry. "In old days, no Serb would dare talk to Russian the way they talk to us," he leaned forward and picked up his knife again. "In old days, we would cut them from ear to ear just for looking at us disrespectfully," he said, motioning with his closed knife, making an imaginary line from one side of his face to the other. Then fell back heavily into the chair. "This is good shit."

"Tank ya, mon," Reggie said. "Your fire went out...ya need to blaze it again."

Elvis brought his joint back to his lips and put the lighter to it again. More than half the joint was still there. He took two deep, heavy tokes and then a lighter third hit before he sat back and relaxed again.

Reggie and I looked at each other for a moment, and he shrugged indicating he didn't know where to go next with the conversation. I nodded.

"So Rodka knows how to drive a big truck?" I asked.

"Pfft. I drive truck better than he does. He's always grinding gears," he said and then made the sound of grinding gears. "*Rrrrrrrannnnnkk. Grrrrrrannnnnnk.* But he can fly helicopter."

"What kind of truck is it? Dump truck?" Reggie continued, trying to draw more information out.

"No, no, no, no. Box truck. For produce. We took it from the dock. Changed the plate so the *musora*...uh cops wouldn't know. And covered the box with canvas," he replied and then paused, thinking. "If they get pinched, it will be the Russians to take fall, not Serbs."

"I wouldn't think it possible for Serbs to give orders to Russians," I said. "It seems...wrong."

"Not 'Serbs,'" he corrected. "*These* Serbs. Especially Vukasin Popovich," he said, lowering his voice as if Popovich could hear if his name were spoken aloud. "That guy scare everyone, with his evil eye and his big scar," he said, putting his finger up to the corner of his ear and letting it trail down his neck, indicating where the 'big scar' was on the Serb.

"Rodka had meeting with Popovich last week. He had eight of us with him. Popovich only two… Popovich say, 'You and your men get clean truck. Truck will be here, your men will be there.'"

Elvis paused to take another hit from his joint. It was nearly gone now. "Vova didn't like the way Popovich was talking to Rodka—like he some dog. So he steps up to him. Rodka tried to stop him. But Popovich hit him—"

Elvis made a quick chopping motion with his hand.

"Hard. Fast. Vova didn't even have time to put hands up. He fell dead," he said, an expression of sadness on his face. "And still, even with all us there, we just stood and said, 'Yes, sir.'"

"Vova was your friend?" I asked sympathetically.

"Vova was *hui*...a dick," he said and spat to the side. "But he was Russian. He should not be treated so. Rodka did nothing. Just watched poor Vova twitch." He did his impression of Vova twitching.

"And then he took the pretty girl," I said, steering the conversation back to the subject of Barb.

"Da. But it was Popovich. Rodka just does what they say. She's on her way to Dusseldorf with my brother," he said, sounding as if he were going to fall asleep at any moment. My heart jumped at the new information. Dusseldorf!

"Dusseldorf? Well they must be there by now," I said, snapping him out of his haze.

"Da. They were supposed to wait in Dusseldorf for heat to die down and get new truck or train or something. Left me here to babysit whores."

"All them whores and just you to watch over them?" Reggie jumped in.

"Me, Dima, and Sobaka. I'm in charge. Those two shit brains," he elaborated, grinning.

Elvis was drifting fast. I looked over at Reggie and nodded my head. He typed something onto his phone and then set it aside.

In a few moments, there was a loud pounding on the door of the apartment. The heaviness of the strikes made it sound as if the door was going to come down. Elvis sat bolt upright as if he had been prodded in the ass with electricity.

"Interpol!" A voice yelled through the door. "Elvis

Sobolev. Open the door."

Not letting Elvis gain his wits, I looked at the phone on the table and pointed at it. "Interpol! They tracked the phone! They'll get your brother!" I shouted.

Elvis's eyes shot open wide, and fear gripped him as he stared at Barb's phone. He reached for it and then pulled his hand back as if it were a snake ready to bite him.

"Do you have a safe place to go?" I asked, trying to sound as desperate as possible.

He looked around the apartment rapidly as if he was looking for a place to hide there. "What am I going to do? You have to help me!" he said pleadingly, shaking in fear and confusion.

"Elvis!" I yelled and then slapped him hard across his face. His eyes turned to me with sudden anger. "My friend," I said. "You need a safe place. You need to warn Rodka. Do you have a safe place to go? I will take you," I said in long slow syllables, my hands on both sides of his face.

"D, d, da—ya…yes!" he sputtered out finally.

I looked at Reggie, and he smiled at me, gave me the thumbs up, and then said, "Go out de back, mon. I will stall dem."

I grabbed my bag from the couch and the phone from the table as Elvis and I ran to the back hallway, and then we turned to go down a narrow flight of stairs in the very back. At the bottom, one door led to the back of Reggie's shop, the other into an alley.

We stumbled into the alley. I was holding Elvis by the arm, keeping him from falling backwards. "Which way?" I asked. "Where are we going?"

"The club," he said haltingly, and then he staggered ahead of me.

I rushed up beside him to help steady him. "Walk normally," I said, "Don't run. It will attract attention."

He straightened himself and slowed his pace. We wobbled along the alley for a way, and when we got to a cross street, Elvis looked in both directions as if he were lost. After a moment's pause, he turned right, back toward the canal. We crossed the bridge to the other side, walked left and then right down a very, very narrow alleyway with glass doors and red lights on both sides. Elvis kept looking over his shoulder to make sure we weren't being followed.

When we got to the next street, we turned left again and then right once more and walked along the sidewalk until we came to another alley. We turned right into the alley and walked to the back of a hotel. Stairs went up from the alley to the hotel and beside them was a short staircase down to the club. When he looked over his shoulder again and saw nothing, he breathed a sigh of relief. "Thank you, my friend," he said, slapping me roughly on my back.

When we entered the club, there was music playing over the speakers though it was still early in the day. There was no one to be seen until we rounded the corner and passed through a beaded curtain into a dark, narrow dance floor, surrounded on both sides by tables and booths. It was a small space. Long and narrow.

It took a moment for my eyes to adjust to the darker environment. The music was typical techno club music—house beat with some old movie dialog dubbed into it. A male singer was mumbling something in Russian in the background. I don't know that I could have made it out even if I spoke Russian, it was that distorted.

At the end of the dance floor was a bar, and there was a man and two women sitting on stools and another woman standing behind the bar. Aside from them, the club was empty.

Elvis said something to the man in Russian I didn't understand, but I understood his name to be Dima. Dima gave him a bored look, but he got up and went back the way we had come. We passed through a doorway beside the bar into a narrow hallway with bathrooms on one side and a door marked "Kantoor" on the other.

We went in to find a man with his pants around his ankles having sex with a woman who was bent over a desk, naked.

"Elvis!" the man said, smiling. The woman looked around the side of the man and smiled at us both as we came through the door.

"Sobaka. Not on the desk. Idiot," he said in English, showing me he was in charge. He spoke to him as he would a beloved pet who had knocked over the trash again.

"Sorry, boss," Sobaka said sheepishly. He pulled up his pants, and the girl stood and gathered her clothes. As soon as Sobaka zipped the fly on his jeans, he turned to face me and Elvis.

He looked at me suspiciously.

"I sent Dima to house to watch the girls. I have to go on business trip. I want you to lock the club up and keep an eye on things here. No one but family gets in," Elvis said to Sobaka as the girl got dressed.

"What about him?" Sobaka said, gesturing towards me.

"Huh? Oh. Alex. He is helping me," he said, and then he

leaned down to reach in the desk drawer, falling forward and catching himself with his hand.

"What's wrong, Yefim?" Sobaka asked, using his given name, reaching for Elvis's elbow.

"Rasta weed." Elvis said, smiling. "The new stuff is good shit."

Sobaka gave a toothy grin, nodding in understanding.

"I have to lay low for a couple of days, so you are in charge till I get back. No partying. Everyone stays sharp," he said, nodding toward the girl Sobaka had been screwing. She had just finishing dressing when she heard this and looked up with a pout.

"You got it, boss. Be careful," he said, and then touched the girl at the base of her back to indicate it was time to leave. I was surprised how he touched her so gently, almost lovingly. With all Reggie had said about the Russians, I half expected to see shoving and slapping.

"He's in love," Elvis said after he had closed the door. "Bad to fall in love with a whore. But he has had bad life. Maybe she make him happy," he said and then shook his head as if that would clear it.

"Money," he said, remembering suddenly, and then reached for the bottom drawer.

When he stood, he was holding a stack of euros and a pistol. My chest tightened as he produced it. He tucked the pistol in his waistband and the euros into his jacket pocket.

"If Interpol catches you with a gun, it could go very badly," I said, hoping to get him to ditch the pistol.

He thought about it for a second and then put the gun back in the drawer, retrieving a phone instead. He shoved the phone into his pocket, grabbed a bag out of the closet, and then walked to the wall, where some keys were hanging on a peg board.

He reached for one set of keys, paused, and then grabbed the ones beside them instead.

We walked back into the bar area, and the two women sitting at the bar were still there, sipping on tall drinks through straws. Elvis and I walked past them, but after a few steps he stopped and turned toward them. I just kept hoping that if I followed along, then he would take me to Barb...or at least to someone who could. I half expected him to look at me, any moment, and say, "It's been nice, now buzz off."

"You two, come with us," he said to the girls. "We're going on a trip."

They were attractive, though over-painted. One was tall and dirty blonde; the other was more average-sized, with an olive complexion and black hair. They hopped off their stools, and the woman behind the counter pulled out two oversized purses and dropped them on the bar.

The girls grabbed their bags and then followed behind us. We went to the front of the club, which happened to be the back of a hotel, and saw Sobaka and his girl behind the counter at the front. She was sitting on his lap, toying with the chain around his neck.

"Lock up behind us. We won't be back tonight. I'll call you if I need you," Elvis said, sounding very much in charge, but still slurring his words quite a bit.

When we exited the club, we turned left instead of the way we had come before. A small parking lot was tucked in between some buildings off to the left, and we followed Elvis to a large Mercedes sedan.

He popped the trunk and threw his bag in and then came around and got behind the wheel. The girls were standing by the back door on the passenger side, so I started to open the front passenger door. I got in, but the girls were still standing outside the car.

Elvis made a rude noise and then got out again. Yelling across the top of the car, he said, "Get in! We must go!"

"But this is Rodka's car," the blonde exclaimed. "He will beat us just for being with you in it." The fear in her face was clear. The olive-skinned girl nodded frantically in agreement. The blonde's accent sounded Italian, but her English was very good.

"I'm on business for Rodka, and my car isn't big enough for all of us," he said, almost pleadingly. The girls looked at the Fiat and then each other, and then they shrugged and got in the back of the Mercedes.

Elvis mumbled something in Russian as he got back in and buckled his seat belt. He checked the mirrors on both sides of the car and then adjusted the one on the passenger side.

He started the car, checked the video display for the backup camera, looked over his shoulder to verify, checked the mirrors again, and then put the car in reverse to back out of the space. As he reached the end of the alley, he signaled with the blinkers and his hand and then inched out into traffic.

"Old woman," I heard one of the girls whisper to the other in the back seat. Elvis glared at them in the rearview mirror.

Once we were on a main street, Elvis sped up—but he still stayed at least five kilometers per hour below the speed limit. We were in the car for only a short time when he pulled off the road onto a service road that ran parallel to a wide channel or river, I couldn't tell. When we pulled up to a tall, iron gate, Elvis pushed the button on a remote hanging from the visor and drove us through.

As we drove around a curved wall and a dense hedge, I saw a large, modern house with an attached, covered dock...a very large one, which accessed the canal with its own man-made cove. It was the house I had seen on the GPS back in Fairfax! This is where Barb's phone signal was the first time we checked it.

Elvis pulled the Mercedes into a covered carport, exited the car, and then went around, retrieving his bag from the trunk. He and the girls walked through the front door after Elvis entered the security code, and then they walked into the large, sunken living room and flopped down on the couch as if they had just run a marathon. I lingered in the foyer and looked around the downstairs.

The house was immense. It was a post and beam modern with stone floors and a glass front, surrounded on two-and-a-half sides by rough block walls. The wide open stairs curved up to a second floor, and on the opposite side of the foyer from the living room, there was a large, formal dining room with a long, heavy, solid oak trestle table surrounded by tall-backed wooden chairs made from the same wood. Through the dining room was an equally large kitchen.

The design brought the kitchen back around to a large, high-ceilinged living room. Against the back wall there was a large, stone fireplace, which rose three stories from the sunken floor to the timber-framed ceiling.

Elvis and the two girls were on the couch in various stages of disrobe and were snorting lines of cocaine from the thick, glass table in front of them. It had taken me only three minutes to take my tour of the downstairs and in that time, they had turned the living room into a miniature version of Studio 54.

"Alex!" Elvis exclaimed. "Come, sit, enjoy. *Mi casa es su casa.*"

The blonde girl leaned back and smiled at me and patted the seat next to her. I wasn't even a little tempted. This was going to get out of hand soon—I could tell.

"I will," I said. "Just need to find the bathroom first."

Elvis pointed over his shoulder toward the foyer without looking away from the girls.

The music was playing, and the girls were stripping and dancing and touching each other and Elvis. Elvis was reclined on his cushion like the King of Persia, and I was doing my best to stay out of the living room as I explored the house.

Off the back of the kitchen was a garage, and off to the rear of the garage was a door to the very large boat house. It was more of a covered dock, but it could easily cover a seventy-foot boat with room left over for several smaller ones.

I suddenly felt very exposed.

I was stepping through the door onto the dock when something hit me on my head. My body failed me, and I could hear myself saying "Shit"—although I don't know for sure if I actually spoke it—and then blackness filled my sight like light receding in a tunnel.

**

When I came to, I was laying on the living room floor with the cold of the stone against my right cheek. I could hear my own pulse in my head along with the crying of the two girls and the pleas coming from Elvis.

"Interpol was at my door!" I heard Elvis pleading.

"And a party with whores was supposed hide you from them?" A man with a deep voice growled back at him.

"*Nyet*! We were staying out of sight!" Elvis complained. "There are—" His words were cut off by a loud slap, which I heard but could not see. Elvis fell to the ground in front of me. His hands were raised in front of him. I had the distinct impression that a gun was being pointed at him, an assumption reinforced by the sudden increase in the hysteria of the girls whimpering.

I looked up to get a glimpse of the other man. But as I moved, a lightning bolt of pain shot down the back of my head to explode into an almost burning sensation at the top of my neck. I moaned. Mistake.

I saw the bottom of a boot descending in almost slow motion toward my face. There was pressure on the front of my skull, starting between my eyes then radiating outward, and then blackness swallowed me again.

**

NICK HORIATIS sat in his sedan outside the safe house. There had been no activity at the house all day. Some incomplete satellite data had indicated the Russians had been playing host to an unknown group the week before, but there was no indication anyone was there at all now.

He was not happy to be stuck alone watching Russian mob hangouts. He had a feeling there was action going on somewhere, and he wanted to be in the middle of it. Normally techs would be sent to survey a location like this, not a trained field agent, but manpower was stretched thin—he'd drawn the short straw on the Russians.

Shortly before sunset, one of the Russian mobsters had showed up at the house with a car full of people. He'd snapped a picture of the occupants as they drove by. He'd inserted the card from his camera into the drive on his computer and then sent them to Langley. Less than a half an hour later, another car had rolled up, parked outside the gate, and sat for a few minutes. The angle was wrong, so Nick couldn't get a photograph.

When the mystery driver emerged from his vehicle, he climbed over the wall instead of going through the gate. *Something is going down*, Nick thought to himself, and he dialed the number for his boss.

"Temple," the voice at the other end answered.

"I've got some activity here at the Russian safe house," he responded without identifying himself.

"Serb?" John Temple asked.

"I don't know yet, but something is cooking. Someone just climbed over the wall, and a little while ago, a car pulled up with what looked like two whores and two men," he replied. "I sent the photos to Langley."

"Can you get audio on the house?" Temple asked.

"No. The wall is blocking the directional," he responded, referring to the high pickup directional microphone, "...unless you want me to go in. I'll be happy to do that."

"No. Observe only. Wait until we get a hit back on the photos," Temple said.

Nick groaned at the thought of having to continue to wait, but he acknowledged his orders. "Yeah. Fine," he said.

"Keep me posted," Temple said and then hung up.

A little more than an hour later, he got a message from Langley. It read:

> *No ID on the girls. The image wasn't clear enough. The driver is Yefim 'Elvis' Sobelev. Brother of Rodka Sobelev, owner of the house. Russian mob. The second we got a hit on with a passport photo. US citizen. Scott Wolfe. Arrived today from US, putting him on top of the pile of flagged individuals. No rap sheet.*

No rap sheet my ass, Nick thought. *You don't hang out with the Russian mob if you're law abiding...unless you are a captive.*

Nick forwarded the message to John Temple and waited for instructions. A few moments later, he got his reply. The message read:

> *Tag their phones. All communications in and out. Law-abiding American citizens don't pal around with Russian mob.*

Shit, Nick thought. *What will it take for him to let me go in?*

six
Four Days Until Event

The wee hours of the morning, Wednesday, May 12th, 2010 - Amsterdam, Netherlands

I was feeling utter helplessness and despair. I was on a rock face, somewhere in the dark, and I felt like crying out, but my voice wouldn't cooperate. I was holding on to Barb's wrist, but she was slipping away. I felt so weak.

She looked up at me. "Let me go," she said.

I was already losing my grip; my fingers were so small that they didn't even go all the way around her arm.

"No," I croaked in a weak voice.

She reached up with her free hand and began prying my fingers off her wrist. My other hand hurt, the stone it was hooked onto was digging painfully into my palm as I tried to bear her weight. She managed to slip her fingers under my thumb and pry it loose, and she plummeted into the darkness below.

From the chasm below me, I heard Barb crying. "I had to leave," she said. "I can't count on you to be there for me." I couldn't see her, but I could feel her drifting away from me until I didn't feel her presence at all.

There I sat in silence, peering into the black, hoping to catch some glimpse of movement. Then another voice came to me. It was mine. Laughing.

"You have to look at the numbers, idiot," *the voice said.*

"Numbers won't bring back the dead," I screamed back defiantly.

"No, stupid. Look at the numbers," *it replied.*

In my mind, my 'other voice' showed me the floor in brief flashes, like a slide show.

It was the floor I had been on when I woke the last time for a few seconds.
A bag on the floor, contents strewn.
Broken glass.
White powder scattered like snow on everything.
Clothes laid there in a heap.
I saw naked female feet.
I saw the iron leg of the table.
I saw a boot, a leg, a belt, a phone. The phone...it was glowing. Pulsing. I understood.

"Now you've got it," *my other voice said. Then it laughed.* ***"Now, WAKE UP!"***

I woke again. This time I was sitting upright. I was in the garage, sitting in one of those sturdy, high-backed wooden chairs from the dining room. My arms wouldn't move. My first thought was that the blows to my head had paralyzed me, but as the fog cleared, I realized my arms and legs were duct taped to the chair. My shirt was missing.

The space was dark except for the light over a workbench in front of me. There I saw Elvis cradling his left arm with his right hand. I couldn't see the girls, but I could hear them sniffling and sobbing in the dark. The other man had his back to me, but I could see something under his arm.

He shifted to one side long enough for me to see that he had a small canister, about the size of a two-liter bottle of soda, and that he was awkwardly twisting something on the top. My heart contracted hard in my chest as I realized it was a propane torch. He turned, looking at me and then set his gun on the workbench and grabbed a spark striker.

"Ah. Good. You are awake," he said as he walked toward me. "Let's see how much the CIA knows, shall we?" He squeezed the striker, and the nozzle on the canister leaped to life. Yellow and orange flame shot out with a tiny cone of blue flame at the base.

"I'm not CIA," I heard myself say, but it didn't sound like me. My voice was broken and gravelly.

He laughed. "It's funny. Every CIA agent you ask, 'Are you CIA?' says, 'No. Not CIA,'" he said as he walked toward me. "It makes you wonder if there are actually any CIA agents at all. And yet, I know they are out there somewhere...so let's start with you."

He let the flame come within inches of the side of my face and then slowly lowered it down to my shoulder, where the heat started to melt away the hair on my upper arm. Then the pain came. I felt, though I could not see, ice so cold that it penetrated all the way to my bones, and then pain exploded up and down my arm. I smelled my hair and flesh. I screamed. And he lifted the torch.

"So. Are you CIA yet?" He asked calmly, as if he were in

no hurry. He could do this all night if he had to.

I was sobbing. I tried to turn my head to see the burn but my head was held tight against the back of the chair with tape. "No. Not CIA."

Tell him Barb was on the boat, I heard someone with my voice whisper in my ear.

He leaned in for another pass with the torch.

"No!" I yelled. "No. My girlfriend was on the boat. I came because my girlfriend died," I spit out desperately.

He paused, looking at my face, and then he cocked his head to the side. "How did you find this place?" he asked suspiciously.

The phone, said the *other* me in my ear.

I hesitated. He leaned forward with the torch again. The flame licked at my chest this time. This time I felt the heat. "Her phone!" I screamed, trying to turn away from the pain, but I was held firmly in place by the layers of tape.

He withdrew the flame. "What about her phone?" he asked calmly.

"I called it after the explosion. It rang and rang and then went to voicemail. So I knew it wasn't destroyed," I lied, not wanting to give away all my secrets. "I hoped there was a mistake, that she was in the hospital or something. So I came to find her."

The man laughed at me. "So you are love sick puppy? How sweet." Then he leaned forward again. "You still did not answer the question. How did you find this place?"

I paused for a long moment. He raised his eyes to let me know he was waiting for me to finish. Behind him I could see Elvis reaching for the gun on the bench.

Elvis! Are you going to shoot me? I wondered. *Do away with me before he figures out you were supposed to get rid of that phone?*

The man raised the torch again, searing more skin from my chest. I yelled in agony. Suddenly, a thought occurred to him, and he stood and then turned to confront Elvis.

There was a shot. It was quieter than I thought it would be—no more than a muffled pop. The man who had been torturing me dropped his torch and crumpled backwards, his head hitting my knee as he fell to the floor. There was a gurgling sound coming from his throat.

The girls began crying more loudly as Elvis walked over to me, slowly. The gun in his hand was shaking. He was pale, staring down at the dying man as he came to a halt in front of him. The man on the floor looked at Elvis with fury in his eyes, his wound oozing dark red across his chest and onto the floor.

"*Picko jedna!*" the man rasped out with a spatter of blood. Elvis raised the gun again, his hand steady that time, and he put another round through the head of the big man. The man twitched once and then was still. Elvis spat on him and then dropped the gun on his chest.

He stood there and stared at the body on floor for a long time, and then he looked at me. "You tricked me," he said calmly.

He squatted down and looked me in the face for a few seconds, as if trying to decide what he should do with me. "But then you let him cook you instead of giving me up." He continued his stare for a moment longer and then leaned close. "She was your girlfriend?" he asked.

I tried to nod, but my head wouldn't move. "Yes," I said, barely audible.

Elvis pulled his switchblade from his pocket, smiled at me, and raised the knife to my head.

My heart sank.

This is it.

I was not going to save Barb, I was not going to marry her and have beautiful children running through the sprinklers on a warm summer day. I could actually hear them laughing and squealing as they hopped through the water on a green lawn behind a white house. I could smell the grass and a charcoal fire in the barbecue. I could see Barb's face smiling at them.

But the darkness didn't come.

Instead, Elvis cut at the tape that bound my head to the chair.

"A man who would do all this for love must be respected," he said as he sawed at the tape on my arms. "And a man who would face flame for woman one second and then face it again for me the next is a friend," he continued as he freed my legs.

When he was done and the tape gave way, I fell to the side. He rushed to catch me. "You are my friend, Alex," he said as he helped me to my feet.

"Scott," I said, correcting him. "My name is Scott."

Elvis smiled. "You are my friend, Scott. I am Yefim."

He helped me walk back into the house and then sat me down on the couch. A pain shot up my side, and I reached for my ribs.

"He kicked you many times while you were unconscious. We thought he had killed you."

I finally got a chance to look at my chest, arm, and shoulder where the big man had burned me. I had expected to see charred skin and gaping, burned holes in my flesh, but found instead only some large angry red blisters with a dark spot in the center of each.

I breathed a sigh of relief, though the pain was excruciating.

"Let's get you fixed up." Elvis said, and then he motioned for the dark-haired girl to come to me. "Go get first aid kit in kitchen," he said to the other girl.

The dark haired girl sat next to me and leaned over to look at my wounds.

"Not *so* bad," she said, but I could tell from her brief expression of shock she was lying. Then she touched my ribs, sending a jolt of pain through my side and shoulder, resulting in a second flash of pain through my head and neck when I tensed.

"You will live," she said and then looked up and smiled at me warmly. "I'm Nyla." Her lip was puffy on one side, and her right eye displayed a blue bruise.

She had put on a man's button-down shirt to cover her previously naked breasts but had not buttoned it. I watched them as they swayed while she worked on cleaning and bandaging my wounds. The softness of her touch and absence of modesty was comforting, calming.

Elvis was speaking Russian on the phone on the other side of the vast living room. When he completed his call, he walked back over and joined us on the couch. "Nyla is good. No? She always fixes wounds for the family—I think she was doctor in other life," he said.

Nyla smiled. "A nurse school dropout—in this life," she corrected.

"I don't think they teach you how remove bullets and fix stabbing wound in Portuguese nurse school," he said jokingly. Elvis looked back at me with a serious gaze. "The big man. His name was Majmun. Serb. He was here to 'sanitize' the house. He was going to kill us all. But he wanted to know who you were first."

I nodded in understanding. The blonde came and joined us on the couch. She was smoking a joint. She took a deep hit and then passed it to Nyla. Nyla took a drag and then offered it to me. I declined, but she pushed it back to me.

"For the pain," she said plainly. I let her put it to my mouth, and I took a deep drag, coughing out most of it. The three of them laughed.

"American can't hold his smoke." Elvis said.

She took a deep hit from it and then leaned over me, placing her thumb on my chin and opening my mouth. She blew the smoke into my mouth, and I inhaled. It was cooler, gentler this time, and I held it for a moment and then blew it out. I felt relaxation wash over me. She handed the joint back to the blonde girl when she saw me relax into the cushions.

"I called Sobaka. He will be here in while to help clean and dispose of de 'Monkey,'" he said, referring to the big man's nickname. "Nyla will take you home. Maria will stay and help me and Sobaka. Then we will all pretend this did not happen."

I looked at him for a moment, hesitant to ask anything of the man who just saved my life. But Barb was more important than courtesy. "Do you know where the hostages are?" I asked plainly, my voice broken and gravelly.

He shook his head. "My brother would never trust me with such information. And I don't even know if Serbs trusted *him* with it." His face softened. "I would tell you if I knew. My brother was wrong to get us involved with this thing. But he is harder man than I am. He has killed people. He hurts the girls. This is his doing, but I am sorry for my part in it. I'm sorry it has hurt you and the one you love. But I cannot tell you what I do not know."

"The phone—" I muttered. He looked at me in confusion. "On Majmun. May I have it?"

Elvis got up and walked away for a moment and then returned with the phone. It was sticky with blood. I opened it and hit recall on the menu. All the incoming numbers said "*UNKNOWN*," but there were two outgoing numbers. One was dialed recently, and the other was dialed many times. I reached for my bag on the couch but my ribs protested. My eyes closed automatically, and I gasped. Maria reached for my bag and handed it to me.

I opened it and found my phone. I noticed that I had several text messages from Bonbon. I hit reply, typed in the two numbers from Majmun's phone, and then wrote "*where?*" and hit send.

It was almost midnight in Fairfax, so I didn't expect an answer till morning. I put my phone back in my bag and handed the bloody phone back to Elvis. "Take the battery and sim card out before you dispose of it. Turning it off doesn't protect you," I said, closing my bag.

Elvis smiled and nodded and then did as I suggested. He and Maria got up and walked away. Nyla lit the joint again and repeated her actions from earlier, blowing cool smoke into my mouth. I was grateful for the relief it brought me and soon let the heaviness in my head pull me into blissful unconsciousness.

**

When I awoke next, I heard Sobaka and Elvis talking in the kitchen. Nyla was still next to me, sleeping quietly and leaning against my good shoulder. She had placed a damp cloth on the back of my neck and was now snoring sweetly, her face pressed against my bare shoulder. It had been a tough night for them as well.

Sobaka looked at me through the bar opening from the kitchen and saw that I was awake. He stopped his conversation with Elvis and came around to where I was sitting, leaned forward, and whispered so as not to awaken Nyla.

"I am proud to know you," he said sincerely. "I know what is love. I hope if my Misha was have trouble like dis, I would be brave enough as you."

He reached over and clasped my hand with both of his. "I also thank you much for try protect Yefim. He is more brother than my own," he said, appearing almost teary eyed. All the talking had wakened Nyla. She sat up, and Sobaka turned toward her. "Get dressed now. You will take him to home and stay with him until he is okay. Car is in front."

He looked back at me and said, "Nyla will take care of you. If I do not see you again, I wish you luck finding your woman," he smiled at me, patted me gently on my good shoulder, and then disappeared through the kitchen door.

Nyla rose from the couch, grabbed her bag, and headed to the bathroom under the stairs in the foyer, shedding her shirt as she walked. A few minutes later, she reemerged looking like a different person. Her hair had been pulled back into a ponytail, her bruised eye had been artfully concealed with makeup, and she wore jeans, a loose-fitting pullover shirt, and a pair of flat shoes. I wouldn't have been able to pick her out of a crowd.

I smiled my approval at her quick change, and she returned it with a playful wink. She looked around the living room, saw no one, and then said loud enough to be heard throughout the house. "We leave now?"

"*Da*. Go. We see you later," I heard Elvis call from the direction of the garage. Then the sound of a saw rang out. The sound diminished greatly when a door closed, and Maria stepped into the living room a second later, making a face and a gesture that reflected her revulsion at what was occurring in the garage. She walked over to Nyla and put her arms around her, kissed her on the cheek, and then turned toward me.

She bent over, kissed me on my nose, and said sincerely, "Good luck, Yankee." Then she walked upstairs with her oversized bag slung across her shoulder.

Nyla helped me to my feet and then slid the shirt she had been wearing over my good shoulder and helped me lift my arm through the hole on my injured side. She put my bag on her shoulder along with hers and then put my good arm around her neck to help me to the car.

My side was throbbing from the pain. She helped me sit on the passenger side of Elvis's Fiat, buckled my seat belt for me, and then hurried around to the driver's side.

"Where you staying, sweetie?" she asked. I had to force the

cobwebs from my head before I could answer her.

"Dam en Warmoestraat, alstublieft. In De Wallen," I said;
my rehearsed line came back to me from the cab ride.

She raised her eyebrows in surprise and approval.

"Don't be impressed," I said. "I practiced it for half an hour
before I landed. It's the Old City Hotel."

She laughed at my confession, started the car, and began to
drive, but Elvis came running out of the side door of the garage,
his hands and arms covered in blood. When he realized how
horrible that must appear he put his hands behind his back and
stepped closer.

"I will call to check you later, my friend. Do not resist
Nyla. She will do what is best for you." Then he looked across to
her. "Stay low, and say nothing to anyone. Park car off street. You
will be safe and out of sight with Scott. If we are lucky, and act
like nothing happen, no one will notice one less Serbian thug in
world. Call Sobaka if you need anything."

Nyla nodded and put the car back in drive. Elvis nodded
and winked at me, and then turned to the gate and clicked the
remote in his hand. The gate swung open, and we zipped out of the
driveway and out into the street. Nyla drove like an Indy car racer,
but I slept the whole trip.

**

I awoke to Nyla tugging on me to pull me from the car. We
were in a dirty garage or shed. The headlights were the only light
in the space, and she had closed the double-wide doors so not even
the street lights were visible. She had our bags already slung
across her shoulder and was pulling on my arm. Groggily, I swung
my legs out of the car and, between the two of us, I managed to

stand, pausing woozily for a second before starting to tip over. She quickly reached around me and grabbed me around my side. I winced as a stab of pain shot up my side, and she instantly shifted her grip to my belt to support me. "Sorry," she muttered as she closed and locked the car.

We exited the garage, and she helped me walk to the street. The sky was still dark, but there was no traffic, so I assumed it was around three or four in the morning—after party time but before early morning delivery times. The sun would start coming up soon. I didn't even bother looking where we were going. I simply put as much of my weight on Nyla as she could handle and struggled to keep my feet under me with the rest.

I had to stop twice before we reached the front door of my hotel. Each time she was patient and doting, checking me every few minutes to see if I was okay. Once we reached the door, she tried to pull it open, but it was locked.

She was about to ring the bell when I remembered what the desk clerk had told me about after hours entry. I asked Nyla to hand me my bag and then fished my electronic room key out and pressed it to the locking mechanism. The light flashed green, and Nyla pushed the door open. We slowly made our way up the stairs to my floor and to my room. Once inside, I sat on the edge of the bed, sending another flash of pain up my side and across my chest.

Nyla closed and bolted the door, and then, after putting our bags down on the dresser, she helped me slide out of my shirt. She fretted over my chest wound for a moment, seeing that it was weeping, and then eased me back onto the bed and went for my pants button and zipper. I raised my head, painfully, in protest.

"Hush," she said. "I am your doctor, and Elvis said not to resist. Be a good boy and relax."

I lowered my head back down, and she deftly removed my

jeans. She then swung my legs onto the bed and covered me with a blanket from the closet. She perched next to me, stroking my head while she peeled back a corner of the bandage on my chest. She made a face. I guess she didn't like what she saw.

"That bad, huh?" I asked.

She shook her head. "Moving rolled the blisters," she said as she went to her bag and pulled out the first aid kit she had taken from the house. "It was bound to happen. It just makes a mess."

She did her healer bit for several minutes, made a satisfied little grunt, and then re-bandaged the wound.

"There," she said with a satisfied tone. "Now you heal properly."

She checked my shoulder and arm next. They were more to her liking, so she just recovered them without new bandages. Then she lowered herself off the bed to the floor next to me. Placing her hands on my side, she said "This will hurt some, but I am only checking. Pain is not doing damage. Damage is already done."

I nodded, and she proceeded to probe my ribs and the tissue between them with her fingertips. The pain was excruciating, and it was all I could do to keep from crying out.

"I know," she said in a soothing tone. "Almost done." She finished her examination and pulled the blanket back over me.

"I don't think you have broken rib. But maybe separated. We will bind them after you wake." She leaned over as if she was going to kiss me, but instead she lifted my lids one at a time to check my pupils—and then she kissed me gently on the lips and placed her hand on my cheek. When she raised back up she smiled warmly at me and said, "No concussion—sleep."

So I did.

**

Barb had returned, at least in my dreams. She told me how excited she was that I had come for her and how proud she was of me for being so brave in the garage. She hugged me warmly, tucked her head into my shoulder, and snuggled up close to me.

I could feel her heavy, soft breasts on my skin and a light kiss from her on my neck. I began to feel aroused from her closeness. Her hand slowly trailed down my belly but came to rest on my pelvic bone, not my erection. There it made soft, loving circles on my skin, heightening the throbbing sensation in my groin.

I awoke suddenly. Nyla was curled up against me on my good side, under the blanket. Her breasts were bare, and one of them was resting on my bare chest. She felt me stir and opened her eyes, smiling. She looked up at my face to see my discomfort, then slowly rose on one arm and flashed a devilish grin.

"You were shivering and calling out," she said soothingly, coyly.

When I didn't respond, she shrugged and hopped out of bed. The sun was up, and I looked at the clock radio to see that it was after 3:00 p.m. I had slept for nearly ten hours. I rushed to sit up but was greeted with a flash of pain in my neck and a renewed throbbing in my side.

She turned her back to me as she slipped her shirt on and then put her hand out in a gesture to stay still. "Don't move until I get back with food. Then I will wrap your ribs." She reached for my wallet. "Compression will help." She pulled out a handful of bills while looking at me with a grin. "I'll need some medical supplies as well," she said, tucking the money into her pocket.

She came around to my side of the bed and pushed me backwards gently with the palm of her hand and then handed me two tablets. I looked up at her suspiciously. "Ibuprofen," she exclaimed innocently. "From the first aid kit." Then she emptied the clothes from her bag on top of the dresser and slung it across her shoulder.

She winked at me on her way out the door. "Back soon," she said, tucking my room key into her pocket with the cash.

I took a moment to gird myself and then rolled over to the other side of the bed so I could reach my bag. I pulled out my iPad and checked my mail. No worthwhile news to be seen there. I pulled my phone out next and began to read the messages from Bonbon and Storc.

The first was from Storc, letting me know he had an update on the Bluetooth app I had already downloaded. "*Faster code cracking,*" he'd said. Next was a message was from Bonbon at 2:00 p.m. yesterday. It read, "*Haven't heard from you. Hope everything is okay.*" The third message was a couple hours later. "*Still haven't heard from you. Still hope everything is okay.*" Message number four. "*Please let us know how it's going.*"

The next two messages were variations on the last. The seventh was a response from Storc about the two numbers I'd sent him. It read, "*Whew! Were worried something happened to you.*" I had to chuckle out loud, resulting in an ache in my side.

"Nope, I'm just fine," I muttered aloud to myself.

The message continued: "*Neither number is showing GPS. Both are cells. May be turned off. Setting up a capture with time stamp. Will display on map as other did...if they pop up.*"

The last message was from Bonbon. "*Someone tried to*

hack your signal to the server at 1:23 a.m. your time. Didn't make it past 1st dynamic. But adding more to be safe. Be careful."

"Shit!" *Too soon,* I thought to myself.

I downloaded Storc's updated app to my phone and then took the prepaid phone out of the bag and began to copy everything on mine to it. While it was copying, I opened the GPS map on my iPad to discover that one of the phone numbers had its GPS signal captured while I slept. It was in Dusseldorf.

No sign of the other one. Barb's phone was flashing on my screen in the same location I was appearing on the map. When the phone copy was complete, I rebooted the prepaid burn phone and tried to connect to the secure server with it. Everything seemed to work as it should, so I shut everything down and shoved it all back into my bag.

I laid back on the bed and rested a few moments. My stomach was rumbling terribly. I realized I had not eaten since yesterday around this time and was suddenly very hungry. Nyla had been gone for more than an hour. Fortunately she arrived soon after with a bag of sandwiches, sodas, and some snacks in one arm, and another bag with medical supplies in the other.

"Food and medicine," she said as she closed the door and then joined me on the bed.

She handed me the bag with the food in it and began to unpack the contents of the other one. She had several elastic compression bandages, some ointments with labels I couldn't decipher, and some over-the-counter pain meds. I grabbed a very nice-looking roast beef sandwich with a horseradish sauce from the bag. The first bite was almost euphoric. I was truly hungry. I tossed the sodas to the side and picked up one of the bottled waters, drained it, and then opened another.

She laid out her supplies for after our meal between bites from a turkey sandwich. She grabbed one of the sodas held it up in an offer to me, and I said, "Thanks, but no. Sugar syrup is bad for you."

She laughed at me, opened the bottle, and took big swallow of its contents. "Ahhhhh," she said, mocking my health consciousness. I shrugged and sat back against the pillows.

We chatted while we ate. She spoke freely and unapologetically about her life as a prostitute and how she'd become one. "I had to quit nurse school—bad husband," she said.

I raised my eyebrow.

"I was too young and foolish. I thought love would make me a housewife," she said. "It was his idea to be prostitute. I wasn't exactly good girl to begin with, so it didn't seem like a stretch."

I nodded my understanding.

"One day he hit me, for money I had," she continued, shrugging once as if it wasn't a big deal. "So I left and came here. The Russians don't treat the 'volunteers' bad, plus I am medical training. It works out."

"Elvis said Rodka hits the girls," I inserted gently, not sure how much leeway I had in the conversation.

She nodded. "New girls, yes," she said. "But this is what it is—sex, drugs, and rock 'n' roll. It's a violent life."

"Elvis is hard to read," I said casually, hoping to gain an insight.

She laughed. "Not so hard to read," she replied. "Elvis

wants to be Rodka, but his heart is too soft. He tries hard to make his brother proud, but Rodka is cold…all business. It's good that Elvis, Sobaka, and Dima take care of us. The others are too rough…I think Rodka knows this. Is why he leaves Elvis in charge of the windows."

"How much medical training did you have?" I asked as I ate the last bit of my sandwich.

"In nurse school? Less than one year," she said and then grinned. "In Amsterdam? Three years intense on job training. There are surgeons who haven't done what I've had to do."

"Ever think of going back to school?" I asked.

She tipped her head to the side and looked into the air. "Think? Yes. Do?" She shrugged. "Who knows? Maybe someone will make that happen."

I looked at my phone and noted the time—it was nearly 6:00 p.m. I started to become a bit antsy as I realized my day had slipped away from me.

When we were done eating, she began checking my wounds again. All my burns seemed to be fine. She seemed pleased with the progress they were making. When she touched my ribs they weren't as sore as they were the night before, but it still hurt to move. She had me sit up, making my head throb, and then proceeded to wrap my torso with the compression bandages.

When she was done, she checked my head, neck, and then the cut on the bridge of my nose where I had been kicked. In the end, she gave me a clean bill of health. I was feeling strong as well. A good night's sleep and food in my stomach had made me feel close enough to human again to go out and prepare for the next leg of my quest.

"I have to leave," I said to Nyla.

"Elvis said to stay low," she said, not realizing that her boss was not my boss.

"Yes, he did," I agreed with her. "But don't you think he was talking to you? He did wish me luck in finding my 'woman.' How can I do that if I'm here?" I asked as gently as I could.

No argument she gave me could make me stay. Too much time had been lost already, and it was time to part ways. She had gone through a great deal of trouble because of me. To my credit, however, had I not showed up, Majmun would have killed them all—even if all I did was show up and get tortured.

Her face said she had resigned her argument. But I noted some disappointment there as well. Was she infatuated with the idea of having her own personal American to play house with?

I stood and hugged her. "Thank you for taking such good care of me," I said. "Maybe it would be best for you to go back to the club and find Elvis and Sobaka." She pressed her face into my chest and gripped me tightly enough that my ribs hurt.

"I hope you find her," she said sincerely. "And I hope she appreciates what you are going through for her."

For the next few minutes she gathered her things from around the room, tucked the medical supplies into my bag, and then walked to the door, turning to say her farewells. "Check your bandages twice a day…especially your chest. Use the ointment in the green tube only if it gets worse. Use the white tube with each changing."

I smiled and walked over to her. "I will. I promise. Thank you for all you've done for me. I will never forget it." I kissed her on her forehead and then released her to go out the door.

On the way out she said over her shoulder, "If she breaks your heart, come back and see me. I can heal those as well." She smiled and winked as she headed down the stairs.

As soon as she was out of sight, I checked the time and went back into the room. I checked the train schedules and realized that I would not be able to catch the last train from Amsterdam to Dusseldorf today. I'd have to take an early train tomorrow. That gave me time to locate some items I needed.

I started to stash my iPad and my prepaid phone in the room safe, but then I remembered the message from Bonbon about the hacking attempt on the site. I powered down the iPad and the prepaid burn phone and wrapped them in a hotel towel. I poked my head out the door of my room and looked both ways down the hall. I needed to find a place outside my room to hide them. Hacks on the phone connection to the encrypted servers screamed NSA. If the government was onto me already, I didn't want to give away my toys.

The coast was clear.

I walked down the hall until I found what I was looking for in the form of a small walk-in closet at the end of the hall: a supply room with an ice machine in it. I pulled the door closed behind me and looked around for a suitable hiding place. Next to the ice machine was a small air return for the central heating and air system.

I took a butter knife from a tray of dishes, unscrewed the vent cover, and peeked inside. There was a turn in the duct. I reached my hand inside to make sure there wasn't a drop after the turn. Satisfied, I pushed the bundle into the hiding spot.

There was plenty of airflow around the bundle, so I didn't have to worry about a nosy repairman coming in to investigate a blockage.

I got the vent cover replaced and then headed back to my room. It was after 7:00 p.m. now, and I had little chance of finding a store with the items I needed, but I had to try. I shouldered my canvas bag and headed down the stairs.

**

AGENT NICK HORIATIS had decided to follow this Wolfe character when he left the Russian compound instead of staying with the Russians. Wolfe had disappeared into the hotel hours before. It looked as if the hooker had been carrying him.

"Too much partying, buddy?" Nick had mumbled as he'd watched them disappear through the front door.

Shortly after sunrise, Nick's relief showed up to take his place. Nick hesitated to leave, but he realized the boy would probably be out for hours...enough time to catch a nap anyway.

He got a secure message around 11:30 a.m. from the NSA. It read:

> *Having difficulty getting any data from Scott Wolfe's phone. It's encrypted, but he is also using a cycling dynamic proxy which is proving very difficult to nail down.*

Nick was certain he had stumbled onto something important.

Nick relieved the day shift watcher hours early and sent him back to the consulate for radio monitoring. Shortly after 3:00 p.m., he got another message from the NSA tech who was helping him. It said:

> *More activity on Wolfe's phone. Am almost positive our*

attempts have been detected. New protocols in place. Never seen anything like this before.

Nick picked up his phone and dialed his NSA tech. "What's your take on Wolfe?" he asked.

"He is using some very sophisticated communications protocols here. Better than we use ourselves," the tech said to Nick.

Nick leaned over to look out the window of his car, gazing up at the window of the room Wolfe was staying in.

"What are the chances of you breaking them?" Nick asked.

"Honestly?" the tech replied. "Zero. The guy is using a combination of defeats I've never seen. He's got awesome tech on his side."

"Thanks," Nick said. "Keep on him. At least we have his location."

"Will do," the tech said and then hung up.

With this new update from the NSA, Nick decided he would raise the alarm with Temple. Nick sent him a text update. A few minutes later, his phone rang.

"Yeah?" Nick answered.

"Okay." John said. "Get a bag team together."

Nick smiled. "Yes, sir."

By 5:00 p.m. everything was in place. It was just a matter of timing. Nick hoped it would wait until after dark, but either way, Scott Wolfe was going to answer some questions.

**

I had just stepped into the alley when I heard an American voice. "Got a light?"

Here it comes, that other voice inside my head said. It startled me, and my heart skipped a beat.

As I turned his direction, two sets of hands grabbed my wrists and shoulders from behind, and a sharp shove sent me to my knees on the cobblestone. My arms were pinned behind me, pulled painfully upward. I could feel the bandage on my chest tugging at my wound, and the movement renewed the sharp pain.

With the pain, a flash of anger exploded into my head, and I kicked out and back with my right foot striking the feet of one of the men, while simultaneously driving all my weight onto my left knee—ouch.

One of the two men behind me fell to the ground, swearing. I felt the hard thud of his face on the back of my head, and my face was shoved down onto the cobblestones, breaking my lip as I had no free hand to stop my fall.

"I will kill you where you lay if you move again," he whispered in my ear.

Then he braced himself against my head and shoulders to stand up, grinding my face, my now-bleeding nose, and my broken lip against the oily stone surface. He jerked me back up to my knees by my hair and was about to smash the side of his hand into my face when the man who had asked me for the light interrupted.

"Enough," he said.

I looked up into the face of the guy behind me as he pulled

my head back by the hair—I could see the seething anger on his face as well as a thin trickle of blood from his nose, which was, now clearly broken. I smiled inwardly but didn't let it show on my face.

The two behind me jerked me to my feet.

They pulled a hood over my head, blocking my vision, and followed with a punch to the gut, sending the air from my lungs and doubling me over.

"What did I say?" I heard cigarette guy ask coolly.

They moved quickly down the alley away from Damstraat, dragging me between the two of them, the toes of my shoes clacking across the stones. The alleyway was quiet this evening. When I had come out of the hotel, only a handful of people had been around. I figured most of them were doing their best to ignore the apparent kidnapping, judging by the lack of voices speaking up in my defense.

I heard an engine start up as I was pulled roughly to one side, and then the vehicle pulled up to us. I heard a metal door roll open—a van.

"Hey! What are you doing?" I heard a woman's voice ask frantically.

I recognized her thick German accent. It was Kathrin—the girl I'd traded bags with yesterday. I heard her boot-clad feet walking toward us.

"Don't come any closer," cigarette man said threateningly. "Official business."

"I don't believe you. ID. I want to see your ID," she insisted loudly.

"This doesn't concern you," he replied, his voice conveying a hint of emotion—annoyance, apparently.

"Help!" Kathrin screamed. "Terrorists! They are killing him! Police! Police!" she yelled.

I could hear cigarette man move toward her and away from me. I heard her boots shuffle backwards on the cobblestones, and then she screamed louder, adding, "They have a bomb! Stop them!"

Her screams had apparently attracted some attention. Within a few seconds, the siren of a police car wailed its approach and then came to a halt at the Damstraat entrance to the alley.

"This is way too much attention, John," I heard a voice in the van say in our direction.

"Shit!" was all cigarette man said. My guess was that he was John.

Kathrin was still screaming for the police when I heard a second police car roll into the alley from the opposite direction, effectively blocking the van from exiting. "Get him inside," cigarette man said.

I was lifted and tossed inside head first, banging my head into a hard metal edge. The contact sent a sharp pain radiating out from my left brow. Someone sat down on me, hard, and then the van door rolled closed with a slam.

I heard more sirens and a man's voice ordering the driver to turn off the engine. He complied. I could hear Kathrin outside the van hysterically carrying on about an abduction and how she thought she saw a bomb in the van.

John was trying to explain that everything was a misunderstanding and that no one was in the van.

The police were not budging. "Open the door!" they yelled. "Open it!"

I decided to help Kathrin's case. I rose up with all my strength, forcing the man sitting on my back toward the ceiling and then slamming him against the side of the van. My damaged ribs screamed from the effort.

"Help me!" I yelled through the bag. "They are killing me!" A fist slammed into the side of my head through the bag.

I heard weapons locking into place outside. I continued to yell. "Help me!"

The door to the van rolled open, and everyone inside was ordered out at gunpoint. One of the passengers delivered a cheap shot to my kidney as he was exiting—I guessed it was broken-nose guy.

There was much yelling and ordering to the ground. I heard John, the cigarette guy, say something about consulate protection. But the police were having none of it until everything was sorted out. Someone helped me to sit upright and pulled the bag from my head.

The bandage had come undone under my shirt, and there was a wet, red spot on my chest. A medic walked up and cut my shirt off to examine the source of the bleeding, and suddenly all eyes were on the ugly burns on my chest, arm, and shoulder, and the compression bandages wrapped around my ribs.

"Oh shit," I heard one of the men on the ground mutter.

"We had nothing to do with that," John said as the medic

began to examine my bloody face.

Kathrin watched me from the crowd with a look of worry on her face. I gave her a wink to let her know I was okay. She seemed to relax a bit, but her brow remained creased with concern.

The men on the ground were handcuffed and stationed against the wall with several officers guarding them. It was a few moments before I was allowed to stand. A shiver ran up my spine from the cool evening air, and I turned to the officer who had been watching over me.

"I'm cold," I said to him. "Can I get a jacket?"

A nearby medic heard the request and held out a blanket. The officer took it and handed it to me. "Does this work?" he asked.

I took it and put it around my shoulders and then shrugged off the corner. It was irritating to my wounds.

"Actually, my room is right up there," I said, pointing up at the third floor window of the hotel. "Would it be okay if I sent my friend up to grab me a new shirt and my jacket?"

I glanced down at my bloody chest to emphasize my condition. He appraised the shredded state of my shirt and wounds and then looked into the crowd.

"Who your friend is?" he asked in a thick Dutch accent.

I pointed at Kathrin. He instantly recognized her as the woman whose screams had drawn the police in the first place, so he gestured to her. As she made her way through the crowd, I dug into my pocket for my room key.

She stepped up to me with a concerned look on her face.

"What is happening?" she asked.

Trust her, my new inner voice whispered into my ear. I jumped visibly, startled, and the officer glanced back in my direction.

"I'm not sure," I said, handing her my room key. "Can you do me a favor and get a shirt and a jacket out of my room?"

"Sure thing," she said and then turned to go.

"Stop her. Don't let her go to his room alone," John shouted from his place against the wall.

The policeman in charge looked at John and then at the girl and decided to send one of the other officers up to the room with her to make sure she only got a shirt and a jacket.

While all eyes were on them, I reached into my bag and pulled out my phone. I tapped the skull and crossbones app and then punched in my four digit code. The screen flashed once and then displayed a status bar.

"Hey. Don't let him use his phone!" broken nose exclaimed.

They all looked in my direction. I gave them a confused and incredulous look, and then put my phone back in my bag to finish running its wipe and restore out of sight. It was dark now, and I still didn't have my shirt.

It was only a few minutes later when a large, black SUV rolled up at the Damstraat end of the alley. It stopped at the entrance of the alleyway as it couldn't get any closer, and several people got out.

They walked toward the sprawling scene flashing badges

and papers at everyone who challenged them. There were four of them approaching—one man in a suit, two in street clothes, and a woman in business attire.

The two men in street clothes reached the van first. They surveyed the situation without speaking and then looked at the four men on the ground in handcuffs. One of the newcomers smiled and shook his head.

"Oh, SB," he said, with mock pity in his voice.

Broken-nose guy turned his head away in disgust. *Broken-nose guy is 'SB,'* I noted, adding to my growing list of names.

The woman approached the van. Her eyes went wide when she saw my chest wound, the bandages on my shoulder and arm, the rib wrapping, and my bruised and bloody face. She spun her attention to the four men on the ground, glaring at them angrily. She opened her mouth to speak, but John spoke before she could form the words.

"Only the bloody nose is ours. The rest he showed up with, ma'am. I swear."

That took some of the steam out of her furry, but she lashed out anyway. "He is an American citizen!" She turned and looked at me, composing herself. "Mr. Wolfe. I'm Beverly Martin, the consul general in Amsterdam," she said in a startling south Texas drawl. She extended her hand, and I shook it, feeling a little uncomfortable addressing someone of her high office with no shirt on.

She continued. "I want to apologize on behalf of the United States Government for your treatment. I'd also like to invite you to ride with me in my vehicle to the US consulate here in Amsterdam."

At that instant, Kathrin showed up with her escorting officer, carrying my shirt and jacket. I thanked her quietly, smoothed the bandage back down over my chest and pulled the shirt down over my head with Kathrin's help.

I looked at Ms. Martin and stood as I tried to pull my jacket on. "I thank you for your invitation, ma'am, but I was about to catch a train."

She softened her stance and took a half a step forward. Lowering her voice, she said "I'm afraid, Mr. Wolfe, this is not one of those invitations you can decline."

"Well," I said, smiling. "In that case, I'd be happy to indulge your hospitality."

As the two men in street clothes turned to go back with us, the consul general spoke to one of them, and he peeled off to talk to the officer in charge. They immediately began releasing the four on the ground. *John* walked back to the SUV with us. I looked over my shoulder and winked at Kathrin but spotted broken-nose guy, scowling at me—I smiled at him as well.

Once in the SUV, Ms. Martin dropped the diplomat's mask. "Will someone please tell me what the *hell* is going on here?" Her matter-of-fact speech and her Texas drawl made her sound quite commanding.

"He resisted arrest." John said. "Then the German girl started screaming for the police."

"Real smooth fellas," she said, and then she turned to me. "Mr. Wolfe, let's cut through the crap, shall we? You were seen leaving the residence of a Russian gangster by the name of Rodka Sobolev. I'd like to know why you were there."

"I'm here to find my girlfriend," I said honestly.

"Is your girlfriend a Russian-owned prostitute?" John chimed in sarcastically.

I looked at him coldly. "Well. I haven't seen her since Saturday, so she could be at this point." Then I looked back at the consul general. "But she was here with her father, so I doubt it. You may know him, ma'am. Robert Whitney?"

All the expressions in the vehicle changed except mine. It took a moment for the depth of my answer to sink in, and once it had, the tone of the conversation changed dramatically.

"Mr. Wolfe, I'm sure you'll understand we will have to verify this, but I want you to know how sorry we are, both for your treatment tonight and for the terrible tragedy that brought you here," the consul general said. But from her sentiment, the missing key words betrayed her deception. There was no mention of death, loss, condolences. They knew. But I appeared to know a little more. I was going to keep it that way.

The first thing I needed to do was to get them off my back. I reached into my bag but before I had my hand through the opening there were two guns pointing at my head and one stuck into my ribs.

"Put those away boys. We aren't measuring anything tonight," Ms. Martin said.

"In my bag. Two phones. Mine and Barbara's." The man to my right reached into my bag, felt around for the phones, and withdrew them. John reached for them, but the consul general grabbed at them first and jerked them from his reach.

"May we examine these, Mr. Wolfe?" she asked politely.

"Please do. If you find anything on there concerning her

whereabouts, will you be so kind as to inform me?" I said smugly.

"Her 'whereabouts,' Mr. Wolfe?" she asked.

"Yes. Since her last text to me was almost twenty minutes after the explosion, I've been working under the assumption that she, at least, is still alive."

The consul general and John exchanged a brief look.

"I think we need to start talking a little more plainly," Ms. Martin said. "We need you to keep this knowledge to yourself. We are attempting to locate—"

She was cut off by John. "Ma'am. I don't think that's wise," he said. "Mr. Wolfe has engaged in covert actions and is in possession of and has used encryption devices to transmit unknown information."

I looked at John. "It's nice to know that our government is on top of the dangerous communications between an American computer geek, his girlfriend, and his friends back home. Too bad the Serbs weren't sending love letters, or you might have stopped them from blowing up Market Square."

John lurched across the seat and grabbed me by my throat. *Strong fingers.* My own hand reached up to his wrist, and I pressed my fingers into the tendon just behind the ball of his thumb as if it were a finger hold on a rock face. His expression changed from anger to confusion and then pain. A split second later, the other two plainclothes security men were pulling him off me. The consul general was raging.

"Enough!" she screamed. "Captain! That is *enough*!"

John sat back in his seat, rubbing his bruised wrist; I rubbed my throat. I looked at John and saw a strange expression ripple across his face.

He did that for my benefit, I thought. *It was an intimidation move to let me know I wasn't safe just because I was in a diplomat's vehicle.*

"Ma'am. I appreciate your hospitality. But if it's all the same, I'd like to be taken back to my hotel."

"Mr. Wolfe. I can understand your concern and your heightened emotional state," she said, her last words spoken while staring directly at *Captain* John. "And I promise you, as soon as we verify your story, you will be released. It shouldn't take long."

seven
Three Days Until Event

1:30 a.m. on Thursday, May 13th, 2010 - US Consulate in Amsterdam, Netherlands

CAPTAIN JOHN TEMPLE sat across the office from consul general Beverly Martin, who was sitting with her stocking feet propped up on her desk. The late night showed its effect on her face, and she was already working on very little sleep since the explosion in the Nieumarkt. Temple was listening to her side of the conversation she was having on the phone.

"So his story checks out, then?" she confirmed from the caller.

"Okay," she replied. "Make copies of both phones and send them to Langley for a deeper analysis, and then bring Mr. Wolfe's phone back up here." She hung up and looked at Temple.

"Our boy is what he says he is," she relayed tiredly, rubbing her eyes with her fingers and then pinching the bridge of her nose. "He's some sort of security software specialist for an outfit called TravTech out of Fairfax. He and Bob's girl have been dating for about three months, and he caught a flight here Monday after the explosion. He has fifty-five hundred in checking and thirty-five thousand in savings, which he cleaned out before coming to Amsterdam, and an eight-hundred dollar balance on his credit card, which he pays off each month. He's been outside of the US five times in his life, never for more than two weeks, and mostly here in Europe."

"Well, the security job explains the encryption," John said, looking down at his wrist where Scott had gripped him—there was more to this kid than met the eye. "Computer geek from Fairfax, huh?" John said, unbelieving. "He played us downtown...expertly. There's something..." He let his thought trail off without finishing his sentence.

Beverly laughed. "It's true. I don't think I've ever seen you lash out like that before. He really knew what buttons to push," she said, and then she took a softer tone. "But in your defense, this has been the week from hell, and it's only going to get worse. We are all on edge."

John nodded without giving his secret away. "Okay. So what do we do with him?"

"I don't know," she said, exasperated. "I'm no spy, but I think we should cut him loose. He's a love-sick puppy lost in terror land."

"Do you mind if I tag him? That's what I'll get from upstairs," John informed her casually.

"Under normal circumstances, I'd tell your 'upstairs' to get a warrant or kiss my ass. But I think I'll look the other way this time. Patriot Act and all," she replied.

John could tell her decision had immediately left a bad taste in her mouth, though. He understood; it was easier to bend the rules now than it had ever been before. It used to be that when you did something dirty, it was the exception, and you paid penance. Now it was so commonplace that the next generation of civil servants wouldn't even think twice about it—it would be considered business as usual.

"You know what? I changed my mind," she said. "If your bosses at Langley want him tracked, they need a FISA warrant. I'm not letting a decent kid from the States be treated like Al Qaeda."

John nodded. His superiors would probably tell him to tag the kid anyway, but he respected the change of heart in the consul general. "Did you get a good look at the burns on his chest?" he asked without pushing the tracking issue further.

"Yeah," she said, reflecting on the dark, crusty flesh she had seen back on the street. "What do you make of it?"

"I've seen it before. He was interrogated by someone. Propane torch, not acetylene," John replied.

"What did he say happened?" she asked.

"Said he burned himself shaving," John replied with a smile and a chuckle.

The consul general laughed in spite of herself. "The kid's got balls, that's clear. Most would've been running into our arms, spilling their guts or begging to be sent back home on the next flight." She rubbed her eyes again. "Do you think it would do any good to tell him to go home?"

"No." John said plainly. "I think as soon as he hits the street, he'll be back on the trail again."

She thought about that for a moment. "Give him your card, John. Tell him to punch your number into his phone," she said. "I have a feeling about this boy. He thwarted an abduction by trained CIA operatives. Cultivated an asset in that German girl in less than

thirty-six hours. He was tortured, yet survived God knows what—
and surrounded by guns and muscle he couldn't hope to overcome,
he provoked a seasoned CIA operative to blow in front of me. He
also knew hours before we did, that our people weren't on that boat
when it blew up."

"He also almost broke my wrist with that grip of his," he
added, rubbing his bruised wrist. "If Tom and Greg hadn't
intervened, I'd be in a cast right now, I have no doubt."

She looked at him through squinted eyes. "We may have
another asset on this," she said. "Make him feel like you're a
friend. Change his mind about you—and for God's sake keep Nick
away from him. Something about that boy rubs him the wrong
way."

John smiled at a private joke in his head.

"What?" Beverly asked.

"That 'boy' is the first person in almost two years to bloody
Nick," John said, referring to Nick Horiatis. "Twice in one night. I
think he broke his nose."

"Well, that would do it," Beverly said with a grin. "Okay.
Let's go cut our boy loose."

On the way out of Beverly's office, they nearly ran into
another man who was about to enter. He was a man of average
height, build, and stature. He dressed like a diplomat, but under the
suit, he carried himself like someone ready to fight.

"Deputy Miller!?" Beverly exclaimed, clearly shocked to
see the man at this time of morning and in Amsterdam. "What
brings you up from The Hague, and at this time of night?"

"We got word that you have a boy here who knows the

Whitney girl," he replied in a tired and stressed voice.

"That's right. We were about to let him back on the streets," she informed him.

"Would you mind if I talked with him first?" Miller asked.

She gave him a puzzled look. "Well certainly, sir. But if you don't mind me asking..."

"I gave Bob Whitney's girl my place on the cruise so the ambassador's daughter would have someone her own age to keep her company," he explained. "I...I'd like to say something to Mr. Wolfe. To apologize or something. Anything. The guilt is eating at me."

"I understand," she said sympathetically, but something didn't sit as being quite right with John. "Let's go down and see him," she continued.

As they turned to walk down the hallway, Beverly and John's gaze met for a second and they exchanged a brief look.

"I have to go debrief my team." John said. "If you will excuse me. Ma'am. Deputy."

"Of course, Captain. Why don't you let Nicholas in on our conversation as well? Okay?" she said.

"Yes ma'am. Good night," he said, and then strode off down an intersecting corridor.

**

Interview Room B

I had been sitting in an 'interview' room with nothing but my thoughts to keep me company for the past three hours. I dozed on the couch for a while after the 'interviewers' left, but couldn't stay asleep for long. I kept jerking awake, feeling like I was supposed to be doing something. But then I would realize I couldn't do anything at the moment and would try to doze again.

When I first arrived, the consulate doctor had been awakened to tend to my wounds. He was somewhat concerned by the burn on my chest, but he'd said that the rest of my issues would cause more discomfort than any real health problems, and that I should be fine if I kept the burns clean and avoided stress on my neck and ribs.

He confirmed what Nyla had said concerning my ribs. They were not broken. Maybe a crack, but more likely a separation and bruise. He said the compression bandage would continue to give me some relief until they healed completely.

The cigarette man, who I learned earlier was a captain—of what I had no idea—and whose first name was John, had sat with me in the small and tastefully, though sparsely, appointed room for about forty-five minutes, asking me questions about my experiences and purpose in Amsterdam. First he asked me to walk him through chronologically and then asked me questions about details in random order.

I was purposefully vague on most of my answers. I gave only yes and no answers when I could, leaving out key details most of the time and resorting to sarcastic jabs occasionally— particularly towards the end of the interview when my frustration had reached its height.

After my few unsuccessful attempts at sleeping, I sat up on the couch and started the machine in my head running again. I had to assume they would let me out at some point. If they didn't, there was little I could do for Barb anyway, so there was no sense in wasting a planning opportunity.

I wondered if the GPS signal for the dialed number on the Serb's phone was still in Dusseldorf. I wondered if I'd be able to pick up their trail again if it wasn't... I wondered if Barb was okay. But I tried to push that worry out of my head quickly as it popped in. There was nothing I could do but focus on finding her.

I heard footsteps moving in my direction, and got my hopes up that I would be released. But the door didn't open. Sometime later, the footsteps returned. *Maybe this time?* But no, still nothing. After the fourth time they came, stopped, and then left again, I stopped letting the sounds of movement be a source of optimism.

My frustration was rising, and I was ready to pound on the door. Before that could happen, though, it finally swung open. The consul general and another man walked in and closed the door behind them.

The man looked at me with a bit of a surprised expression and then turned to the consul general. "Beverly?" he said incredulously.

"I know, Deputy. He has seen a bit of trouble in the past twenty-four hours," she said defensively. "But the security team didn't do near any of it. Mr. Wolfe has been the guest of some rather unsavory types recently."

She then turned to me. "Mr. Wolfe, this is Mission Deputy Chief Dwight Miller. He is Charge d'Affaires at the Embassy at The Hague."

"Mr. Wolfe, I want to apologize for your detainment and your treatment. But I also wanted to talk with you about Barbara if I could," he said and then turned to the consul general. "Beverly, can I have a moment alone with Mr. Wolfe?"

"Of course, sir," she said and then left the room, closing the door behind her.

He looked at me intensely. Pain on his face. It took him a moment to form his first words. I could tell there was a conflict going on within the man. "I understand that you are in a relationship with Barbara Whitney," he began. "Is it serious?"

I was taken aback by his question. He shook his head as if he were shaking a bug out of his ear. "I'm sorry. Of course it's serious, otherwise you wouldn't be here." He paused a long moment, regrouping his thoughts.

"I want to apologize to you. I want to apologize to Barbara, but she isn't here, and it's my fault." I could see the pained sincerity in his face.

"I don't understand," I replied.

He composed himself. Some of the agony he had been displaying just shifted to some place more private within him. He was a little less pained when he continued. "I gave Barbara my place on the tour boat...and I did so at the ambassador's request." *Deception.* "He had been concerned that his daughter wouldn't have someone her own age to engage with. My effort to please the ambassador put another innocent person in harm's way."

The formal shift in the tone of his explanation and the way he said "another innocent person" was put in harm's way made me believe there was more to this than a simple apology or collateral guilt. He was somehow responsible for this...or at the least, tangled in it. It was interesting that my new onboard inner voice had confirmed my suspicions as well.

"There's no need to apologize to me," I said.

"I feel I must make amends somehow, nonetheless." He paused again and then sat. I followed his lead and sat opposite him. "I understand you have been searching for her. And though you have not been very forthright in sharing what you have discovered, it appears you have made some inroads."

"I'm not sure what I've discovered," I said, giving him a vague half-truth in keeping with the rest of my answers.

"I don't suppose that there is any way I could convince you to abandon your efforts."

"No," I said plainly.

"That's what I thought." He stood to dismiss himself. "Well, Mr. Wolfe, it was a pleasure meeting you." He extended his hand to shake mine. I replied in kind. "I wish you luck in your goals and hope you meet with more success than we have."

More deception, came the whisper in my ear.

He's afraid of my involvement? Then why is he letting me go? He clearly outranks the consul general. Then it hit me. *If he is involved, then he likely thinks that it's better that I'm out there and not in here sharing my information with the CIA.*

I got a mental pat on the back from my *other* self.

As Deputy Miller walked out the door and down the hall, the consul general came back into the room. It was the first time I'd really seen her in full light. She was an attractive woman. Younger than I'd thought when she was in the dark of the street and in the SUV. But that probably had more to do with the fact that I had always pictured diplomats to be middle aged or senior citizens, given appointments like this as rewards for political service.

Though her hair was flecked with some gray, it was still quite blond. She was not tall. No more than an inch or so over five feet. I would guess her age to be around forty, and she seemed to be fit, if not athletic, in carriage and appearance. Her smile came easily—a trait most suitable for a foreign service officer, and her Texas drawl along with her confident presentation made her ideal for the diplomatic corps and command. I found it impossible to dislike her, though her purposes seemed to be at odds with mine.

"Mr. Wolfe. Again, I'd like to apologize for the events of last night and for your detainment." She handed me my phone. "But as promised, you are now free to go. Captain Temple is making arrangements for your transportation back to your hotel or wherever you would like to go."

I guessed it would be too much to ask for a ride to Dusseldorf, not to mention it would give away my next steps.

"Captain Temple?" I asked.

She smiled. "The man who accosted you in my vehicle," she said with a grin. "John."

"Thank you, ma'am," I said sincerely, noting the addition of the last name to my growing list of players. "Where is Barb's phone?" I asked, hoping.

"I'm sorry, Mr. Wolfe. Ms. Whitney is a family member of State Department staff. I can't give her phone back to you. It may also be vital evidence in our investigation," she stepped closer to me. "Once again, for your safety, I would implore you to cease your independent efforts toward finding Barbara. It may also...put us at cross purposes."

"I thank you for your concern, ma'am," I said, clearly not moved by her sentiment.

She pursed her lips tightly together. There was frustration there, I could see, but beneath it was something she wanted to say.

Her face was instinctively pressing her lips together to stop her. I decided to help her loosen them.

"Ma'am. I understand exactly what you must be going through right now. I will promise you this: If I find myself in any situation that would be improved by the engagement of the United States Government, I will call you."

She tilted her head to the side, squinting her eyes and measuring me, and then she turned and slipped her arm through mine. "That would make me very happy Mr. Wolfe," she said as we started to walk down the hallway to the stairs. "I have to admit, any assistance in our investigation would be much appreciated. We seem to be at a disadvantage, and it's not a position we usually find ourselves in," she said honestly, surprising me with her candor.

I hesitated. I didn't want to disclose anything to these people, but I couldn't resist the urge to help this woman. She was too damned likable. Before I could talk myself out of it, my lips were moving. "The man who did this," I said, putting my hand to my chest and ribs, "was a Serb by the name of Majmun." She stopped mid stride and turned to look at me with surprise. "I'm sorry, but I don't know his real name," I continued.

"Do you know the whereabouts of this man?" she asked hopefully.

"He's dead," I said plainly.

"Mr. Wolfe! You didn't—"

"No ma'am. I did not."

"Who...?"

I smiled at her, tight lipped, indicating that was all she

would get from me. She smiled in reply, reading my expression perfectly with her diplomat's skills. "You, Mr. Wolfe, are quite...surprising," she said, resuming our arm-in-arm stroll to the covered carport in the rear of the consulate. There, Captain Temple and a black SUV were waiting for me. She stopped as we got to the vehicle.

"I wish you good luck, Mr. Wolfe. I believe you will need it." Then she reached out to shake my hand. "I hope you are reunited with that girl of yours—soon. I've never met Barbara, but I know her father. He is a good man, an honorable man. I hold him in high regard—and I can't say that for many," she stated plainly, letting her folksy Texan drawl wrap her words with sincerity. "Take care of this young man, John. We don't meet many like him," she said—though I suspected the comment was more to flatter me than to inform the Captain of my character. But there was sincerity to her voice.

I stepped into the back of the SUV, followed by Captain Temple. As soon as he closed the door, the SUV lurched forward. I looked up at the driver and saw his reflection in the rearview mirror. There was a bandage across his nose. He glanced up and caught me looking at him and then scowled.

"Mr. Wolfe. I want to apologize for earlier. You seem to have a talent for bringing out the violence in people," Captain Temple said, smiling. I heard our driver grunt agreement.

"Thank you for the apology, Captain. I'm sorry as well. My provocation toward you was not deserved." I spoke stiffly, but sincerely.

"No need. You played that situation well," he said flashing me a knowing grin. "But it's your proclivity for attracting violence that I would like to talk to you about."

"Captain," I said, cutting him off, and then I switched

gears. "What are you a captain of, by the way?"

The driver looked up in the mirror to see if I would get my answer.

"It's an old title. I used to be a captain in the Navy," he replied simply, easily. He was making friends. I would play along.

"Ah," I said.

"Your proclivity," he said returning to the subject. I sat back to hear his lecture. I was surprised not to get one.

"We aren't babysitters, Scott. This is serious business," he said, his tone somber and frank. "But if you find yourself in a situation over your head, or something you think we could handle better, I want you to call me," he said, handing me a business card.

"Thank you, sir," I said, not committing to anything.

"Don't thank me. Before this is done, you may wish we had kept you in the basement of the consulate," he replied and then grinned. "And here," he said, reaching into his jacket pocket, pulling out a wad of euros. "Petty cash in compensation for your trouble and injuries."

"Thanks," I said, surprised. But I glanced up at the mirror just in time to see the trace of a smile on the face of our driver disappear.

Deception, I thought. *What are you two up to?*

I tucked the cash into my jacket pocket, and we rode in silence the rest of the way to the hotel. The sun wasn't up yet, but it wouldn't be long. I'd need to hurry—I was a day behind schedule.

**

4:10 a.m. – Damstraat in Amsterdam

The SUV pulled up in front of the alley entrance to my hotel. John opened the side door, and we both got out. He handed me my bag and reached out his hand to shake.

"Be careful," he said sincerely.

"I always am," I replied with a grin, grasping his hand firmly—though not too firmly.

He got back in the SUV and sped away. I walked back to the hotel and headed up to my room. I was just about to open my room door when a door down the hall popped open and a head looked out.

It was Kathrin.

She rushed up to me, barefoot in a t-shirt that covered her to her thighs. At first I thought she was going to jump up on me, but she stopped short, looking at me curiously. "Are you well?" she asked quickly.

I looked around the hall to see if we had disturbed anyone else. I brought my finger to my lips indicating quiet and then opened my room door. We went in, and she immediately started with the questions.

"Oh my God! Who are they? Did they hurt you? Are you a spy? A criminal? Why did they let you go?" Except for the German accent, it reminded me a bit of Bonbon's tirades.

I raised my hands to try to slow her questions. "They were US government. I'm not sure what part of the government," I said, starting to answer what questions I could. "They didn't hurt me...after the abduction anyway." Then I paused and looked her in the eye. "Thank you for that. You are a very brave girl."

She smiled and blushed.

"As to spy or criminal. No to both. And they let me go because I didn't do anything wrong," I said, answering all of her questions.

"Then why did they take you?" she asked pleadingly. She knew there must be more to the story.

I hesitated. She punched me in the arm. "Tell me!" she said. The punch woke the pain from my burns. I grimaced. "I'm sorry!" she exclaimed, suddenly remembering the wounds.

"It's okay," I said and then turned to my duffel bag on the dresser. I closed it and made a cursory check around the room to be sure I hadn't forgotten anything. When I was satisfied I was all packed, I turned and saw that she was still standing there, looking at me.

"You didn't answer me," she said defiantly.

She would not be dissuaded—I could tell.

Trust her, my other voice whispered into my ear. This secondary presence, although helpful, was beginning to be disconcerting. I was quite sure I didn't like it.

"Someone I know was on the boat before it exploded. I came to look for her," I explained. "My actions sent up some red flags." Her face showed she was puzzled. "Red flag. Warning. *Achtung,*" I elaborated.

Her eyes flashed understanding. "Who was this person?" she asked.

"My girlfriend," I stated plainly.

Her expression didn't change. "And did you find her?"

"Not yet."

"Yet?" she repeated.

"Yet," I confirmed.

She studied me for a moment and then said, "Can I help you with anything?"

"Do you know Dusseldorf?" I asked with a grin.

She was taken aback. "I meant I would carry a bag or tell you were the train station is!" she exclaimed. "Not going for terrorists."

I laughed. "Okay. In that case, no, I'm fine." I winked at her.

She hugged me gently and then turned and left my room. I waited to hear her door close down the hall and then slipped out the door carrying my duffel and shoulder bag. I quietly walked down the hall to the closet I had stashed my backup phone and iPad in. Silently, I removed the grate, withdrew my bundle, and then reattached the cover.

"Are you sure you aren't a spy?" I heard behind me.

She scared the shit out of me. I spun around to see her standing there, fully clothed, boots unlaced, tucking her t-shirt into her olive drab fatigue pants.

"Shhh." I said pressing my finger to my lips.

I found it odd that this strange girl was so persistent in her pursuit of me. *Why is she doing this?* I asked myself.

Trust her, came my other voice.

Yeah, yeah, yeah. Trust her. I replied within my head. *And why should I trust you?* No answer. It had been worth a try.

Her backpack, formerly mine, was hanging from her fingertips.

She followed me down the stairs to the foyer, where I stopped at the desk. She laced up her boots while I placed my room key in an envelope and wrote my room number and a brief note explaining that I was checking out early. I tucked in a couple hundred euros from the wad Captain John had given me, and then sealed the envelope and placed it on the desk.

We walked out of the building and into the street. I looked at her as she marched beside me with a determined look on her face. She was still trying to figure out if she should be with me— so was I.

We turned left on Damstraat and headed for the Dam. We were nearly to the National Monument at the Dam by the time I managed to flag down a taxi. We got in and I said "*Centrall alstublieft.*"

We were silent on the way to train station. I sorted through the bills that the captain had given me to take an accounting. When we arrived at the train station, I handed one of the hundred euro bills to the driver, saying, *"Dank u wel."*

He looked frustrated at the size of the bill, not wanting to cut change for that much. I indicated he should keep the rest. *"Heel erg bedankt!"* he said exuberantly.

Kathrin and I walked into the station and found the commuter train platforms. I walked to a ticket vending machine, looked up the rate for a ticket to Paris, and inserted two of the one hundred euro bills that the Captain had given me.

The ticket printed and was ejected from the machine along with my change. I handed Kathrin the change.

She gave me a curious look. "Paris?" she asked.

I winked at her and went through the motions a second time. The machine again spit out the ticket and change. I handed Kathrin the change again.

I walked down the platform a short ways, Kathrin close behind me. I alternated between looking at the ticket and up at the ceiling as we slowly walked along the corridor. I was looking for another vending machine that wasn't in direct view of the cameras, but I made it look instead as if I were looking for platform numbers.

There was a cluster of cameras with no red lights on the opposite side of the tracks. I stopped at a small magazine and coffee kiosk, ordered two lattes, a bag full of muffins and sandwiches, a magazine, and several bottles of water. I handed the cashier the last hundred the captain had given me and stuffed the change in my pocket.

I handed Kathrin's coffee and one of the bags to her and then strolled over to the back-to-back ticket vending machines across from the dead cluster of cameras. We stopped and loitered, munching on muffins and drinking our coffee, waiting for the Paris train. I asked Kathrin to sit on the ground by the machine.

I set my bag on the ground next to her. Then I went around to the "dark" side of the electronic vendor. I took bills out of my wallet and procured two tickets to Dusseldorf. The train to Dusseldorf was already sitting on the track two platforms over. It would leave in five minutes. The Paris train was late. But I could see it moving slowly down the track in our direction.

I motioned for Kathrin to prepare to board the Paris train as soon as it arrived. I looked her in the eye and asked, "Are you sure you want to do this? This is your last chance to abandon me before we reach our destination."

I wonder if she woke her friends to say goodbye. The Paris train pulled to a stop in front of us. She looked up at me nervously, but she nodded that she was going to continue. "Did you say anything to anyone?" I asked. "Your friends?"

"I left a note," she replied, and a strange expression rippled across her features for a split second.

"You didn't tell them where you were going, did you?" I asked.

She shook her head sharply. "I didn't know where I was going."

I winked as the doors on the train opened. With only two minutes left before the Dusseldorf train departed, we pushed our way onto the Paris train, prompting several curses in French and Dutch as the travelers began to exit the train.

We pushed through the crowd and then down to the other side through a closed but unlocked door that opened onto the tracks. Before exiting, I spied an access panel with a fire extinguisher inside. I jerked the door open, reached into my bag, retrieved my phone, and tucked it in behind the extinguisher, closing the door once it was secure.

"Come on," I said, and I looked both ways before leaping.

We walked across one set of tracks to the Dusseldorf train, which was preparing to leave. Holding Kathrin's hand in mine to make sure she followed safely, we arrived at a train door from the track side. I felt a sudden stirring of warmth in my chest as her fingers curled around mine.

I pounded on the door, and a conductor came to the window. He seemed upset with us, but he opened the door, saying something angrily to us in Dutch.

I showed him our tickets saying, "I'm sorry. We were on the wrong side of the track."

He looked at our tickets and handed them back to us scowling, but he let us in. We found two empty seats just as the train was departing and sat with a sigh of relief. Kathrin burst out laughing. We sat for a while enjoying the rest of the muffins, and I explained to her why I had done all that I had to get us on the Dusseldorf train.

"I assumed the bills were tagged with something that could be tracked. Something that didn't come off when touched, or they would be chasing ghost signals all over Amsterdam," I said. "The tickets to Paris were purchased with those bills. I bought them one at a time so I could get clean change from each transaction."

She reached into her pocket and fished out the change and then handed it to me.

"I did it in full view of the cameras in case security footage was checked," I said as I slipped the change into my pocket. "I left my phone on the Paris-bound train because the government is tracking it. I have a backup anyway."

She nodded her understanding.

In reality, there were a few other reasons I'd ditched that phone. First, I had no use for it now that my special apps had been erased. Second, the government now knew I was looking for Barbara and could use my number to track me, and third, they'd had my phone in their possession for hours. It could also be infected with spyware. I didn't have time to scan it to be sure.

"How often do you run off with strangers in the middle of the night when on holiday?" I asked with a grin.

"More often than I probably should," she responded, mirroring my smile.

"Your friends won't be worried?" I asked.

She shook her head and then looked out the window as we moved slowly out of the station. "They've come to expect me being unpredictable," she said—and there was that flash again. Something…private.

Trust her, my other voice said.

I mentally shrugged. I didn't have time to question her motives or my new mental co-pilot. She was German, she wanted to help, and I didn't speak the language as well as I needed to in order to do what had to be done.

As soon as we had finished our muffins and hydrated, I pulled my prepaid burn phone out of my bag and checked the GPS signal from the numbers I had given Storc. There had been several new hits on them.

There was one hit on the number that the Serb had previously called once, and four new hits on the one that had been called multiple times. The last one had been three hours ago, and it was still in Dusseldorf.

I then checked my messages. Bonbon had sent me one letting me know there had been new attempts to crack the encryption and router path on communications. It read:

They are persistent, but still aren't any closer to finding origin. I have to admit though...   it's making me nervous.

I wrote back and told her to get with Storc. I typed:

Prolly won't see any more attempts. Had to wipe mine. Am on new 1 now. They have   no way of knowing about it. But, JIC, add a couple more dynamic switches and send me the sync file before he activates it.

I checked the news and the weather in Dusseldorf and then tucked the phone back into my bag.

When I turned back to Kathrin, I saw she was asleep, so I put my head against the window and tried to do the same. The rhythmic clacking of the tracks helped push me into slumber.

I dreamed of Barb.

"This is your fault, Scott Wolfe," she said in my dreams.

"I know," I replied.

**

Kathrin shook me about two hours later as we were pulling into the station in Dusseldorf. I wiped the sleep from my eyes and stood, grabbing my duffel bag and jacket from the overhead. She hefted her pack, and we slowly made our way to the door.

Once free of the crowd, she stopped, adjusted her straps and asked, "What next?"

She looked like a soldier standing at attention and waiting for orders. She didn't look old enough to have been in the military and be out already. I asked her about this. "Boots, uniform trousers, standing at attention. Were you in the military?"

She laughed at me. "You Americans and your powerful sense of individuality," she said, shaking her head. "School children in some countries march to classes, stand at attention when waiting, and do not speak unless spoken to."

I shot her a look of disbelief.

"Okay. Boarding schools. I was what you would call a 'troubled' child," she said smiling. "So my parents sent me someplace to give me 'discipline.'"

"Did it work?" I asked.

"It disciplined my actions, not my 'attitude.' As far as I'm concerned, it made me more dangerous," she said, winking. "After all, I'm keeping company with a fugitive." She flashed a toothy smile in a quirky manner.

I laughed with her as I pulled my phone from my bag. I pulled up the map display and zoomed in on the marks near the Rhine River.

"There," I said pointing at the mark on the map. She reached over and pinched the image with her finger, zooming in closer. She then moved the screen to the left and then the right to see the surrounding labels on the streets.

"Okay," she said confidently and then set off for the taxi area with me following close behind.

We stepped into the cab and she said, *"Stromstrassa. Rheinturm, Bitte,"* and we were on our way.

When we arrived at the tower Rheinturm, we set out on foot to the river walk, which followed the Rhine.

"What are we going to do once we find them?" Kathrin asked me quietly as we approached a large, elaborate, suspension footbridge across a protected harbor.

I found it interesting that this little adventure was now a "we." I have to admit, I felt more confident with a partner in crime. "We have to find out what's going on," I said as I scanned the scene. To our right was a bend of the Rhine River, and to the left were several manmade coves trenched into the point of the bend.

"We have to figure out as much as we can about what's going on without being discovered," I said. "The only thing I know for sure is that we don't know anything yet. Before we *do* anything, we have to know *everything*."

"How can we know everything?" Kathrin asked.

"We can't," I replied. "Which makes it all that much more important to try."

We continued along the trail until we were near the marker placed on the map.

I looked at the signal once again to verify the location and then looked up to get my bearings. The mark seemed to be centered on one of a handful of warehouses along the water's edge. I could make out the high windows and metal roofs just beyond a small, fenced scrapyard next to the foot path.

"The signal is coming from over there," I said, glancing to my left.

Kathrin nodded her acknowledgement, but we kept moving

along the path. Once we had gone beyond the line of sight from the building, I paused.

"I saw a metal building with no windows at ground level," I said.

"That's what I saw as well," she replied.

"I'd have to climb the fence if I wanted to get closer on this side," I said. "I'd rather not be that obvious if I can avoid it. Especially in the daylight."

She nodded. "Let's take a closer look at what's on the water side," she suggested.

I nodded and then turned around, going back the way we had come. We paused at the foot of the bridge so we could see the buildings facing the warehouses from the other side. I noted a Hyatt Regency hotel on the point, and on the finger of land beyond that was a German sports shoe manufacturer.

"Cameras," I said.

"Huh?" Kathrin replied and then looked where my eyes had gone. "Oh. On the hotel?"

"And on the sneaker factory," I said, nodding toward the other building.

"Yah," she said quietly.

We walked back across the bridge and sat in the small park at the other end. While we ate our sandwiches, I pulled my phone from the bag and tested for Wi-Fi signals. We were on the far edge of the signal for the hotel, but one bar would be enough for what I wanted to do.

"We'll need business attire," I said as I stuffed the wax paper into the trash. "And we need to find an electronics store...one that takes traveler's checks."

She nodded without any sign that would be a problem.

"Are you sure you want to do this?" I asked.

She looked genuinely hurt that I would even ask. "Are you having second thoughts?" she asked.

"I've had second thoughts since I decided to get on the plane," I replied with a grin. "But no. No second thoughts about you."

She smiled and nodded. "I'm in," she said.

I pulled out my tablet and sent a text to Storc requesting assistance getting into the hotel and the shoe factory. I typed:

I need to be on the 'invitation' list for both the hotel and the shoe company as a security   specialist. Can you arrange for them to have an immediate need for one? It would be   most helpful if they needed one desperately.

As soon as he texted me back in the affirmative, we headed for the city, where Kathrin quickly located stores for us to procure what we needed.

We spent the rest of the afternoon making our purchases. Clothes, briefcases, routers, an additional prepaid phone, a multi-tool, binoculars, duct tape—anything we thought we might need was purchased with traveler's checks. Once our shopping was complete, we checked into a small hotel near the university so we could prepare for our 'business.'

"How will we get the hotel and factory to give us access to

everything?" she asked as we unpacked our purchases in the room. "Won't they be suspicious of tech support showing up so quickly?"

"The bigger the mess, the less a client pays attention to detail," I replied, laying out our business attire. "Storc will make sure they are more concerned about getting back up and running than about who showed up to fix it."

She nodded and held up her business suit, wrinkling her face.

"Not my usual style," she said.

"You are the respectable one," I said with a wink.

She grinned. "That's not usually my style either," she said and then turned to strip off her shirt and put on her blouse.

I turned my back to her and pulled up my messages on my iPad. There was a message from Storc:

Both the Hotel and the shoe company have experienced sudden and unexplained difficulty   with their networks. It is affecting operations. They are expecting a network security   technician sometime in the next twelve hours. Both companies requested expedited   service.

Attached to the message were details about the security company they were expecting a visit from, including a badge with a blank image and security verification letters.

"How do I look?" Kathrin asked behind me.

I turned to see her in her blouse, but she was still wearing the military-style trousers. I grinned just as another message chimed through, and I held up my finger for her to wait just a second.

It was another message from Storc. It read:

I have no doubt you could find and easily squash the little bugger, but I assume you have   other reasons for wanting access.

Attached was a script to hunt down and kill the virus he had infected the systems with.

I turned back to Kathrin. "How attached are you to those piercings?" I asked.

She immediately began removing them. As soon as she was done, she pulled her hair back. "How is this?" she asked.

"Perfect," I said, holding up my phone to snap a picture of her.

I then pulled a copy of my badge photo from my images directory and transferred both images to a memory card.

"I'll be back in a few minutes," I said. "If you are hungry, go grab us some food. Don't use a credit card."

She nodded.

I took the information about the security company and went to the copy center down the street while Kathrin finished assembling our clothing and picked up some food.

I used the computer, the photo printer, and the laminating machine at the copy center to create credentials for us. It took ten minutes for the first one, but the second one took less time, as I already had the template made.

Once I was done, I went back to the hotel and our room.

When I entered our room, I had to check the door number because the woman standing before me looked nothing like the girl I had left less than an hour before.

Kathrin had made an incredible transformation. She no longer looked like some militant hipster. She had donned her business suit, put her long, blond hair into a very precise bun, and her face was made up to look so professional that I could have mistaken her for a lawyer.

I whistled. "Now *that* is a disguise," I said, letting my surprise show in my voice.

"*Vielendanke!*" she said sincerely, a blush forming on her cheeks. Then she dipped her shoulders back and forth in a flirty manner, modeling her look. She walked past me twice, spinning each time like a model on a catwalk.

I handed her ID to her.

"This still looks enough like you to be convincing," I joked and then went into the bathroom to get dressed myself.

I left the stubble on my face as she suggested but combed and gelled my hair. When I had finished dressing, I went in to see if she approved.

She put her hand to her chin and shook her head. "More... more geek," she said.

She placed a pair of clear-lensed glasses on my face, pulled one corner of my shirttail out of my trousers, and then splattered a drop of gravy from our dinner on my shirt and took a step back.

"Now you look the way all Germans think American techs look," she said.

I was about to protest, but I realized there was a reason for the stereotype.

"Sit," she said firmly as she pulled her makeup case from the shopping bag.

"What?" I asked.

"I need to cover the marks on your face," she said as she extracted an applicator.

I nodded and let her do her work. Within moments, she had me looking close to normal.

"Do I look pretty?" I asked with a grin.

"If we get caught, you will be the most popular boy in prison," she laughed.

We ate and then gathered our belongings and headed out to hail a cab.

"How is your German?" Kathrin asked in the taxi.

"*Ich habe keine Deutsche,*" I replied, saying, very poorly, that 'I have no German.' An exaggeration, but functionally, I had no way of expressing complex concepts to a non-English speaker.

"I'll handle the introductions," she said with a chuckle.

We arrived at the hotel and went to the front desk. The woman behind the counter greeted us in German.

Responding in German, Kathrin quickly explained who we were, produced a work order and showed the woman her ID. I followed her example and showed the front desk clerk mine, which was hanging from my neck on a lanyard.

The woman asked me something in German, but Kathrin was quick to explain that I was an American, that I spoke no German, and that I was a specialist on loan to them from the New York office—I knew this last part only because she said "New York office" in a stream of otherwise-unintelligible German.

"She says there were some strange problems that have been popping up recently," Kathrin said to me. "And the guestroom door system is not allowing people into their rooms."

I nodded. "Show me where the server room is," I replied. Kathrin translated, but the woman had already begun leading the way. She took us to the back to introduce us to the night manager, who quickly gave us access to the computer systems.

Once we were alone, I slipped the flash drive containing Storc's worm killer into the system and began to unpack the hardware I needed.

"Can I help?" Kathrin asked.

"Just keep them out of here until I finish," I replied.

She exited the server room and struck up a conversation with the night manager.

Once Storc's script routine was complete and the worm had been eradicated, I started a download of the last three days' of security videos, and then began to build an encrypted tunnel between the security camera system and the firewall. It took me a bit longer than I had intended because all the files were in German, but the underlying system structure was familiar to me.

When I was done, I isolated one IP address outside the firewall, tied a more powerful, narrowband, wireless router to it, and then tested the signal from my phone. I was not only able to access the video but was also able to remotely control the cameras. "*Wunderbar,*" I whispered.

I then took the one camera facing the warehouses off the main security feed so it would only be viewable from the new Wi-Fi I'd set up.

"All done!" I said, prompting Kathrin and the night manager to enter the server room.

He asked something in German. Kathrin translated. "So what was the problem?" she asked as I began to pack up my tools.

"There was a virus that made it through the firewall," I explained. "It came in through one of the wireless cameras that had a flaw in the BIOS. I took it offline until it can be replaced."

Kathrin explained the problem to him. He looked totally confused—as expected.

"Tell him we'll special order a replacement unit," I continued. "No charge to the hotel."

He looked relieved after Kathrin had explained it all to him.

"Tank you, very much," he replied with a thick accent, shaking my hand enthusiastically. "Tank you. Tank you."

Another happy customer, I thought.

We said goodnight, and then we were on our way to our next stop—the shoe company.

"That went well?" Kathrin asked as we climbed into the taxi.

"Yeah," I replied as I adjusted my fake glasses. "And they'll have their camera back in a couple of days."

"What if the real security company comes out?" Kathrin asked.

"They never got the call," I replied. "And Storc already added a log entry to their sales computer. Complementary emergency service with a discount to the hotel on next month's bill for their trouble."

Kathrin looked at me with a shocked smile.

I shrugged. "It was their security system. If it hadn't been so easy to hack, none of this would have happened," I said with a grin, defending Storc's little jab at the security company.

Kathrin laughed.

The taxi dropped us at the entrance to the shoe facility. We showed our credentials, and then we were escorted to the manager's office by the security guard. We repeated the performance from the hotel—first extracting Storc's worm from the system and then tapping the two cameras facing the warehouses.

Kathrin gave him the same explanation as we did at the hotel, but he didn't seem to be as enthusiastic as the hotel night manager had been, saying something quite cross.

"What's the problem?" I asked.

"He isn't happy that he will be without two cameras. He wants an assurance it will be back up and running," she replied.

"Tell him that if the new cameras aren't installed within two days that I will personally come back out and replace them with a better model from our stock." I said.

She relayed the message, and that seemed to pacify him, so we turned in our visitor badges and left the building.

In fact, the cameras would go back to working in two days on their own. I set a timed routine to undo all of the code I had programmed. In two days, their system would work better than it had before.

The cab that Kathrin had called from inside was waiting for us when we exited. We got in and asked to be taken to the university. Once there, we walked the remaining two blocks to our hotel. It was the first time we were truly alone since our deception began.

"Even with the gravy, the desk clerk at the hotel was drooling when she saw you. Especially when I told her you were American," Kathrin teased.

"That's okay," I replied. "I think the night manager at the shoe factory had his eye on you."

The joke didn't go over well. She made a face and simulated a shiver. "No thanks."

While Kathrin was in the bathroom changing out of her business clothes, I was reviewing the video footage from the previous three days, starting from the time of the explosion. I zipped through the hotel video loop at high speed and discovered only one truck pulling into the far warehouse and none pulling into or out of the other.

I backed the video up to the point the truck went in. The time stamp on the video said it pulled in at 6:23 p.m. on Monday. It was a box truck with canvas covering the back, just as Elvis had described. Kathrin reemerged from the bathroom back in her canvas trousers and boots, but she had kept her hair up in the bun. The makeup was gone.

"Can you see them?" she asked.

"This is just the video playback from the footage I downloaded," I explained. "We'll have to be much closer to get the live feed."

I pulled my iPad out of its protective pouch and powered it up. It had been charging all evening so I was sure I'd have enough battery to last me the night. Beyond that, I'd have to wing it.

At around 10:30 p.m., we set out on foot down the streets to the Rheinturm, and then back down the foot path to the park across the water from the hotel. It was about a thousand feet across the water to the hotel and about another two hundred to the transmitter I set up. It would be no trouble getting signal from the hotel camera.

I used the remote function to center the camera on the warehouse across the water and then zoomed in to the max. I switched the signal to infrared and began watching the feed. I told Kathrin that she could get some sleep if she wanted.

Without a word, she pulled her jacket around her, pulled her feet up on the bench and leaned against my shoulder.

After a moment of scrunching down into her imaginary nest, I felt her head move against my shoulder. "Are you afraid for her?" she asked after a moment.

"I am. But I'm trying not to think about it. There's nothing I can do until I can safely get in," I replied.

"Are you afraid for us?" she asked more quietly.

"I'm trying not to think about that, either," I said.

She turned her head down into her jacket and drifted off to sleep. I wished it were that easy for me. Kathrin had been invaluable to me, but the next step was something I had to do alone. I couldn't ask her to risk herself for me or Barb.

eight
Two Days Until Event

12:01 a.m. on Friday, May 14th, 2010 - Dusseldorf, Germany

I studied the video feed for a while and discovered a man on a loading dock smoking a cigarette. When he opened the door to go in, another came out to replace him. The images were faint through the open side door, but I could make out several figures in the distance sitting on the floor back to back while others appeared to be sitting against the far wall.

There was little light in the warehouse, and when the door closed again, there was none. The windows near the roof line must have been painted over because there was no light escaping from them, either.

There was no other activity for several hours. At around 2:30 a.m., Kathrin stirred and then sat up.

"Would you like a break?" she asked, sleep in her voice still. "I can watch the video and let you know if anything happens."

I had watched the video feed for more than three hours and had seen little in the way of outside activity. So far I had no idea what I was up against except for an outside guard during night hours.

"Think you can manage on your own for a bit?" I asked. "I want to take a closer look."

She nodded.

"Keep an eye on the water side of the warehouse," I continued. "I'm going to try to get close enough to see inside."

I put my phone on vibrate and pulled out the prepaid phone we had picked up during our shopping trip. I punched my number into her phone. "Text me if it looks like something is happening," I said and then handed it to her.

"Be careful," she said.

I headed off down the path and across the bridge. After a few minutes, I was behind the scrapyard I had seen earlier.

I crossed over to the road on the other side and walked up to the fence surrounding the two warehouses. I followed the fence down to the water's edge and climbed over the bulkhead down onto the heavy rubble piled against the bulkhead wall. From down there, the bulkhead was nearly as tall as I was, so I was able to move along the edge of the water without stooping.

I walked alongside the bulkhead for about a hundred feet and then popped my head over the edge to sneak a peek. I saw no movement and no sign of people. That worried me, because I had seen at least one person on the water side loading dock since we started watching.

Just then my phone vibrated. For vibrate, it was horribly loud in the dead of night. I grabbed it quickly and popped open the message. It was from Kathrin: "*Man on dock went inside. You are clear right now."*

Whew! I sent her a quick message: *"That was LOUD on vibrate. Only send in emergency."*

I waited a few seconds to make sure there was no reply. There wasn't, so I turned and waved at the security camera, knowing she could see me, and then continued on.

I poked my head over the edge again and pressed myself up and over the bulkhead. It was clear ground between me and the loading dock, so I crossed as quickly as I could without making any noise.

When I reached the loading dock, I saw that most of it was solid concrete, but closer to the end, it was a raised wooden platform. I 'duck walked' down to that end and crawled in under the decking. I moved as far as I could to the back wall and listened intently for any sound on the other side.

I heard voices arguing...in broken English. I wondered why they were speaking in English until I remembered that it was a mix of Russian and Bosnian Serb men who had taken the hostages. Some of the men may not know the language of the others, and English was a pretty universal language for communicating with other Europeans.

"Vee are goin' to be caught!" I heard someone say.

"You will do as told and shut your mouth," came the angry reply.

It sounded as if there was a scuffle. I pushed away from the wall and slowly worked my way around to the backside of the warehouse.

There was a piece of metal siding that had been curled

outward a few inches at the base. There was an indentation at the bottom of it. Some clumsy forklift operator had punched through at some point in the past. This hole was probably a constant entry point for rodents of all sorts.

I lowered myself down to my belly and inched toward the hole. I looked inside, and in the dim light, I could see several people sitting against a wall at the far end. I scanned the group the best I could from my limited position, but I could not see Barb.

I heard more arguing, with multiple voices joining in the heated conversation. Much of it was in a language I didn't recognize.

I caught the English word 'monkey' in one exchange and 'chill' in another.

I pulled myself back to my feet and walked down a little farther. Turning the next corner put me on the 'path' side of the warehouse.

Next to the electrical box mounted on this side of the building was a hole through the metal siding where the conduit went inside. The caulk around the hole had dried and was peeling, so I grabbed an edge and pulled a chunk away from the wall.

I looked through. It was a narrower view than the other opening had provided, but I was closer to them than I had been before.

My heart jumped as soon as I spotted her. *Barb!* I had to bite my tongue to keep myself from yelling her name. She was leaning against her father with her head on his shoulder and her eyes closed. It was all I could do to keep from rushing in and scooping her up in my arms.

My heart was beating so quickly that I had to pull back

from the crack and take a couple of deep breaths to calm my heart rate. It took a few moments.

Don't get caught. Don't get caught. Don't get caught. I repeated the words in my head as if the mantra alone would make it so.

Once I was calm, I peeked through the hole again. I had to force my gaze away from Barb to look at the rest of the scene.

There were two men leaning against a large garage door with automatic rifles in their laps. Another leaned against the back of the truck that the hostages had been brought in on. I looked harder, trying to see around the conduit, and I could just make out a second truck with a cargo container strapped to a flat bed. The back doors of the container were open, but the door closest to me was blocking my view of the inside.

What's the container for, boys? I asked myself.

I glanced back at Barb for a moment, soaking in every detail to see if I could discern any injuries. Outwardly she seemed fine, at least as far as I could tell. The stress on her face was clear, even in her sleep, but that was to be expected.

I heard her voice in my head as I had so many times in my dreams.

This is your fault, Scott Wolfe.

My heart started to race, and I had to pull away from the hole again.

I know!

This time I stood and walked along the back wall of the warehouse until I was at the opposite end from where I had started.

I had to walk around a shed bump out. It appeared to be some sort of equipment shed built onto the side of the warehouse. The structure was no more than eight feet square…possibly a climate control or a compressor room.

On the back of the shed was a louvered fan vent. I quietly lifted the louver to look in. The fan was off and the louver lifted easily. It was dark inside, but I could see a dim light coming from the crack beneath the door leading into the warehouse.

I looked around the shed. *An air compressor…a big one.*

On the opposite wall from the big machine was an exterior door. I quietly lowered the louver and walked around to the door. I tested it gently. Locked. But a cheap lock. This might be a way in.

I went back to the louver and looked toward the side with the exterior door. There was some junk piled against it. A wooden pallet and a dock ramp. From the light through the crack under the door, I could see that there were fresh scuffs in the dust by the pile.

Shit, I thought. *They anticipated that. Hinges on the inside.*

I would not be able to open that door without making a great deal of noise. I'd have to focus on the fan louver.

I looked closely at the frame of the fan. Two screws on each of its four sides held it to the shed wall. I looked at the motor and followed the cord down with my eyes as far as I could. I reached my hand in carefully, grasped the cord, and pulled it gently. I heard and felt the plug rattle against the wall. I froze. I waited, standing there for a long while before I was comfortable letting the cord back down. I was careful not to make any noise as I lowered it back to the ground.

Now that I had established that the fan was non-functioning, I had a potential entry point. I decided to check the rest of the perimeter before continuing. I walked to the edge of the building.

I poked my head around the corner, thought I saw movement, and froze. Fire lit the face of a man on the gate side of the warehouse. When it was extinguished, I could see the orange dot at the end of his cigarette brighten and then float away from his face.

Gotta love a smoker, I thought ironically.

I stood motionless for several long moments and then quietly retreated the way I had come. I walked back to the compressor shed and pulled the multi-tool out of my shoulder bag.

I lifted the louvers once again and carefully started to loosen the screws attaching the fan and louver to the opening in the wall. The screws had been there a long time. The first three came out with no trouble, but the fourth was stuck hard. I lifted my elbow to get better leverage and turned hard. There was a squeak. A short burst of sound that made me flinch. I froze, waiting to hear any approach.

I lowered the louver and skulked back over to the front corner of the warehouse. The guard was still there, sitting at the top of the ramp smoking his cigarette. I turned and went back to finish removing the louver.

I listened carefully for movement before entering and then placed my hand on the opening, pressing up slowly, trying not to drag my feet against the metal siding.

I hovered there for a second, listening. Once I was sure I hadn't attracted any attention, I pulled my legs through the opening and lowered myself to the ground inside.

I'm in! I thought excitedly.

I bent to look under the crack of the door, but all I could see was feet.

I put my hand on the knob and gently turned it less than a quarter of an inch to see if it would turn. It did, with no noise. I then slowly let it return.

Near the ground to the side of the door was a hole in the metal siding. No light was coming through because there was a rag stuffed into the opening.

I lowered myself to the ground and gently tugged on the rag to see if it would come free easily. It popped out in my hand with the first light touch.

Shhhhhhhh, I thought.

I stopped to listen to see if anyone had noticed. When I was satisfied that no one was coming my direction, I breathed a sigh of relief and lowered myself down to look through the hole.

I could see nearly the whole warehouse from this vantage point. I could clearly see four armed men standing or sitting around the perimeter of the warehouse. A fifth man was sitting against the truck in which the hostages had been smuggled out of Amsterdam. A sixth man was exiting the cargo container, which was sitting on a flatbed trailer hooked up to a beat-up looking yard tractor, not a truck as I had thought.

Six, I thought. *That's a lot.*

I could see chemical toilets and wooden pallets stacked and covered for sleeping; there were several hostages on them. There weren't enough sleeping spaces for everyone, so it looked as if they had placed the more elderly hostages on them.

Many were left on the floor, including Barb and her father, who sat near the center of a group of about twenty hostages. I now saw another young woman asleep with her head in Barb's lap.

That must be the ambassador's daughter, I thought. *Michelle Babbage.*

I looked for several minutes longer, cataloging all that I saw. Weapons, clothes, locations of the hostages, food, and water—judging by the empty containers and packages, they had nearly exhausted their food supply. The SUV must resupply them each day.

There were several injured hostages, but they looked to have been bandaged. Some seemed to be sitting comfortably.

There were four hostages who were tied up. They seemed to be the only ones who were restrained in any way. All four were in their late twenties to early thirties and in good shape. I deduced that they had been the security detail for the group, and that they were being treated differently than the others because they had or were expected to cause trouble. Two of them were among the wounded and bandaged.

A third was laying on his side, coughing and breathing heavily. I could see his shirt had been ripped open, revealing a large bruise that radiated out from his side that covered nearly all of his left side and torso.

None of the hostages had shoes. Some didn't even have socks.

I heard yelling coming from the cargo container. The man who had exited before came back up to the opening and started arguing with the voice inside. I couldn't understand what they were saying, but the man in the cargo container was throwing debris out of the back in what appeared to be a temper tantrum.

I heard a mocking tone coming from the man on the ground and recognized a word—Majmun.

It seemed that some part of their plan had relied on the man Elvis had shot in the garage of the safe house. I hoped it wasn't something that would make them more desperate...unless I could use it to my advantage.

Elvis, did you do Barb a favor or not? I asked myself.

The cargo container was decked out with ventilation and utility boxes hanging compactly from the walls. It said "Livestock" on the side in several languages, including English. I could see blocks of explosives and wires tucked in around the inside edge of the container opening.

I left my spot after drinking in a few more moments of Barb and then crawled out of the hole in the wall. I placed the louver back in its position, but re-attached it with only two screws so that I might enter that way more easily next time.

I walked back around the rear of the warehouse and then stooped low to walk back to the bulkhead. As I was ready to lower myself over the edge, the side door on the loading dock opened and a man stepped out, arguing with someone inside. I dropped down quickly onto the ledge below the bulkhead.

The voice inside was saying something in a commanding tone. Reprimanding.

The man on the outside made a rude gesture and said something that sounded like a word Elvis had used.

"*Zalupa,*" he exclaimed, accompanied by the universal

finger gesture for displeasure.

Then, just as the door was closing, I got a text message. The vibration ended at the instant the door closed.

I quickly pulled the phone out and hit "view" so the vibration would stop. I peeked over the edge to see if the man had heard my phone.

SHIT!

He was walking to the edge of the loading dock and looking toward me. He pulled out a flashlight and shined it in my direction.

I started to slide along the bulkhead as quickly as I could without making any noise. My heart was racing as I tried to rapidly traverse the concrete water barrier in complete silence, fearful of accidentally kicking something with my foot.

I was a good thirty feet away by the time he reached the edge. He was searching the area directly below him with the flashlight, when a loud splash occurred on the opposite side of the water, followed by loud honking. The light had apparently disturbed a pair of geese sleeping in the current-free cove. They splashed and honked their protests at the inconsiderate man.

He turned off his light and walked back to the loading dock. I continued down the bulkhead until I was well past hearing range and then climbed up and crossed back over to the foot path. I walked quietly and calmly down the path and across the bridge, letting the cool night lower my heart rate and adrenaline levels.

When I arrived back out our command post in the park, it looked as if Kathrin was on the verge of crying. She looked up at me and shook her head, unable to speak. "What's wrong?" I asked.

"I thought I could warn you," she said.

"You did," I said, trying to put her at ease. "It's my fault. I should have thought about how loud vibrate mode is when there is no other noise."

She nodded with her head down, not looking me in the eye.

"I did tell you emergencies only. That seemed like an emergency," I said, lifting her chin so I could see her eyes. "But we have to find a better way to communicate when we come back," I said, winking at her.

"Did you see her?" she asked excitedly.

"Yes," I said, smiling. "She looks healthy. That should put some of my fears to rest."

But it didn't.

Sunrise was only an hour away, so I packed up our equipment, and we headed back to the hotel. I had a plan started, and this would be the mother of all designs. It would have to be.

On the way back to the hotel, we passed a bakery that had just opened for the day, so we stopped and got some food. The warm bread and pastries filled our nostrils all the way home. Neither one of us could wait, so we each pulled one out and ate it on the way. I had nearly abandoned all my eating habits. Calories had become more important than anything else.

I kept seeing Barb's sleeping face. I had seen that face on a few occasions when she had drifted asleep in my arms watching a movie on TV or sitting on a bench overlooking the tidal basin at night in DC. It broke my heart, and it took all my will to keep from turning back to the warehouse. We got to the hotel and Kathrin immediately fell into bed and dozed, snoring softly.

I plugged in my iPad and started to go through the daytime footage of the warehouse. It was time to plan.

**

Going through the footage, I discovered that men only sat watch outside at night. I guessed it would be too obvious to have men sitting outside of a supposedly empty warehouse all day long.

Occasionally, an SUV would drive up. After a few seconds, someone would come out of the warehouse, unlock the gate, and let the SUV back up next to the warehouse. It never went into the warehouse. It had happened three times since they arrived, once each day around 2:00 p.m., starting on Tuesday. The driver of the SUV looked like he could be one of the Serbs. I was only guessing, but he looked to have the same complexion and hair, and his face was unshaven for roughly the same amount of time.

When it arrived each day, five men would come out and carry boxes back inside. The driver usually leaned against the vehicle and smoked while the other five were unloading. That left three inside for a total of eight, plus the driver of the SUV.

If I was lucky, at least one would be on a sleep cycle after standing guard duty all night. If I was *very* lucky, two of them would be asleep. During my reconnaissance, I'd noted that all of the overhead garage and dock doors had been bolted from the inside, preventing anyone from opening them from the outside. There were four hinged doors. Two on the loading dock side, one on the ramp side facing the gate, and the one through the shed that opened into the main warehouse.

One of the doors on the dock side was blocked with pallets. All of the doors had bars that could be dropped across them, but the door by the ramp had a glass window. It was painted over, but that wouldn't stop someone from breaking the glass and lifting the bar.

The back side of the warehouse was windowless and door-free except for the compressor shed. I wished I had discovered the warehouse at least one day earlier. Had I not spent the better part of the day sleeping after my torture, I might have one more day of information on the goings on in the warehouse.

I scanned through both sets of saved surveillance video and found nothing else of interest on the outside of the building except the arrival of the cargo container on the day we arrived. There were no routines when others were outside except the daily resupply visit. And no other building weaknesses that I could see.

There was power to the building. The fan was unplugged in the compressor shed. The compressor itself had been plugged in, but the long lever for the power was off. I had to assume the compressor worked. I hoped. It would make a great distraction if it did.

Ice requires eighty calories per gram of water to melt. Melt rate depends on the external factors controlling the application of those heat units. Heat flows by conduction, convection and/or radiation. $X = I x (R = 80 x F)$.

All the men wore boots, black jeans or trousers, long-sleeved pullover shirts, and black or navy blue jackets of some sort.

Easy enough to duplicate, I thought.

Ice, clothes, and a huge set of brass balls would be what I required.

**

8:55 a.m. on Friday, Friday, May 14th

I must have dozed while re-watching the video footage, because the next thing I heard was the shower in the bathroom. I panicked for a moment and looked for the time. 9:00 a.m. *Good.* I had only dozed for a couple of hours.

When Kathrin came back into the room, she was wrapped in a towel and brushing out her hair. She sat on the edge of the bed, and I tried to ignore her naked legs.

"Are you hungry?" she asked and then tossed the bag of pastries to me before giving me a chance to respond.

"*Danke*," I said absently, rising from my chair, still trying to avert my eyes.

"*Bitte*," she replied with some amusement in her voice as she pulled my iPad to her.

It felt odd sitting with an almost complete stranger, who was wrapped in only a towel, eating some of the best pastry I had in my life.

"Why did you come with me?" I asked.

She didn't even bother looking up from the tablet. "You required assistance. I thought it would be fun," she said. "Stop analyzing. We have hostages to free." Then she went to get dressed in the bathroom.

Avoidance, I thought.

Trust her, came the whisper from my other voice.

"Yeah, yeah, yeah," I muttered.

This auditory hallucination was starting to worry me, but I

didn't have time to figure it out. I had lived my whole life with visual hallucinations—in the form of my flow charting and memory recall—perhaps the 'voice' was just a stress-induced addition.

"Did you say something?" Kathrin asked from the bathroom.

"Just talking to myself," I said—totally true.

She wore the same thing she had the night before, with the exception of a fresher t-shirt. I realized that both of us had been wearing the same clothes for quite a while, and we were starting to get a little ripe. If she was going to be smelling fresher, it would only be polite if I did as well.

As soon as she was done, I took my turn in the bathroom and took the first shower I'd had in a while. It felt good to let the warm water run over my tight muscles. The pain on my chest was a bit uncomfortable but manageable. When I was done, I asked Kathrin to hand me my bag through the bathroom door.

While I was changing and re-bandaging my ribs, she sat on the floor outside the bathroom. "What are we going to do?" she asked.

"I figure that most of the gunmen go outside when the SUV shows up each day," I replied as I smoothed a fresh bandage over my chest and shoulder wound. "There is a manual release on the overhead garage door. If I can get the remaining couple of Serbs away from the release with a distraction, I can come in on the other side and drop that door…effectively trapping the bad guys outside."

"What about the ones who stay inside?" she asked.

"That's the tricky part," I replied. "The ones doing the

loading seem to leave their weapons inside. It's a gamble, but if their guns are close enough to the manual release, I can grab one and get the last two guys."

"You could shoot someone?" she asked.

Good question, I thought.

"If I have to," I said with more confidence than I was feeling. "But that door dropping will cause a commotion. With all the weapons inside, I might be able to cut a couple of the security team loose to help."

"Once the two inside are down, the only way in will be through the side doors." I said, "And we'd have their guns. If they tried to come back in, they'd be cut down. They'd be smarter to just hop in the SUV and take off."

"Good plan," she said.

"Thanks," I replied sincerely as I came out of the bathroom.

"It just seems strange," she said.

"What does?" I asked.

"They have resupply, transportation, shelter, arms, hostages, a flatbed with a livestock container," she mused. "But why no surveillance, alarms, daytime guards?"

"I'm not one hundred percent sure, but it seems the warehouse was supposed be a temporary stop," I replied. "Judging by the empty food and water cases, they had only planned on being there one or two days, tops."

She nodded her agreement with my observation.

"The daytime guards would draw attention from across the cove," I said. "Don't forget that there's a hotel, a factory, and other businesses there. I think they had no plan for a delay. Cameras and alarms would take planning and installation—not something you do if you were only planning on staying out of sight for a few hours."

"Makes sense," she said. "But I would have carried wireless cameras with me."

"You'd make a better criminal than they would," I chuckled.

She shot me a sly grin. "Maybe when this is over, we should consider a career change," she said, barely containing her laugh.

"I have a hard enough time sleeping as it is," I replied. "I wouldn't want my conscience keeping me up at night as well."

"Good point," she replied with a knowing grin.

There it is again, I thought. *That flash of 'I know something you don't and I think it's funny that you don't know it, too.'*

"Can you get some ice from the machine down the hall?" I asked.

"Yah," she replied and then got our ice bucket off of the dresser and went down the hall to put ice cubes in it while I finished packing our items into my shoulder bag and her backpack.

It was 10:35 am. Time to head back to the warehouse.

**

The communications issue from the night before was remedied with a simple purchase of hands-free, earbud-style headsets for the phones. We would stay in constant communication rather than relying on texting.

By 12:15 p.m., I was on the path behind the warehouses, and Kathrin was looking like a lunchtime lounger in the park while she watched the video feeds on my iPad.

"How am I looking on the water side?" I asked.

"All clear," Kathrin replied into my headset.

I walked along the edge of the fence all the way to the water and then slipped down the bulkhead and climbed back up onto the ground just on the other side of the fence.

"That was good," Kathrin said into my ear. "No one noticed."

Walking like I belonged there, I made my way back to the compressor shed to peek through the louvers.

Once I was satisfied that nothing had changed from the previous night, I walked to the edge of the building and peeked around the corner toward the gate side. Seeing no one, I went back to the compressor shed.

"Okay," I whispered. "I'm going in."

"Be careful," Kathrin replied.

Climbing through the opening in the wall the way I had done in the dark, I was careful not to make any noise. Once in, I peeked through my peephole and saw the hostages and their captors in pretty much the same locations they had been the night before.

Several of the abductors were sleeping in corners around the warehouse, some with hats pulled over their faces. It would be perfect if those fellows were the ones to stay behind when the SUV was unloaded, but I couldn't count on that.

The compressor seemed to be holding air—according to the gage anyway. I could only pray the motor would start when I wanted it to. I reached behind the machine and unplugged it and then flipped the power lever back and forth a couple of times to ensure it was working freely.

I reached into my bag and pulled out the insulated pouch containing the ice and then placed a cube on the switch base, flipping the lever over to rest on it. The temperature in the shed was very warm with the sun beating directly on it. It shouldn't take long for it to melt.

I was watching the activity, or lack thereof, through the hole. My eyes kept drifting back to Barb. She was in the same place she had been the night before.

This is your fault, Scott Wolfe. The playback of her voice looped in my head.

She was awake now, talking quietly to her father and the ambassador's daughter. She was smiling, touching the girl's hand. I heard the click of the lever behind me.

Six minutes and twenty-five seconds.

I retrieved another ice cube and repeated the experiment.

There was a lot of activity around the entrance of the cargo container. Two men were carrying boxes and cases of water into it. One carried a stack of ratty-looking cargo blankets, and then another one followed behind him. Something was going to happen soon.

"Kathrin," I whispered into my headset.

"Here," she replied.

"Turn the shoe company camera around to face the road leading to the warehouses," I whispered. "Focus it all the way down the road. I want as much notice as possible."

"Yah," she said. Her usual chatty nature had been replaced with no-nonsense communication—clear, precise, and clipped. She had really taken to this line of work. There might be a job for her with the BND, the German Foreign Intelligence Service, in the future. She truly seemed to enjoy it.

Click. The lever engaged.

Six minutes, thirteen seconds.

I set it up again. I looked back through the hole. It was after one o'clock now, and the SUV could be pulling up at any time. A knot was forming in my stomach, and I was frantically checking and rechecking the locations of the guards, mentally noting who was sleeping and awake, where the weapons were sitting, who seemed most awake, who seemed most tired, least disciplined, most disciplined etc.—any hints or clues that might help.

My mind, unbidden, provided what data it could. *The average human body requires seven and a half to eight and a half hours of sleep to remain optimal. Stress increases the need for sleep. Loss of one and a half hours of sleep can result in a thirty-two percent reduction in waking alertness, impaired memory, and cognitive and information-processing ability. Extended periods with reduced sleep can result in reduced immune efficiency and increased desire for nicotine, sugar, sex, or other dopamine-*

releasing surrogates.

I heard something. The yard tractor was starting up. I looked in the direction of the machine and saw one of the armed men driving it in a tight circle toward the front of the warehouse.

Click. The lever engaged.

Six minutes and twenty seconds.

As soon as the tractor had finished turning the trailer, the armed men started ushering hostages through the doors of the cargo container.

Oh, shit, I thought.

"I see the SUV." Kathrin said into my ear.

"The plan is changing," I said, trying to run a new flow chart, but there were too many unknown variables for me to create a logic flow that was useful.

"Why?" she asked, a note of panic in her voice.

"They are moving the hostages into the container. It looks like they are leaving," I said, a tinge of anger in my voice; anger at myself for not getting here a day sooner; anger for not coming up with a plan that I could have acted on last night.

I had to wing it. It was getting pretty clear that I would not be able to free the hostages right now.

Calm is your friend, I heard my other voice whisper in my ear.

"There is another car coming," Kathrin said. "Gray sedan."

The garage door was opening as the last of the hostages were being herded into the cargo container.

"The black SUV has arrived at the gate." Kathrin said. "One of the men motioned for it to come inside." A few seconds later, she spoke again. "The sedan pulled through the gate and stopped outside. Three of the men placed their rifles in the back of the SUV, and then got in the sedan."

"What are they doing?" I asked.

"They just drove away," she replied.

"Kathrin," I said.

"Here," she replied.

"The fence on the back of the warehouse," I said.

"Yes," she said.

"I need your phone. Go now! Run!" I said desperately.

"On my way," she said.

I could hear her heavy breath in my ear and then her footfalls on wooden planking as she ran down the path and across the bridge.

I hopped out of the hole in the wall and ran to the fence just as she came into sight around the corner of the path. She was running full tilt, her legs making long strides, her arms pumping furiously up and down. She arrived at the fence, winded, and then tossed the phone over.

I pointed at the bag she had slung on her shoulder. "Tape," I said in an elevated whisper.

She reached into her pack, pulling out a roll of heavy duty utility tape, and then tossed that over as well. I caught it and signaled for her to get out of sight, and then I ran back to the compressor shed.

I pulled the louvered vent back into its opening behind me and jammed a rusty nail into the space between the frame and the vent to hold it in place. I looked through the hole in the wall.

Two of the men had closed the door on the cargo container, latched it, and then locked it with a heavy padlock. Then the rest of the guards started getting into the SUV, with the exception of the one man who was driving the old, beat-up yard tractor. Once they were in, the SUV pulled out of the warehouse. I wish Kathrin could tell me how far the SUV had pulled ahead, but I now had the prepaid phone she had been using. I'd have to chance it.

I placed an ice cube under the lever of the compressor switch and then plugged the machine in. I went to the hole and saw the cargo container as it started to slowly pull toward the large opening.

I pushed the door open and then crept forward, looking to see if I could spot the SUV. It drove slowly down the road and then stopped beside a freight crane next to a set of train tracks at a dock for river barges.

The man on the tractor had his back to me and was slowly towing the trailer with the cargo box through the large overhead garage door with the concrete ramp. I ran over to the back of the cargo container and tugged on the lock in the fleeting hope that it might not be latched.

Wishful thinking.

I pulled a long length of the sticky, heavy duty duct tape

from the roll, attached it to the phone, and then reached through one of the slots used to lift the box with a fork lift. I stuck it securely to the inside edge and then pulled off a second and a third piece of tape to make sure it would truly stick.

The trailer was slowing as we passed just beyond the opening of the door. Then it banged to a stop. I looked around the corner of the box and saw no one on the tractor. He was coming around the other side to close the garage door, I suspected. I hopped down off the back of the trailer and then slipped under it just in time to watch his legs pass.

I accidentally drug my toe, moving further under the trailer—it made a scuffing sound.

You didn't hear it, you didn't hear it, I thought, trying to will my thoughts into reality. After all, the engine of the tractor was running.

He paused.

I wasn't going to be that lucky. If I came out from under the trailer on the other side, the men from the SUV would be able to see me. I watched as the man's legs passed only a few inches from me, next to the rear tires.

He stopped again and began to bend to look under the trailer. My hand tightened into a fist, and my body went taut, preparing for a strike. Suddenly there was a loud and horrible whine, like a metal rake being pulled across a chalk board, followed by a loud thrumming and clacking.

The compressor! I thought, relieved, as the man jerked back upright and ran in the direction of the noise, withdrawing a pistol from under his jacket as he went.

I rolled back out from under the trailer and then hurried

quietly across to a pile of pallets that were stacked near the wall opposite the compressor room. I watched as the man jerked the door open, pointing his gun into the small room. He flipped on the light switch in the dark room and leveled his gun at the source of the noise. He walked in and then, reaching down, he flipped the switch on the compressor.

It rattled once more in protest and went quiet.

He emerged from the room and brought his finger up to smell and then taste. *The water from the melted ice,* I realized. Then he wiped his hand on his pants and looked around the warehouse slowly.

A voice called to him from outside. He paused. The voice called again, louder, more insistent. *"Da. Da, da, da!"* The man yelled. He re-holstered his pistol, pulled the garage door closed, and then exited the warehouse through the door facing the gate.

I breathed a sigh of relief as the door closed. I heard the tractor rev up and heard it and the trailer with the hostages move away from the closed door. I hopped up from my hiding spot and ran back to the compressor room. Hopping up, I popped the louver out with my feet and then ran around to the back corner of the warehouse. There I crouched at the corner and watched the activity by the crane.

One of the men was starting up the crane. The roar of its diesel engine blocked out the other noises in the area.

I looked around behind me and to both sides to see if I could spot Kathrin. I saw the tip of her head peering out from under the wooden stairs on the dock side of the platform in front of me. She looked back and saw me and then motioned me to come to her.

I looked beyond her toward the group by the crane. Their

attention was on a rail car that was being pushed along the tracks running along the water's edge by a small gas-powered vehicle. I ducked down low and scurried over to the stairs and then dove under next to her. She stared at me for a second, waiting, listening.

I suddenly remembered we still had a video feed.

"My iPad," I said in a whisper.

She quickly pulled it out of her backpack and handed it to me. I pulled up the video feed and zoomed the camera in on the dock area where the crane was.

Kathrin crawled around to my side so she could see as well.

We could clearly see the yard tractor as it towed the trailer to the base of the crane scaffolding. To the casual observer, it would simply seem like workmen loading cargo on a rail car. No weapons were visible, no one was acting suspiciously—it was just another day of work in Dusseldorf.

One man was shouting. He was smaller than the man he was yelling at. The one who was being shouted at stepped forward threateningly, but he was quickly restrained by three others standing near him.

The smaller man stepped forward and poked his finger in the other man's chest, prompting the larger man to spit in his face. The small man slapped the larger man with the back of his hand, sending the larger man into a rage. The other three pulled him back roughly, preventing him from lashing out. The smaller man turned and walked away.

The three released their grip, and he started kicking and shouting at them. They reached out, but not to strike. They were trying to calm him.

"Russians," I said aloud.

"What?" Kathrin asked.

"Elvis said the Russians were being treated disrespectfully by the Serbs. Something that was difficult for them to accept," I said. "Those four there…I bet those are Russians."

She grunted her understanding.

While the men had been arguing, the remaining handful had been attaching cables and hooks to the cargo box and preparing to move it to the flat bed rail car. By the time the four Russians had calmed down, the cargo box had been placed gently on the bed of the car.

Two of the four men stepped up onto the bed of the rail car and ratcheted down the chain 'dogs' to hold the box securely to the bed. Two of them stayed on the bed of the rail car as it started moving down the track. The remainder piled into the SUV and drove away.

I pulled out my phone and sent a secure text to Storc. It read: "*Have found Barb. Haven't got her yet but working on it. Need GPS tracking this number.*" Then I sent him the phone number of the prepaid phone I had attached to the container.

He sent a reply almost immediately: "*Tracking is on. First ping should be up in a few minutes. Re: Barb. Bonbon almost wet herself. Stay safe.*"

"We have to find out where that container is going," I said matter-of-factly.

"We could follow the signal to the rail yard and see which train it is hooked to," she offered.

"That's a plan. Let's go get our stuff and then head for the yard," I said.

We left our hiding place just as the rail car was pulling around the long curve on the opposite side of the bend. Back down the path and across the bridge, we left at a trot.

**

2:10 p.m. on Friday, May 14th - US Consulate in Amsterdam

BEVERLY MARTIN's phone rang while she was in the middle of a meeting. She looked down at the screen on her phone to see it was John Temple. She answered in a quiet voice. "Yeah. Just a second." Then she excused herself from her meeting and pulled the door closed on her office. "What's up?" she asked.

"I just wanted you to know that our amateur isn't in Paris." John said plainly. "Our team found his phone on the train—just his phone."

The consul general chuckled. "I guess your tag isn't working either if you had the Paris team check the train."

John was a bit annoyed that the Consul General was so quick to assume he had tagged the boy after she forbade it. But of course she was right, which made it sting all the more.

The cash with the tracking filaments worked into each bill had proved useless before the Paris train even left. John had thought it strange that the boy would spend all of his money within an hour of receiving it. It was clear: enough credit wasn't being given to young Mr. Wolfe. He was demonstrating real tradecraft.

She took the long pause as his admission without an admission. She would not force him to lie to her. She knew he was under orders. "Any clue at all, as to his whereabouts?" she asked.

"None. He's evaporated." John replied.

"Where are we then?" she asked, frustrated by the dead end.

"We still have our feelers out in Prague. Everything went quiet there with the Serb network just before the explosion. We are trying to interview all of our regulars there, but a lot of them disappeared around the same time. Two just turned up in the Vltava with bullets in the backs of their heads."

She let that digest. "Okay, John. Is there anything I can do to help?" she asked.

"I wish there was. We're just treading water at the moment," he replied.

"Okay. Thanks for the update. Keep me posted when you can," she said, her exhaustion clear in her voice, and then she added, "And John... Thanks for keeping me in the loop on this. I know you don't have to."

"My pleasure, ma'am," he responded and then ended the call.

**

JOHN TEMPLE sat down hard on the bank of the Vltava River after stuffing his phone back into his pocket. He looked over at the Czech police and emergency crews as they hauled the second of the two bodies from the water and up the bank on stretchers. Nick Horiatis walked up to John with a thermos of coffee and handed it to him. "What did the old lady have to say about the punk?"

"You know, Short Bus, you should be careful about what you call other people." John said, driving the point home with the nickname Nick hated.

When Nick joined the agency, it leaked out that his mother had driven a handicap bus for the public school system and that Nick would ride to school with her each morning. That kind of information is just the sort of fodder the instructors loved to use to break the ego of a new candidate. And to Nick's everlasting resentment, the moniker had stuck.

"Whatever," he said absently. "I told you we should've kept that kid locked in the basement," he continued, staring disapprovingly at his boss. His nose was blue and black where Scott had broken it two nights earlier. There were also four stitches in his scalp, just above the hair line, from where his head had been smashed into the side of the van door.

"That 'kid' went to ground with us watching him with both eyes and appears to be the only one with any leads in this cluster fuck." He paused to take a sip of coffee. "He might be the best hope we have of finding the hostages alive."

Nick scoffed. "Wouldn't that be something," he said sarcastically.

"He confirmed the Jovanovich Family connection when all we had were suspicions," John reminded him.

"Yeah! Because he got captured and tortured!" Nick said incredulously.

John looked at Nick sideways. "Yeah... But he escaped, and Majmun is dead."

Nick shook his head. "Well if he's so fucking on top of things, it would be nice if he'd clue us in a little bit."

John turned and stared back out over the water of the Vltava River, taking another sip of coffee.

"Yeah...that would be nice," he said, more to himself than to Nick.

**

Afternoon of Friday, May 14th - Hauptbahnhof, Dusseldorf

We arrived at the hotel, packed up our clothes and equipment into two small rolling suitcases, and called a cab. While on the way to the train station, Hauptbahnhof Dusseldorf, I checked the signal on the cargo container. It was still on the main track line heading to the train station.

I sent a text to Storc with the car and cargo container numbers, hoping he'd be able to get into the system and discover a destination, but he informed me that the numbers weren't in the system. He said he'd keep checking to see if they popped up.

Once we arrived at the station, we put our luggage in a locker and then started searching for the container. When we located it through a window, we saw that the two men who had ridden with the container were overseeing the connection with another car...a passenger car.

"Down there," I said to Kathrin. "Let's see if we can get into the yard."

We went down a flight of stairs and attempted to exit into the yard, but were blocked by a security door requiring a pass card. I was tired, and I was having a hard time keeping the panic at bay.

"Neine!" came a voice behind us.

A security guard.

Kathrin said something to the effect of, "Isn't this the door to the platform?"

The guard shook his as he replied, and then pointed up the stairs.

Kathrin nodded and smiled, *"Danke,"* she said and then pulled me back upstairs by the arm. My heart was pounding in my chest so hard, I could hear it in my ears. The locked door and the guard had only made it worse.

I was starting to feel like I was in over my head for the first time. The lack of sleep along with the constant pain in my chest and shoulder were making it exceedingly difficult to concentrate on forming a plan.

Barb is here, only yards away, I thought. *Seriously, a locked door and a security guard are going to stop you now?*

We went back upstairs looking for an alternate way into the yard.

I stopped to think, Kathrin watching me expectantly. But nothing was coming to me.

Kathrin reached out, putting her hand on my shoulder. "I have an idea," she said.

She walked across the floor of the station to a food Kiosk and ordered a sandwich, a soda and a cup of coffee. She walked back to me carrying the bagged meal in one hand and the coffee in the other.

She handed me the coffee.

"I'll be right back," she said, smiling confidently, and then she disappeared around the corner. A few moments later I saw her out in the yard.

"She smiled upon them and the doors were opened." I said to myself in a whisper.

She walked over to a gray-haired man in orange coveralls. He was rotund, to say the least, with a broad paint brush of a gray mustache hanging down over his lip. As she approached him he turned and waved his hands indicating she wasn't supposed to be here. She held out the bag and the soda saying something to him.

He turned and looked down the track then up at the control tower and shrugged.

She said something else to him and he nodded, taking the bag and soda from her. She continued to talk to him, and he gestured around the yard and then pointed off in one direction then another. She pointed at the car carrying our cargo container—it had just been hooked up with a passenger car.

He turned to look where she was pointing and then looked down at the clipboard he had tucked under his arm, flipped a page, and then said something back. She threw her arms around his thick neck, kissed him on his cheek, and then walked back to the terminal.

All I could do was shake my head. Any hesitation I might have had about dragging Kathrin along with me had just evaporated.

When she returned, she stopped in front of me, smiling.

"Who was lunch for?" I asked with a grin.

"*Meine bruuder*," she said through a toothy grin. "It seems he is at another yard, but the nice man with the big mustache is going to make sure he gets it."

I laughed. "What else did the nice man say?" I probed.

"He explained how difficult his job is and how he had to keep track of all the cars in the yard lest passengers or cargo end up in Greece instead of France or Switzerland instead of Turkey," she replied. "I asked him about that strange box car with all gadgets hanging on it."

"And?" I asked.

"There are two cars on that manifest...one passenger and one climate-controlled stable box for prize stallions—going to Prague on the night train," she said, shifting herself around to my side. "Apparently they are a troop of equestrian performers."

"How fortunate for us that we are on our way to Prague! We might catch a performance," I said.

Kathrin's eyes lit up and her smile widened—I thought her cheeks would burst from the pressure. She threw her arms around me and said, "I thought for sure you would send me on my way once we were done in Germany." Then she backed up to look at me.

"No way," I said. "I'd never leave my German super spy behind." Then I winked at her.

She hooked her arm through mine and pulled me forward. "Come! We must purchase tickets for the night train!" she said gleefully.

We purchased tickets for a sleeping berth. The night train departed from Frankfurt, so we also purchased tickets on a commuter train to take us there. Before boarding, we ordered a small meal of wurst and kraut at a terminal restaurant. I found it difficult to enjoy my meal while Barbara was locked inside that container, but I hadn't eaten or slept for a while, so the change of pace did much to refresh me.

Once our meal was done, we walked leisurely toward the platform to board the train—it was nice not to rush.

"So what do you do when you aren't on crazy adventures with Americans?" I asked as the train pulled out of the station.

She grinned. "Oh. That is my job," she said, trying to pull a straight face. "It's a service I provide."

"Really?" I replied ironically. "How's the pay?"

"Wait until you get my bill," she said and then she broke into a broad grin that spread to her whole face.

I chuckled.

"I'm a gopher, mostly," she replied, finally giving me a half-straight answer. "I deliver packages for a company, do some dispatching, driving...sometimes I just sit around and listen to the phones."

"Oh, like for a delivery company?" I asked.

"They do lots of things, but yes, they do deliveries as well," she said. "It's sort of like a concierge service."

"Okay," I replied, not familiar with the concept, but I assumed it was a European thing.

"Do you do this much?" she asked.

"All the time," I replied. "This is just a little side job I picked up for vacation. Usually my assignments are much harder."

It took her a second to realize I was joking, and then we both laughed.

The trip to Frankfurt was uneventful as both of us napped more than anything else. It was a short trip, but it was nice to have a stress-free conversation with the chatty girl I had met at the hotel. But as soon as we were quiet again, I remembered that Barb was in a box on a different train, without comfortable seats, with no giggly conversation and no window to look out. Her voice came back to mind.

This is your fault, Scott Wolfe.

I know, I replied.

When we arrived in Frankfurt, we immediately made for the train to Prague. We located the correct platform and strolled along the edge, looking for the two target cars.

Kathrin bumped my arm with her elbow and nodded toward the back of the train.

I looked down the track and saw the cargo container and the attached passenger car containing our hostages and their guards.

The back end of the passenger car facing the container had a glass-covered landing. One of the captors was sitting in a chair, watching the doors of the cargo container. No doubt they would be taking shifts watching the container.

The private passenger car the Serbs had obtained was situated between the rest of the passenger cars and the cargo container. There would be no way for me to access the container without going through the Serb's car—or over it. But I had seen enough movies to know I wasn't up to that sort of acrobatic spy work, especially knowing there were explosives lining the inside of the box doors. That wouldn't do at all.

"Hi Barb! I'm here to pick up you and your friends."

BOOM!

Though I was a quick study in most things, there was no way I was going to make an inaugural attempt at bomb defusing on a box containing my girlfriend.

We would have to wait until Prague.

We boarded the train and found our sleeping compartment. The thought of sleep made us both ache to lie down even though there was some sunlight left. But after we settled into our compartment, we decided to explore the train.

We headed toward the engine first, passing through other sleeper cars and the dining car.

"Maybe we should get something to eat after we explore," I suggested as we entered the dining car. It smelled wonderful.

"Please," she said in an amazing release of sincerity. "I'm starving."

Now I know how sincerity really *looks on you,* I thought.

Then we headed back, seeing how close we could get to the bad guy's car.

"Careful," she whispered as I reached for the handle.

I looked up through the double windows and saw the

passage blocked by two men arguing. "You're right," I said, defeated. "Let's go get some food."

**

8:47 p.m. on Friday, May 14th - the night train to Prague

After getting a bite to eat, we arrived back at our sleeping berth. The train had been underway for several minutes, so I was expecting tickets to be called for any time now.

Moments later, there was a knock at the door. The steward was there to punch our tickets and collect our passports.

"Why do I have to give up my passport?" Kathrin complained.

"Only the seated passengers keep their passports. Those with sleeping berths aren't disturbed during the trip, so the passports need to be kept in the safe," the steward explained. "I assure you, they will be returned prior to our arrival in Prague."

I had been aware of this because I had taken night trains in Europe before. I was surprised by Kathrin's response.

Once he was gone, we prepared for bed. I laid down on my bunk fully clothed, but Kathrin stripped to her underwear and then pulled a long t-shirt over her before climbing up to hers.

About the time I started to drift the first time, my phone chimed, indicating that I had a message. I pulled it up and read the text from Storc. It read: "*City Night Line, Night Train Frankfurt Hbf to Prague HL N. One livestock car and one passenger car. Scheduled to arrive Praha Hlavni Nadrazi at 8:09 a.m.*"

I texted back. "*Thanks pal. I don't know what I'd do without you. I'll keep you posted.*"

It would have been cruel to let him know that a girl with a bag of wiener schnitzel and a soda got the information hours before he did.

"Good news?" Kathrin asked from above.

"Yeah. It looks like the cars are going to Prague," I replied.

"We should get right on that," she said, giggling. She paused for a long moment and then said, "I can't wait to meet the woman who inspires such heroism."

"Or insanity," I offered.

She leaned over the edge of her bunk and smiled. "This is the most worthwhile thing I've ever done in my life," she said softly. "Thank you for letting me be a part of it."

"I've been meaning to ask why you are doing this." I said playfully, but I truly wanted to know.

"Are you joking? Cute American boy on international adventure? Who wouldn't?" she said, winking at me, and then she rolled back into the center of her bunk.

I thought about it for a second. "Seriously, though. You didn't come because you were hoping to hook up with me, did you?" Joking, a bit.

There was a burst of laughter from above me. Something I said must have been very funny.

"Although you are very cute and charming when you aren't buzzing like a computer, I'm not even remotely attracted to you," she laughed again.

"Not at all?" I asked playfully.

"Nope," she said, giggling again.

"Come on," I said with mock incredulity. "Not even a little?"

"Not even a little...I like girls," she stated firmly, but I could hear the smile on her face.

"Really!?"

"Really."

There was a long pause "I don't guess I have to worry about you slipping into my bunk overnight."

She burst out laughing.

"You think you know someone..." I continued.

More laughter.

We needed the laughter and the sleep. We were underway for only a short time when a heavy rain began. Thunder and lightning made me huddle under the covers more deeply and aided in a sound sleep. And I did sleep, well and hard—dreaming of Barb.

And once of Barb and Kathrin—but that ended in laughter too.

nine
One Day Until Event

5:15 a.m. on Saturday, May 15th, 2010 - On the night train to Prague, Decin, Czech Republic

I was awakened by a sudden jolt—a bump that shook me in my bunk. I opened my eyes slowly and stretched, checking the time on my phone. I looked out the window and saw that it was still dark and that the train wasn't moving. I pulled my hoodie over my head and stepped into my boots. Without lacing them, I opened the door on our compartment and poked my head out. I saw a steward at the far end of the car and walked down to ask what was happening, wiping the sleep from my eyes as I approached.

He was speaking on the cabin phone. His tone indicated he was scolding someone on the other end. He was speaking in German, however, so I couldn't understand the conversation. I waited until he finished and hung up the phone.

"What's going on?" I asked sleepily.

He responded in very good English without a second thought. "I'm very sorry for the disturbance, sir," he said sincerely. "We will be arriving in Prague behind schedule. There was an emergency stop."

I looked out the window and saw we were just outside a town in a large train yard next to a small rail depot. The train was just beginning to move.

"Where are we?" I asked.

"Decin, sir," he said. "Just over the Czech border."

I looked out the window again.

"What was the emergency?" I asked without looking away from the window.

"It was veterinary in nature. It appears that we were forced to stop here to detach a stable car," he said with disgust in his voice.

I was awake now. I felt adrenaline being dumped into my bloodstream.

"Someone must have a great deal of influence," he continued. "This train doesn't normally stop."

His last words were directed to my back, as I was already running down the hall to our sleeping compartment. I burst through the door, sending Kathrin sitting up in bed, awakened by the ruckus.

"Grab your things," I said.

"Why? What's going on?" she asked as she grabbed her bag and swung down from the bunk.

I looked out the window. From the light of the security lamps in the train yard, I could see that Barb's container car was being pushed slowly onto a branch line by a small yard engine.

"We are about to lose our container car." I replied, stuffing my belongings into my bag.

Kathrin looked out the window and then packed more quickly. She pulled her pants on, quickly tucking in her sleep shirt while slipping her feet into her boots. The train had stopped again, sending us askew.

She grabbed her pack and the small, wheeled carry-on bag and then we dashed out of our compartment just as the train started moving forward again.

We ran down the corridor to the end where the steward had been standing. We pulled the inner door open. The steward stood inside the door to the left, so we broke to the right.

"Wait. You can't exit here. This is not a stop!" he yelled.

Kathrin pulled back on the door handle and slid the door open as I turned to him. "They are stealing our horses!" I yelled as I felt the cold air from outside.

When I turned around Kathrin was gone, so I followed her through the door.

The train was still going relatively slowly when we exited, but without a platform, it's a decent drop from a moving vehicle. When I reached the ground, my boot came off, and I hit the ground hard with my knee. It took me a moment to assess that no real damage had been done, but when I turned to look for Kathrin, she was several feet behind me, on the ground and holding her ankle.

I ran to her.

"I should have taken a second to lace my boots," she joked through her grimace.

I pulled her boot off and felt her ankle and the top of her foot. She grimaced again.

"Move it," I said.

She circled it all directions, grunting in pain when it reached a certain point, but she managed to move through it.

It wasn't broken. That was the good news—but it was sprained.

I pulled my hoodie and t-shirt off and began to uncoil one section of compression bandage from my chest. I then wrapped her foot with it, careful to add support around the arch.

I put my shirt and hoodie back on before I helped her pull her boot back on, and she laced it loosely. She tried to stand on it. Tested it with some weight and then a little more, and then she walked a few steps and nodded that she was okay.

I reached into my map bag and pulled out a handful of bills, handing them to her.

"Go up to the station and buy a ticket back home." I said, pointing at the depot building.

She blinked at me, staring dumbfounded. "No," she said finally and firmly. "It is a sprain. I've had them worse than this before and hiked through the Alps. I will not leave."

"Kathrin," I said firmly. "You're a faithful and dedicated friend. We will be great friends for many years to come, but your part of this adventure is over."

An angry look appeared on her face. She moved toward me and shoved me.

"Stop," I said.

She threw a punch. I blocked it, pushing it to the side. Then she threw another, faster than the first…then more.

She was throwing punches and kicks at a furious pace, and I was starting to fall behind when she leapt from the ground, spinning, her bad foot flying within an inch of my nose. She landed gracefully, standing, poised for another strike. She held that pose for a moment.

"I'd say I'm in pretty decent shape for continuing. I dare you to say otherwise," she said willfully.

I stared at her—blinking.

"You've convinced me," I said ironically, flashing a smile.

She laughed. I laughed. Then we shook off the tension created by her quite impressive display and started walking toward the hostages' container, which was rolling slowly away from us down a branch track.

As it left the yard, it began to pick up speed and pull away from us. I started to trot, but I quickly realized that Kathrin would not be able to follow with her sore ankle. I began looking around for some alternative form of transportation.

We walked as quickly as we could, watching as the container car drifted further and further from sight, turning onto another branch that led across a bridge over the river.

In the small dirt and gravel parking area to the right of us, a young man in blue coveralls was just pulling in on a noisy two stroke scooter. We jogged over to him. He was just setting it up on its stand when he saw us approaching.

Kathrin asked if he spoke German. He shook his head apologetically.

"*Koupit,*" she said—the word 'buy' in Czech—and pointed at his scooter. He looked at his scooter and then at us and shook his head.

I reached into my pocket and pulled out four hundred-euro bills. "*Koupit,*" I said.

His eyes flashed wide and a broken-toothed smile appeared.

Within moments, our bags were strapped to the rickety luggage rack on the back, and we were riding out of the lot onto a connecting street. We merged onto a highway and crossed the river bridge riding on the sidewalk. We scanned ahead and to our left, trying to catch sight of the two train cars. When we had crossed the water, I began moving through streets, taking us closer to the direction they had gone.

We reached a dead end at a chain link fence. The tracks were on the other side of the fence. I hopped off and leaned against it, looking both ways and then spotted it several hundred yards to the east. It had already passed this point.

"It's already gone by," I said as I reached into my bag and grabbed my phone.

"How far?" she asked.

"Less than a minute," I replied, handing her my phone after pulling up the map. "Here, navigate. They are headed that way," I said, pointing.

I turned the scooter in a tight circle, and then we took off back down the street, reversing our course.

"Do you see the tag for the phone?" I asked.

"Tag?" she replied.

"Yes…the GPS marker on the map," I said.

"No. It's not on here," she replied and then held it up for me to see.

"Shit!" I exclaimed. "We can't lose it. If we do, we'll never find it again without that GPS signal."

By the time I made our next left, she had the map zoomed in to detail and was guiding me through the streets, tapping me either on my left or right side and pointing before each turn.

She was guiding us to a larger train yard than the one we had departed from.

"We need to catch up with them before the next yard, or we won't know which way they went," she said into my ear, her breath and the vibration of her voice giving me a momentary calm despite her urgent message.

We turned onto a road that ran parallel to the train yard and both of us scanned it for the two cars being pulled by the small yard engine. When we were reaching the end of the yard, the road veered off to the right, but a small dirt drive continued to run along the last three sets of tracks.

I craned my neck up trying to see down the line and spotted the back of our target moving down the center set of tracks.

I stopped the scooter. "They're on the center track," I said.

Kathrin pulled up the satellite view on the phone's map. Looking at a daytime aerial photo of the train yard, she searched the line on the map out to the next town where it could branch out.

"Ceska Lipa. Thirty-one kilometers." She mapped out the road that seemed to be fastest to Ceska Lipa. "Turn there and take a right at the stop sign," she said.

I complied and we backed off the dirt road and then made for Route 262, which followed nearly the same path as the rails, veering away only occasionally.

I checked the fuel gage on the scooter and saw we had nearly a full tank, so we sped off in a puff of oily smoke, through the streets toward Route 262.

It was only about eighteen miles to Ceska Lipa, and it was unlikely the scooter would go as fast as the small utility engine towing the two train cars, so we had to make up time where we could—at the beginning and the end of the trip when the acceleration and deceleration of the train gave us an advantage.

I gunned the engine, throttle open all the way. If I had thirty minutes to spare, I could clean the spark plug and the fuel filter and get a bit more speed, but we were stuck with the scooter as it was.

We pulled ahead of the train just outside of Decin, but after a few minutes, it passed us again in the dark. I could see the safety lights on the back of the rail car as they got smaller and smaller, pulling further away. They finally disappeared around a turn in the track as it followed a narrow river.

It was almost another half an hour before we entered Ceska Lipa. No sign of the train.

We had to gamble. There were two places on the other side of the small city where the track branched off, and we estimated that if it slowed down as it entered town, then it could be no more than three quarters of a mile ahead of us.

There were five directions it could go. The closest branch would take the train north with only one destination we could discern by looking at the map. The next branch was close to the road on Route 9.

On the southern branch, we would be able to see nearly two miles when at the top of the hill, judging by the satellite image on the map. If we didn't see it on the southern spur, it would have taken the eastern route, and then we should be able to see in both directions far enough to tell which way it had gone when we arrived at the next spur. If not, it meant that they had taken the northern branch and we'd have to backtrack.

It was a gamble, but it was all we had.

When we crossed the bridge near the station, we saw no sign of them, so we continued east at full speed until the road intersected with Route 9, which ran north and south. It was nearly a straight shot for us going south to the next branch but for the train it would have required several slow turns through the city. That should help us catch up if they did pass this way.

We stopped on the road near the next branch. We looked down the long hill from the top of the bridge over the tracks.

"Do you see anything?" I asked.

"No," she replied.

There was no way they could be so far ahead of us as to be out of sight from that vantage point. That meant they had either gone east or north on the first branch we passed. I pulled on the throttle and moved us forward at top speed again.

One last chance, Scott, I thought.

The next track branch would be our make or break moment. If we didn't see them, even if it was because we were late, we would have to flip a coin...north or south.

I gunned the engine and guided the scooter down a shallow embankment and then up a hill a few hundred yards from the highway. The hill was little more than a barren bump of dirt, but it gave us enough height to make out what we were looking for.

On the eastern spur of the last branch, just visible before entering a wooded area, we saw our train.

"Thank God," Kathrin exclaimed.

"Tell me about it," I muttered.

We looked at the map.

There was still no GPS signal from the phone, but the next town the tracks would reach would be Zakupy, followed by Mimon.

I throttled up and sped down the hill, bouncing roughly across a shallow ditch and back onto the road.

I'm coming Barb, I thought to myself.

**

Something about the name Mimon was familiar. I couldn't put my finger on what it was, but I knew I had skimmed across something recently in my research.

We decided to go back to Route 262. The train would have to take a long loop to get through Zakupy and another small town before they reached Mimon, which was where the next branch was.

If we didn't get to Mimon in time to see which spur they took, and if we didn't get a GPS signal from the phone, we would have to guess which direction to follow—one of three. At that point, any hope of catching up would be based entirely on chance.

The poor little scooter had probably never been pushed as hard as we were pushing it. We still had better than a half a tank of petrol, but the black cloud of oily smoke was getting thicker with every start.

We zipped past the two small towns. Kathrin watched along the roadside for any sign that they had stopped in one of them.

"I don't see them," she said as we zipped by the train yard.

"We'll catch them in Mimon," I said, still trying to remember where I had seen the name.

Route 262 became 268 in Zakupy and then split into three other directions once it reached Mimon. Each branch snaked back and forth across one of the three spurs that radiated out from Mimon.

The sun was up then. It was early morning, and it was going to be a clear, sunny day. If we were anywhere near the train, we should be able to spot it as we crossed each line of tracks.

The first line showed us nothing for more than a half mile. It was possible the train was further ahead than that, but we had to continue. If it was gone, there was no way to know. We had to keep going and try to catch a glimpse.

When we reached the center of town, we had three road choices: 270 North, 270 South, or 268 Southeast. Three choices, one train—with no guarantee that we hadn't missed it on the northern spur behind us.

Then I noticed a tall hill to the northeast of us. The ridge had the ruins of a castle. I was getting desperate, so I was ready to take a gamble. I pointed at the hilltop and got a positive nod from Kathrin, so we set off in that direction.

"If they are on the north route, we won't see them from there," she said.

"If they didn't slow down going through town, we won't see them in any direction," I replied.

"Don't be so negative," she replied, squeezing my waist tighter with her arms. "Remember, we are here and there is no sign of CIA. You have an angel on your shoulder."

I couldn't help but notice her chin resting on my shoulder as she spoke into my ear. "You're on my shoulder," I laughed.

"Like I said..."

I smiled at her reply, suddenly feeling much more encouraged.

It took longer to get to the top of the castle mound than I had anticipated. The scooter was not suited for trail travel, especially with two riders aboard. But we reached the flattened area in a few minutes, just below the walls of the ruins of Ralsko Castle, according to a sign at its base.

I rapidly dismounted and grabbed for the luggage to fish the binoculars out.

I climbed as high on the ruins as I dared and started scanning the three rail lines coming out of the city. For five minutes, I rapidly scanned for movement, and then spent ten additional minutes on a more thorough search, following each line out as far as I could see.

Nothing but a single commuter train and a lumber train, which was sitting still, on the southern spur.

The gamble had not paid off.

At that point, Barb could have been heading in any compass direction, and I wouldn't have a clue as to which.

Why couldn't you have been riding a Harley? I complained to the yard worker in my head. A motorcycle would have cost all my remaining cash, but we would have been able to follow the train every inch of the way.

I slowly climbed down off the ruins of Castle Ralsko, feeling defeated. I looked across the horizon for any sign: a cloud in the shape of an arrow, a flare or rocket, sky writing, or *anything* that might indicate my angel was truly looking out for me—but all I received was a chill from the cold wind on the barren hillside.

I walked back to the scooter. Kathrin was waiting there, sitting against a rock, drinking water from a bottle. She handed it to me, and I took a long drink as well. As soon as the moisture hit my mouth I realized how thirsty and now hungry I was.

She looked up expectantly. She could tell I had not spotted the train due to my sudden lack of vigor and direction.

"What next?" she asked.

I shrugged. "All we can do is wait and hope the phone

finds enough signal to send GPS data." I wasn't sure what else we could do.

We sat at the ruins snacking on trail mix, silently scanning the horizon for any sign that we might have missed. All the time my head turned through complex scenarios and probabilities. My flow chart was stuck on Mimon. I couldn't help but feel like I was missing something.

"Why would they risk detection, stopping a train in the middle of its journey?" I asked aloud. I thought about it for a moment. "And why take such a high profile train configuration into the countryside when all they would have to do is get on a regular cargo manifest and go through normal train routes?"

Kathrin looked at me but didn't respond. She had seen me like this enough in the past couple of days to know I was working on the problem myself.

"It stinks of desperation," I said and then paused, turning other pieces over to fit. "Majmun was a critical part of their next step. That's clear. Maybe he was supposed to procure the transportation to their next stop."

I looked out over the bright landscape stretching out to the horizon. My eyes came to rest on a bright patch of ground about four miles away.

"They stayed in Dusseldorf too long," I said firmly. "It made them nervous, but something else delayed them. It would have been easy enough to get a truck or a bus to move the hostages. So something is missing. What else was Majmun supposed to do?"

It was clear that Elvis had put a wrinkle in their plans by killing the big Serb. Certainly they were afraid they had been discovered. And it's possible that they had no backup plan in place if Majmun failed to arrange for the next leg of transport. But what held them in one place for more than three days?

It hit me like an electrical charge through my body.

"Of course!" I exclaimed, and Kathrin whipped her head around to stare at me. "They had transportation lined up for themselves. But they didn't plan on anything other than failure or success."

She looked at me with a puzzled expression.

"They had no plan for a delay, no plan for Elvis killing their messenger!" I said to her.

"What does that mean?" she asked.

"It means the release, if it had happened as planned, would have resulted in the hostages being freed in Dusseldorf. If it hadn't happened on schedule, the hostages would have been killed in Dusseldorf. But they lost Majmun, so something about that delayed them. Leaving them exposed for too long in that warehouse. They had to change their plans."

"Why did they bring the hostages here, though?" she asked.

"I don't know. They needed to move them. That's certain. Three days in one place is a long time when you are hiding from CIA, satellites, and every other intelligence agency on the planet," I said, rubbing the back of my head as if it would stimulate more data.

"Maybe they always planned on bringing them here, but the timing got screwed up. It was risky though. Two train cars being pulled by a small yard engine would be noticeable. That probably explains the speed. They were pushing that thing hard. They didn't want daytime eyes seeing it."

I looked out over the horizon again. That patch of bright ground caught my attention again. "Are there any airports here?" I asked Kathrin.

She pulled out my phone and tapped and swished her finger across the face of it for a few seconds. "No. There is nothing listed for Mimon. But the satellite view does show a runway…a big one."

As soon as she said that, I remembered why Mimon was a familiar name. During the Cold War, Jovanovich had worked for the Soviet military. Mimon was listed as one of the Cold War bases on a cross reference list that Bonbon had linked to my research files.

"Look up 'Mimon Base,'" I said.

She tapped and swished her finger. "A Soviet training base was located here. It was abandoned in 1992—huh," she said.

"What?"

"It seems the name Mimon translates to 'purposely forgotten,'" she said, musing.

"Well someone didn't forget it," I said, letting her in on my newest theory. "I bet Jovanovich was stationed here."

She raised an eyebrow. "It's worth checking," she said.

"Okay. Let's go down and snoop around," I said, mounting the scooter.

Kathrin stopped and looked around the ruins and the vast view before climbing on back. "It's beautiful here," she said and then held up my phone and snapped a couple of pictures.

Once on the back of the scooter, she held the phone out away from us, snapping a photo of the two of us with the vista in the background.

We rode down the hillside and into town, where we located a petrol station and a small restaurant. Kathrin went in to tidy up in the restaurant bathroom as I filled the tank on the scooter. It didn't take long; it barely took three liters.

When I was done, I strolled in and met her at a table by the window. She leaned close to me across the table. "They will not be surprised by a German tourist here, but an American will draw attention. You will be the talk of the town in an hour if you open your mouth," she whispered.

I nodded and made the 'zipped lip' motion across my mouth.

Kathrin ordered for us in German and informed the waitress that we would be taking the food with us instead of eating in. The waitress seemed to understand well enough when asked for sandwiches, coffee, beer, a few extra hearty rolls, and some sausages to tuck in the bag for later.

It was a few minutes before our order was ready. While we were waiting, Kathrin was doing her best to make out a conversation two tables behind her. Several old men were sitting around the table eating slices of cold sausage and drinking coffee.

She looked at me and smiled as she adjusted her head to listen in.

When our food arrived, Kathrin paid and we rose to leave. The waitress said something to us. I saw Kathrin smile and nod, so I did the same and then repeated "*Danke*" when Kathrin did, so the woman wouldn't think I was a mute.

Before we walked out, Kathrin turned back to the waitress and asked her a question. The woman pointed out the window and down the street and made a curving gesture with her hand as she answered her in halting German.

Outside, I turned to ask what that was about, but she gave me a warning look, indicating that we were still too close to the restaurant. I pulled the empty thermos from our carry-on bag, and Kathrin poured both cups of coffee into it. She stowed it back in the bag, followed by our food, zipped the bag closed, and hopped on the scooter.

As we sped out of town, she leaned forward and pressed her lips against my ear.

"Go right here," she said, pointing at a side street at the edge of town.

I complied, and in a few moments we were in front of a sprawling mill facility. It seemed to be abandoned except for a small building at the end closest to town.

There were several small pickup trucks in front of the building and men carrying what looked like bags of agricultural lime from the building and stacking them in the backs of the vehicles or on wagons.

Farmers, I thought. *Picking up fertilizer.*

"Why are we here?" I asked.

"In the shop, the old men were talking about Russians at the mill," she said. "I don't speak Czech, so I only caught a few words, '*Mlynske*,' '*Ruske*,' and '*krute*.' They didn't seem to be happy about the visitors."

I drove the scooter down the road a little further so we were out of sight of the farmers and then pulled up to a large warehouse structure. We got off and I leaned the scooter against the wall.

The tracks running beside the mill were overgrown with tall weeds, but I noticed that some of them had recently been crushed on the rails.

I pointed at the crushed grass on the rails. "Something came through here recently," I said. "The grass is still wet on the rail."

She nodded her agreement.

We walked along the tracks until we reached a spur that went behind a covered loading dock, and then we approached the side wall of the building carefully and looked through a window.

The rail cars!

We ducked back quickly and silently celebrated a moment of glee. When I had settled my heart rate, I raised up to look again. The doors of the container were open. I looked from side to side and saw no one.

We crept further down the outside wall and peeked in the window.

Nothing.

There was no one to be seen.

We quietly walked to the back of the building and found a door with no door knob. I looked through the hole and once satisfied there was no movement inside, I pushed it open.

The hinges squealed loudly.

FUCK, that was loud!

We froze and paused a few seconds to see if there was a reaction to our entry. When we heard no guns, yells, or footsteps running toward us, we entered the building.

I carefully approached the shipping container, which was chained to the flat bed car, and then hopped up on the deck. I looked around the inside of the box entrance and saw that the explosives were all gone.

I walked around to the side and reached my hand into the hole I had placed the phone through. It was still there. I pulled it out and shook it. Water came out. I turned to show Kathrin, but she was sneaking onto the passenger car.

I followed her up the steps and looked around the compartment. In the corner was a rifle and an ammunition belt. Kathrin walked over to it and started to pick it up when behind her the bathroom door opened and a large dark-haired man walked out.

He paused, surprised, and then tried to reach for the gun, but Kathrin was closer and grabbed it first. The man kicked it away.

She jumped up and flung her boot-clad foot toward the man's face, but he caught her by the leg and slammed her to the ground with a bang, dropping his weight on top of her.

He hadn't noticed me at the far end with his attention focused on Kathrin, so he didn't see me racing down the aisle toward them until it was too late. He reached for his belt, fishing for the knife there, but he looked up just in time to see me flying through the air at him.

All he could do was put his arm up as my foot went crashing down on his head. His arm caught most of the blow, but Kathrin used the freedom to punch him in the throat.

The reflex action of putting his hand to his throat gave me a clear shot at his head, and I punched him in the temple with all my weight behind me.

POW!

He went limp on top of Kathrin. "Get him off of me!" she yelled in anger and panic. She was kicking and pushing to extract herself. I flipped him onto his side, and she scooted backwards away from him.

That was a strong emotional reaction, I thought, but I didn't waste any time pondering it. "Are you hurt?" I asked, squatting down next to her.

She checked arms, legs, head. "Ouch," she said.

I pulled her hair up and looked at the back of her head. There was a lump, but the skin had not been broken. The man on the floor moaned and started to roll off his side. I punched him hard in the face again.

It really hurts to punch someone in the face. It doesn't feel much better to be punched, but my hand was aching and skin had been pulled from my knuckles.

When Kathrin was able to get up under her own power, I began trying to locate something to tie the big guy down with.

"Help me find something to tie him down," I said.

I found nothing suitable in the passenger car, but Kathrin

had left the rail car to search around the floor of the mill building. She found a roll of baling wire in a corner, grabbed it, and returned. Our prisoner was still out.

I set him up in one of the high-backed seats and began wrapping the baling wire around his limbs, using my multi tool to cut the heavy gage metal wire and then twisting the ends together with its pliers.

By the time he woke the next time, he was securely wired to the seat, including his head. I had learned this was an important consideration when restraining someone—a lesson taught to me by Majmun in Amsterdam.

I had a piece of duct tape ready for his mouth if he cried out. He did not. He looked at me and then looked at Kathrin and a crease formed in his brow.

"CIA?" he asked.

I looked at Kathrin. "Why does everyone think I'm CIA?" I asked.

She shrugged.

I looked back at the man. "No. Not CIA. Computer programmer," I stated plainly.

The crease in his forehead got deeper. He was confused. The accent had sounded Russian to me, but I'm no expert. I decided to test my theory.

"Serbian?" I asked him.

"Bah!" He spat in disgust. "Russian." His chest puffed out against the wire.

"Rodka?" I asked.

He was stunned. "How do you know this name?" he asked, bewildered, looking as if he had been left out of some important conversation.

"I know Elvis," I said, starting to build the boundaries of the game. Now was the time for the puzzle master to turn the tables.

He was suddenly angry. "That bastard betrayed us."

"No. Majmun betrayed you," I stated coldly. "Right before he died." Not a complete lie. It had been Majmun's phone that gave me their location.

He blinked again. "The Monkey?" Again shocked by my information. "I can tell you are American. Are you sure you are not CIA?" he asked.

I smiled. "I'm sure." I sat across from him, face softened and hands open, signaling honesty. "Majmun went to the house in Amsterdam. Elvis, the girls, and I were there," I said, weaving the story in a way that benefited me but would stand up to scrutiny if it was checked out. "Majmun was to kill all the Russians left there after the lot of you left for Dusseldorf."

"I don't believe you. These are just names you heard. You are on fishing trip," he said, looking hard to see my reaction.

I pulled my shirt off and then tore the bandages away from my chest, arm, and shoulder to show him my burns. His face softened and he nodded as best he could with his head wired back. He recognized the work.

"Is Elvis alive?" he asked, genuine concern in his tone.

I nodded. "He saved us all."

The Russian's eyebrows went up. "Elvis killed Majmun?"

I nodded. "He told me to find Rodka if I could and tell him, 'We were betrayed.'" I looked at him, holding my eyes steady for him to read the 'truth' in them.

The pieces were slowly starting to come together for our prisoner. It would be easy for him to believe anything negative about the Serbs. I recognized him as the big man who had been arguing with the shorter Serb on the dock in Dusseldorf. In fact, I'd bet I could get him to believe anything I wanted him to about them.

His eyes stared out into nothing, darting back and forth, trying to grasp all that had been said, and then a hesitant look spread across his face. One last assault of skepticism—half-hearted.

"I don't believe you. This is trick. I will not speak any more," he said with finality. But I could see he was nearly there.

I pulled out my phone and dialed.

"*Da*." Elvis answered on the other end.

"It's Scott," I said. It took him a moment to reply, no doubt because he still thought of me as Alex.

It registered. "Scott! How are you, my friend? Did you find your girl?" he asked cheerfully, genuinely happy to hear from me.

"Almost. We are close. I have a friend of yours here. I was trying to explain to him about Majmun, how you saved us all and asked me to warn Rodka when I found Barb. But I think he needs to hear it from you."

There was a pause. His mind wrapped around what I was telling him. "*Da*! Put him on."

I pressed the phone against the big Russian's ear. "*Da*," he said, his face hard, looking at me suspiciously.

I could hear the voice of the other end. A short statement and then a "*Da*" from the big man. Each new piece of information softened his expression a little more. The tone of his voice became more questioning, less harsh.

He looked up at me from time to time. Trying to picture the *Scott* in the story he was being told, no doubt. Then something was said that made him very unhappy. His face got hard again, and I heard Russian words which must have been some sort of swear. Then he nodded, said. "*Da*," and looked at me.

I put the phone back to my ear. "Elvis?"

"My friend. I must thank you. I have been crazy trying to think of way to warn Rodka. You have again shown you are good friend. The man you have is Daniil. He is enforcer. Very dedicated to my brother. He will help you if it means saving him."

"Thank you, Elvis. I hope your family is with you again soon," I said sincerely.

When the call was completed, I looked at the big man in front of me, waiting for some indication of his state of mind. "Well, untie me, lover boy! We have to find way to get Serbs away from your girlfriend." His face broke into a broad, toothy grin.

I cut him loose with my multi tool and stood back while he rubbed the circulation back into his hands and arms.

"I'm Daniil," he said finally, reaching his hand out to me.

"Daniil. I'm pleased to meet you. I'm Scott," I said.

Kathrin was a little less enthusiastic about the sudden change in tone, but she joined in with the new pleasantries. "Kathrin," she said curtly.

Daniil looked at her and smiled. "You hit good for girl."

He turned his neck from side to side and winced when the side of his face touched his shoulder. "You hit pretty good too," he said to me, working his jaw back and forth.

Daniil proceeded to tell us everything he knew. "Popovich, the one in charge, said for me to hide train cars and engine," he said. "Then go in town and listen for if we got clean away."

"Elvis said Popovich doesn't really trust you and the others," I said, adding more division to the stew. "Why would he send you alone?"

"Serbs would stick out here," he replied. "Russian is like second language in towns like this. Rodka even knows this town, he was going to go, but Popovich said, 'No, you stay with me. Send Daniil. He causes trouble anyway.' So they send me."

"Rodka knows the town?" I asked.

"*Da*. He was stationed here," Daniil disclosed. "And Jovanovich had business here for Soviets. Popovich as well."

That's the connection, I thought. "What sort of business would Jovanovich have with the Russians?" I asked.

"Civilian militia," Daniil said, curling his lip in disgust. "No more than informer and criminal using work for army as excuse to rape and pillage."

I nodded my understanding. There had already been a level of distrust between the groups before the hostages were taken.

I looked up at the cargo box the hostages had been in.

"The explosives are gone," I said. He looked at me, his eyes reduced to suspicious slits. "I followed you from Dusseldorf," I replied. "I saw the container in the warehouse there."

Daniil laughed. "Rodka said to set up cameras outside," he said with a grin. "Serbs said 'No. We won't be here that long,'" and then winked at me.

My heart skipped a beat thinking how differently this would have gone if they had listened to Rodka.

"Da. Explosives were packed up and taken with hostages," he said. "And all the food, water, blankets, yah, yah, yah," he replied. "But I don't think they use them. I think they go soon."

"What makes you think that?" I asked.

He shrugged. "Just hunch," he replied. "But when they send me here, they told others to walk airfield. Clear any debris."

I nodded.

"I figure they bring plane and take everyone with," he continued. "But looks like they plan on killing us along with hostages," he said, shaking his head, a sneer building on his face. "I have to go back and warn Rodka."

"Is Rodka the type to fly into a rage and do something crazy?" I asked.

Daniil shook his head. "Not Rodka, but others will. They

would start shooting at hint of betrayal."

"Then do us both a favor and wait until you can get Rodka alone to tell him," I said.

He thought about it second and then nodded in somber agreement. He knew hot heads would not prevail. I had to give him credit—for an enforcer who had just been subdued by a girl and a computer geek, he seemed fairly clear-headed himself. I guessed we were lucky it was him we nabbed in the train and not one of the others.

"Come," he said. "I show you sneaky way back to the base."

"We have to grab our stuff," I said as we exited the passenger car.

I let Daniil walk in front of us, just in case there was any lingering resentment. Better safe than sorry.

**

I rolled the scooter into the mill, and then Kathrin and I began transferring supplies from the carry-on bags to our pack and shoulder bags. Before shouldering mine, I also rolled a generous portion of bailing wire into a loose spool and tucked it in.

When we were ready, Daniil led us down an overgrown road to the back side of the base.

Cracked asphalt, barely visible through the grass growing through it, led us past ruined buildings and mounds of dirt surrounded by wire fencing—contaminated soil no doubt. Russian military bases were not famous for ecological friendliness.

We stopped well away from the barracks.

"Wait here until dark." Daniil said. "There is old command building." He pointed at a one-story building at the center of several barracks, and then he set out toward the barracks by himself.

We watched as he approached the building. As he got closer, two armed men came out to greet him. They talked for a moment.

Voices were raised. Something was wrong.

The men talking to Daniil lifted their weapons and pointed them at him. He protested loudly but finally dropped his weapon. As they escorted him away from the door they had come out of, two more men came out, and then a third.

Russians, I thought to myself.

One followed the two holding Daniil, shouting after them. There was a heated exchange but the first two men turned and continued to usher Daniil down the pathway to another entrance in the same building.

The man who had run after them stopped and watched, puffed on his cigarette, and then threw it angrily to the ground.

"That must be Rodka," I whispered to Kathrin. He stormed back into the barracks, followed closely by the other two.

Kathrin and I waited, not knowing how to react. Our inside man had been captured and might be tortured to reveal us any second now. We decided to stay on plan for the moment. We checked and rechecked our gear, waiting for dark. If nothing else, we'd be closer to the hostages in the other building.

We watched for signs of any additional activity outside the

barracks. There was none. When dark finally came, we crept to the back side of what appeared to be a small administrative office building and entered through a broken window on the side away from the barracks.

Inside, there were metal desks and filing cabinets overturned, emptied, broken. There was graffiti covering nearly all the interior walls and signs of a campfire or two in the center of the floor in a couple of the offices.

We moved through the building quietly, careful about where we stepped for fear of breaking glass or knocking into anything which could make noise. Once we were on the side facing the barracks, we peered through a window to see if there was any activity.

Through one set of covered windows, we saw hints of firelight in the barracks across the yard. The light danced on the walls through the window. We saw very little else.

Occasionally one of the men—we assumed he was a Serb—exited the door they had taken Daniil through. He would walk down to the other entrance and chat with someone there and then return to his own door. Around 11:00 p.m. Rodka walked out of the building, striding toward the other door with purpose in his steps.

"Uh oh," I whispered.

Kathrin nodded. "Yah," she whispered in reply. "This will be ugly."

Rodka entered and there followed all manner of raised voices and crashing noises. After a few minutes, both men came out, arguing. The Serb who had been guarding Daniil was falling backwards over himself yelling at the Russian. He raised his rifle threateningly, but hesitated. Rodka stepped forward, pushed the rifle aside and slapped the Serb hard across the face.

This is a change, I thought to myself.

The Serb fell to the ground, rubbing his face, and reached for his rifle, but Rodka had his handgun pointed at the man's head before he could complete his action.

The man raised his voice again. Rodka replied by spitting on the ground and then waved his gun at the man on the ground, indicating he should leave.

The Serb grabbed his rifle and ran, looking back over his shoulder to be sure he would not be shot in the back. Rodka watched as he left and then ran to the door that Daniil had been taken through as soon as the runner had disappeared into the other end of the building.

"Rodka is a badass," I said.

"He won't be able to help us if he gets himself killed," Kathrin replied.

"True. But if Rodka gets killed, the rest of the Russians will be next," I replied. "If nothing else, that reduces the number of bad guys we have to deal with."

It suddenly occurred to me how cold and calculating I sounded…and even more startling to me was how easily it came out. Kathrin nodded her agreement of my assessment. It made me look at her with raised awareness as well.

Trust her, whispered my other voice into my ear. I could feel my mind relax that time.

Quite right. No time to worry about imagined issues.

There was a lull in action for a few minutes, and then the Serb reemerged from the barracks followed by two others. It was dark, but I could tell that one of the men had some sort of deformity or scar on his jaw and neck.

"Popovich!" I whispered.

Kathrin nodded her agreement.

The three Serbs strode into the far door and reemerged, shoving Rodka. Rodka turned, yelling at the three of them. The argument was heated. I was beginning to wonder if there was going to be bloodshed, but I was surprised a few minutes later. While Rodka and the three Serbs argued, Daniil came walking out of the door, rubbing his wrists.

Rodka had been with Daniil long enough to learn about what had happened with Elvis, Majmun, and myself. I wondered how far Daniil had gotten before the Serbs interrupted. Daniil had fresh bruises and cuts on his face that hadn't come from me.

Then it dawned on me. "Damn!" I said.

"What?" Kathrin asked.

"The bruises on his face. That's what gave him away," I whispered.

Her eyes went wide. I couldn't believe I missed such an obvious detail. He probably told them he fell. Nothing like a bad lie to raise suspicions.

"He seems to be free now, and they aren't storming us. Do you think Rodka knows now?" she asked.

"I would think so. There'd be no reason for Daniil not to tell him, especially since he was tied up and obviously beaten."

The men continued to argue as Daniil joined Rodka at his side. The volume of the argument gradually decreased and a fragile peace seemed to take hold as the Serbs walked past Rodka and Daniil into the barracks.

Rodka leaned close to Daniil and placed his hand on his shoulder, saying something to him in confidence. Daniil nodded enthusiastically and followed through the same door the Serbs had just walked through.

Rodka turned to follow but turned his head in our direction as he walked. For a moment I thought he was looking right at us.

"He knows," I said.

"What will we do if he betrays us?"

"I don't think he'd do that. He now knows the Serbs probably plan to do away with them as well as the hostages if things go bad," I said, pausing to run a couple of scenarios through my head. "But even if he does, I'm pretty sure the cavalry will be here soon...if they aren't already."

"What does this mean—'cavalry?'" she asked.

"Backup. The good guys charging in to save the day," I explained.

"What good guys? How do you know this?" she asked incredulously.

"I sent our friends at the CIA a message."

"When did you do that? Why didn't you tell me?" she asked, annoyed.

"You were right there when I did it," I said with a grin. "Before we left the train, I told the steward that our horses were being stolen."

"Is that code? How is that a message to the CIA?" Kathrin asked, not seeing the connection.

"Where is your passport?" I asked.

She patted her pocket and then her eyes went wide as she remembered that they were taken by the ticket collector when we entered our sleeping compartment.

"The train," she said, still not understanding.

"When the train arrives at its destination, the passports left over will be reported to the US consulate in Prague and the German government," I said, letting that sink in before I continued. "As soon as the passports are entered in the system, it will alert the CIA—they've been trying to track us…or at least me, anyway."

"So they will know we got off the train in Decin. How does that get them here?" she asked.

"When we left the train, I told the steward, 'They are stealing my horses,' my guess is he was on the radio to the police before we bought our scooter. But even if he wasn't, the CIA would interview him because he was the steward on our car."

A look of understanding passed across her face. "So if they know we got off when the livestock car was detached, they can use their satellites to look back where the train cars ended," she said, piecing it together.

"Right! They probably even have great footage of us on the scooter following them."

"The Russians will not play nice if they know the CIA is involved," she said, a dark tone in her voice.

"I agree. But we had no way of knowing the Russians would be an asset. I think we ought to—"

I was interrupted by a vehicle approaching. Two Range Rovers pulled up to the barracks beneath the covered entryway and eight men piled out, stretching talking loudly. Laughing!

Shit, I thought to myself. *More Serbs.*

Some of them went inside, and a few moments later, some came back out, laughing and back slapping with the new arrivals.

Reinforcements? I wondered.

Several of the men walked to the back of the Range Rovers and began unloading boxes, taking them inside the barracks where the hostages were. Inside it sounded like a party. It seems the new arrivals had brought good news of some sort.

I pulled my burn-phone out and slipped the earbud into my ear. I pressed the icon for Storc's Bluetooth emulator. The status gage showed a scan taking place, and after a few seconds, it popped up with two viable Bluetooth connections—one was active. I clicked on it to see if I could listen in.

"I'm st-ll in the fucking city," a man's voice protested. The voice sounded familiar, but the range on the Bluetooth was at its maximum distance—the signal was very broken and digitally squelched.

"Then I'd sug--st you -et out of the city before the passengers an- -he package arri--," said the other voice.

"You -an't jus- -ake this des---on unitlateral-. We -ad –n agreement." The signal began to break up.

"There ar-- three more ----ages. w- stil-- ave a deal." The signal died.

I tried to reconnect. I hit the link a dozen or more times with no success. He must have moved.

Someone was being warned out of the city.

What city? Mimon? I thought. *I wouldn't exactly call that a city.*

Someone had made a unilateral decision.

An agreement broken.

Three more? Still have a deal? I wondered. *Three more what?*

I added the new data to my flow chart. Too many missing pieces to get an answer.

Kathrin and I sat in silence, watching as men drifted in and out of the building. Some had bottles of liquor, taking heavy draughts and then passing them along to the next man.

"Looks like they are celebrating something," I said.

"Drunk men are easier to subdue." She replied as if she had done it before.

"But there are more now than before," I added.

"Yah," she replied. "There's that."

After a while, three of the Russians exited the front door, rifles in hand, to take up post at the corners of the building. They were to be on guard duty while the Serbs celebrated their news...whatever that news was.

The Russians seemed unfazed by the slight. Truth be told, they seemed a bit relieved to be away from the new influx of Serbs. They watched the activity from a distance, lighting up cigarettes and alternating between watching the tree line around them and the party behind them.

A short while later, we heard screaming and some ruckus from inside the barracks. A moment more, and one of the Serbs exited, clearly drunk, dragging a woman by the arm behind him. They were heading our direction.

He would take a step or two forward, then the woman—no, a girl—would pull backwards, sending him off balance. He would jerk her forward again. This happened several times on the way toward our hiding spot.

When he'd finally had enough, he turned and struck her across the face.

I almost jumped up out of my hiding place.

She shrieked in pain and fear and then submitted and followed the rest of the way without struggle.

As they got closer, I could hear her sobbing. It was Michelle, the ambassador's daughter. I'm ashamed to admit I had a moment of relief that it wasn't Barb. Then it dawned on me that if it had been Barb, I could have her free in only a few moments.

Kathrin backed away from the window quietly, anger in her face. I looked at her and shook my head. "Wait for it," I whispered.

She nodded, swallowing down her fury.

I quietly walked to the front room, careful not to make any noise, and then ducked behind the door just as the Serb and his prey entered the room.

He shoved her roughly, positioning her face down over a metal desk in the foyer, and then he began to unfasten her pants. He pulled them down to the middle of her thighs and began undoing his own.

I silently stepped out from behind the door and approached him from behind. She was thrashing and kicking, forcing him to hold her with one hand while he fiddled with his own belt with the other.

I was about to jump on his back when I saw the gun on his belt.

It tipped backwards toward me as he unfastened his belt and began to let it fall. He was still blissfully unaware of me, his mind instead focused on his spoils. I reached down quickly and lifted it from the holster. He turned just as I lifted the gun to his head.

He stopped motionless. Then his hands slowly started to rise. When they reached the midway point he made a quick motion to turn, but he failed to complete it. Kathrin had come down hard on his head with a piece of wood, sending him sprawling to the ground face first, unconscious, pants down around his ankles.

The girl screamed and twisted away from us, pulling her pants up with one hand and supporting herself in her retreat with the other.

She fell over the opposite side of the desk and then looked

around—first at her attacker, lying sprawled on the floor, and then up at me and Kathrin.

She jumped up, running to Kathrin, and then threw her arms around her.

Kathrin shushed her. I shushed her. She stopped crying long enough to look at me, measuring me as I rolled the big Serb over and started to bind him with the coil of bailing wire I had taken from the mill.

She watched me for a moment, blinking her tears away. "Are you CIA?" she asked.

Kathrin and I couldn't help but chuckle. Confusion spread across her face.

"No," I said. "I'm Barb's boyfriend."

Her eyes opened wide. "Scott?" She asked, unbelieving. "Why are you here? Where is the rescue team?"

"I believe they are on their way," I replied comfortingly.

"How did you find us?" she asked.

"Shhh," I said gesturing for her to lower her voice.

"Low friends in lower places," I whispered. "But more importantly, as far as they are concerned," I said, gesturing with my thumb toward the barracks. "he is still in here having a private party with you."

She broke free of Kathrin and walked over to the Serb and stared at him for a moment, a blank look on her face—and then suddenly began kicking him in the side and head. Kathrin and I rushed to restrain her. She started crying again.

"Shh. Shh, shhh," Kathrin shushed. "It's okay, it's *okay*. It's over now."

ten
The Event

Shortly after midnight, Sunday, May 16th, 2010 - Ralsko Airbase, Czech Republic

Kathrin sank to the floor with the girl's head cradled to her breast, stroking her hair and placing her lips to the top of her head. She began to rock the girl back and forth as if she were an infant being lulled to sleep.

Kathrin looked up to watch as I moved the Serb into our office. I finished wiring him to a metal chair, wrapping duct tape around his head and covering his mouth. In Majmun fashion, I stuck a board behind the man, wiring it to the back of the seat, and then I wired the man's head to the board. There would be no movement unless he decided to turn the chair over on its side, more than likely resulting in broken fingers, thanks to the way I had bound him.

"What will we do with her—and him?" she asked, nodding at our uninvited visitor.

I thought for a moment. "I think we need to talk to the cavalry and let them know what's going on," I said finally.

A thoughtful look crossed her face, and she nodded once.

I pulled my phone out, reached into my pocket for John Temple's card, and dialed.

"Temple," he said in almost a whisper.

"Captain," I said. "It's Scott Wolfe."

There was a pause. "Scott. It's good to hear from you. Where are you?" he asked.

"I suspect you know where I am if you got my message," I said, taunting. "Where are you?"

Another pause. "Close," he whispered.

"Before you do anything, there are some things you need to be aware of," I said, hinting that he didn't have all the data I did.

Another pause. It occurred to me that the pause was happening because of a time delay. His communications were most likely being relayed through some communications server and encrypted—possibly all the way to Langley.

"Okay," he said and then hung up.

Strange, I thought.

Just then, four dark figures rose out of the darkness as if they were shadows rising from the floor. Startled, Kathrin began to move to her feet, but I put my hand out to her, signaling calm.

She relaxed her stance a bit, and then Michelle stirred, looking around, a look of panic on her face. She was about to cry out, but Kathrin put her hand over her mouth gently and said in a whisper, "It's okay."

Two of the shadowy figures moved to the center of the room and two took up guard positions, one at the door, and one at the window. The two closest to us lifted night vision goggles off their heads and pulled off their hoods. I recognized one of them.

"SB," I said, nodding to the man who had roughed me up in the alley in Amsterdam. Quiet chuckles came from the other three—a snarl came from SB.

"I'm sorry. I don't get the joke," I said sincerely. Apparently SB stood for something insulting. "What should I call you?" I asked.

"Nothing," he said in disgust and turned to kneel next to the ambassador's daughter and Kathrin. The other man who had uncloaked in front of us turned to me and smiled. "Don't mind him. He's still smarting from the broken nose you gave him," he said in a whisper.

So I *had* broken his nose! Good for me.

"Lieutenant Marsh. US Navy," he said, extending his hand to shake mine.

SEALs! "Pleased to meet you, Lieutenant. Scott Wolfe," I replied, shaking his hand.

"You've done a hell of a job, Mr. Wolfe," he said turning and looking at the Serb wired to the chair. He spoke into his throat mic. "Momma, this is Arrow. Monkey Wrench gift wrapped a bad guy for us. Instructions, over," he said quietly.

"Monkey Wrench. That must be me," I said smiling.

Marsh smiled and nodded. "A useful tool that can fix many things or smash them to pieces."

I nodded, smiling. I approved.

We were close enough I could hear the voice in his earpiece. "Arrow. Condition of bad guy. Over."

Marsh looked at the man, lifted an eyelid with a thumb, and then spoke. "Momma. Bad guy is unconscious, wired to a metal chair. Over."

"Wait one," the voice replied. A few seconds later. "Arrow. Is location secure for forward movement? Over."

"Affirmative Momma. Location Secure. Over."

"Moving forward. Out."

SB was giving Michelle water from his CamelBak water reservoir and checking her physical condition. Marsh was looking the prisoner over. He injected something into his neck and began cutting the wire from his arms, legs, and head. He looked at the cut and raised bump on his head and then turned and looked at me with a smile. I motioned my head toward Kathrin to let him know that I couldn't take credit for it. He looked at her and chuckled.

He slipped back towards me. "You two take the prize for best amateur operatives," he said with an amused smile.

Just then four more men showed up through the back of the building. There was a huddle and then two of them moved to guard positions elsewhere in the building.

One of them approached me. His hood came off, revealing John Temple. His clean-shaven face and square jaw smiled broadly as he surveyed the scene. He extended his hand to me. "Scott, I'm glad you called when you did. Things were about to get loud around here."

"There are a couple of things you need to know," I said quietly.

"Okay. Shoot," he said

"The vehicles that pulled up a while ago. There were eight more Serbs in them."

"Damn." Temple swore. "We saw the vehicles," he said, pointing up to the ceiling.

Satellite. I understood his meaning.

"But the porticos built by the Russians were designed to hide entry and exit from above."
Temple looked at Marsh, prompting Marsh to come over and squat down next to us.

"Bad odds. That brings the total to seventeen bad guys," Marsh said.

I quickly interjected. "Maybe not." They looked at me, ready to hear more. "The five Russians may be assets," I said.

"Explain," Temple said.

"See that big Russian on the corner? The one with all the bruises on his face?" I asked. Temple nodded.

"That's Daniil. Nice guy. A little slow, but faithful. We bumped into him back at the mill."

Marsh and Temple's eyebrows went up in unison.

"Kathrin and I sat him down and had a little talk with him. The Russian boss has a brother in Amsterdam. He's the one who killed Majmun. I called the brother, Elvis, and let him talk to Daniil. When we let him go, he came back here, and the Serbs reinforced my propaganda by beating him more."

"Risky," Marsh said.

"Agreed. But if we play it right, at the very least we might be able to get the Russians to sit out the fight," I replied.

Marsh and Temple looked at each other for a beat, and then Marsh turned back and looked at me. "Are you sure you aren't CIA?" he asked with a grin.

I couldn't help but chuckle.

"That still leaves twelve." John said.

"Eleven," I corrected, pointing at the lump on the floor.

"Right," he said. "Better. But we should try to whittle it down a bit more before we move in force."

"In force" is what worried me. I needed to try and inject some non-violence into this discussion.

"Let me try and get the Russians either out of the picture or on our side."

"I don't like it, boss," I heard SB say from across the room.

"I tend to agree with you on this one, Nick." John replied.

Nick, I thought, making a mental note. "If I can get Daniil over here without him seeing you, I can let him know it's going down. Maybe we can figure out how they stand."

John thought about that for a moment. Then he clicked his

throat mic. "Papa, this is Momma. Over."

"Go for Papa," I heard through his earpiece.

"Monkey Wrench informs five Rusky bad guys may be assets. Instruction. Over," he said quietly.

There was a long pause and then I heard a different voice. "Momma. This is Papa actual. You're on the ground. It's your call."

John exchanged a look with Lt. Marsh, who shrugged. "Papa—will advise. Out."

"Okay, Scott. You've got one chance to get them on board, either out of the fight or in the fight on our side. No hesitation, no waffling, no time to decide. Once chance." John said with a serious warning tone to his voice. "If it doesn't go your way, we take the Russians first since they are clued in, and then the Serbs."

I nodded, and then something occurred to me. "Why are the Serbs celebrating?"

John paused a second, trying to decide if he should tell me. "Jovanovich was released."

I couldn't believe my ears. Everything I've ever heard about how the US deals with terrorists suddenly turned upside down. My flow chart started self-filling; answers were starting to pour into my head. "I didn't think we did that kind of thing," I said, confused.

"We don't usually," John said. "But the deputy mission chief pushed hard at State to exert pressure on The Hague."

"Deputy Chief? Miller? How did he manage that?" I asked.

"Miller is in charge. The ambassador's daughter is a hostage, so he's stepped aside. The deputy chief—the Charge d'Affaires—is second in command." John replied, his flat tone revealing his disapproval.

"When was Jovanovich being released?" I asked, a pattern forming in my head.

John looked at his watch. "He's already gone. Left more than two hours ago."

"How is he leaving the Hague?" I continued.

He hesitated a second, then relented. "There was an old Russian cargo helo waiting on a chopper pad for him just outside the city. Armored SUVs would have convoyed out to the pad and then he would have taken off for destinations unknown," he said.

"Do you have tracking on the chopper?" I asked.

"Where is all this leading?" he asked, getting impatient with my data-gathering process.

"We are on an abandoned military airbase out in the country with no active bases anywhere nearby. They chose a cargo helicopter, when a small transport chopper or a jet would be faster and easier to lose on radar," I said. "How many personnel can it carry?"

John had enough info to keep him interested. "About one hundred including the crew."

"Do you know of any other movement by the Serb mob?" I asked, speeding up my process.

"Movement?" John asked.

"Movement. Abandoned operations, weapons shipments, groups of men moving out of one place and into another, synchronized showering, anything unusual. Movement!" I pushed.

"Prague was cleared out. Not even our informers were left. Most were killed or disappeared," he replied, swallowing some agitation.

"And what is the arrangement for the return of the hostages?" I asked.

"Same chopper returns with the hostages and lands just outside the Hague." John replied, showing his frustration with how this was shaking out. "We were pretty pissed off about that, but Miller negotiated the exchange terms. He wouldn't even take the calls from Langley advising him."

A noise in John's earpiece distracted him. "Acknowledged," he said into his throat mic. He looked up. "We have incoming air traffic."

A confused look passed across Lt. Marsh's face. "It's too soon for the chopper."

Just then, there was a roar overhead. Everyone looked up in unison. Heavy aircraft. Not a chopper, a plane.

We looked out the window just in time to see the field landing lights fill the night air with a sheen and the dark shadow of a large, four-engine plane disappear below the roof line of the row of barracks between us and the runway.

"Secondary transport?" Marsh offered.

"I don't know." John replied.

My flow chart flashed before my eyes and the auto-fill

process started again. All the new information coalesced with the arrival of the giant transport plane. New pieces of data suddenly jumped into places that had been blank before. Hostages, cargo helicopter, arms dealers, new cargo plane, Miller's secret, the words "package" and "three more."

And then there was the new oddity in my head, that voice, which simply said, *nuke*.

"This is a setup for a terrorist attack," I said confidently.

All eyes turned to me. "Explain." John said plainly, open to any explanation for the turn of events.

"How did Jovanovich get caught? Weapons theft?" I asked, leading him down my line of logic.

"He got caught in Bruges. No bombs, no chemical weapons, no bio weapons," John replied.

"No weapons, no depot?" I asked.

"Captain," Lt. Marsh interjected. "I was in Gori when the Russians rolled in. They were almost an hour getting to the Georgian base after they bombed it. And one column of Serb vehicles did make it off the base before the tanks started shelling."

"Gori," I said to myself.

"Yes," Marsh replied firmly. "The Russians bombed the shit out of Gori, moved in, and then left three days later. Crazy shit."

My flowchart popped up new data for me to see.

"Nadiradze," I said, staring blankly at the floor as my brain pulled some old line of information from an article on the fall of the Soviet Union.

"What?" John asked.

I looked at him. "Alexander Nadiradze. Father of modern mobile nuclear missile design," I replied. "He was born in Gori. He worked in Gori."

"I don't need wild supposition. I need facts and I need them fast, because unlike you, I don't have the ability to magically look into that plane and see a terrorist attack!"

"I think you'll find that one or more tactical warheads just landed on this airfield," I replied, jumping to the conclusion my flowchart had just come up with.

There was a pause as everyone absorbed that information. "Cargo chopper, mystery cargo plane, Bosnian Serb war criminal and arms dealer in Gori, window shopping at a base during a bombing campaign, now being released and coming here," I said and then paused, letting the pieces come together in his head. I could tell by the look on his face he wasn't convinced. "Where is Deputy Miller?"

"What? What difference does that make?" he replied incredulously.

Marsh looked at John again. "The name of the agent in charge of the Gori detail was 'Miller,'" he said, as belief started shaping his responses.

"The Deputy Chief used to be CIA," John said quietly. "We worked with the same station chief."

"He set up the boat tour, he negotiated the return of Jovanovich, he may have been in Gori. Where is he now? I'll bet you a steak dinner he's not in The Hague." I said forcefully, feigning more confidence in my theory than I actually had.

A light of understanding clicked in John's eyes. He depressed the switch on his throat mic. "Papa, this is Momma. Request location Tulip. Over."

"Momma, Papa. Verify, request location Tulip Actual? Over." Came the voice.

Not knowing the call sign for the Charge d'Affaires, John had to improvise. "Papa. Negative. Tulip Junior. Over."

There was a pause and then a different voice came over the headset. "Momma. This is Papa actual. Why the hell do you need to know that?" There was frustration in the voice.

"Sir, no time to explain. Is he in the crib?"

No communication protocols now. *He's showing urgency*, I thought.

"Momma. Negative. Tulip is en route home," the gruff voice relayed.

Eyebrows raised, all heads were up, and a look of shock washed over John's face. Miller was on his way back to the States.

"Papa, this is Momma. Do you get a hot read from the air traffic just arrived this location. Over," John continued.

There was a long pause. "Negative, Momma. But there is a blind spot approximately two meters by four meters that's not even allowing ground heat to show. You've got something shielded down there. Over."

"Fuck me," John said.

"Crow, this is Momma. Do you have eyes on aircraft? Over," John said into his mic.

"Momma, Crow. Affirmative. Duce and half exiting aircraft with twelve new Tangos," came the reply. A two and a half ton truck.

"Crow. What's on the duce? Over."

"Momma, Crow. Metal box. It fills the back." John looked at me, and then to Lt. Marsh. "I hate to say this guys, but I think the hostages just became secondary."

The blood drained from my face. I could feel it hit my feet like boiling water. The weight of that statement reminded me why I didn't want to help the CIA to begin with.

"You can't do that. They are tied together," I said desperately.

"This changes the rules, son," he said impatiently, clearly not used to a voice of dissent in the field.

"Bullshit," I said, snapping him out of command mode long enough to speak. "The cargo chopper is coming here. They are going to load the hostages and that box. I'll bet you anything a Russian is going to be flying it, and he hasn't been let in on the plan. If we get to the Russians, this whole thing turns around."

John lifted his head and looked out the window toward the runway and then across the compound. When he lowered himself back to a knee he looked at me and snarled. "Find your Russian. Get them on board now, or we take the field."

I looked at the unconscious Serb on the floor. "Strip him out of his clothes," I said as I started undressing. We were about the same size, or at least close enough not to be noticed in the dark. John handed me a small radio, throat mic, earpiece, and a 9mm pistol with a silencer. "Do you know how to use this?" he asked.

"Sure! I've used radios before." I said sarcastically, but I took both items, tucking the pistol into the holster that came off the Serb.

I looked at Michelle and Kathrin. "Kathrin?" I started, but she cut in before I could even ask.

"I'm in. What do you need?" she asked pointedly.

"Can you switch clothes with Michelle?" I asked.

She didn't hesitate a second; she was pulling her khaki pants and jacket off and prompting Michelle to do the same. The men in the room all turned their backs abruptly, startled by the sudden strip show.

In a matter of seconds they had switched outfits. Kathrin walked over and kneeled next to me. I looked at her hair and then at Michelle's. The color was close but Kathrin's was much longer. She saw what I was looking at and reached up to pull her hair back and tie it up.

"Give me his bottle," I said to no one in particular.

Nick reached for it, took a sip, and then handed it to me.

"You ready?" I asked Kathrin.

"Yah," she said firmly.

I looked at John, who clicked on his throat mic. "Crow this is Momma. Friendly in bad guy dress leaving forward position with friendly female. Cover. Over."

"Acknowledged." came the reply, now not only in John's speaker but in my ear as well.

"Okay. Let's go," I said, standing up and placing my arm around Kathrin's neck as if I were holding her against her will, a bottle of vodka in the other hand. We exited the building and started to walk toward Daniil's guard position.

"Struggle a little," I whispered in her ear.

She responded by throwing an elbow into my poor bruised ribs, knocking the wind out of me.

"Not that much!" I snapped. She resumed her wiggling, but dialed it back to something a drunk Serb could handle.

We walked up to Daniil's position. The scowl on his face vanished as he recognized me. I reached out drunkenly and handed him my bottle. The others outside the barracks who had been watching and waiting to see if there was to be a fight, resumed their conversations.

Daniil took a drink. "What are you doing?" he asked, his eyes shifting back and forth, worried about my presence.

"The plan is changing fast. I need you over in that building now. Take Kathrin—gently please—and I'll follow you back to the building," I said.

Daniil nodded, took Kathrin around the neck as I had, and walked her back to the building.

I squatted next to the corner of the barracks waiting until he was about halfway there and then started to follow, weaving drunkenly.

I was nearly halfway to the door myself when another of the drunken Serbs approached me from the Barracks. He had his own bottle and was weaving toward me…no doubt wanting his turn with the girl. He was speaking to me in Serbian. I didn't understand anything he was saying.

"Say '*Jebi se*,'" came Nick's voice in my earpiece. "It means 'fuck yourself.'"

I wasn't sure that was the best course of action to take, but I wasn't really in a position to argue the point. "*Jebi se*," I said gruffly. The Serb responded by grabbing me by my shoulder and giving me a half turn. He immediately recognized that I did not belong there.

My hand went to the 9mm in my holster, but I had no need for it. There was a squishing sound and my face was sprayed with a mist of warm blood from the man's throat. Crow got his shot off. The Serb was about to drop, but I reached my arm around his waist in a half stumble and grabbed his bottle with my free hand.

"Say '*Pijani svinja*' loudly and laugh," came Nick's voice in my ear.

"*Pijani svinja!*" I said loudly and then laughed as I dragged the lifeless Serb through the door of our building.

Daniil was on his knees in the small office where John, Lt. Marsh, and Michelle were. Nick and one of the other men had rifles trained on Daniil's head.

I walked between Nick and Daniil, helping him to his feet.

"Back off guys. Daniil is going to lose brothers tonight if we don't help him. He's here on his own." I said, trying to make him my friend again.

"I knew you were CIA," Daniil said, half-smiling.

"No. Not me. Not her," I said pointing at Kathrin, "and not her." Pointing at Michelle. "And not this guy." I gestured toward the Serb I had dropped just inside the doorway. "But the rest of these fuckers I can't vouch for," I said, smiling.

"What now?" Daniil said.

I turned to Nick and the other man, gesturing for them to lower their weapons. They looked at John, and he nodded. Everyone relaxed a tick.

"Daniil. Which one of you knows how to fly a helicopter?" I asked.

A confused look washed over his face. "Rodka used to fly helicopter for army."

"Anyone else?" I asked.

"*Nyet.*" Daniil replied. "Funny you ask. Popovich says we go to Hague with helicopter. Rodka flies."

I looked at John, gaging his response to this new information, which confirmed at least part of what I had theorized. John nodded at me.

"This is going to sound real bad, but I need you to hear me out before you respond. We've got one chance to make this work," I said.

"Okay," he said pensively.

"The Serbs are going to kill you and the hostages on that helicopter," I said plainly.

His eyes opened wide. "How do you know this?" he asked.

"The plane that just arrived? We believe it brought in at least one nuclear bomb. The Serbs are going to send it to The Hague with the hostages and you."

Fear washed across his face.

"So we need to find a way to get you, the nuke, and the hostages out of here before you take off in that helicopter," I said.

"Half of hostages," he said, correcting me.

"Half?" John and I asked at the same time.

"*Da*. Half go with us to Hague, half go with Serbs on plane," he said.

"Shit!" John exclaimed.

This changed things.

"We don't have the manpower we need." John said. "We can take the helicopter with minimal collateral losses, but if they split the hostages, up we can't do both."

"Then we have to move before the helo arrives." Lt. Marsh said.

There was a click in John's earpiece. He turned his head to listen, then "Acknowledged."

"It's too late," he said as he turned back to us. "The chopper is ten minutes out. Even if the Russians help us, we now have twenty-two Serbs to deal with," he said, accounting for the one that Crow had killed.

I was already in the zone. This was only a little wrinkle—an adjustment. I just had to convince John.

"Let them leave on the chopper," I said.

"What? Do you seriously think I'm going to let the Russian mob fly off with hostages and a nuclear device?" John exclaimed and then turned to Daniil. "No offense."

Daniil shrugged.

"Yes. Three of their guys and two of your guys dressed as theirs," I said, explaining. "Fifteen hostages and five guys with guns strolling in the dark. Most of the Serbs will be well away from the chopper as soon as the nuke gets loaded. The person arming it would have come in on the transport and probably doesn't even know what the Russians all look like."

"Is true. New guys don't know us, old guys all drunk." Daniil offered.

"Once the chopper is off, you can take the cargo plane. No loud noises around the nuclear device. That's better anyway," I said, appealing to his common sense. "And at least half the hostages would be free with no shots fired."

John thought about it for a minute. He was coming around. I pulled out my iPad and brought up the map of the area. I zoomed in on the hilltop Kathrin and I did yesterday's surveillance from.

"Here. Ralsko Castle. It's on a big hill. You can set down on the other side in the field, here," I said, pointing at the map. "You've got roughly three hours before the chopper is supposed to arrive at The Hague. That's plenty of time to get the hostages off and your specialists in to deactivate the bomb."

John looked at my map. "What's the terrain like?" he asked.

I switched the map to terrain view.

He studied it and then stood. "We need Rodka," he said.

I looked at Daniil. He nodded and left the building, walking into the growing chaos outside the barracks where several new Serbs just showed up. He returned a few moments later, Rodka following behind him.

I met him and Daniil in the entrance. Rodka looked on the floor, seeing the dead Serb, and then looked at me.

"Daniil says you can help us." He looked at me for a second and then pointed his gun at me. "Daniil trusts too much."

Before his sentence was finished, there were four laser spots on Rodka's chest. He froze. Anger washed across his face.

Daniil jumped in quickly. He said something to Rodka in Russian that I didn't understand, but several others in the room did.

John added something in Russian. Rodka looked behind him at the truck rolling up in front of the barracks.

"How do I know you tell truth?" Rodka asked John.

"Why would they be in charge the whole time and then send just the Russians off in the chopper with the hostages? And why would they need to fly in a special truck just to move hostages from the barracks to the chopper?" John replied.

It made perfect sense to him. I saw it on his face. Resignation.

"We need to dress two of our guys like two of your guys," I said. "The rest goes as planned. You get in the helicopter, fly away from the base and land here on the other side of this hill. You'll pick up our bomb team and then the hostages and the rest of your guys are free."

"But I need to fly, for talk on radio," Rodka stated more than asked.

"I'm afraid so. But our techs can defuse the bomb." John said sympathetically. "And even if they can't, we'll run the engines hot and get there early, go out over the ocean and ditch it. But I doubt it will come to that," he said, trying to down play the danger.

Rodka thought about it for a second. He dropped his gaze to the floor as he sorted all the information. "What choice I have?" he began. "If I yell, everyone dies, including us. If I ignore you and take chopper, it blows up, either by Serbs or by your jets. If I go with your plan, maybe I live but my men are free—"

He paused, looking first at Daniil, then me, and then back to John.

"Your offer sounds best," he said finally. "I go with you."

"Great. We need two of your men to switch with our guys," I said.

Rodka nodded. I looked at John and then John looked at Lt Marsh. "Okay! Let's move this Charlie Foxtrot along," he said finally.

Daniil and Rodka left. While they were gone, John called in the plan and requested the techs to be at the coordinates on the opposite side of Ralsko castle along with transport for approximately fifteen hostages and two Russians.

A few moments later, Daniil returned with two of the other Russians. As they arrived, the chopper could be heard approaching the tarmac.

"Hurry! Change into their clothes." John said to Lt. Marsh and one of the other men.

Once changed, Daniil and the two impostors walked out of the building, blending into the chaos of the hostage-loading procedure and then climbed into the back of the truck with the hostages. A few seconds later, they were gone.

I hadn't gotten a chance to see if Barb had been loaded into that truck or not. I waited until everyone had settled down and the truck was being backed onto the chopper before broaching it.

I clicked the switch for the throat mic I was still wearing.

"Arrow, Monkey Wrench. Is Barb with you? Over," I asked.

John flashed me a hard look, but he kept quiet.

There was a long pause and then a barely audible "*Nyet.*"

I swore silently to myself. No such luck.

As soon as the chopper was airborne, the attention shifted to the plane. John, Nick, and one of the other guys were arguing about how to take the plane when we heard the engines start up.

Time had just run out. They had already decided that if they couldn't come up with an effective assault plan that they would just track the plane and follow it to its next location. I wasn't happy with that. The Serbs had what they wanted; they didn't need the hostages anymore.

Kathrin quietly worked her way around to me. She bumped my arm and nodded toward the tarmac.

I raised an eyebrow in question.

Is she asking what I think she's asking? I thought.

She was still dressed in Michelle's clothes. I was still in the Serb's clothes.

I looked at her pensively. She lifted her eyebrows and nodded toward the tarmac again, more insistently.

The engines on the aircraft revved.

It was put-up or shut-up time.

While John and Nick had their backs to us, we snuck out of the office and into the entry way. The area in front of the barracks was clearing out and everyone was headed toward the airfield.

I looked at Kathrin. "Are you sure?" I asked.

"Am I or am I not still your hostage?" she asked, grinning.

"Okay. Let's go," I whispered, and we headed out the door.

I pulled the black hood up from under my jacket and Kathrin put a hand to her face as if she were crying. I was dragging her along by the elbow as we walked quickly to the airfield.

When we arrived, I held back so we were the last ones on board and then stumbled up the ramp as the plane started to move, head down, dragging Kathrin behind me.

Out of the frying pan, into the fire, I thought as the ramp started to close.

**

I drunkenly pushed past a handful of Serbs. They laughed and shoved back, grabbing at Kathrin's behind as I pulled her forward. I looked at her, quickly catching her attention by gripping her elbow, warning her not to strike back.

I could tell by the look on her face that it was difficult for her to restrain herself, but she nonetheless continued in her role as the weeping rape victim.

I pushed her roughly toward the small cargo container strapped to the center of the cargo area. The door was open. I shoved her toward the opening and she stumbled inside. I couldn't hear what was said over the roar of the engines, but I could see hands reach out to comfort her, and then confused looks, followed by Kathrin putting her finger to her lips as the door clanked shut.

I fell over heavily against the bulkhead between the door and a bundle of something soft, and immediately put my head between my knees as if I were sick.

I looked sideways to see if anyone had noticed the strangers in their midst. They appeared to have been fooled—at least for now. Then I saw another Serb running for the back of the ramp as it was coming up. He leapt onto the ramp and pulled himself over. His hood was up as mine was, as many of the Serbs' were, but as he pulled himself drunkenly toward the bulkhead, I saw his face.

Nick! I realized.

He tucked his head into the corner and fell over as if he was passed out. Then I heard a voice in my ear.

"Momma, Spartan. On board. Package in sight. Monkey Wrench and Gretel are under the radar."

"Roger, Spartan," came John's Voice. "Monkey Wrench. If you can still hear me, you and I are going to have words when this is over. Momma out."

I looked down the aisle at Nick. He was convincing as a passed-out drunk, but I could see one of his eyes flitting back and forth, looking around the cargo bay. There were roughly eighteen Serbs back here with us. I had no way of knowing how many were in the seats forward of us from my viewpoint, but by guessing, I came up with an additional eight count plus flight crew.

Very, *very* bad odds.

What was I thinking? I asked myself.

I slumped against the bundle next to me. It took me a moment, but I figured out what it was. It was an equipment parachute.

The hooks were neatly lined up to attach to a cargo sled. I looked across the bay and saw another one just like it on the other side.

I looked up at Nick and nodded in the direction of the chutes. He looked. Then he looked back at me and nodded.

Just then one of the drunken Serbs walked up and started talking to me in a belligerent tone. I tucked my head deeper between my legs.

"He wants to know if she was good," Nick said into my ear.

I nodded without raising my head. He persisted, throwing more words at me that I didn't understand.

"He's pissed at you for sharing her with the Russian instead of your friend," Nick said.

I leaned forward, putting my finger down my throat, and retched on his boots. That backed him off for a second, and then he came toward me more aggressively.

"You aren't going to get rid of him," Nick warned.

I waved my hand gesturing for him to leave me.

Two of the sober Serbs came over and tried to talk him into sitting down and sleeping it off. But he insisted on being belligerent.

"We can use this if you play it right," Nick said into my ear. "If he doesn't back off this time, start a fight. I'll need thirty seconds on each side to hook up the chutes."

I nodded.

The poor drunk bastard wouldn't give up. This time, when he came at me, he pushed at me with his boot. I stood up, head still down, but glad for the darkness in the cargo area. Only a tactical red light was on.

When he approached again and shoved me, I pushed him to the side and hit him in the ribs. He stumbled but didn't fall. It took him a second to realize he was in a fight, but once the adrenaline was in him, he became a bull.

He charged me, fist swinging high. I easily side stepped the drunken punch and delivered another hammer to his other side.

Now he was pissed. The men in the cargo bay were starting to enjoy the show, yelling at him, encouraging him to go back for more.

He came charging back at me, but this time he threw his body into me and wrapped his arms around my waist, slamming me into the cargo container. I saw Nick out of the corner of my eye; he was snapping the heavy snap links of the chute onto the cargo sled the hostages were strapped to.

I brought my elbows down hard on my opponent's back, loosening his grip and allowing me to shove him backwards. He stumbled but got to his feet again.

"I need to get on that side now," I heard Nick say into my ear.

When the drunken Serb returned to his feet, he stumbled toward me again, and I threw a punch that sent him spinning to the other side of the cargo container.

There two of the sober onlookers caught him. He appeared to be unconscious, but they were shaking him and egging him back into the fight.

"I need more time," Nick warned.

Shit, I thought to myself. *This is going to hurt.*

I stepped forward drunkenly as if I were going to punch the man again, but I let my swing miss my target, instead striking one of the sober men holding him—a big guy.

Oops! I should have thought that out a little longer, I realized.

A loud whoop rose from the men in the cargo bay.

The man rubbed his face with the back of his hand then smiled at me.

There is nothing scarier than hitting a guy in the face and getting a smile in response.

This man was not drunk and was not small—but he *was* pissed. I barely saw the fist that hit me in the side of my head. I staggered against the cargo box. He stepped forward, fists raised. I raised my hand as if conceding my mistake, but he moved forward anyway.

I ducked under a punch, letting his hand slam against the side of the cargo container. This just enraged him more.

He attempted a round house punch, but my elbow rose of its own volition to catch the strike and then my foot lashed out and caught him at the knee. I guess old muscle memory is better than no muscle memory. It was hard to believe that a couple years of karate as a kid had made such a permanent alteration to my reflexive motor skills, but I had no other explanation for the automatic response.

He stepped back for a second, somewhat surprised by the coherent counter, but determination washed across his face. He would not be undone by a drunk.

He responded with kicks in the air, followed by another round house punch. I was able to dodge the kicks, but all I could do with the punch was raise my shoulder to protect my ear. Most of it glanced off my skull, but enough of it connected that it rung my bell a bit.

I would have been able to shake it off if it hadn't been for the sweep of the leg.

CRASH!

I went down hard on my injured ribs, slamming to the

floor, my shoulder colliding with the wall next to the container.

He wasn't done yet.

He stepped forward and brought his boot down over my head. I crossed my arms and pushed back hard as he made contact, sending him backwards a few feet.

"You need to hit the emergency drop on the ramp. The guide chute release is on my side," came Nick's voice "When the light flashes, you have to be strapped onto the sled or you are going home with these guys," he said just as the angry Serb stepped in for another kick.

"Busy!" I said.

The kick was making for my head. I raised my left elbow to block it and then executed a nearly perfect roundhouse sweep with my leg, following with a knee to his chest, which sent him bouncing to the deck.

I took the moment's respite to look around for something to strap myself to the container with. I saw a long heavy strap tucked into a cargo pouch on the wall.

The Serb saw me looking for something; I guess he assumed I was looking for a weapon. He pulled a long military knife from behind his back.

He charged. I dodged his first slash, but on the back slash he caught a piece of my left forearm. I felt the blade cut through my jacket and bite into my skin.

His next stab was slower, so I kicked his hand as it came around, the tip of my boot catching him at the wrist and sending his knife skidding on the floor behind him. He turned and went for it.

While he was away, I reached for the cargo strap. It was about twelve feet long and heavy, with large metal clips at both ends.

He returned with his knife in hand. I spun my body, whipping one end of the strap out toward his head. He ducked it, but it caught his shoulder on the retreat. He stepped forward again. I whipped both ends of the strap around in front of me, letting it pass once around my body.

"Anytime you're ready." Nick said.

When the strap came back around, I lifted my arm and let it pass under again and then whipped my whole body around like a helicopter blade, flinging the heavy clip across the man's jaw.

The man went sailing to the floor, his teeth flying across the cargo bay.

A great roar of laughter and whoops erupted from the men. One of other Serbs was cautiously approaching me, scrutinizing my face.

I'd been made.

"It's now or never!" I heard Nick say, just as the curious Serb was realizing I was not who I should have been.

He was about to sound the alarm when I whipped the cargo hook back around, striking the ramp release and smashing the control panel.

The ramp began to descend.

Confused looks spread across the bay. The noise in the cargo bay was incredible as the ramp continued to open.

Most of the Serbs became acutely aware that they were not strapped in and started moving toward to the front of the plane, away from the ramp.

"I hope you are strapped on." I heard Nick in my ear again just as the large guide chute exploded backwards through the open ramp.

Just as the sled started to slide, pulled toward the door by the guide chute, I slammed myself against the container box and flicked one end of the clip over a bar welded to the side. It immediately began dragging me toward the ramp.

Many of the Serbs were under the impression that this was some sort of freak accident and began trying to grab at me and the sled. But in the split second that I clipped the second hook onto the box, realization entered their eyes—just as the box left the plane.

For three of them, it was too late; they were being pulled out of the back of the plane by their own momentum.

I watched as their expressions were replaced by terror as they fell with me for a few moments. I looked back at the plane in time to see several more of them being jerked out of the plane by the parachutes as they began to open in the cargo hold.

Because the chutes were engaged from the sides of the plane instead of the center, anyone having the misfortune of being between them and the ramp was knocked out the rear.

A few more tumbled out the back and receded into darkness before I was jerked up by my strap when the chutes engaged. It was too dark to see the falling men for long. For a brief moment they were dark spots against the countryside, and then they were gone from sight.

I hung there for a few seconds, dangling with my back to the container.

It was the most calm I'd felt since this whole thing had started. The strap dug painfully into my injured ribs, so I shifted my weight by pulling up on the welded bar. I felt above me and discovered two more bars. It was a ladder—no more than pieces of rebar welded to the corrugated panels of the box.

Hooking my arm through one, I unclipped one end of the cargo strap and attached it to itself under my arm, effectively creating a chest harness. I gripped the rung tightly and unhooked the other end, leaving me for a moment without a safety.

I quickly snapped it several rungs higher and began to climb.

I guess this is officially my highest climb, I thought to myself as I smiled.

"Did you make it, Monkey Wrench?" I heard Nick say through my earpiece. He was strapped in on the opposite side of the container.

I clicked on my throat mic. "AHHHHHhhhhhhhhaaaaaa. Over," I said and laughed after I released the mic switch.

It actually felt good to scream. I felt more tension melt away.

"Smartass," he said, but I think I detected a hint of amusement in his voice.

By then I was over the top of the container and looking down at him on the other side. He looked up and I caught a glimpse of a grin before it disappeared into a sneer.

"This is a slow ride," he said. "There's enough chute here for a tank. This box is nothing."

"Good," I replied. "There are people in this box who have no way to prepare for a hard landing."

He nodded. Then he climbed up to where I was, scanning the dark horizon as he moved. "Momma, this is Spartan. Over," I heard in my earpiece and in front of me.

"Spartan, Momma. Over," came John's voice.

"Momma, Spartan. Be advised. Monkey Wrench, Gretel, and package are in hand, floating slowly toward a field about six clicks from your location. Over."

"Spartan, Momma. Good to hear it, but you've got to tighten up. Tangos rolling your way on the ground. Over."

"Shit!" Nick exclaimed under his breath. "Any details, Momma?"

There was a pause. John must have been getting information from his com-link that we weren't hearing. "Spartan. Papa informs me you have a truck with four maybe five bad guys en route to your location. Wait."

There was another pause, and then, "Spartan, be advised. Heavy is changing course to intercept. Over." John was referring to the cargo plane.

And the bad news just keeps coming, I thought.

"Momma, Spartan. Any chance of support? Over."

"Affirmative Spartan, but you'll have to deal with the ground hostiles yourself. Our ride is fifteen mikes out, then another five to you. Over."

Fifteen minutes didn't used to seem like a very long time, but *this* fifteen minutes seemed like an epoch.

"Momma. ETA on the heavy. Over," Nick asked.

A pause, then, "Fifteen mikes. Over."

"Momma, tell your ride to push it up. We've got zero maneuverability on this box. Out."

Nick looked at me. "Do you know how to pull a trigger?"

I did, so I nodded. In truth, I am a fair shot. I grew up on a farm and had hunted and target practiced like most farm boys.

But pulling the trigger on a man...that would be a test. The fact that I put myself in this situation, though, and that I had come as far as I had, made me believe I would do what I needed to do.

Nick looked back down the length of the cargo container. It was small compared to the one on the train. He held his hands out to both sides, grabbing straps in the front.

"Get back there and hook up to the box. Do you see these?" he said, pointing at the coupling and retainer pins for the chute straps. "When we hit, jerk the pin out and pull down hard here. The last thing we need is a gust to drag us around this field while were being shot at."

"Got it. Jerk, then pull down," I replied.

We were only a few seconds from touching down when Nick spotted the vehicle John had told us about. It was still about half a mile away as we hit the ground with a crash. It was a hard jolt. I lost my footing and ended up on my belly.

Quickly righting myself, I grabbed for the latches on the chutes and freed them.

Nick was on the ground, running toward the SUV, by the time I hopped off the top of the box. The brush was high, about chest height. The field hadn't been plowed this year, so last year's fall growth had gotten tall.

I ran in the direction Nick had gone, but I had lost sight of him.

"Get down. Let them pass. We'll hit 'em from behind," I heard Nick in my ear when I was about fifty yards away from the container.

A few seconds later, I could see the headlights of the SUV through the tall grass. They were bouncing hard over the rough plowed field and completely unable to see through the brush.

The vehicle went past me and then pulled to a sudden stop ten feet further away. I guess I was lucky it didn't run over me. Five men spilled out, rifles raised in the direction of the cargo container.

"Now!" I heard Nick hiss in my ear.

On the other side of the Range Rover, two men tensed and then dropped. I didn't even hear the shots that killed them.

The third Serb on that side squatted down low. I aimed my pistol at the closest man to me, hesitated, and then dropped my aim to his shoulder.

I squeezed the trigger and he screamed out, his rifle dropping from his hand. The second man spun around, rifle pointed directly at my chest.

I hesitated.

The next second seemed to stretch out for minutes.

A flash came from the end of the rifle in the Serb's hands.

Almost simultaneously, I saw a flash come from the end of my pistol.

There was pressure against the palm of my hand.

I heard a small clack and then caught a glimpse of the brass casing flying away in my peripheral vision.

Suddenly it felt like someone had hit me in the chest with a hammer.

I noticed, as I was spinning to the ground, that the Serb had developed a dark spot in the center of his forehead.

Flinging himself backwards, falling flat-backed on the ground, the Serb was horizontal before I was. I landed hard on my right shoulder with my back to the SUV and then rolled onto my back thanks to gravity.

Suddenly there was pain.

I turned my head toward the SUV and saw the first man I shot grabbing his rifle with his other hand.

It felt like hours before my body responded, but somehow I managed to roll onto my throbbing left side. The pain raced down into my arm and gut like hot liquid as I swung my right arm over, pointing my pistol at the face of the man who was now holding his rifle with his good arm.

I squeezed.

Another flash of light, pressure in my palm, and a small glint of metal flying away from my pistol.

This time there was no reply from the other rifle. I laid there staring at his open eyes, a dark spot between them leaking black fluid down his face.

What was I feeling? Was there a change in me?

All I could feel was pain.

I released my pistol and brought my hand up to feel where I had been struck. Warm, sticky blood greeted my fingertips. The wound was higher than I thought it had been.

I took a deep breath. Lots of pain, but no bubbling.

Good. It didn't get my lung, I thought.

I tried to reach back with my other hand to see if there was an exit, but it hurt too much so I dropped my arm back to the ground.

I spoke into my throat mic. "Nick. You alive?" I asked.

"Affirmative. No names," Nick said quietly.

"I'm down. No bad guys my side," I said, grunting. Then I saw movement to the front of the headlights.

"Are you to the front of the SUV?" I whispered into my mic.

"Negative," he whispered.

I reached to my side for the pistol. Felt around in the grass for a second before my fingers touched it. I brought it up quietly, my hand steady as a rock.

I can't express how amazed I was at the sheer mechanical movement of my hand as I lifted that weapon into place.

I heard a whisper from the man in front of me. Something in Serbian, I assumed.

"*Oopomoc*," I heard Nick say in my ear.

"*Oopomoc*," I called out in a horse whisper.

The man appeared in the headlights of the SUV.

I squeezed my trigger.

This time there was no pause, no slow motion, and no elevated heart rate. There was only a muted clack, and then I saw a spray of pink mist in the headlights along with two dark spots that had appeared in his throat and cheek.

Nick and I had shot him at precisely the same moment.

Nick ran around the SUV to my side, looking at each of the three downed men, popping another round into each of them to insure they were dead, and then he kneeled next to me.

He pulled back the jacket and ripped my shirt open at the collar to see the wound, then roughly rolled me on my side to see my back.

"It went through," he said, and then laid his ear to my chest. "Any trouble breathing?"

"No," I said weakly.

"Hurts like hell, doesn't it," he said, smiling, and then he began unwinding the compression bandages from around my ribs.

"Spartan, Momma. What's Monkey Wrench's status? Over," John asked into our earpieces.

"Momma. It's a scratch. Clean through. He'll live." Nick said, making light of my trauma.

It certainly didn't feel like I would live. "I'm sorry about your nose," I said in a hoarse whisper. He smiled and continued to unwrap my ribs.

"Status on Heavy. Over," he asked as he began re-wrapping the bandage around my shoulder, compressing the now wadded up halves of my shirt.

"Spartan. Eight mikes. Over."

"Momma. Acknowledged. Will advise status of package. Wait," Nick said as he tied the end of the bandage and then grabbed the rifle belonging to the man closest to us.

I pushed myself up and dizzily wobbled along behind him as he ran toward the cargo container, holstering my pistol and picking up a rifle myself.

By the time I reached him, he had the door unlatched and was pulling it open.

"We're Americans." Nick said as I reached the opening.

Sounds of delight came from inside.

"Is anyone injured?" I asked.

I heard a couple of people say they were okay. Others were checking on their fellow boxmates.

When it appeared that no one was seriously injured from the 'jump,' Nick picked up the pace. "Okay, everyone out. We need to get you all to that SUV over there," he yelled into the box. "The plane is on its way back."

That got them moving.

The former hostages started exiting the container. Kathrin was helping an older woman to the front. When I saw Barb, she was standing in the center of the entrance, jaw dropped, eyes wide.

"Scott? What? How?" she sputtered.

Nick interrupted. "Hugging and kissing later. We're escaping now. The bad guys are on their way back."

Barb's father came forward, helping one of the other hostages. He looked up and saw Barb's expression and then looked at me.

"You know each other?" he asked as he left the container.

"Enough talk!" Nick shouted. "We have to move!"

Just then there was an explosion of light and noise. The cargo plane burst over the hill flying so low that everyone but Nick dropped to the ground.

Nick picked up the woman Mr. Whitney had been helping, and then slung her over his shoulder. She looked none the worse for the treatment, despite being in her sixties.

Eight people were at the vehicle when he arrived with the woman; one more ran behind him. By the time those people had crammed themselves inside, the plane had turned around and was headed directly for us.

He ran toward the box again, and then stopped, realizing there was no time for more, not to mention no room in the SUV.

"Get them clear," I said into my throat mic. "Gretel and I will take the others through the woods."

The plane was deafeningly loud as it approached. There were seven of us—Kathrin, Barb, Mr. Whitney, a man from the security detail, another middle-aged man, and a woman.

I urged everyone to run hard for the tree line in the opposite direction of the SUV. Once they were all moving, I took up the rear. The bodyguard was moving slowly. He was one of the wounded men I had seen in Dusseldorf.

As we made it to the trees, the big cargo plane touched the ground, its landing gear bouncing over the rough field, throwing dirt and brush far and wide. The gear must have hit a very irregular spot of ground because all at once it lurched up. We could see the landing gear on one side fold under itself.

When it came back down, it came down hard, sending a tidal wave of soil into the air. It smashed over the cargo container and continued bouncing across the field.

I could see the headlights of the SUV were disappearing around a hill as the monstrous hulk finally came to a complete stop.

"Monkey Wrench. Keep moving. Don't stop until you rendezvous with the extraction team," Nick said into my ear.

"Acknowledged," I said.

Mr. Whitney looked at me. "I don't know if you noticed or not, but they took our shoes. We aren't going to make great time."

"I know. Do the best you can. We'll all stay together," I said as we ran.

To be honest, I was grateful for the slower pace. My chest was throbbing and every movement was sending streaks of pain down my arm and torso like hot lead was being poured on me. It suddenly occurred to me that Kathrin was probably having difficulty with her twisted ankle as well.

The dressing Nick had put on my chest was starting to work loose and blood began trickling down my belly again.

Kathrin was in the middle, helping the wounded security man, but she looked back over her shoulder to check on the others. Seeing the blood running down my chest and torso, she slowed in front of me.

"You're hurt!" she exclaimed.

I handed her the rifle I had slung across my shoulder. "Let's get down this hill and out of sight. We need to keep moving," I said with labored breaths.

I looked over my shoulder and saw men pouring out of the cargo plane. They were splitting into small groups and going in all directions.

Good, they haven't seen us, I thought as we started descending down a steep embankment.

Just then a piece of tree splintered over our heads.

"Move!" I yelled.

Everyone picked up their pace as we crested the hill and then began to slide down the slope toward a fast moving stream below. When we reached the bottom, there was a moment of indecision. I quickly took stock of the situation: I'm wounded, hostages have no shoes, hill on both sides, water running rapidly.

The water was our best hope.

"In!" I yelled.

No one hesitated. Everybody was suddenly in the water, splashing and trying to keep their heads up as the current swept us along. It had been the best option, but I failed to guess how difficult it would be to hold my head above water with only one working arm or how painful it would be to try and use my wounded side if I had to.

The water took us around a bend just as I looked up and saw several men reaching the top of the hill we had gone down. A couple shots were fired, but they impacted nowhere near us. I could see Kathrin trying to help the wounded security man keep his head above water.

I could hear, though not yet see, rapids in front of us. I looked back to see if any pursuers were visible. They were not.

Thank God, I thought. I *need a fucking break at some point.*

It would be a few minutes before they could run around the stream's edge to get a view of us. If, however, they decided to jump in, they would be much closer behind.

I saw the older man drop out of sight in front of me, followed by the woman, Barb, Kathrin and the security guy, and finally Mr. Whitney.

When I went over, I landed in deep water with a smack to my exit wound. My feet were no longer touching the bottom, and it suddenly occurred to me that I was not able to swim in my condition.

Thankfully, the current continued to drag me forward until my feet touched bottom. I pushed with my feet so that my head popped above the surface for a breath.

The stream continued to move rapidly, and we had just created a few extra moments of invisibility going over the fall. But I was starting to have difficulty keeping my head above water.

"Monkey Wrench. This is Momma. Where are you?" John's voice spoke into my ear.

I opened my mouth to answer but instead swallowed a mouthful of river. I coughed and spit, wheezing, trying to clear my throat. "In the water!" I gasped.

Just then I heard a helicopter pass over. *The cavalry!* I thought joyfully.

But there was no way for them to land near us with all those trees and the steep bank. We had to keep moving.

"Monkey Wrench. There's a clearing half a click downstream from you. We'll extract you there." John said.

"Momma. Be advised. Mean fuckers in pursuit," I gasped.

"Acknowledged," he said.

Fifty meters. We can make that, I thought to myself.

Then I realized that didn't seem right.

Is it fifty? I've lost too much blood. My brain isn't working right. Five hundred meters. Whoa, that's way worse.

The other six were still moving rapidly down the stream. The water was gaining speed, which was good news for us as a group, but bad news for me. I was already having difficulty keeping my head up. I began swallowing more and more water.

The others were much farther ahead now. I was slowing down as I hit each rock, unable to navigate around them.

"Three hundred meters," I heard in my ear. "Monkey Wrench."

Another bump. I looked up just in time to see Barb and her dad go around another bend.

Good. They're making good time, I thought.

"Two hundred meters," someone said, but when I looked around, I didn't see anyone.

"Monkey Wrench!"

I know that tune, I thought to myself.

I felt sand on my neck. Sand and water. It felt really good. The cool water splashing on the side of my face, the sand on my back and neck. I was feeling better already.

"Monkey Wrench! Please advise," I heard from a distance.

"Don't want to be your monkey wrench," I sang weakly. "One more indecent accident. I'd rather leave..."

The Foo Fighters fucking rock, I thought, and then saw someone on the bank. *Oh look. Someone's here to help me up.*

Four men with rifles approached me, walking down the bank. A man with a scar on his face lifted his arm toward me.

Is he offering me a hand?

A voice screamed in my ear. *"SHOOT!"*

My hand felt for the pistol on my hip. My arm was underwater.

"Monkey Wrench! Shoot that mother fucker now, or he is going to kill you," I heard someone say.

"Momma? Is that you?" I said weakly.

The men turned to each other and laughed.

Do guns work underwater? I wondered.

I squeezed the trigger to find out.

Blood gushed from the man's throat. A flash of light came from his hand and then something hit me in the stomach. The other three men lifted up their arms...

No. Wait. They have guns too, I thought. *But theirs are dry.*

Pops and cracks filled my ears, and then one of the men fell on top of me. He was really fucking heavy.

It hurt. And worse than that, he was holding my head underwater with his weight. I could taste blood in my mouth. It was not pleasant at all.

I decided to sleep until the dream was over.

**

I could hear voices. Screaming. It sounded like Kathrin screaming, "No! No!" But I couldn't be sure. I tried to tell her it was okay—that the pain had stopped—but my mouth didn't move.

There were hands on me. Dragging me.

Oh yeah, I thought. *It does still hurt.*

Someone poked my chest and it felt like fire.

Ouch. Stop it. That hurts.

But they kept doing it.

Then I realized I hadn't actually said it. More hands. Pressure on my chest. Someone was pushing on it.

I really wish you would stop doing that. It hurts, I said.

"Nope. No sound." A voice in my head said. **"When you speak, there is sound."**

Then the pain stopped.

I couldn't hear my heart in my ears any more.

I was floating. I heard splashing, more screaming and crying. Or was it laughter?

A moment later, the pain came back for a while and someone was pressing on my chest again. I heard *whump, whump, whump, whump.*

I wondered if it was my heart, and I thought how fast it was beating. *I better try to slow it down.* I thought, then the pain went away again.

"That's better," the voice in my head said.

I recognized the voice. It was me—or rather the *other* me I remembered from the torture garage in Amsterdam.

I began to float. This was very nice. I felt warm and all my stress was gone.

I heard a woman's voice calling me. "Scott. Where are you?"

It was Kathrin! I saw her walking through a field of tall grass and wildflowers, calling out to me as if we were playing hide-and-seek. The ground was soft and warm. There was a gentle breeze, and the sun was on my face. I was so content. I didn't want to play, so I called her over.

"I'm here, Kathrin!" I chirped lazily. I thought, Ah, I must have my voice back. She's coming toward me.

She was wearing a long, flowing, beige skirt—the kind you see stoner girls wearing at music festivals—and a loose-fitting white peasant blouse with puffy sleeves.

She should wear girl clothes more often*, I thought. Her hair was flitting gently in the breeze, her long, golden curls glowing and dancing in the sun.*

She was smiling at me. Hmm. Where are her piercings? *I wondered. No matter. She's beautiful and she's coming toward me.*

"You can always count on Kathrin," she said softly into my ear. It was a comforting thought... Someone who would stay with me always, no matter what, no matter how tough it got, no matter how confusing.

Her face materialized above mine.

"There you are," she said smiling.

Then something occurred to me.

Suddenly I was standing in front of a house.

I'm here to see Barbara! We have a date, *I realized, panicking.* I have to get ready for my date. I'm not dressed.

But wait.

That bitch left me...and after I got shot! FOR HER!

I was standing on her doorstep. I heard her walking toward the door on the other side.

I'm not dressed. This is all wrong. I have to hide before she sees me. I dove into the bushes—Kathrin laughed at me.

The door opened. Barb called out. "Is someone there? Hello? Scott, is that you?"

How could she not see Kathrin standing there?

"If it IS you, you better be ready in ten minutes, or we won't be going out tonight," she said. "I have it all worked out, and there is no room for lack of commitment, mister."

I stayed quiet. She looked at her watch. "Nine minutes out and not responding," she said, and then she turned around and walked back into the house, slamming the door behind her.

I ran. Behind the house, over the hedge, through the neighbor's yard. I jumped the fence...

Then I heard a shot.

A shot.

Oh shit. I shot someone. I wonder if I'll get in trouble for that. I'd hate to go to jail.

"You can't get in trouble for that," *the other me said.* **"They were bad guys."**

Then I felt guilty for thinking of myself when someone's son or husband or brother was dead because I shot them. I thought, I'm so fucking selfish. I don't deserve Kathrin...I mean Barb.

I started to cry. I robbed some poor mother of her baby boy. Somewhere, right now, a mother is crying because of me.

Then I saw Kathrin's face again. She was smiling at me. Holding my hand. Comforting me. "You stayed with me the whole time! Why did you do that?" I asked.

"Because I love you, silly goose," she said, her accent like music in my ears. "Still no pulse, hit him again."

That was an odd thing to say.

The sun and sky silhouetted her smiling face and her long, golden curls. They were tickling my nose.

Then her hair started to go into my nose. "That's not comfortable. Please stop," I said.

A thump on my chest. BOOM. Then another. BOOM. That one hurt.

Then suddenly the pain in my body returned.

"Would you please stop doing that," I said.

Did I say it?

Yes! Said my other voice. **There was sound that time.**

As I started drifting into dreamless darkness, I could hear the *whump, whump, whump* again and someone said. "He's back."

Who's back? I wondered. *I hope it isn't the bad guys. I'm too tired to fight again.*

Then, the darkness swallowed me.

eleven
Aftermath

6:25 a.m., Tuesday, May 18th, 2010, two days after rescue -
Landstuhl Regional Medical Center, Landstuhl, Germany.

When I woke, the first thing I noticed was the pain in my shoulder and chest. In fact, I believe that's what brought me out of my slumber.

The second thing I noticed was a jungle of wires and tubes coming out of my body, hooked to various machines and bags. I was in a hospital. The sun was shining through the window and though it had not filled the room yet, I could feel the first warm rays kissing my toes beneath the sheet.

I saw Barb sleeping in a chair at the corner of my bed. I tried to turn toward her but a sudden flash of pain through my abdomen stopped me and sent one of my monitors squealing. Barb opened her eyes at the sound and lurched toward me.

She saw my eyes were opened and then turned to lean out the door. She called for assistance. A nurse ran in and came to my side. She moved her hands over one of the gadgets behind me and the alarm ceased.

As she turned her attention to me, she smiled. "Well hello, sleepyhead," she said sweetly.

I tried to respond but quickly realized there was a tube down my throat.

"Just a second and the doctor will have that out," she said, indicating I shouldn't attempt to speak.

A moment later a doctor came in. Barb moved to the side and was peering over her shoulder nervously.

"Good morning, Mr. Wolfe," she said. "I'm Doctor Chhatre."

She was a short woman with shoulder-length, coal black hair and a bright, broad, white smile across cocoa brown skin that made her likable at first sight.

"I think you don't need this anymore," she said as she placed a piece of gauze over my mouth and began to withdraw the tube.

The gagging reflex was strong as it left my throat. I tried clearing my throat and hocked up what seemed like a pint of phlegm.

I tried to speak. It hurt. "Day." The single word was all I managed to grind out of my gravelly voice box.

"It's Tuesday, Mr. Wolfe," the doctor said. "You've been through a lot, so I need you take it easy. Can you answer some questions for me?"

I nodded.

"Do you know your name?" she asked.

"Wolfe," I rasped, smiling.

An amused but impatient look appeared on her face. "Your first name, Mr. Wolfe."

"Scott," I said.

"Do you remember your birthday?" she asked.

"May 20th," I responded.

"And what do you do for a living?"

"Her Majesty's Secret Service," I said, smiling.

"Okay, Mr. Wolfe, you are clearly in a better place than you were twenty-four hours ago. I'll come back to check your dressings in a while," she said and then turned to Barb. "He really needs to rest, so not too much all at once."

Barb nodded, looking at me pensively. She looked as if she were about to explode a million questions at me.

"It's good to see you looking so well, Mr. Wolfe. I'll be back to check on you shortly." Dr. Chhatre said, and then she left the room with the nurse.

The nurse touched Barb on the shoulder as she left and winked at her.

Barb walked cautiously to my bedside. "Hey," she said smiling.

"Hey," I croaked back at her.

"You sound awful," she said, tears welling up in her eyes.

"Well at least I look awesome," I joked, prompting a nervous burst of laughter from her.

"Why?" she asked. "Why did you put yourself in so much danger?"

I felt as if she were asking me to say, "Because I love you." But I could tell she wanted a real answer.

I was not feeling right. I suddenly had no answer for her. Then I realized that I never had an answer. I did what I did because I felt it needed to be done. There was no emotion behind it. "Girlfriend" was an excuse for being there, not the reason.

But I couldn't tell her that.

"I had to," I rasped. "You owe me twenty bucks for breakfast."

"You've put me in a difficult position, you jerk," she said jokingly. "Now I have to totally re-evaluate what I think of you."

"Don't go to too much trouble. I'm still an asshole," I said with a smile.

She laughed, tears streaming down her face. "Rest," she said. "I'll be here when you wake up."

And I did. I slept for nearly four hours before I was awakened by Dr. Chhatre peeling my bandages back.

I was able to get a good look at what the big deal had been all about. I was surprised to see a long line of staples across and up my abdomen. The sight was a bit of a shock.

"What happened to my stomach?" I asked her.

"You were shot, Mr. Wolfe," she said, stating the obvious. "You had a penetrating abdominal trauma. We had to go in to control the bleeding in the branches of the portal and hepatic veins as well as the hepatic arterial radicles. You also had a pretty nasty through-and-through gunshot to your chest. You lost a lot of blood."

"Will I live?" I asked, half sarcastically.

"You will now. I don't know if you realize it, but you died in transit," she said with a disapproving grin, like Mom when I made a mess of her kitchen, "three times…the last time for more than eight minutes." The shock on my face must have been obvious. "Don't worry. It's not a record," she said.

That provided little comfort.

The doctor looked over her shoulder at the sleeping figure in chair at the foot of my bed and then returned her gaze to my wound, smiling.

"That one has been here since you arrived," she said, her eyes rising to meet mine for a second before returning to her task. "Pulled some strings to get that seat as well. Non-related civilians don't usually get to do that here."

"Where is 'here?'" I rasped.

"Landstuhl Regional Medical Center, Germany. It's a military hospital," she replied as she continued to work.

She gave a satisfied grunt at her handiwork and covered it with fresh dressing.

"I don't know what you did, Mr. Wolfe, but you have made quite an impression," she looked at Barb again, "on a number of people."

She turned to walk out and touched Barb on the shoulder as she passed the chair she was sleeping in.

"He's awake, dear," she said gently, and then she exited.

Barb rose and walked to my side, grasping my hand gently and smiling through nervous eyes.

"So what happened while I was out?" I asked.

"Besides dying?" she asked through her weak smile, tears welling up in her eyes again.

"Yeah...besides that."

"I don't know much. I was on the helicopter with you back to the Russian airbase and then from the airbase on a plane to Ramstien and then from Ramstien to here," she said before touching my face softly with her lips. "They didn't fill me in on much."

She reached over, pulled her chair closer to my side, and then sat, placing her head down on my hand at the edge of the bed.

When she looked up again her tears had been wiped away. "They wouldn't let the girl who was with you come. She seemed very upset. What's her name? Gretel?" she asked.

I smiled. "Kathrin," I replied. "Gretel was the code name the assault team gave her."

"Ah. And they called you Monkey Wrench, huh?" she asked, flashing a mischievous smile. "I can sympathize."

"Hey..." I complained. "Go easy. I just found out I died."

Then I winked at her.

"They told me that if it hadn't been for you that none of us would be here now."

I was taken aback. "Don't believe everything you hear, sweetheart. I think I caused them as much grief as help."

"That's not the way they were talking on the plane. I heard one of them saying that you and Gretel, I mean Kathrin, climbed into the back of that cargo plane like you owned it..." She tightened her grip on my hand. "'Hard core shit,' I believe was the term he used."

I just grunted acknowledgment, not knowing exactly how to respond.

"I'd hit you if you weren't in such bad shape." Her emotions welled up in her again.

"I might not feel it. They've got me on some good drugs," I replied, smiling.

She adjusted her position, trying to compose her face again, wiping her eyes. "There are some men who asked me to let them know when you were coherent enough for a chat. Do you feel up to that?"

I nodded. She stood and then bent, kissing me on my forehead.

"Okay. I'll be back in a little while," she said with a supportive smile. "Can I get you something while I'm out?"

"Cheeseburger," I said, smiling broadly.

"I think you'll have to be satisfied with a magazine," she

replied, patting my hand.

"Okay. Climbing-related if they have it." Then an overwhelming desire hit me. "Or guns."

She cocked her head to the side and shot me a worried look, and then she shook it off and turned to leave, blowing me a kiss as she exited the room.

A few minutes later, Captain John Temple entered the room with another man.

"Awake at last, you annoying little fuck," he said with a broad smile on his face. "How are you feeling, Scott?"

"Like I've been shot," I said, matching his original tone. "If that's the level of protection our government offers tourists, I'll be staying home for a while."

"Glad to hear it," he said, but I could tell it was a jest. There was affection in his tone. "In all seriousness though, I'm authorized to express gratitude on behalf of the Secretary of State and the President for what you've done and for your sacrifice in service to your country."

Wow, I thought. *The president knows my name.*

Too much seriousness. Had to tone it down. "That's funny. I was half-expecting to be handcuffed and dragged out of here by my heels."

"There was talk of that as well. But only from someone who is about to see a world of shit fall on his head. Even Nick asked about you," John said with a knowing smile. "If you could turn him, the rest of them didn't have a chance."

"That's good to know. I'd hate to wake up to him paying

me back for the broken nose." I said.

John laughed. "Yeah...well don't expect a pass on that. But I think you're safe for now."

"I'll sleep with one eye open," I replied, grinning.

"We need to debrief you properly at some point. But in the meantime, I don't think I have to tell you not to speak of this to anyone. Your involvement is not to be made public—despite the rumors already flying," he said, taking on an official tone. "We'd like to debrief the rest of your team as well, but we have been unable to ascertain who they are."

I smiled. "I think they might like to keep it that way."

John looked at me for a moment, hesitating, and then caving to the moment. "Okay. We can discuss that at another time."

"What happened? I'm not aware of anything after the stream," I asked.

"You were right about the device on the helicopter." John began, but he was interrupted by the man he came in with.

"Sir," he said, "Mr. Wolfe isn't cleared for this."

John looked at him with fire. "Mr. Wolfe is the reason we have any of *this*. And he is lying here like shredded beef because of it," he said and then leaned in close to him, "and if your sensitive nature won't allow you to witness the disclosure, I suggest you leave the room."

The man sat back, suitably chastised to keep his mouth closed for the rest of the conversation.

John looked back at me and continued. "They were able to defuse it outside Mimon. What we didn't know was that there were others. One was on the cargo plane. We aren't sure where the others are yet, but we know what to look for now, so we should be able to track them down."

I nodded my understanding. I didn't really think there was only one. You don't rob a tactical nuclear storage facility and only take one—I wouldn't anyway.

"You know Popovich is dead, but what you might not have known was that when you and Nick left the cargo plane, you dragged Jovanovich out the back with you. Ironically, he would have lived much longer if he'd stood trial."

"Wow. Of all the dumb luck. But I didn't know Popovich was dead. How did that happen?" I asked, stupefied.

"Well..." John started, shooting me a curious look. "You killed him. Don't you remember? You shot him in the throat while you were lying in the stream. He was standing above you? I yelled, 'Shoot?' Any of this sound familiar?"

"Vaguely. It was a blur," I admitted, shifting my weight to try and ease the discomfort in my chest.

"Understood. Hell of a shot though. Side armed, half-drowned, bleeding out, and all that..." he said rapidly.

"In the state I was in, I could have just as easily shot my foot off," I said. Then it occurred to me—not counting the Serbs who fell out of the plane, I had killed four men.

It must have shown on my face because John changed gears.

"I know it's hard. I've been there as well," he said

sympathetically. "We've got resources back home who you can talk with, frankly, without worrying about spilling secrets. Sometimes it's just good to say it out loud." He shook his head. "Anyway. That's all stuff we can go over later."

"The hostages are all okay?" I asked.

"Yes. Yes. Everyone is fine. Two of the security detail who were wounded were down the hall from you, but they were released last night. Everyone else is fine."

"Kathrin?" I asked.

"She's okay as well. She wanted to come and see you here, but there are some irregularities in her backstory that prevented it." He looked at me pensively.

"Backstory irregularities? Like what?" I asked angrily.

"I wasn't filled in on the details," he replied. "I was just told there were 'irregularities.'"

Anger flashed through my mind. "Fuck that!" I said raising my voice and then choking. "You—" Then I had a coughing fit.

"I'm already working on it," he said, trying to calm me. He turned to call for a nurse.

Before he could open his mouth, she ran in, pushing past John to check my monitors and help me lay back.

"We can do the rest of this later," John said. "I'll be around for a few days." Then he turned to leave. At the door he stopped and looked back at me. "By the way. You were right about Miller, too. That's being taken care of as we speak."

I nodded at him through my coughing fit, watching the

nurse press a button on one of my machines.

A second later, I drifted back to sleep.

**

Several hours later - 2201 C Street Northwest, Washington DC, the US State Department

DEPUTY CHIEF DWIGHT MILLER pulled into the VIP parking garage of the State Department at 8:45 a.m. He presented his credentials to the guard and then pulled through the gate to the first available parking space. Exiting his Mercedes, he grabbed his briefcase and jacket from the back seat and then started walking toward the elevator.

Standing in front of him was a man in a black suit who was also waiting for the elevator to descend. The man turned and smiled as the deputy approached. Miller thought about how odd the man looked with his cut and swollen nose and bruised forehead. There was something familiar about him as well.

"That looks like it hurt," Miller said to the man.

He smiled without looking away from the elevator. "It's nothing compared to what the other guy got," he said, a strange tone in his voice.

Miller heard an engine start behind him, and tires squeaked against the smooth concrete in the distance. A second later, a van rolled up behind him and stopped.

He turned as the door opened. Three men in FBI jackets got out. Miller tensed and turned to flee toward the stairs, but the man who had been beside him was now in front of him. He didn't see the fist that hit him.

The next thing he experienced was being pulled backwards into the van, looking at the man in the black suit.

"If you boys need any help with the interrogation, just let me know," he said, winking at them.

"We'll call you if we have any trouble with him," one of them replied, smiling.

Miller wet himself as they pulled away. "I'm a diplomat!" he screamed. "You can't treat me like this. I know the Secretary."

"Sorry pal. You don't know her anymore. She made the call," one of the men replied. "You have the right to remain silent. Anything you say can and will be used against you in a court of law. You have the right to consult an attorney and have that attorney present during any questioning. If you cannot afford an attorney, one will be provided for you at no cost."

He paused and laughed. "You may need that 'provided attorney,' actually—now that all your assets have been seized."

**

NICK HORIATIS turned from the elevator and walked back into the parking area toward a black Ford Explorer. It was his own vehicle, but he liked the black SUVs he worked in so much that he purchased one that was similar. He climbed into the front seat and flipped open his phone.

"Hey, Boss. It's done. He didn't have a clue he'd been blown," Nick said.

"Good. Finish up your report and send it to me, then take the rest of the week since you're already back home. I'll see you at Langley next Monday," John Temple replied.

"Got it," he said, glad for a few days of his own. "How's Monkey Wrench?"

"He's awake and being a smart ass," John replied.

"No surprise there." Nick said.

"He was pretty hot about Gretel not being allowed on base," John said.

"I told you," Nick replied. "I wouldn't be surprised if he dumped the princess for her. I know I would. That high kick is hot."

John laughed. "I think the strings that got pulled to get Ms. Whitney in that hospital room were the same ones that got tugged to keep Gretel out. I'd hate to be in the room if Monkey Wrench finds out."

"The kid can't catch a break, can he?" Nick said sincerely.

"He might get one yet," John said, hinting. "Hey! You aren't going soft on the kid, are you?"

"Ha!" Nick replied. "Not till I pay him back for my nose."

"Let's hope you get the chance. I like him too," John said.

"Ok, Boss. Have a good one."

Nick hung up the phone and smiled. He really did like that kid. He had balls and a clean sense of right and wrong. There was a shortage of real good guys...if he could get past the shootings. That was yet to be seen, but Nick hoped for the best.

**

*8:15 a.m., Saturday, May 22nd, 2010, six days after rescue -
Airfield, Ramstien Air Force Base, Landstuhl, Germany.*

The Ambulance delivering me to Ramstien pulled through
the gate at the small aircraft hangar area and onto the tarmac.

Barb had been with me nearly every minute since I
regained consciousness in the hospital. She ran errands, fussed
over me, and even snuck in a cupcake with a candle on my
birthday two days earlier.

To be honest, I had forgotten about my birthday, and that
had been one of the first questions the doctor had asked me.

She rode with me in the ambulance.

"I've already checked, and I can transfer to Georgetown for
the next semester," she said. "I'll have to take a few classes over,
but it the doctorate will still be from the Harvard program."

I nodded. I wasn't really in the mood to talk about life
changes. Every movement sent fresh flashes of pain through my
body, and all I wanted was to lay in my own bed.

"I think it's time for me to get my own place, as well," she
said, looking at me sideways.

When I didn't comment, she continued.

"Having a roommate is nice, but—"

I knew she was fishing for some indication of my feelings
on her living arrangements—I just nodded and smiled.

"So apparently, the State Department has already been
sending out enquiries about me," she said, shifting gears. "It's nice
to know the options are open. I understand there's some interest in

you as well."

I smiled. "I like my job," I said.

"I know," she replied gently. "But there is more room for advancement at State, and with Daddy there…" She smiled and shrugged, hinting that strings could be pulled.

"I just really want to go home and sleep," I replied tiredly.

"Yes," she said, suddenly snapping herself out of her fantasy life. "First we have to get you healed."

The 'we' made me feel like I was a project.

When we arrived at our designated departure point, the ambulance personnel lifted me out of the back of the vehicle in my wheelchair and lowered me carefully to the pavement.

Barb hopped down behind me and took the handles.

"I've got it from here guys," she said to them. "Thanks." Then she wheeled me to the small, executive-style jet awaiting us.

We rolled to the foot of the stairway, and she set the brake. There was an attendant there to help me up the stairs, but as I was about to attempt rising, a black SUV sped up alongside us and stopped. John Temple jumped out of the driver's side.

"Good! I was afraid I'd missed you," he said as he jogged towards us. "Hello Ms. Whitney. Scott," he said, nodding.

"You said goodbye yesterday," I reminded him, smiling. "After you spent the day grilling me in the debrief."

It hadn't been that bad. Mostly I just told him what I saw, who I saw, and when I saw it—and promised not to tell anyone—

although he did a great job of filling me in on the details that I hadn't been present for.

"I actually have a couple more things we need to go over before you head home," he said, and then he turned to Barb. "It shouldn't take more than a few minutes." He stared at her, a hint to give us some privacy.

"Okay. I'll just be up here if you need me," she said, and then walked up the stairs to the plane door.

"Yours and the gentleman's luggage have already been loaded, ma'am. We'll depart as soon as the Captain gives clearance," I heard a crewman at the top say to her.

"You aren't the captain?" she asked.

"I'm flying the plane," he replied and then smiled.

It only took her a second to realize it wasn't the plane's captain he was referring to.

As soon as she was aboard, John turned back to me and pulled a passport and the phone I had sent to Paris out of his pocket. "I think you lost these," he said. "I arranged for a Prague entry stamp. I remembered that you didn't get a chance to."

"Thanks," I said smiling.

"And one more thing. Somebody—I don't know who—went to some trouble to make sure this didn't happen," he said, lowering his voice. "But teammates watch out for each other. I've been around long enough to know how to get around the *proper channels.*"

"What are you talking about?" I asked.

John turned toward the SUV and waved. The door opened and a familiar face emerged.

"Kathrin!" I shouted despite myself.

She ran over and squatted next to me, giving me a hug.

"I was so worried about you, but they wouldn't let me see you," she burst out as she continued to crush me, sending fresh streaks of pain through my shoulder. "I was so afraid I wouldn't see you."

I sucked in my breath from the discomfort, and she backed away quickly to arm's length.

"I'm so sorry," she said. "I'm just so glad to see you. I didn't think I was going to be able to, and I had no way of contacting you, and that was driving me crazy thinking about not having anyone I could talk to about all this."

"Uh. Gretel hasn't been debriefed to the same depth that you have so you'll have to refrain from..." John started to say, but he realized neither one of us was paying attention to him. "I'll be right over here if you need me," he said wandering back over to the SUV.

"I like that," Kathrin said.

"What? Gretel?" I asked, laughing.

"Yah. Monkey Wrench *und* Gretel. International antiterrorist superheroes," she said, smiling. "Sounds like a TV show!"

She looked over her shoulder toward the plane and saw Barb trying very hard to ignore us. "I know you have to go, but I'm so glad I got to say goodbye properly," she said, her eyes starting to glisten. "It wouldn't have been right if I'd just lost track of you."

"I know. I was pretty pissed about it, too," I said. "But they've had me pretty well immobilized the past few days."

"Bah. A little gun shot or two couldn't keep you down. You'll be fighting bad guys in no time," she said laughing.

"I hope not. My life of international intrigue is over," I replied sincerely.

"We'll see," she said through suspicious, slitted eyes. "Besides, we need to join up again. Even John said we are a great team."

"I don't even know your last name," I said.

A whistle sounded behind us. We looked and saw John making the universal 'wrap it up' signal.

Kathrin reached into my map bag, the one I had traded her in Amsterdam the day we met. She extracted my phone—the prepaid phone I'd had through most of the adventure—and proceeded to tap her information into it.

Before she handed it back, she held it up to get a picture of the two of us, and she kissed me on the cheek just as she snapped the picture.

"It's Fuchs," she said into my ear. "It means fox."

She shot me a mischievous grin as she emailed the photo to herself using my email account.

As she tucked my phone back into the bag, she leaned close and whispered in my ear. "I lied on the train."

Then she kissed my cheek again, turned, and walked back to John's SUV without looking back until she got there. As she got into the vehicle she blew me a kiss.

"*Auf Wiedersehen*, Scott Wolfe! Be well!" she shouted.

"*Auf Wiedersehen!*" I yelled back, smiling.

I would truly miss her. I liked the way the W in Wolfe became a V when she said it.

John came over to help me out of my wheelchair and up the stairs. "I'll be in DC in a few days," he said as we walked up the stairs. "I'll stop by and check on you."

"Okay. Maybe we can grab a beer and talk about the old times," I joked.

"Be sure to call the Agency shrink I gave you," he said with a warning tone. "I'm going to follow up on that as well."

"I will," I assured him. But I didn't feel like I needed it.

"Have a good trip, and tell Bonny and Storc thanks for their service," he said mildly. "I'll have them debriefed as well."

I raised my eyebrows.

"Don't worry. They aren't in trouble," he said. "But both of them might get a recruiting call from NoSuch. Your COMSEC was top notch."

No Such Agency is what many government personnel call the NSA.

"What gave them away?" I asked.

"Barb called Bonny and between the two of them, they spilled all the beans. She may be a genius with encryption algorithms, but she can't keep a secret for shit," he said, smiling.

We both laughed.

"Thanks for everything, John. I appreciate it," I said, nodding toward the SUV. He understood.

"My pleasure. And it's been my honor serving with you," he said sincerely. "You've reminded me why I do this."

We shook hands and he patted me gently on my back and then turned and left. I watched as he drove away and waved just before they turned out of sight.

On the plane, they had a special seat set up for me so that I could recline with my feet up.

I still hadn't had much in the way of solid food, but hunger was getting the best of me as we hadn't had any breakfast. So when I was asked if I'd like something to eat, I said yes.

I sat next to the window, watching the countryside go by as we wheeled down the runway and then lifted into the air.

Barb was chatting away, but I was absorbed by the landscape. I only caught bits and pieces of her monologue.

"…and we can make sure someone is there, at least in the beginning, so you can get to your appointments, physical therapy, and such," she said. "I'm sure Bonny will want to help."

I nodded absently as she went on. A moment later she was saying something about school.

"…as soon as classes start," she said. "Don't you think?"

I nodded again, not knowing what I had just agreed to.

She talked more about physical therapy, school, work, Bonny, Storc, and rock climbing during the trip back to the States. Notably missing from the conversation was her abduction, Serbians, guns—and Kathrin.

I just stared out the window and nodded.

**

After a few hours, she tired of talking and drifted off to sleep in her first-class seat. While she was napping, I pulled my phone out and tried to get a signal to check email. No such luck. Then I flipped to my photos.

The photo of me and Kathrin on the tarmac was first. I stared at it for a few seconds before flicking my thumb across the screen to see the next one. It was a photo of Kathrin with her arm around the Serb she had knocked unconscious in the admin building at Ralsko Airbase. She was making a war face. The next photo was of me wrapping wire around Daniil on the train in Mimon.

Before that was a picture of me filling the scooter at the gas station in Mimon, taken through the window of the cafe. There was the one of us on the scooter at Ralsko castle and some of the scenery, but there were two of me climbing on the ruins of the castle as well. Then several of us while riding on the scooter...all of them were of her looking at the camera, pulling faces and me oblivious to her photography as I drove.

The last one was of the two of us on the night train to Prague. I was clearly asleep and she was hanging upside-down from her bunk, hair dangling, kissing me on the cheek. I saw Barb stir out of the corner of my eye and quickly closed the photo window before shutting the phone off and returning it to my bag.

She leaned over and grabbed me around the arm, resting her head on my shoulder.

"Any mail?" she asked.

"No signal," I said. "I'll have to check again when we land."

She took the bag from my lap and set it on the floor beside us. "Later. You have to heal before you can get back to doing much of anything."

"I know. I'll behave. I promise," I said.

"You're sure? You'll behave?" she asked, staring as she tipped her head down as if she were looking over the top of reading glasses.

"Yes ma'am," I said, smiling.

Deep down, I wondered if I could keep that promise.

Epilogue

Monday, May 31ˢᵗ, 2010, fifteen days after rescue - Zurich, Switzerland

HEINRICH BRAUN sat in a chair opposite Frau Racine Loeff. The nervousness he elicited from her was mildly arousing. But his purpose for being there would be to her benefit if she would simply fall in line. He had been sent to make the case for that.

She had been building an interesting client base over the last few years and had drawn the attention of Heinrich's employer. Having done so, her services were sought to create a number of accounts. Her particular method of account management allowed companies and individuals to have the origins of their funds hidden—an ideal model for criminals, arms dealers, countries labeled undesirable, and corporations who funded political movements with a desire to stay anonymous.

It had come to Heinrich's attention that some of their transactions through Frau Loeff had been traced to one of the deposit banks in Zurich. Heinrich was there with her to ascertain the level of penetration into the veil that she had created.

"As I have assured you many times, the transaction

numbers have no correlation to the origin accounts," she replied confidently. "Anyone having those transactions would have information only on those who received the payments through the corporate entities which paid them."

Heinrich could hear a tremble in her voice. It excited him. "And when the trail of those entities leads back to the source...?" Heinrich probed.

In reply, she turned her computer screen around to face him. She showed him the complex route the flow of money took. All funds terminated at a company named ARG Banti Inc. after bouncing through several dozen other "corporations"—none of them real.

"What is this 'Banti?'" Heinrich asked.

"You are sitting in the offices of ARG Banti right now," she replied.

"And where do the funds that supply Banti arrive from?" he asked, already knowing the answer.

"They are collected through a series of cash withdrawals as payments from multiple accounts that are not associated with this office," she replied, with a sly smile on her face.

"I don't see those accounts here," Heinrich stated plainly.

"Nor would anyone else," she stated firmly, almost insulted at the idea. "Those accounts are only accessed by me from another similarly-veiled shell company that makes dividend payments on behalf of some three dozen corporations."

"How do you access those?" he asked her.

She produced a handheld device for his inspection. "All the

accounts are managed through web interfaces. I have the account numbers and passwords memorized. I am the only person who, one, is able to access them and, two, is able to withdraw from them. The path to all funds begins, ends, and then begins again with me. Simply put, there is no trail."

"Very well," Heinrich said. "We require you to end your relationships with all your other clients and cater exclusively to us. Your fee will be doubled, and in addition, you will be eligible to collect all interest produced by the accounts that you manage. That sum should be upwards of several million euros per quarter."

The discomfort was clear on her face. The sums he was talking about were huge in comparison to what she was currently making, but some of her clients were quite dangerous to cross.

"I'm sorry," she said. "That will be quite impossible. I have far too many clients who rely on my services. Many of them would be loath to let me abandon them."

Heinrich smiled. His employer had already anticipated this dilemma and made arrangements to "help" Frau Loeff sever her connections.

"We have taken the liberty of freeing you from some of your responsibilities already," he said, handing her that morning's Washington Post. On the front page was a story about an explosion in Spain, which had killed a known drug kingpin and the majority of his family and staff.

The Frau raised her eyebrows in shock. She certainly recognized the name as one of her more dangerous clients.

"You will find that several more of your clients have met with similarly tragic ends," he said as he rose from his seat, smoothing his jacket lapel with his fingers. "We are very concerned about your safety and your continued benefit to the organization. We couldn't have any 'loose strings' mucking up our plans."

"Mr. Braun," she replied nervously. "I will have to reflect on this before I could act on such an undertaking."

"I understand completely," he replied. He looked at the outer door of her office and then back to her. "I will give you ample time to consider your options. I would suspect the time it takes for me to travel to that door should be sufficient." Then leaned forward to shake her hand.

"It's been a pleasure doing business with you," he said with finality in his voice, and then strode slowly, leisurely to the outer door.

Braun saw the color leave the woman's face. There was no choice at all. It was clear; these people would have her or no one would.

"Of course we will continue our business. I can notify you as soon as the remainder of my accounts have been settled," she expressed, trying to retain some dignity in her voice. The effort failed.

"Excellent," Heinrich replied coldly. "*Auf Wiedersehen*, Frau Loeff. Thank you for your time."

As he walked down the corridor to the elevator, he dialed his employer. "Yes," the other party answered.

"It is Heinrich," he said.

He was placed on hold without any further conversation. A few moments later, William Spryte answered. "What is the verdict, Heinrich?" Spryte asked.

"The source of the funds is quite well protected. Our little nosy bird can fish through all the transaction IDs he wishes to. None of them will lead back to you or to Combine," Heinrich replied.

"Excellent news." Spryte said. "And did she accept our terms?"

"She did," Heinrich replied. "But I would recommend a stop gap measure in the event that Frau Loeff were ever to draw attention to herself from outside. If she were to be compromised, it would theoretically be possible ascertain the source of her funds—as untraceable as they are otherwise."

"Very well. We will give her Mr. Harbinger's contact information as a contingency," he replied. "He will be her 'security' contact."

"Yes, sir," Heinrich said.

"Now that we know our transactions are quite safe, let us work on uncovering and dissuading our snoop." Spryte said.

"Understood. I will be back in the States tomorrow evening and will begin on that task immediately," Heinrich replied, excitement building in his chest.

"Perhaps something that looks random to the rest of the world. But clear enough that he understands it is about him."

"Yes, sir," Heinrich replied. "Excellent idea, sir."

"Have a good journey back, my friend." Spryte said, and then he ended the call without waiting for a response.

Heinrich was pleased. He had not done so much field work since he had served in the Stasi. This was bound to be an exciting year for him. He could feel his erection stir at the thought of it.

On the elevator ride to the lobby, he decided that he would reward himself tonight. Someone of a tender age, perhaps.

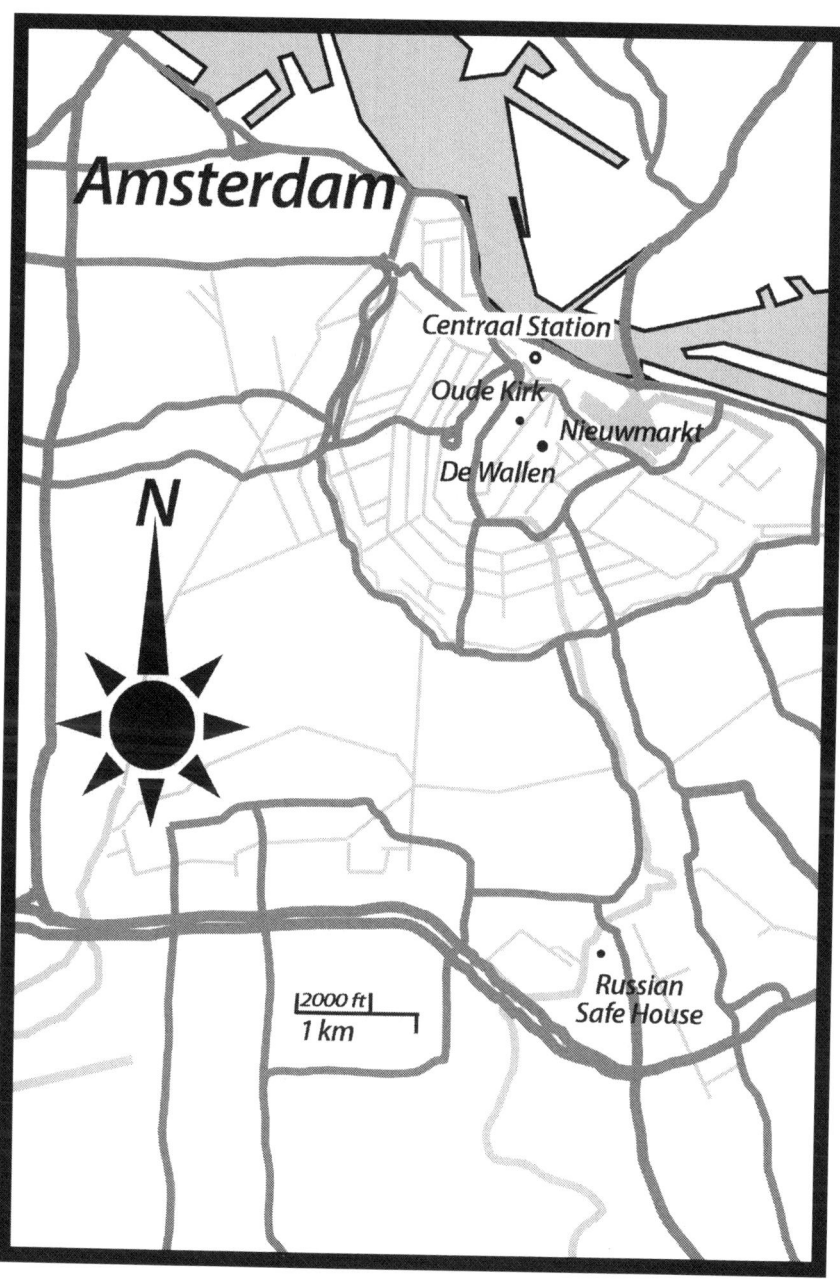

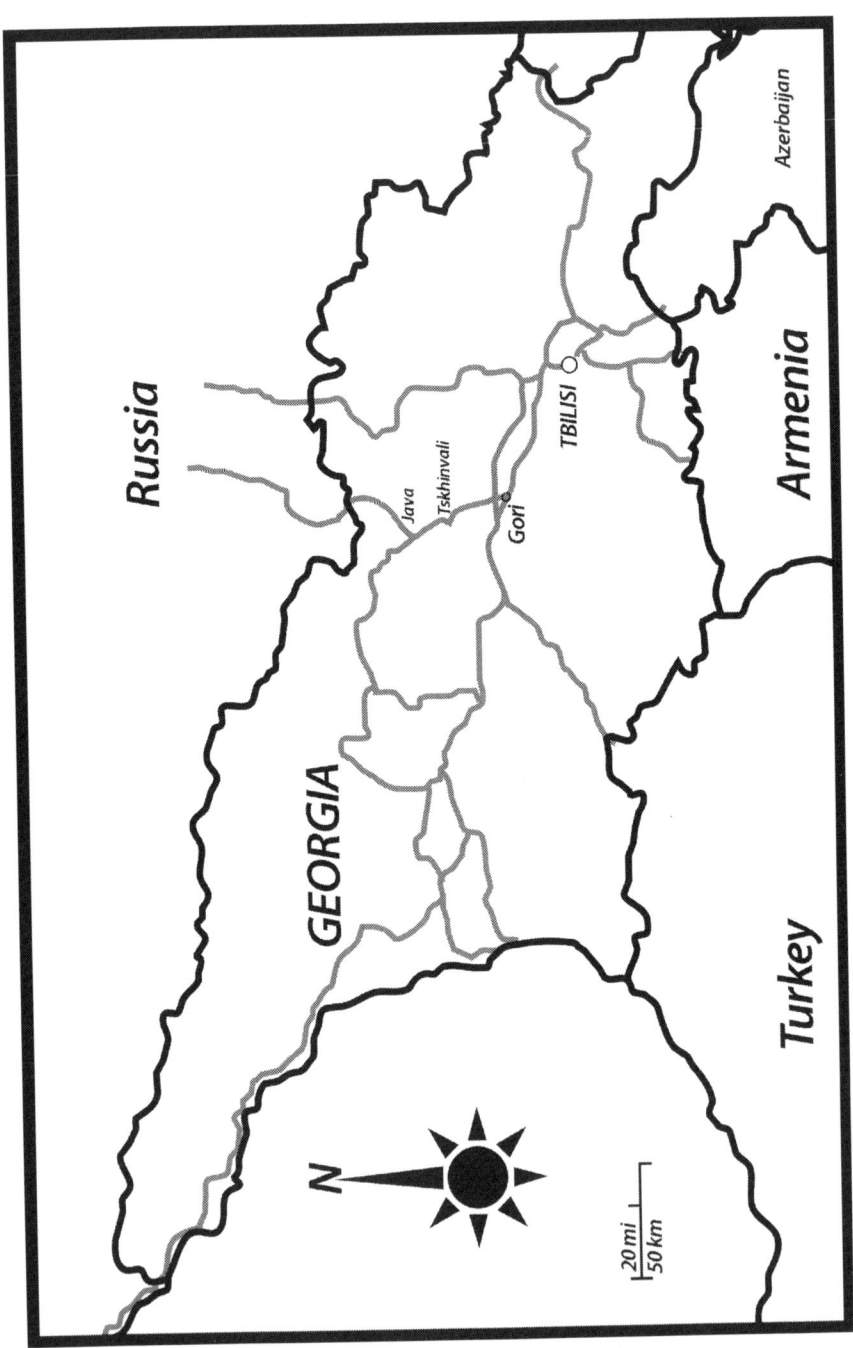

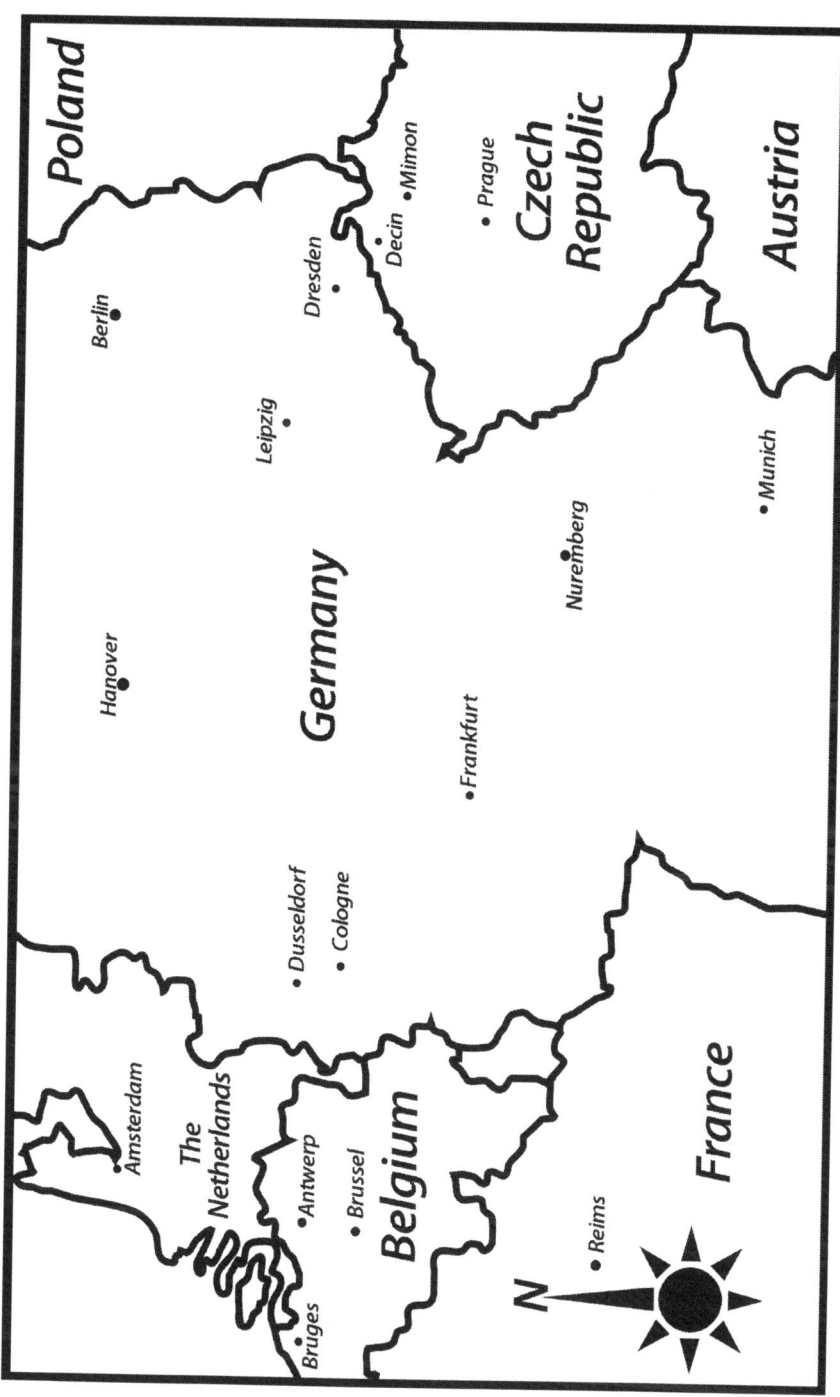

Acknowledgments

A debt of gratitude to my editor, Brenda Errichiello, for her tireless efforts in taking my first, very raw, novel and helping me turn it into a reality.

To my wife Diane, who has provided me with more support than I ever thought possible and certainly more than I felt I deserved. If not for you, this story would still be knocking around in my head instead of being real.

To my friend Don Cooper, whose fount of wisdom seems inexhaustible. In matters of law enforcement, military, world events, chemistry and so much more, I thank you for being my sounding board, encyclopedia, and friend.

And finally a big thank you to my former business partner, Jo Ann. If it hadn't been for what we started together all those years ago, I wouldn't have had the opportunity to fulfill this dream.

Look for Scott Wolfe's return early 2014 in

2nd Amendment Remedies

Made in the USA
Charleston, SC
27 December 2013